WHITE MOUNTAIN SPIRIT

THE LANGESFORD LEGACY BOOK 2

DORIS LEMCKE

ISBN: 978-1-68046-562-4

Published by Satin Romance
An Imprint of Melange Books, LLC
White Bear Lake, MN 55110
www.satinromance.com

Published in the United States of America.

Cover Design by Shelley Schmidt

I'm happy to dedicate this book to Mid-Michigan Writers, who believed in my dream of being published and helped me develop the skills to make it happen. And to the Southwest Florida Romance Writers who more than a decade later, opened their hearts and shared their talent with me. Because of their generosity and mentorship, I found the dream again.

Thank you MaryLou Bugh and Chris Lucka at MMW for showing me the way. And authors Karen Auriti, Karen Benson, Heather Burch, Lynnette Hallberg, Jean Harrington, Diane O'Key, as well as the other members of SWFRW for their critiques, friendship, support and reviews.

CHAPTER ONE

$\mathcal{E}$lena Santiago sat alone in the cool, quiet hall of the Charles Carter School for Indians. "An Apache doesn't cry." Yet as soon as she said the words, her white blood betrayed her, flooding her eyes with tears.

Why now? She'd held them back three days ago when the wood peddler brought home the broken and bloody body of the only good white man she'd ever known. She'd even kept them at bay as she stood over a newly dug grave, wishing Marcus Williams a smooth journey into the spirit world.

"Earth to earth, ashes to ashes, dust to dust," his widow Judith, recited, clutching her cracked and dog-eared Bible to her breasts. "Be gracious unto him and give him peace," she prayed to her god as the desert went silent.

As if out of respect for the old frontiersman, no breeze whistled down through the foothills of the Sangre de Christo Mountains. No bird of prey shrieked in the cloudless blue sky, no noisy prairie dog scolded them. Then, "Amen," floated to heaven on a sudden gust of wind that stirred the desert soil into frantic dust devils around the mourners.

As swirling grains of sand stung Elena's ankles and eyes, her skin prickled from the chilly touch of a ghostly finger. She knew then that the man she called Grandfather hadn't died falling from his horse into a ravine. Something terrible had happened. The hoot of an owl from a lone juniper tree, told her someone else would die. "Not yet," she answered the tempting call to reunite with her murdered father and brother—and Marcus. She had to protect Judith.

Now, waiting outside her adopted mother's office, the salty taste of grief choked her with memories of other violent deaths. If she gave into it, her heart would be crushed by the weight of her sorrow.

She'd kept memories of the day her village was slaughtered hidden behind a sulfur-smelling fog in the back of her mind. It was eight years ago, but every night since Marcus died, the fog lifted a little until the night before his burial. That night, she'd dreamed of the day the frontiersman and the missionary saved her life.

Her head covered by a burlap bag, she was slung over the rump of a soldier's mule. Her sweat had long-since dried into a crust on her skin and her breath was shallow. She would see her father and Little Wolf again. Soon.

Instead of the sweet voice of her dead bother calling her to him, what sounded like a growling bear ordered, "Halt! What's on the mule?"

The tether holding her to the animal broke free. Strong, gentle hands that smelled like lye soap guided her to the hard-packed ground and the feed sack split beneath the point of a Bowie knife. An instant later, she was pulled into the billowing folds of Judith Williams' skirt.

While Judith held a canteen to Elena's parched lips, the soldier dismounted. "Troublemaker," he announced. "Pulled a knife and killed one of my men. I'm taking her back to the reservation at San Carlos."

Marcus cocked his Winchester rifle. "Well then, you're a mite off course, Colonel. Last I checked Arizona's west o' here. We been followin' your bloody trail from Squaw Peak an' you bin headin' due east."

With his white beard and piercing blue eyes, Elena had thought he was the white man's god, sent to take her into the next world. Instead, he aimed the rifle between the soldier's eyes. "If you don't want to face trial for tradin' in Indian slaves, you an' yer men'll turn yer yellow asses north now, or try to outrun a bullet later." A warning shot from the Winchester sent all but the one called Colonel to the trail.

Instead of running for his life, he looked down on them. The sun behind him shadowed his face. "Watch your back, old man." Then he turned to Judith. "She belongs to me. You can't hide behind that Bible forever. One day, I'll have both your ragged white scalps and the girl, too."

Now, Elena's dreams told her he'd finally gotten half of his revenge, and she made her own vow. When Marcus' Comanche partner, Jesse Woods, returned from the Pueblo to protect Judith, she'd find the Colonel and avenge Marcus' death the Apache way.

Revenge heating her blood, she wiped the traces of her weak, white-woman's tears from her cheeks, straightened her blue, homespun shirt over her striped skirt, and entered the cluttered room without a sound.

Judith stood with her back to the door, staring through a tiny leaded glass window facing El Royale St. "It should be raining, Elena," she said without turning. "You need rain to mourn properly."

Elena smiled at the woman who had faced down an Army to save a ragged half-breed girl, and approached the window. "Marcus hated rain, Madre. The clear sky and bright sun of the West gave him strength. This is his spirit's home, as it is mine."

Judith turned. In eight years, her hair had grown more silver than gold. And her shoulders sagged from the burden of supporting Apache and Navaho students on the meager donations from her New England benefactors. Yet the courage, faith, and intelligence in her cobalt blue eyes had never faded.

After a quick embrace, she motioned for Elena to sit opposite her at a scarred old desk in a corner of the room. "It's true he loved the West, dear," she said to the pain behind Elena's mask. "But unfortunately, he—we, have unfinished business. Back East."

She removed Marcus' saddlebag from a nail on the wall behind her and pulled out an envelope. Taking Elena's hand in hers, she gazed into her eyes. "My husband had intended to post this with Wells Fargo, but he was too late. There is no time now to wait for the post. More than ever, it must be delivered quickly to our dear friends, Patrick and Camilla O'Grady, in Georgia."

Elena sighed with relief. If Judith visited her friends in the East and Jesse managed the school, she could search for Marcus' killer, knowing her adoptive mother was safe. Still, her mind reeled with questions. With Jesse still gone, who would manage the school? "When are you leaving?"

Judith leaned closer to whisper, "I cannot go. You must be my messenger."

This time Elena didn't fight the tears spilling from her eyes. Struggling to breathe in without being able to breathe out, her lungs burned. Her heart beat fast in its effort to survive.

No. The man who killed Marcus was in Santa Fe! She knew it. The desert breeze had whispered, "He's here" when the last clump of earth covered his coffin. At first, she thought it meant Marcus' spirit had stayed behind to protect them, but her dream told her it was the man who murdered him. She couldn't leave Judith alone for him to kill her, too. She pulled her hands free. "No. Please, Madre. I cannot."

Tears followed the weathered landscape of Judith's face, to stain the envelope on the desk. Her voice weary, her hands still holding Elena's, she spoke. "There is no one else to send. I'm too old to travel and I have work to do here. Many lives depend on the fast and safe delivery of this letter."

In the space of only a few days, Judith seemed to have grown old. As if the indomitable spirit that had buried three husbands and two children, and endured nearly a year as a Comanche prisoner, was fading. Elena longed to reach out and hold her in her arms. To give her own strength to the woman who had given her a new life, but Judith wouldn't welcome it. They had work to do, and work always came first.

"I need your help, *Querida*," Judith said. "Like the Century Plant blooming only once in a generation, an evil from long before you were born has returned. I can't stop it without your help."

Elena's heart broke for the only mother she'd known since she was ten years old. As if reaching back in time, she touched the silver cross at her neck. Her Spanish mother gave it to her before she died giving birth to Little Wolf. "Protect him, *Querida*," were Maria Concetta Santiago's last words.

But she had failed. Held kicking and screaming by a soldier, she'd watched as another one ran a bayonet through the four-year-old boy's chest and took his hair for a fifteen-dollar bounty. What could be more evil than that?

"What evil, *Madre*?" She whispered lest she call forth the embodiment of the voice that haunted her sleep.

Judith shook her head and dabbed at her cheeks with the same linen handkerchief that had washed the dirt and blood from Elena's face so long ago. She rose and walked around the desk to pull her into her arms. "The story is too long to tell, my dear. Just know that I will never, ever, let you pay for the mistake I made twenty-five years ago. I only ask for your help and forgiveness as I set you on this mission."

"To Georgia?" Elena whispered against Judith's broad shoulder.

She knew about Georgia. The soldier who murdered her village was going to take her to a place there called Atlanta, and when she learned to read English, she looked it up. It was far to the east, near the other sea. A place where it never snowed. Where white people made slaves of those with dark skin. To her, it was the white man's hell. There must be another way.

She pulled away to offer an alternative. "You can send Jesse when he returns. He is half white and lived among them in the East. He knows their ways."

Ashamed of showing her fear of going into the land of her enemies, she lowered her gaze. "*Por favor, Mi Madre,* save for you and Grandfather, I cannot walk among the whites even here, without feeling their hate and hating them also in return."

When she looked up, Judith was smiling. "Strong words for an eighteen-year-old girl. There is good and bad in every race, Elena. Don't forget that, like Jesse, you are half white. Perhaps the time has finally come for you to learn the ways of your mother's people."

She raised the lid of an old trunk to pull out a stylish green gown the color of a pine forest in summer. Leading Elena to the oval mirror in a corner of the room, she held it in front of her and pulled her long, ebony braid up to the crown of her head, resting her other hand on Elena's shoulder.

"You can be whoever you want to be Elena: Indian, Mexican, even a Spanish lady like your mother. The world is full of choices, but until you see them, how will you know the right one?"

Then she winked. "The O'Grady's will welcome you. In fact, Patrick and Camilla have two sons not much older than you. I'm told that like you, Clay loves horses and has a gentle hand. The oldest is Sean. He is...well, Sean is like a panther, a restless loner, still looking for his place in the world."

Elena understood then that like any good mother, Judith was trying to give her a better life. However, she only wanted her own life, a home and family of her own. A life without fear that the Colonel would find her. She stepped away from the gown that had turned her reflection into a stranger.

Anger replaced her fear. "Is that what this trip is about? Is there really a letter or is this just a way to find a white husband for me? Must I repay you for saving me from the slave trader by becoming a slave to your friends?" She clasped her hand over her mouth at the pain on Judith's loving face.

The older woman sighed and went back to face the window. "We both know better than that. Come here and take a good look."

When Elena joined her, she pointed to the cowboys ambling toward the saloons on Front St. Then to a few Indians sleeping in doorways, and finally to Juan Pedro whipping his burro loaded with wood.

"This is your future if you stay here. Do you want to wed Juan Pedro and let him beat you like he does his burro? Or would you rather work in one of the saloons for the likes of Alex Dooley, the faro dealer?" She touched Elena's cheek. "You are far too beautiful, intelligent, and talented to waste your life here without knowing what choices the world holds for you."

As if the speech had taken too much of her strength, she returned to her desk and folded her hands. "All I ask is that you deliver this letter to the O'Gradys and stay with them for thirty days while Jesse and I finish...other business. I will send you money then. If you don't like it there, you can come back to your old life—and I will welcome you with open arms."

CHAPTER TWO

*A*fter a tearful goodbye to Judith at the school, she boarded the train alone, grateful for a seat at the back of the last Pullman car. She spent five days traveling on the giant, snorting machine into the land of her enemies, where the cities and countryside seemed as foreign to her as the moon. The stops along the way were the most frightening. Despite her mourning black, squinty-eyed white men looked at her as if she was a feast, while their pasty-faced women pretended she didn't exist.

She heeded Judith's advice to pose as a Spanish widow who spoke little English. When they stopped to eat and spend the night at the Harvey House hotels along the route, she pretended not to understand the cruel things they said about her. At night, she slept fitfully, thinking about Marcus' letter and what important news it held. To open it would dishonor them both, so it remained safely on the bottom of the little carpetbag she never let out of her sight.

"An Apache doesn't fear," Elena whispered as the train steamed toward the tiny station outside Jeffers, Georgia. Yet the part of her that wasn't Apache feared what would greet her when she stepped onto the platform that loomed larger with every rapid heartbeat.

The train slowed until black smoke clouded her view through the soot-stained window. When the train whistle screamed like a dying buffalo, she closed her eyes against the memories it revived, and took a deep breath. She must be strong to deliver Marcus' letter.

She smoothed the unfamiliar lines of Judith's suffocating traveling dress amid the clatter of people preparing to leave the train. Be still, she willed her quivering hands and adjusted the bothersome, feathered hat on her head.

Touching her mother's silver cross on her neck, she acknowledged that despite the mysterious purpose of her mission, Judith only wanted to give her a choice. But there was no need. She'd already made her choice. She was born Apache and she'd remain Apache.

~

Sean O'Grady leaned against the whitewashed siding of the Omer Depot, awaiting the noon train. It was already 12:45, and he idly scuffed at the scarred wood platform. His fiancée, Mary Louise Fairchild, would be peeved at missing tea with him, but meeting a real-live Indian from Santa Fe was an experience he refused to miss. There would be plenty of time for tea and biscuits after they were married.

Frowning at how dull the prospect sounded, he bade farewell to his dream of heading out West for a piece of the wilderness while there was still some of it left. He'd waited too long, and a promise was a promise. It could be worse, he thought.

While the marriage wasn't a love match, he'd known Mary Louise all her life. After her parents died in a carriage accident, he was all that stood between her and the scavengers who'd caught the scent of money before the funeral flowers wilted. If he hadn't offered her the protection of marriage, God only knew who would. One name came to mind, and imagining Roscoe LaPorte's filthy hands on the innocent Mary Louise made him sick.

"Besides, it's about time, Boyo," he muttered. He was twenty-five years old and owned the largest plantation in the state. And as his mother had put it, "It's time to redeem your misspent youth and become an upstanding citizen."

With a heavy sigh, he acknowledged that if his father could leave the exciting life of a Pinkerton detective to become a Southern horse breeder, the least he could do was honor the life he was born into by running the largest plantation in the state.

Pulling a cigar from his jacket pocket, he bit off the end and spit it out in the nearby alley. He lit a match on the sole of his boot and watched the flame ignite the cheroot, turning it slowly between his fingers until the ashes turned white. Putting the match out just before it singed his fingers, he leaned back against the depot siding to let the rich, Virginia tobacco restore his wellbeing.

The sound of heavy footsteps on the steps broke the peace of the moment. With no outward sign of alarm, Sean looked through the smoke at Billy Berens and his cousin Cyrus, followed as usual by Billy's hulking brother Rupert.

"Mornin' gentlemen," he drawled, wondering if they understood that it was neither morning, nor were they gentlemen.

Billy raised a hand to halt his troop and cocked his head, grinning. His gold eyes glowed with feline cunning as they took in Sean's spit-shined boots and white, linen suit. "Well, well. If it ain't Seany Boy O'Grady." He spat a wad of chew onto the platform, barely missing Sean's boot.

"Where you bin, boy?" He stepped to the side, as if to circle his prey, but the depot wall stopped him from completing the circuit. "What's the matter?" he taunted. "Too good fer yer old friends?"

He looked to Cyrus and Rupert for support and they obliged with a chorus of, "Yeah, Seany Boy, where you bin?"

When he still didn't reply, red patches of color dotted Billy's pock-marked face. "We bin missin' you up at Roscoe's."

"I've been busy," Sean exhaled into a gentle, southwestern breeze.

Billy blinked as the pungent cigar smoke wafted into his face. "That so?" He took another step closer, overpowering the pleasant scent of tobacco with his sour body odor and rancid breath.

"Well, you bin missin' some big games," he hissed through rotting, broken teeth. "Roscoe's mighty pissed off. He wants the money you owe him. Now."

Billy and Sean stared at each other. Sean didn't hide his disgust while hate and jealousy radiated from Billy.

When the whistle of the approaching train died, Sean spoke. "You go on and tell Roscoe that you can't owe money to a cheat. What I know about Savannah, New Orleans, and Santa Fe more than covers what he says I owe him."

He also knew that nobody walked away from Roscoe LaPorte. Very few people were aware that the former hero of the Indian Wars-turned-politician had business interests in brothels and gambling dens from Georgia to New Mexico. Those who did, and tried to pull out of what he called his, "Ring," rarely lived to tell the tale. That was the reason for Billy's visit. To deliver a warning.

Billy's face contorted with rage. "So gittin' all engaged to the rich little gal next door makes you think you're better'n us." He made a lewd gesture toward the buttons on his pants and nodded toward his mates. "Maybe we should pay a little visit to Rosewood. Meet Miss 'Fairy Chil' an' smell that sweet little flower our—"

Blood spurted from Billy's nose before he could finish, and two of his teeth flew sideways, hitting Rupert in the cheek. In a fair fight, Sean's compact build, strength, and agility would have held the advantage over the taller, rangy Billy. But the Berens clan never heard of a fair fight. Before Sean could press the advantage of drawing first blood, Rupert jumped him and held him while Cyrus slammed a fist into his ribs. A lucky jab opened a cut above his eye that bled more than it hurt.

Sean's elbow to Rupert's groin sent him to the ground. Then he hurled head first into Cyrus' midsection, throwing him into the side of the building, knocking him out. Finally, he turned to see Billy grinning through bloody gums as he pulled a gutting knife from his boot. When he lunged, Sean kicked the knife out of his hand.

They both dove for it, with Billy's longer fingers finding the blade first. He grunted every time Sean slammed his arm onto the hard-packed earth, but didn't release the knife until the report of the Station Master's gun called the fight a draw.

With the menacing blade now lying harmless in the dirt, Sean kicked it across the alley. Billy spit another tooth and fingered a deep cut Sean's ring had carved into his cheek.

"I'll kill you for this," he hissed. "If Roscoe don't do it first."

Barely winded from the scuffle, Sean brushed the dirt from his trousers. "Don't push me, Berens. You may not be so lucky the next time you insult a lady."

By the time the Station Master holstered his gun and hobbled toward them on his wooden leg, Billy and Rupert had collected Cyrus, scuttling away like rats. Sean shook his torn and bloodied jacket, ripping off a piece of his shirt to dab at his left eye. "O'Grady, this little lady says you're s'posed to be fetchin' 'er."

Sean turned. Nearly eye level from the raised platform, a tiny young woman stared at him from a face that could have been carved from golden marble. It was framed by the thickest, shiniest, blackest hair he'd ever seen. Eyes the color of Georgia peat shimmered with a spark of recognition.

Had they met? No, he'd never forget that face, that skin, that hair. Or the perfectly proportioned body made to fit a man's embrace. He looked around at the emptying depot. Where was Judith Williams' Indian student?

She'd only written, "E. Santiago," on her telegram. Could it be a woman? He instantly forgot about the pain, Billy, and Roscoe LaPorte, to limp toward her.

"E. Santiago? Are you E. Santiago from Santa Fe? We were expecting a man. An Indian, actually," he added, wiping a dirty hand on his trousers before holding it out to her.

The girl hesitated as if considering getting back on the train. Acknowledging she probably never expected to be greeted by somebody fresh from a brawl, he watched her appraise him until a hint of color flushed her cheeks and she stepped down from the platform without his help.

"You are almost right, Senor O'Grady," she answered.

"I am Elena Santiago, and I am an Indian. Apache, actually."

He cocked his head. "You don't say."

After a moment's speculation, he turned to a nearby rain barrel to wash his face with his ruined jacket, thinking sadly that if an Apache girl could look, sound, and act like a Spanish lady, then the wilderness was truly gone. He'd wasted most of his life dreaming about something that existed only in dime novels and his own imagination. For once in his life, he'd made the right choice.

CHAPTER THREE

*E*lena had stepped through the crowd with the Station Master, surprised to see a young man in a white suit fighting off three rough-looking attackers. She couldn't look away. He moved like a panther to outmaneuver his opponents every time they made contact. With his straight black hair and compact build, he reminded her more of an Apache warrior than a spoiled, white gentleman.

When the fight was over and he looked at her, something deep inside her recognized the untamed spirit behind his stormy gray eyes. The feeling of being touched by a spirit subsided when he turned away. She dismissed superstitions from her mind. She was going home in twenty-nine days.

He touched her gloved hand for just a moment and she felt no ghostly chill at the contact with his flesh as she had with his gaze. "This way," he said as if he he'd just stepped out of a drawing room instead of being picked up off a dusty street with a bloody face and bruised knuckles.

They were just out of sight of the depot when he suddenly turned pale and doubled over to lean against an open carriage. She touched his bare arm. "You are hurt."

After a few quick, shallow breaths, he nodded. "A rib. Cyrus must have gotten in a good punch." He straightened slowly. "Just bruised, I think. I'm not coughing up blood, so nothing's broken or punctured. I can breathe if I take it easy." He reached out for her little carpetbag, and grimaced at the sudden movement.

Instead of pain, Elena saw fury in his frown, and instead of a muscular arm barely covered by a tattered white shirt, the blue sleeve of a soldier thrust toward her with a ham-sized fist. She clutched the bag to her chest, stepping back against the wheel of the carriage and shaking her head to be rid of the nightmare that until now, had only haunted her dreams.

As if recognizing the terror in her eyes, Sean dropped his arm and reached out again, slowly this time, with his palm up, as if to a frightened pony. "Then let me at least give you a hand up."

She stood rooted in place, horrified and humiliated. Only the carriage had saved her from shaming Judith and her Apache ancestors by running away into the nearby forest. Now, she saw that his eyes had cleared from stormy gray to bright quicksilver, and his smile was warm, kind. Still shaken by the sudden intrusion of memories that had been buried for eight years, she appreciated that kindness—even from a white man.

Judith had told her that the present is the best defense against the past, and now she saw the wisdom in those words. Senor O'Grady was not a renegade soldier reaching out to drag her away from her murdered family. He was just a beaten young man trying to hide the pain of his injuries. The Apache could be kind too.

"No. You do not know how badly you are hurt. I can drive a team." She tossed the bag inside the carriage and gathered her skirts to climb into the driver's box without help. But when Sean swayed with his foot on the step as he tried to join her, she jumped back down to help him.

He shook his head, nodding toward the remainder of the crowd that had gathered to watch the fight and was now staring at them. The pale faces and wide eyes reminded her of prairie dogs standing outside their holes, heads cocked curiously to one side. She was tempted to stamp her foot and scare them all back into their little homes.

Instead, she stepped away to steady the perfectly matched pair of chestnut mares. From beneath lowered eyelids, she watched his white neighbors let him struggle up the step alone. When he was settled, she climbed back into the box beside him and took up the reins, clicking her tongue to urge the horses away from the station.

With the magnificent team of horses under her hands and a sweet, floral-scented breeze in her face, Elena smiled at the young man who was obviously not at home in his own skin.

"Now you will give me directions to your home. Then you will rest. No?"

"There's no need for direction. The horses know their way. We can both sit back and enjoy the view." To demonstrate, he settled against the tufted leather seat, and dozed until a wheel hit a hole in the road, throwing him against her.

His shoulder knocked her hat askew, freeing a thick tendril from its pins to lay across the bodice of her dress. She pulled the horses to a stop and turned to him, meeting eyes that held more than the pain of a beating in their steel colored depths. If eyes were truly the windows to the soul, she thought, Senor O'Grady's soul was very old, very angry, and very sad.

Immobilized by those quicksilver eyes, she let him tuck the wayward strands of hair back into place. Her heart beat faster at the touch of his fingertips along her neck, and an unfamiliar warmth crept down to her stomach. It called her attention to the layers of petticoats that clung to her sweating thighs and the corset pressing painfully against her ribs.

He was too close! Whatever was inside her that called out to him had to be silenced. He was her enemy, but common sense told her it wouldn't do to push a wounded white man out of his own carriage. To break the spell of both his touch and his gaze, she moved away, making a pretense of straightening her hat.

"I didn't see the hole. Have I hurt you?"

He looked at her a long moment as if judging her sincerity before taking the reins. "I'm fine. That dip in the road is a marker. The turnoff to Langesford is up ahead. I can't have our guest driving herself up to the house."

The sudden chill in his voice surprised her. Even the horses noticed the different hand on the reins, tossing their heads before continuing. With nothing to occupy her attention, she looked closely at her new surroundings. The unfamiliar trees and plants fascinated her, but the gray moss that hung down from the tall pines like loose skin on a bear, made her cringe.

"Your horses are *magnifico*—I mean beautiful." She cursed herself for the mistake. Judith wanted her to improve her English.

"My father's passion. He's Irish, you know," he answered with a hint of mischief in his voice.

She didn't, but nodded as if she did. "Horses are also very important to The People. On the trail, a horse carries all our goods. On the desert, they may even feed us."

He chuckled and turned to face her, a spark of humor in his good eye. "Very resourceful, but don't let my brother hear you say that. He'd die before eating his horse, and likely consider doing it a hanging offense."

At her gasp, he patted her hand. "Don't worry. It's just that Clay shares my father's passion for horseflesh as a work of art rather than a work animal

—or food. While I run the farm, they're building Morning Bird Stables into one of the finest ranches in the state. They're breeding the strength, endurance, and agility of the wild mustang with Georgia, Kentucky, and Tennessee thoroughbreds."

Oddly comforted by the warmth of his hand, Elena shook her head. "You can breed an Indian pony with all the fine-boned show horses you want, but you will never capture the spirit in the pony's heart."

"Why is that?"

She was happy to explain what every Apache knew. "A mustang's strength comes from the land, the clear mountain streams, and the cloudless western sky. The high mountains and barren deserts gave them the stamina to outrun the white soldiers until…" She couldn't continue.

She was spared further questions when he pulled the horses to a stop at the end of a long drive lined by flower-tipped trees. They formed a sweet-smelling canopy leading to a house nearly as long as a Santa Fe block. Elena stared in awe down the drive at the O'Grady family home rising behind pillars three stories high.

Shuttered dormers jutted out of the third-floor roof, while on the main floor, tiny panes of glass shimmered in the sun like waves on a mountain lake. It was truly a white man's palace. Despite Judith's assurances and the young O'Grady's consideration, she still didn't know if she'd be welcome. A glance at him told her he was also in no hurry to face his family.

As they moved ahead slowly, she wondered about the battered man beside her. If his brother was Clay, he had to be Sean, the oldest son. The one Judith said was trying to find his place in the world.

She wondered why anyone with such a grand hacienda would brawl in an alley with men like those who slept in the streets of Santa Fe. Would his brother hang a person who ate a horse to stay alive? And finally, how would Senora O'Grady, who had been a slave to the Comanche with Judith, welcome an Apache into her home?

The horses stopped just short of the wide front steps of what Judith called a verandah. Several people stood on the broad expanse, staring at them. Sean took a deep breath before stepping down and walked slowly around the carriage to Elena's side. When he reached out to help her down, his face turned gray and sweat liquefied the dried blood above his eye.

Because his family was watching, she allowed him to put his hands on her waist when she jumped down on her own. Before he could reach for her bag, she took it herself.

"Good idea," he whispered, nodding toward the woman on the veranda whose horrified gaze was fixed on his bloodstained clothes and the ugly cut above his left eye.

Without thinking, Elena pulled his arm around her shoulder, bracing her body alongside his, her arm around his waist as he leaned into her. "Please help him. He fought off three horrible men who bothered me at the train station."

The woman, a young man, and a girl a few years younger than Elena rushed toward them with offers of help and sympathetic words. Behind them, an older man with a crooked smile on his still-handsome face approached more slowly.

Elena recognized the stunningly elegant Camilla O'Grady instantly. Except for a few strands of gray in her chestnut hair, the years had done little to fade the beauty Judith had described. With every shining hair in place and their dresses without wrinkle or stain, she and the young blonde girl looked like beautiful china dolls. Elena felt dirty and shabby by comparison.

Dirty, shabby, and guilty. She had lied to her hosts before even meeting them. She didn't even know why, except that something about Sean O'Grady made her forget he was her enemy. What if he exposed her lie, even at the risk of his own punishment? Though he was in her debt, she was at his mercy.

When everyone had gone into the house except the older gentleman, she again fought the cowardly urge to turn and run. Instead, she stared at the toes of her dust-covered shoes on the crushed clay and shell drive.

Seconds ticked by in silence as he waited for her to find the courage to look at his face. Finally, when her heart stopped hammering in her chest, she raised her head.

She met eyes the same shade of gray as his son's, recognizing what his son would be in thirty years. While Sean's eyes were like smoke from a forest on fire, filled with both passion and pain; his father's were like antique pewter, refined, and resilient. She corrected herself. He was what his son could only hope to be in thirty years.

The gentleman smiled, extending his hand to her until she cautiously held out hers. He pressed her wary offering between both his palms. "I assume you are the messenger sent to us by our dear old friend Judith Williams."

She searched his eyes for signs of the white man's contempt, but found only kindness. It gave her the confidence to smile back. "*Si*. I am Elena Santiago. May I assume you are Judith's dear old friend."

"No, that would be me," came from the woman on the veranda, now only a few steps away.

Senor O'Grady's smile broadened when his wife reached them and put a dainty hand on his arm. "I hope you didn't frighten our guest," she scolded, yet when he placed his arm around her waist, she melted into the embrace without hesitation.

Elena sensed their bond. Like the earth meeting the sea; impossible to tell where one ended and the other began. It was the same with Judith and Marcus, and with her own parents, Maria Santiago and Wah-Kee of the White Mountain Apache. When she wondered if she would ever feel such oneness with any man, eyes that flashed like silver daggers crossed her memory.

"To what do we owe this honor?" the senora asked, looking over her husband's shoulder as if for someone else."

"I doubt a soft Southern horse breeder could ever frighten our visitor, Cammy," he answered. "This is Elena Santiago, Judith's student from Santa Fe."

Surprise, disbelief, and curiosity followed one another on Camilla O'Grady's fine features. "But I thought Judith's students were Navaho."

Elena acknowledged that Judith's plan to fool Senora O'Grady into thinking she was of Spanish descent was working. The right answer would pave her way into the white world; but it would be a way paved with lies. There had been enough of those for one day.

She avoided Camilla's intense green eyes to speak to Patrick's gentle smile. "*Si*, most of them are from the Navaho tribes, but I am White Mountain Apache. The Senor and Senora Williams saved me from white soldiers eight years ago, and raised me at their school."

Patrick nodded in understanding and sympathy, but Camilla turned pale, swaying just enough for her husband to tighten his arm around her waist. "I see," she said before taking a deep breath and continuing in a voice cooler than before, "Well, you must be exhausted after your terrible experience at the depot. Please, follow me."

She led Elena up the steps toward the mansion's open double doors. Once inside, the young blonde girl emerged from the shadows, a blush at being caught eavesdropping coloring her porcelain-pale cheeks.

"Elena, this is Lily. Our youngest child." Then she said to the girl, "This is Miss Elena, our visitor from Santa Fe. Please show her to the room next to yours. Perhaps she would like to borrow one of your dressing gowns while she refreshes herself and Chloe unpacks her things."

She turned back to Elena. "You can rest until supper. We'll talk later."

Following Lily's bouncing blonde curls up the stairs, Elena felt the chill of Camilla's stare on the back of her neck. The moment the Senora had heard the word, "Apache", the warmth had disappeared from her eyes as well as her voice. It was clear that as much as Elena hated being sent into the world of her enemies, Senora O'Grady hated receiving one of hers into her home.

"There's good and evil in both races," Judith had said, and Elena tried to understand her hostess' feelings. While Judith had saved her from becoming a slave to the whites, the senora and Judith had been slaves to the cruel Comanche for nearly a year until Patrick, Marcus, and Jesse freed them. Would Camilla O'Grady have the forgiving heart Judith had assured?

She hoped so, but Judith hadn't seen the senora in twenty-five years. People changed. Would Camilla O'Grady seek revenge against a White Mountain Apache for what the Comanche did to her?

CHAPTER FOUR

*D*r. Montrose bandaged Sean's bruised ribs and put several stitches above his eyebrow. "No permanent damage," he assured Camilla. "A week or so on the verandah should fix him up fine."

By six o'clock, a dose of laudanum and a hot bath had soothed Sean's bruises and sore muscles. He dressed carefully, looking forward to dining with E. Santiago from Santa Fe. Stopping to check his appearance in the mirror, thoughts about how Mary Louise would react to his interest in Elena dulled his excitement.

"I just want a little conversation. News about the Wild West," he muttered to his reflection. However, instead of Mary Louise's vacant blue stare, he pictured Elena's doe-soft eyes revealing a concern he'd never seen in a woman before. It was almost as if someone knew just what kind of woman he'd always dreamed of and sent her to him—after he'd promised to marry someone else.

The timing troubled him. Avoiding temptation was never his strong suit, and one man knew that very well. The possibility of one of Roscoe LaPorte's stable of sad-eyed Indian girls posing as the messenger from Santa Fe darkened his mood. It didn't matter, he tried to convince himself. Nothing would stop him from keeping his word to Mary Louise. It was time to stop looking for shadows in the sunlight.

The memory of the spirited young woman who greeted him at the station made it hard to hide his disappointment when he sat at the table opposite Elena. While still an exotic beauty, the breathtaking vision was gone, replaced by a tiny little dormouse in a gray cambric dress with black velvet piping around a high collar. Even her lustrous black hair was neatly braided into loops at either side of the nape of her neck.

As Clay droned on about the birth of a new cross-bred foal, Sean missed both the beautiful smile and musical voice that had charmed him earlier in the day. Watching her barely raise her eyes or speak, except to answer questions, he began to think he'd imagined it all.

Indeed, he wished he had, and this lost little creature warily picking at a baked pullet and steamed okra, was the reality. Then he could forget that her natural scent of the forest and sunshine was more alluring than the most expensive French perfume. He'd forget her strength as she'd pulled him to her side, and how her soft little body had fit against his on the painful walk to the veranda.

He refilled his wine glass several times to erase the memory of the lovely siren who had unearthed yearnings he'd tried so hard to bury; but with every goblet, the image grew stronger.

~

While the wine only added to Sean's torment, the unfamiliar drink helped Elena swallow the strange and delicious food. It also helped ease her nerves before answering Camilla O'Grady's rapid-fire questions.

"You look so young Elena, not much older than Lily's fourteen, I'd say. Why on earth did Judith send you here alone just to deliver a letter?"

She dabbed at the corners of her mouth with a linen napkin before answering, "I saw eighteen years this spring. Jesse Woods was gone when Grand…Marcus…died. Judith said the letter was very important, so she sent me."

Not wanting them to judge Judith harshly, she continued. "She provided for me very well. I traveled on the Santa Fe Railroad and was very careful. The Harvey Houses at the stations where the train stopped were clean and safe." She didn't mention the knife strapped to her calf.

Patrick nodded as if it all made perfect sense. "Judith has her own ideas about things, all right. I've heard that the Harvey Houses have greatly improved trans-continental travel since our…my, last trip."

Camilla glanced sharply at him and leaned forward. "Jesse gone? Where?"

Elena remembered that Jesse's mother, Morning Bird, had befriended

Camilla and Judith before they were rescued from the Comanche. "Jesse became ill after visiting Morning Bird's lodge in the Pueblos. He could not even return for Marcus' burial."

At the mention of the Comanche wise woman, Camilla suddenly leaned back in her chair, folding her napkin with great care.

Clay saved the awkward silence. "Morning Bird? That's the name of our stable." He looked at his mother. "Do you know her?"

"I did...do." Patrick replied. "Jesse was a guide for me...after the war."

Camilla then picked up the thread of conversation. "Judith wrote about them. How helpful they were in... gaining the trust of the Indians. I hope he recovers quickly."

It didn't surprise Elena that they'd kept the senora's time among the Comanche a secret from their family. It seemed that lies and secrets were the way of the white-eyes. She vowed it would never be hers, despite what she'd done for their oldest son.

"I do too," she told them, trying to hide her worry.

Unless something terrible had happened to him, Jesse would never have missed being with Judith during her time of need. All along the trip, she'd worried about what Judith hadn't told her. It grieved her that it would be a month before she could return home to find out.

As if following her thoughts, Lily spoke up. "How long can you stay, Elena? Sean's engagement ball is on Saturday next. Wouldn't it be wonderful if you could stay, and maybe you can..."

"Lily." Camilla spoke so sharply the girl's jaw snapped shut and she leaned back in her chair to sulk.

"We'd be pleased to have you stay, Elena, if it fits your plans." Patrick covered the embarrassing silence.

How she wished it didn't. She sensed that Camilla O'Grady also wished for her to leave soon, but she was trapped. She folded her napkin as her hostess had, and stared at her half-eaten plate of food. "Judith had only money enough for a ticket here. She has asked for me to stay for thirty...I mean twenty-nine...more days. She will send me a return ticket in that time."

Pride made her look squarely at Patrick. "I will repay your kindness to me with work. I'm skilled at sewing and though I cannot cook food such as this, I will be happy to help your cook." Then her confidence deserted her and she lowered her gaze. "If I could, I would give you the letter and return by the next train."

Several voices blended as one to tell her that she was welcome to stay, however long she wished. She was a guest, an emissary, and was welcome indefinitely. They'd hear nothing about working for her room and board. Only one voice was absent from the chorus.

"Well, it's settled then." Camilla finally sighed. She rose to signal that the meal was over. "Lily has been practicing diligently on the piano pieces she'll play at the ball. Shall we retire to the music room?"

From their groans, it was obvious that Clay and Sean preferred to pursue their own interests on the warm, May evening, but they obediently followed their mother. Patrick offered Lily and Elena each an arm, escorting Lily to the piano and Elena to a leather reading chair.

After three soothing sonatas, Sean snored softly in the chair beside Elena. He jumped when Clay applauded. "Wonderful, Lily. You'll be on the concert tour before you're sixteen. Is that all? I hope."

Lily stuck her tongue out at him, but before it got out of hand, Camilla spoke for the first time since entering the room. "Elena, I remember how important music was to Judith and I'm sure you've had lessons. Do you have any favorite tunes you could play for a change of tempo?"

She nodded. "*Si*, Judith taught me the piano."

"Then will you honor us with one of your favorites?"

Amid murmurs of encouragement, even from the barely stirring Sean, Elena sat at the most magnificent piano she'd ever seen. It dominated a room cluttered with heavy furniture and tables decorated with silver picture frames and tiny porcelain figurines. As the warm ivory keys played "Amazing Grace," she was certain there was magic in them to sound so wonderful under her novice touch.

The magic even extended to her voice as her normally weak contralto rang out clear and unaffected by the butterflies playing in her stomach. At the second stanza, Patrick joined in with his baritone, followed by Lily's young soprano. Then Clay's tenor made it a quartet.

Finally, Camilla rose and stood with her hand resting lightly on Elena's shoulder. Her gaze fixed on her husband, she sang solo, "'Tis Grace that brought me safe thus far, and grace will lead me home."

Patrick dabbed at a sentimental tear in his eye. "My mother's favorite."

"You have a lovely voice," Camilla conceded. Though her eyes were curiously sad, it was a welcome change from the cold green stare that had unnerved Elena throughout supper.

"It's been a long time since I've heard a voice so..." She poured another sherry. Looking past Elena to meet her husband's concerned gaze, she lifted her glass. "Haunting."

Lily clapped daintily. "It's beautiful. You could be in the opera."

A laudanum and wine-induced chuckle rumbled from Sean's throat. "You should be on the stage all right," he slurred. "You're a regular little hummingbird."

Elena met his gaze, wondering what was tormenting this proud and rich young man. "I think you mean nightingale," she corrected him. "And there are no opera houses in Santa Fe."

"A pity." He rose awkwardly from the chair. Bending low, he whispered, "You're a natural performer."

Everyone stared at Sean's departing back until Camilla spoke. "Lily, perhaps you should retire as well. Clay, I know how anxious you are to see to that new foal."

Like Camilla, Clay had hair the color of the dark, red Georgia soil, and his laughing bright, blue eyes were just like Lily's. He kissed his mother on the cheek. "It was better than a night at the Palace." With a wink at Elena and the promise of friendship in his smile, he left her alone with Patrick and Camilla O'Grady.

"The letter is in my bag," she said without waiting for them to ask, and turned to leave the room.

Patrick followed her and pointed to wide, double oak doors across the hall. "Please bring it to the study."

CHAPTER FIVE

$\mathcal{T}$he envelope lay at the bottom of the carpetbag that until now, Elena had always kept with her. Anxious to finally be rid of the mysterious letter, she pulled it out and ran her fingers over Marcus' familiar scrawl, frowning. From its weight, it was a long piece of writing for a man who preferred actions to words.

It puzzled her. She'd never seen Marcus write anything longer than an errand list. Still, she wouldn't satisfy her curiosity by opening it, or even holding it up to the lamplight. Out of respect and love for her adopted parents, she'd deliver it with the seal unbroken. It would be testimony to their trust and her honesty.

When she stepped into the hall and turned toward the staircase, a hand snatched the envelope from her grasp. Instinct stifled her urge to scream and she faced Sean with clenched fists. "What are you doing?"

His height and outstretched arm kept her from reaching the precious package. He stood straight now, his hand steady enough to make her wonder if he'd only pretended to be drunk, but the wine was still on his breath when he turned her question back to her.

"I could ask the same thing. You come here looking like a Spanish lady and tell us you're an Indian. You handle horses like a teamster, then act like a lost kitten all evening. Then, while you can barely speak at dinner, you turn around and sing like an angel afterward.

"But you're no angel, Hummingbird," he pronounced. Looking deeply into her eyes, his voice caught when he finished, "You're a curse." He stepped back into a corner by a large potted palm and turned his attention to the envelope. "Maybe this will explain things."

Elena lunged at him hissing, "No! That is for your father. You can't..." Her attack upset his balance and the papers flew out of his grasp, landing in disarray on the floor around the palm.

Before her fists could connect with his injured ribs, he caught her wrists and pulled her to him. "Who are you, E. Santiago?" he said softly, his breath warm against her neck.

While she remained silent under his scrutiny, her body answered his questions. Her eyes blurred with angry tears and her face felt burned from the desert sun. Her pulse beat fast against her throat.

She couldn't move. Couldn't fight what her own body told her it wanted, and waited for whatever violence...or tenderness lay beneath his white skin. Then he released her, his arms falling to his sides before he shook his head and brushed his fingers through his hair.

She looked up to see the glaze of alcohol finally cleared from his eyes, but the sadness in them kept her still. When she looked down, she was surprised that her hand still rested against his heart.

He followed her gaze, and the tense muscle in his jaw relaxed. She wondered if he might kiss her, and what it would be like if he did. Then his mischievous half-smile slowly appeared and she realized what he already knew. She'd had the chance to get away from him and didn't take it.

Why? The question in his smile echoed the voice in her brain. It seemed that just being near him forced her to think and do foolish things. She pulled her hand away. *You* are the curse, she wanted to scream. Instead, she shrugged.

"You are loco."

~

Was God tormenting him for proposing a loveless marriage, Sean wondered. Or was the Devil himself trying to keep him from doing even one decent thing with his life? Without saying a word, her body had answered his questions.

Her bright eyes, filled with angry tears, showed no seductive intent, and her flawless skin had flushed like burnished gold touched with rose. Her pulse beat fast against the soft skin of a throat he knew would feel like velvet under his lips. But most of all, he felt her tremble. Roscoe's women didn't blush or tremble at a man's touch. His own weakness was the curse, not Elena Santiago.

Fortunately, his sanity returned just in time. The nap in the music room had helped the combination of the doctor's drugs and wine wear off. He could see more clearly now, if only out of one eye, and realized his disappointment that she wasn't the stunning Indian princess of his fantasies had led him to treat her boorishly all evening. If he'd treated Mary Louise like that, the whole house would be in an uproar.

Either Elena was exactly what she said she was, a mission girl unschooled in the use of feminine wiles, or she was the best actress he'd ever seen. Which one? For the moment, either was damned troublesome.

"Maybe so, but you have to admit I've a right to be suspicious."

He crossed his arms over his chest just in case she changed her mind about going for his bruised ribs. "First, who in their right mind sends a young girl across the country alone just to deliver a letter? How do we know you're even the real E. Santiago? A real lady would have brought the house down with her screams just now. And why did you lie for me today if you didn't have something to gain from it?"

Elena turned to pick up the pages of her letter, answering his questions, one at a time. "I told you the letter was too important for Judith to trust with the post and there was no one else to send. If you doubt who I am, you may telegraph her for my description."

Facing him with the loose pages clutched to her chest, her voice lowered. "If I had screamed, who would they believe? The white gentleman or the half-breed Apache? And I lied for you today because your father looked like he wanted to finish what those men in the alley began."

She stepped away from him, "I lied for you out of kindness before, and I will this time to save myself from shame. It will be the last time."

This time, her head cocked to the side as she studied him. "Does your family know about the men named Billy and Roscoe who have vowed to kill you?"

Without touching him, she'd struck an open wound. His hand curled easily around her upper arm as he leaned close to her ear. "If you are who you say you are, you won't even think about either Billy or Roscoe. If you're not, it's still the best advice I can give you."

She pulled free of his grasp. "I don't need your advice," she hissed. "If you are so afraid of your enemies, perhaps you should stay away from me."

"What do you mean by that?"

She smiled. "The Apache know how to torture a man so that he will beg for death."

He believed she had the power to make a grown man beg all right, though he doubted it would be for death. Yet for an instant, her face had darkened and the light in her eyes was fueled by hundreds of years of hatred for white men. He decided to yield her the point and stepped aside.

When she turned toward the stairs without glancing back, he smiled at her rod-straight back and the braids that bounced with each step. Then he bent awkwardly to pick up a broken palm frond and noticed something leaning against the wall. He chuckled as he pulled out a battered dime novel by Ned Butler, one of his favorite authors. "Lily," he smiled. Apparently, she took after him in her choice of reading material—and in hiding it from their disapproving mother.

The worn cover showed a Confederate flag draped over a pile of what must have been the "Rebel Treasure" of the title. It had obviously been read often. He smiled and slapped it against his thigh. Perhaps a romp through the fictional Wild West would take his mind off the puzzling Indian maiden.

CHAPTER SIX

*a*t dawn on the morning of the engagement party, Elena sat on the window seat of her room. As she sewed lace on Lily's pink, taffeta gown, she tried to make sense of what had gone on in the days since her arrival.

She was confused that Sean's fiancée hadn't visited him after his beating. Rather, he lounged on the verandah while Clay visited Mary Louise in his place. Lily told her that Miss Fairchild rarely left Rosewood since her parents' deaths.

To Elena, such a loss seemed all the more reason to be concerned about her injured future husband. Finally, she decided it was Sean O'Grady's problem if he was marrying a weak and selfish woman.

She was more concerned about his parents. They had changed since receiving the letter. It was as if a barrier had been put up between the earth and the sea. The warmth in their eyes for each other was replaced by a coolness that chilled Elena. It grieved her that she was responsible for it.

Still, she sensed the letter was only partially to blame. That first night, when she stopped outside the office door to compose herself, she'd heard Camilla say "It's the curse. Now Marcus is dead. We can't let what my brother did destroy…"

Patrick answered her timid knock and when she entered the room, tears glistened in Camilla's expressive eyes. Elena held the ruined package out to

Patrick and again protected Sean. "I...tripped on the carpet upstairs and the seal broke. The pages spilled out and now they are mixed up. I am so sorry."

She couldn't meet her hosts' eyes after lying to them again, and waited for them to accuse her of violating Judith's trust. But Camilla remained silent.

Patrick's voice was gentle when he spoke. "That's quite all right, Elena. We'll manage. In the morning, please show Chloe where you tripped and we'll have it fixed." Then he sat down in a worn leather chair behind a huge, polished mahogany desk built for a chair on either side, and politely dismissed her with a nod.

Since then, Patrick had missed nearly every meal and spent many hours closed inside the office or away on business. When he did join the family, he looked tired and often, when he approached his wife, she left the room.

Questions nagged at Elena. What was the curse? What did the Senora's brother do and what could it destroy? She decided that after the ball, she'd find a way to go home and get the answers. Then maybe she could help them.

A knock on her door startled her and she pricked her finger. She sucked a drop of blood from the wound. "Come in."

Camilla O'Grady entered with a muslin-covered bundle in her arms and laid it across the huge feather bed before sitting down next to it. She ran a hand over the smooth, satin coverlet as if she knew Elena slept on the Persian carpet, covered by a bright quilt from the trunk.

"You're up early, Elena. It's a habit of mine too, for many years now."

Elena joined her on the edge of the bed. "*Si*, the rising sun calls to me. Though here, with the morning mist, the call is not so clear."

Camilla's nod acknowledged the difference between the sapphire-bright morning sky in New Mexico, and Georgia's pastel pink and white dawn. "The best laid plans of mice and men often go astray," she sighed. "And time does *not* heal all wounds."

"I do not know much about mice or men," Elena confessed with a smile intended to dispel the cloud of sadness surrounding the Senora. She also agreed that even an eternity couldn't heal some wounds. Wounds she suspected Senora O'Grady still carried in her own heart.

Camilla nodded. "I didn't think so. Apache girls are well protected. You were ten when Judith rescued you. Did you have your rite into womanhood yet?"

It didn't surprise Elena that the senora was familiar with the rite during which young Apache girls were welcomed into womanhood. It was a cherished tradition among all the tribes. Even on the desolate San Carlos Reservation, she had looked forward to when she would take on the role of Changing Woman, the mother of all Apache women.

For months, her mother would have prepared for the Sunrise Ceremony in the summer that followed her first bleeding. There would be a separate camp, a special meal and a ceremonial dress decorated with beads, shells, and sacred yellow pollen. An eagle feather would be placed in her hair, her face painted with sacred clay. She would pray, fast, and dance with the spirit dancers for four days. On the final morning, she would leave the tipi a woman, blessed by their creator, Usen.

She had missed that blessing. "No. I became a woman among the whites, but I have held to the morals of my people and no man has touched me," she added proudly. At least until Sean O'Grady's eyes touched her soul. The beat of his heart under her fingers had awakened feelings for which she had not been prepared. In the custom of her people, she was still pure, but in her heart, she wondered.

"Yes, you are an innocent," Camilla sighed. After a moment's hesitation, she continued. "My son's fiancée is an innocent too and an orphan, like you. Sean, as my oldest son, inherited the Langesford from my father on his twenty-fifth birthday, two months ago, around the time Mary Louise's parents died in a tragic carriage accident. He's the only suitor Mary Louise can trust to keep her family's fortune intact for her children. It's all very civilized, very practical. The way things have been done here for generations."

With a wistful smile, she spoke again. "Even my own marriage was engineered by my father." For a moment, the smile faded as if powerful memories overwhelmed her. Then she recovered and cleared her throat. "Anyway, this engagement was Sean's idea and he's been faithful to it, so far. However, a man's good intentions can sometimes be overruled by his passions. You're a very beautiful young woman, Elena. I need to know the truth."

Elena held her breath. If Senora O'Grady knew she was a liar and turned her out of her home, what would happen to her? She couldn't go back to Santa Fe with that shame on her head. Before she could respond, Camilla leaned closer. "Why did Judith really send you here?"

She couldn't lie again to the woman who allowed her to stay in her home after delivering misery and sadness. "My mother was a white Mexican from Spain," she explained. "I think Judith wants me to choose between my white blood and my Apache spirit. I think she hopes for me to choose a white man to marry, and to live as one of them, I mean you."

"What do you want?" was barely a whisper.

"I just want to go home." To kill the man who murdered her family and her guardian.

"I see." When Camilla smiled this time, eyes that were so often a somber forest green, flashed with golden lights in the morning sunshine. "I knew Judith well...once, and I think she simply wants you to know both races that share your blood. I think she hopes you'll meet a man to whom you won't have to lie."

She touched Elena's arm. "We could send you back to Santa Fe today if you really want to go, but Judith had a reason for wanting you to stay with us longer. Times have changed. The world of the Apache is dying. Think about the good you could do for your people by walking in both worlds."

Reaching for the bundle on the bed, she added, "Once, when I was not much older than you, I was in an unfamiliar and frightening place. A woman there taught me how to blend in, when to speak and when to keep silent. She taught me to see each sunrise as a blessing and showed me how to survive from one day to the next. I owe her my life."

"Morning Bird?"

Tears flooded Camilla's eyes when she nodded. "So Judith told you."

She blinked them away and unfolded the sheet to reveal a stunning emerald green ball gown. "I don't know what the consequences will be," she confessed. "But tonight, you will meet the best that Georgia's white society can offer. If Judith wants you to make a choice, there will be choices aplenty."

Elena looked at the gown, understanding what she was being offered. She never intended to go to Sean O'Grady's engagement ball. It was enough to watch the elegant guests arrive and listen to the music as it drifted down from the third-floor ballroom. Now, like Judith, the Senora was inviting her to masquerade as one of them.

Yet what about after the ball? Fear danced under her skin. Would she be able to shed the evening's experience like she would ultimately shed this dress? After wearing this silk gown, how would she feel in homespun?

At the risk of sounding ungrateful, she felt compelled to ask, "Why are you doing this for me?"

Instead of taking offense, Camilla smiled. "It's a small payment on a long overdue debt I can never fully repay. Just do me this favor. Choose anyone at the party tonight, except Sean."

Elena lifted the gown and held it in front of her, facing the mirror as she had with Judith only a short time ago. This time she didn't step away from the exotic beauty facing her. Instead, she planned how to make the dress match the styles she'd seen in the fashion magazines that came to Santa Fe.

"Do not worry, Senora," she told Camilla's reflection. "Senorita Mary Louise is welcome to him." She attributed the sudden chill she felt at the thought of Sean in another woman's arms to the excitement of testing Judith's ballroom dancing lessons.

When Camilla left, Elena went down the back stairs to the verandah where Sean had settled into a chair with his feet up, alternately napping, sipping cool drinks, or reading a tattered old book. She paused at the threshold, knowing that before she could to go to his ball, she had to prove to herself that he had no power over her.

"I won't bite you, Elena," he said as if eyes in the back of his head could see her while he faced the broad, tree-lined drive. "Please, join me." He waved without turning around.

She cautiously sat on a wooden stool by the door and he lifted his legs from a tufted footstool, twisting in his chair to face her. The cut above his brow was healing and the bruises on his face had faded to reveal how truly handsome he was. As it always did, her heart beat faster when he fixed his amused gray gaze on her.

He put his book on a table next to a hand-painted glass pitcher and two empty crystal tumblers. "Can I offer you a drink?" At her hesitation, he continued. "It's not firewater, if that's what you're afraid of. It's a little early in the day for that, even for me."

Truth be told, he hadn't touched anything stronger than cider since the night Elena arrived. He'd been so violently ill the next morning he worried he'd cracked a couple more ribs vomiting. It'd be a long time before he touched either alcohol or laudanum again, let alone together.

Instead, he used his recovery time to sort out his feelings, doubts, and suspicions about Miss E. Santiago. Yet every time he saw her doing chores, walking with Lily in the gardens, or sitting under an old pine with a piece of mending, he wondered more about the contradictions surrounding her.

She behaved like a lady, yet claimed to be a member of one of the most violent Indian tribes. It was a combination that would intrigue any man. His enemy, Roscoe LaPorte, knew that very well, and made a very handsome living from the trade of women who intrigued men. With his mind set on political office, the blackguard would do anything to gain the wealth and the social acceptance marriage to the last of the Georgia Fairchilds would bring him.

Now that Mary Louise had spurned Roscoe's advances in favor of marrying Sean, he wondered how far Roscoe would go to break up the engagement. If one of his connections in Santa Fe had let him know about Judith's messenger, would he stoop to killing the real E. Santiago and replacing her, or him, with a very skilled actress?

Watching Elena shake her head at his offer of a drink, he admitted that sending an impostor to Langesford just to break up his engagement was pure melodrama. It'd be a whole lot easier for Roscoe to just kill him like he had the Fairchilds.

"A sweet tea?" he pressed. At her nod, he poured them both a drink, thinking that the best way to deal with this situation might be to start over. After a deep sip of the cool, sugar-sweetened lemon tea, he began, "I really should apologize for the other night. I'm told I made quite a scene. I embarrassed you and nearly disgraced the entire family after the recital. Unfortunately, I'm afraid that between the laudanum and the wine, I don't really remember what happened."

The tension appeared to drain from Elena's body as she pulled her stool a little closer. "Yes, you were a little loco, I mean crazy. It was not your fault."

Remembering everything clearly, including the enticing smell of her hair and how she'd trembled against him, Sean doubted Mary Louise or any other lady he'd ever courted would have seen things that way. "A forgiving woman is a rare and wonderful thing."

Also a dangerous one, he reminded himself before becoming lost in her earnest, dark brown gaze. Then he offered up his innocent glass of tea in a toast. "To the benefit of the doubt."

"Your mother has invited me to the ball," Elena spoke.

He leaned toward her. "Of course."

"I, I thought you should know."

Her lips trembled just enough to make him shift in his seat. If he didn't move, he'd kiss her and again send her running away. "Why?"

"Uh, I...do not want to cause any problems, so I wanted to..."

"To what?" He set his glass on the table without taking his eyes from hers. "Ask my permission? There's no need, Hummingbird," he said softly. "As our guest, we're honored to have you attend. I hope you have a fine time."

He meant it. Actress or innocent didn't matter anymore. No matter who sent her, she was here. It would be the devil's own test of his strength to spend the evening with both the chattering chickadee, Mary Louise, and this exotic wild bird. He stood. "Now if you'll excuse me, I seem to be out of tea." He left her to search for something a little more substantial to drink.

CHAPTER SEVEN

*E*lena's anger grew with every stitch she applied to the secondhand gown. Sean had lied about not remembering that first evening, or he wouldn't have called her Hummingbird. It told her he still didn't believe she was the real messenger from Judith. Now it was too late to tell his parents what happened at the train station and in the hallway. She'd have to fight her battle with this loco Gringo alone.

She took her dinner in her room to avoid upsetting Camilla's precise seating arrangements, as well as Sean, until the moment she chose to do battle. Chloe brought up a tray after she served the guests and made herself comfortable on the edge of the bed.

Elena smiled at the large woman with bright brown eyes that sparked with humor, and full red lips that rarely frowned. Her coffee and cream-colored skin was lighter than most Mexicans, but everyone said she was a Negro. It was all very confusing.

"I am from St. Lucia," Chloe told her. "It is a small island in a warm sea called the Caribbean. My Papa, he be the master of our sugar plantation, and my Maman, she a house servant. My Papa die when I was younger than you. We cannot abide de son who take over in his place, and so we come, first to New Orleans. When my maman die, I come here. An' here I will stay."

She watched Elena absently push the succulent roasted veal around her plate. When it became obvious she was going to let the delicious food go to waste, Chloe produced her own cutlery from deep inside her apron pocket and took a bite. "U y mwe." She gestured first to Elena and then to herself. "We be different dan dem whites, and so dey be 'fraid of us sometime.

Dey t'ink when de blood o' diffrent colors is mixed up, we get powers dey don' have. Dey t'ink we have de sight and can see into der souls. Dey be 'fraid o' what we know 'bout dem." Then she laughed. "An' dey be right. Only de power, it don' come from de blood. It come from der fears. Only not de O'Gradys. Dey see through the color."

Then she rose. "*Alors.* Time to fix you up, mamselle. Now get yo' body up and take off dat robe. Tis time to show de white folk what you got."

Elena rose and removed her robe, revealing her modest linen camisole and pantalets.

"Ohhh no," Chloe sighed, "Dis won' do at all." She laughed and hiked her own full skirt up to reveal several layers of brightly colored underskirts adding to her already ample proportions. She pulled up one layer after another until reaching a sparkling white petticoat made of fine batiste, with a row of wide white lace along the hem. A few quick motions of her nimble fingers released it from her waist to fall like a diaphanous, white cloud to her feet.

An instant later, the petticoat floated down over Elena's head. Chloe adjusted the drawstring at her waist, pausing a moment to ponder her next move, then ordered, "*Enleve' ca.* Out of dis."

Elena gasped when Chloe pulled her arms above her head and tugged her camisole up over them.

"No," Chloe said when Elena lowered her arms to cover her breasts. "You must not be ashamed of your body, *Cherie.* Eet is lovely, and may be a woman's only weapon in dis cruel, world."

Elena again obeyed, lowering her arms and standing in front of the mirror. Her dark hair lay smoothly down her back, emphasizing her long, slender neck. Her breasts were firm and full above a small waist and gently rounded hips. When did that happen? She'd never thought about being beautiful. She was simply a woman, and someday a man would claim her. She could only hope he'd treat her kindly. That was the Apache way.

"That way is gone now," she whispered to the girl in the mirror. Tonight, she'd dress as a gringo woman again and walk their false road. At Senora O'Grady's urging, she would masquerade as the Spanish-American daughter of an old family friend from Santa Fe.

The old silk gown sighed in satisfaction as it slid over Elena's naked shoulders and shaped itself to the curves of a body that scarcely needed the bothersome corset. Thin, black velvet straps positioned slightly down from the top of her shoulders held the bodice firmly in place, highlighting her bosom without exposing it. Matching black velvet bows topped the scallops that Elena had sown into the hem, contrasting with the sparkling white lace of Chloe's underskirt peeking between them.

Chloe clapped her hands. "You must really have de sight to sew dem scallops. Dey would be pretty without de petticoat, showing a bit of ankle, but *mon Dieu*, by showing de undergarment and no leg, you create de mystery."

She walked behind Elena to look at the back of the dress. Fabric that had once covered an old-fashioned, crinoline now draped over a half-cage to form a small train that began slightly below the line of her hips. *"Oui,"* Chloe whispered. "No bustle."

Her appraisal complete, Chloe placed her palms on wide hips and pressed her lips together. "Next, de hair." She grabbed a hank of Elena's thick hair with one hand and a brush with the other. Then she pulled and twisted and jabbed at Elena's head until her poker-straight hair coiled up to the crown of her head, one long tendril cascading down to curl provocatively along the top of her bodice.

Then Chloe pulled two delicate white flowers from a vase on the dressing table and fastened them above Elena's ears. "De fragrance of real flowers is better dan any perfume," she explained, leaving Elena giddy from the scent of gardenias floating around her.

"Oh, listen," Chloe whispered. "De music has started. You must go now." She smiled at her creation. "De young master will have eyes only for you, Cherie. One look and he will see de foolishness of dis marriage."

A rare dip in the corners of Chloe's ever-smiling lips revealed her concern. "Like you, chil', he is different from t'others. He be an old soul, that one. Now it is time for him to step into the sun or live in de shadows forever."

Elena had no desire to stop Sean's marriage plans. Indeed, if he was making a big mistake, she wouldn't stand in his way. A smile curved her lips as she pictured herself surrounded by handsome, rich and adoring white men who had no idea that she was Apache.

The smile faded at the thought of Sean dancing with his beautiful, rich, and adoring white fiancée. She would forget Sean O'Grady someday, but after tonight, he would remember her for a long time. Understanding only a little of what Chloe told her, she reached for the silk stole she'd made from the extra fabric of the skirt.

Quicker than a cat catching a sparrow, Chloe snatched the wrap away. "No. Do not cover yourself."

"But I look so...so...bare."

"True beauty needs no decoration." The older woman chuckled. Then she seemed to think better of it. "Well, perhaps just a little somet'ing. Do you have a necklace?"

"One." Elena crossed the room to her little bag and pulled out the delicate silver chain holding her crucifix. Her mother had worn it as a symbol of her God's protection. Even though Maria's God had turned his face from the Apache, Elena wore it as a reminder of her mother's love. Perhaps here, with the people the white god loved, the magic would return.

Chloe's smile told Elena she approved. She fastened it at the back of Elena's neck. "Eet's exquisite! I have seen fine silver work such as dis come to de islands on ships from Spain. Where could a poor Indian girl have gotten such a t'ing?" she said with a sly wink, "You did not take a scalp to get dis treasure?"

Elena didn't understand. White Mountain Apaches didn't take scalps. It was the Mexicans who offered a bounty for Apache scalps, even those of children. She pushed the thought of Little Wolf's shoulder-length hair hanging from a soldier's bloodied fist out of her mind. "No. It was my mother's. She was wearing it when my father stole her from her Rancheria in Sonora."

The older woman looked at it more closely. "Den your maman must have been of noble blood. Dis chain is antique silver. Handmade. The cross as well. If your mother had been kept on her land, you would be a rich senorita today." Then she clicked her tongue and shook her head. "Ah, *ma cher*, if 'ifs' were 'ises' the world would be a diff'rent place."

Elena still had no idea what Chloe was talking about. If her mother had not been taken by Wah-Kee, then she would not be anywhere. What is, simply is. But instead of questioning Chloe's logic, she touched the warm metal and felt her strength grow. She was finally ready for battle.

"Should I go now?"

Chloe nodded and opened the door. "Straight up de main staircase, Cherie. May God go with you."

CHAPTER EIGHT

*E*ach step toward the ballroom eroded Elena's confidence. Despite the necklace and beautiful gown, she felt nearly naked and completely vulnerable. She almost turned away when she saw her hosts still greeting guests, but Patrick's raised eyebrows, appreciative smile, and little bow gave her the courage to continue.

At Patrick's nudge, Camilla turned toward her and froze for just an instant before taking Elena's hand. "You do wonders for that dress," she said graciously. The warmth of her smile confirmed she would stand by their agreement. "Come along. I'll introduce you to Georgia's most eligible bachelors."

Elena didn't respond to Camilla's gentle tug on her arm. The light shining from gas lamps set in the old candle niches along the walls and the heady smell of flowers mixed with ladies' perfume, dazed her. Seeing the colorfully dressed dancers whirl to music that sounded like it came from heaven, made her dizzy. She swayed on her feet.

Patrick was at her side in an instant with a strong arm around her waist. "You have to breathe out as well as in, Elena." His grin erased years from his handsome face. "That's how you survive at these affairs."

She hadn't realized she was holding her breath and exhaled slowly. Looking from one to the other of her hosts, she saw that they had put aside whatever was haunting them, at least for the evening. She hoped it was forever.

"Not to worry, my dear," Patrick told her in a voice accustomed to soothing frightened, high-strung thoroughbreds. "You look absolutely radiant." When she was steady again, he winked. "You'll have these country squires on their knees before the night is over."

As if summoned, a deep voice came from behind them. "Who is this ravishing creature?"

They all turned to face a tall, immaculately groomed gentleman wearing a superbly tailored black silk suit. He looked at Elena with a wide smile on his full lips, his hand extended.

"LaPorte." Patrick stopped smiling and stepped between them, forcing the man to lower his arm. "I didn't think you'd have the gall to come tonight."

The man named LaPorte didn't flinch from Patrick's cold reception or even blink his coal-black eyes at being told he wasn't welcome. "Wouldn't have missed it for the world, O'Grady," he answered, sounding more like an orator or an actor than a country squire. Then, with the grace of a dancer, he side-stepped Patrick to face Elena again. "Now, are you going to tell me this beautiful woman's name, or am I going to have to guess? Athena? Aphrodite? Or is it Eve straight from the Garden of Eden?"

Camilla interrupted the awkward confrontation between her husband and the younger man by speaking. "This is Elena Santiago, Colonel LaPorte. She's the daughter of an old friend, visiting us from New Mexico." She glanced at Elena and continued. "This is Col. Roscoe LaPorte, Elena. He's a new neighbor who many think will be Georgia's next Senator-elect, come the fall elections."

Roscoe? The man who wanted to kill Sean? Yet his parents had invited him to the engagement ball *and he came*. She would never understand the ways of the whites. Grateful the Senora had told as much truth about her as possible, she slowly extended her gloved hand to him.

"Colonel LaPorte," she said carefully.

He leaned over and grasped her hand. Without taking his eyes off hers, he lifted it slowly. His thumb caressed the sensitive flesh of her palm through the lace glove at the same instant his lips touched the back of her hand. Then his black eyes lit with amusement as she tried to pull out of his grasp.

"I believe the orchestra is calling for us to dance," he told her and without waiting for an answer, tucked her arm under his to join the dancers on the polished marble floor.

"You are a graceful dancer, Senorita," Roscoe said softly, guiding her to the center of ballroom.

"*Gracias*," Elena whispered, concentrating so hard on following his long strides she forgot her vow to speak only English.

An eyebrow rose at her use of the Spanish word and his smile changed into a smug grin. "So you're from New Mexico. Where exactly, Elena?"

No one had ever said her name quite the way he did. It sounded like an endearment and a title all in one, as if only he had the right to call her that. Rather than being flattered, a chill raced through her body. Every part of her wanted to run, but she kept dancing.

She fought the temptation to tell this arrogant white man she was born in an Apache winter camp near the Gila River in Arizona, and that she considered all the land west of the Mississippi River to be her home. "Santa Fe," she said while his strong arms guided her body's movements.

"Ah, yes. Santa Fe. A very agreeable place." His black eyes reflected the light of the gas lamps as he smiled broadly. "We must get together soon and discuss the landscape, so to speak."

When the dance ended, he returned Elena to Camilla, who now stood alone at the entrance to the ballroom. "I look forward to our next meeting, Senorita Elena," he said smoothly and kissed her hand again.

Her gaze followed his tall, straight back as he strode to a group of older couples nearby. When he turned and their eyes met again, she shivered in the overcrowded room, wishing she hadn't given up her silk wrap to Chloe.

Clay appeared at his mother's side and whistled low at Elena. "So, you're the mysterious Spanish woman," He said. "What's going on?"

Camilla silenced him with a look. "Elena is simply a visitor from Santa Fe tonight, Clay. No one needs to know anything else."

"I am not ashamed," Elena said, suddenly feeling dishonest—again.

"You shouldn't be," Clay answered with a grin. "Half the people here are part pirate or scalawag." Nodding toward Colonel LaPorte, he added, "Or worse." His good-humored wink told Elena her secret was safe with him.

How different he was from his brother. Besides their appearance, their spirits seemed to be from different worlds, as if one brother was made of sunshine and joy, the other of storms and gloom. Like the Apache spirits of Light and Darkness, Life and Death.

"A reel." Clay said when a livelier tune began. "Are you up to it?"

"Yes, I know that one."

"Then come with me." He took her hand and they joined the other young dancers on the floor.

At the end of it, Clay dabbed the perspiration from his brow with his handkerchief. He tugged on Elena's arm to guide her to the refreshment table, joining Sean and a beautiful, young blonde woman who looked as fragile as a bird next to Sean's powerful body. "You haven't met Mary Louise."

"New Mexico is so far," Miss Fairchild giggled and blushed when Clay introduced Elena. Her white silk fan fluttered when she peeked over the top of it at her future husband. "I don't know if I could ever travel that far, especially alone. I swear if Sean or Clay didn't come to visit me, I'd just die a lonely old homebody."

Standing with Miss Fairchild made Elena feel strong. Despite being an orphan, Mary Louise was rich and well protected; yet when she spoke, she blinked and giggled, her tiny fingers toying with her curls. Elena could smell the fear beneath her lilac perfume and wondered what, or who, frightened her.

She declined Clay's offer of another dance and accepted a glass of punch while Sean and Mary Louise took to the floor. She watched Sean hold his bride-to-be stiffly, at arm's length. They were both silent throughout the beautiful waltz, and whenever their eyes met, Mary Louise was the first to look away.

Was she only marrying Sean because she needed a protector? If so, Elena felt very sad for Mary Louise. Even to her inexperienced mind, a marriage without love, no matter how wealthy, would be empty.

The couple soon returned. "Let's change partners," Clay suggested. "It's time I danced with my future sister-in-law."

The delight on Mary Louise's pale face surprised Elena. Sean nodded and gave his brother a good-natured warning. "Just remember she's my fiancée."

A shadow crossed Clay's handsome features. "How could I forget?"

Clay and Mary Louise moved as one body on the dance floor; his rust-colored head bending low to hear her little-girl voice above the music. Sean frowned and poured two more cups of punch.

He held one out to Elena. "It's spiked you know."

She accepted the drink more out of the need to hold something in her hands than thirst. "Spiked?"

"There's liquor in it. Aren't you afraid I'll turn into the devil?"

"That damage has already been done."

~

He laughed, noting again the savage spark in her eyes. It was the only sign of her Apache birthright that remained after yet another miraculous transformation; this time into a stunning ingénue. Who is she, he wondered for the thousandth time. Virgin or vixen?

He admitted on the dance floor, she had looked uncomfortable in Roscoe's arms. And even in the reel, she missed just enough steps to be convincing. Or genuine. It was time to find out for sure. He put his untouched glass of spiced rum down and held out his hand.

"My brother promised me his partner. Let's dance."

She stepped back, bumping against the heavily decorated table. "No. You do not have to do that."

"Are you telling me an Apache is afraid to dance with the devil?"

She pointed to the crucifix. "I have my protection." The orchestra began a Brahms' waltz and she smiled. "I know this piece from Judith's piano music. It sounds like heaven with so many instruments playing together." Linking her arm with his, they stepped onto the dance floor.

She closed her eyes and Sean felt the tension leave her body. A dreamy smile lifted the corners of her mouth as a woman might in the throes of ecstasy, her body following his movements flawlessly. He knew he had to say something or he'd end up kissing her right there in front of God and everyone.

"You dance well for an Apache," he teased. "You also seemed to get on very well with old Roscoe. What do you think of him?"

She stiffened in response to his challenge, but didn't miss a step. "Senor LaPorte is a very charming man. A real gentleman. I can see why you do not get along with him."

Recognizing the vixen in the flash of her dark eyes, Sean tightened his grip around her waist. "Is that so? Well let's go somewhere more private and I'll tell you about your new friend."

His steps sped up in response to a playful rise in the music's tempo and Elena's agile feet kept pace until she saw that he was steering her toward one of the open balcony doors. "Oh, no," she gasped, stopping so abruptly she fell against him, mussing Chloe's carefully arranged hairstyle.

"I seem to have twisted my ankle," she said loud enough for nearby dancers to hear. She began her limping escape from the floor.

Sean watched her limp on the wrong ankle and smiled just before he swept her up in his arms and carried her to a chair. Along the way, a string of Spanish and Apache epithets rolled off her tongue in a continuous low mutter only he could hear.

He didn't need to understand the language to know what she meant. Once she was seated, he continued the charade to gently remove her dancing slipper and examine a clearly uninjured ankle.

Finally, proof. Any of Roscoe's girls would have welcomed the chance for a romantic tryst on the balcony, especially if seduction was her assignment. Yet this woman risked attention by feigning an injury to avoid it.

"You little fool," he whispered. "Why did you do that?"

She pulled her leg from the warm fingers that had left her ankle to wander up her calf. Then she carefully rearranged the folds of her skirt. "You are the fool, you stupid Gringo. You are a fool not to believe me, and to think you will be happy if you marry for land instead of love. Most of all, to not see that Mary Louise is afraid of you."

She pushed him away. "Now stop squeezing the life out of me and go back to your betrothed."

As if summoned, Mary Louise's concerned face peered around Sean's shoulder. "Are you all right, Elena?"

"*Sí...* Yes," she stammered. "I am not an accomplished dancer, and I have twisted my ankle. I think I will rest a while."

Mary Louise accepted the answer without question and turned her interest back to the ballroom. "Oh, look," she exclaimed. "Lily is almost ready to play. They're setting up the chairs."

When Clay moaned, she slapped him playfully on the arm. "Oh stop," she laughed, then froze when she noticed Sean staring at her, his head cocked slightly to the side. She giggled nervously. "I can find our seats if you want to stay and help Elena, Sean."

Elena stood up, unnecessarily leaning on the back of her chair. "No. I am fine. You do not want to be late for Lily's recital. She is very talented."

"Not as talented as some," Sean muttered.

"You go right ahead," he said to Mary Louise. "I'll help Elena to her room and join you in a few minutes." His gentle smile and light kiss on her cheek brought a happy smile to Miss Fairchild's lips and she left with Clay to find their seats.

"You know I am not hurt," Elena whispered. "Just let me go alone."

"Yes, O'Grady. Let her go." Elena stiffened and Sean bristled at the threat in Roscoe LaPorte's voice.

The older man stepped between them and smiled at Sean. "Have you forgotten which woman is your fiancée?" He gestured casually toward Mary Louise and Clay. "She's the blonde over there with your besotted brother."

Sean stared into Roscoe's fathomless black eyes. "I haven't forgotten anything." His tone said he wasn't talking about Mary Louise.

"Perhaps you should."

Sean ignored both Elena's presence and the threat in Roscoe's words. "It's over, LaPorte. You can't steal Rosewood and I won't ruin you. I'd say we're even."

Roscoe's jaw tensed, but he recovered quickly to glance at Elena. "Do you really believe you can beat me? Think about it, boy. At your own engagement ball, nearly everyone has seen you flirt shamelessly with this lovely young woman, even to the point of fondling her ankle. And your fiancée seems happier with your brother than you."

He leaned closer. "The wedding is still three weeks away, O'Grady, and we're a long way from even." He turned on his heel and left the room.

Fortunately, most of the guests had already lost interest in Elena's faked injury and were taking their seats for Lily's recital. She touched Sean's arm. "You were right," she whispered. "He is someone to avoid. There is something evil about him. I have felt it only once in my life, but I remember it well. You are in danger, no?"

Yes. He covered the hand on his arm with his. Again, he saw the soft glow of concern in her eyes. After how he'd treated her, how could she still be concerned about his safety? "Not to worry," he said with confidence he didn't feel. "Roscoe is just a lesson learned a little too late. I can handle him." The doubt in her eyes told him she saw more than he cared to show.

A drumroll from the orchestra announced Lily's approach to the grand piano in the center of the ballroom floor. Mary Louise turned and waved for him to join her. He dropped Elena's hand to wave back and nod.

"You may have a point about my escorting you to your room," he admitted, and left her to join his fiancée.

CHAPTER NINE

*E*lena avoided Sean after the ball by staying inside to help Chloe with the household chores. Though she'd never let him know it, she forgave his behavior that night. Her part in creating the regrettable scene couldn't be denied. She'd been playing a role, and like all lies, it led to disaster. Yet, instinct told her there was more to the confrontation between Sean and Roscoe LaPorte than jealousy over Mary Louise.

After three days, the scent of the forest beckoned. When the moon rose at night, the bright stars that had seemed so close on the desert winked playfully from behind misty clouds. She had to get away from the house or she'd go insane.

As the sun rose, pink and yellow in the sky the next day, she watched Sean leave for his daily rounds of the plantation. He wore heavy denim jeans and a simple homespun shirt. There was nothing to distinguish him from a common vaquero as he rode out sitting tall in a Western-style saddle. Except for his horse. The magnificent black stallion pranced as if proud to carry the owner of Langesford to his work.

She forced herself to look away when Sean's image grew smaller in the distance. If he held to his routine, he wouldn't be back until nearly noon. Then he'd wash, change his clothes, and call on Mary Louise, as he'd done faithfully since the ill-fated ball. It was the perfect opportunity for her to escape from the house for a little while without the risk of meeting him.

She offered to collect some special herbs to help Chloe with her indigestion and stopped by the stables where Clay tended their thoroughbred horses. The familiar scent of fresh straw, hay, saddle soap, and leather refreshed her. She entered feeling confident.

Clay was grooming Valiant, the prize of Morning Bird Stables. She admired the tall, broad-chested Arabian stallion, reminding herself not to let Clay know how many people a horse this size would feed. The giant lowered his head to her hand and she stroked his velvet-soft nose. "He is beautiful, Senor Clay."

He barely looked up from his work on a hind hoof and grunted. "Try to keep him steady, will you? I'm working here."

She obediently held Valiant's muzzle. "But he is so big. How could he run down a steer, or carry a rider down a steep ravine? Or live on the desert where there is little water? I wonder if he would survive when the trail became hard." She peered around Valiant's head to see that she finally had Clay's attention.

He released the hind leg, frowning at her from behind the horse's rump. "These happen to be among the finest horses in the world. For any purpose."

"Oh, I don't know about that," she pretended to wonder out loud. "With his head so far up there, how could he see a prairie dog hole, or a rattlesnake? How would he be in battle, where swiftness is more important than strength?"

Hiding a smile, she shook her head doubtfully. "The desert is a hard master." Then with perfect timing, her voice filled with homesickness. "Oh, if only you could see an Indian pony at work, Senor Clay. Then I think your heart would leave these giants."

He stepped around Valiant to stand in front of her, his hands on the hips of his leather apron. "Are you saying an Indian pony could outrun this champion?"

She bit her lip to keep from laughing. Clay was so easy to understand, not at all like his puzzling older brother. "No, it's just that these animals make me miss those of my home."

His frown melted at the longing in her voice and he willingly told her what she already knew. Among his fine thoroughbred racers, he had several Indian ponies whose multi-colored markings had earned them the name, "paints." He took her to the newest mare that had come from New Mexico.

The pony, a dappled brown, white, and black beauty seemed to recognize her when Elena stepped up to the stall door. She stamped and whinnied until Clay led her out. "Her name is Spirit Dancer."

"Spirit Dancer," Elena repeated, laughing when the pony nuzzled her. "Is she broken?"

"Only to bareback."

"May I ride her?"

"I don't know. I don't want you to get hurt."

"I won't. See how she nudges me. She is restless and needs to run." They both did. If only they could run the many miles back to their home.

"Well I have been spending a lot of time on Valiant and the new foal." Finally, he relented. "Well, maybe just a little run. Come outside. We'll see how she takes to you."

Elena followed him to the exercise yard and shook her head. "Not here. To run around in circles will make her loco. I could take her around the land for a little while and bring her back, happy to return to her little stall." Another lie. A taste of freedom only made the hunger greater.

His arms crossed over his chest as he considered her crisp white shirt-waist and straight, navy blue skirt. "You'd have to ride sidesaddle in that, and she isn't used to that much weight on her back."

"I can ride bareback. And I have something to wear. May I return in a little while to ride her?"

Valiant snorted impatiently inside the stable. "Suit yourself," Clay conceded. "However, you should know that the boundaries to Langesford are the river past the woods to the north; the edge of the cotton fields to the south; and roads on the east and west. Not all the neighbors know you're a guest here, so it's safer if you stay on Langesford land."

His smile showed he had some idea he'd been hoodwinked. "Sean's at the cotton field," he added and chuckled when Elena blushed.

It took only moments to change into the blue shirt and striped skirt she'd tucked into the bottom of her carpetbag. She was happy to discard the white woman's shoes that painfully pinched her feet and pull on her long, buckskin moccasins. Then she padded soundlessly down the back stairs and out to the yard. Clay was there to help her mount, but soon saw it was unnecessary.

Rubbing her cheek against the mare's soft pink nose, Elena whispered to Spirit Dancer in her native language. The horse seemed to nod in understanding and lowered her head to help her kindred spirit mount. Once seated, the tears shining in Elena's dark eyes said more than a simple "thank you" ever could.

Her heart felt like it was bursting from pure joy when she pulled the pins out of her hair and shook it to tumble down her back. With an imitation war whoop, she nudged Spirit Dancer's flanks with her soft heels, sending them down the drive at a gallop.

She turned north, toward the river that would renew her spirit. After her failed masquerade as a white woman, she wanted to be alone in the forest to speak to the four winds and to the god of her mother and Judith. To pray to leave this place where people married for land, lied about their blood, and entertained their enemies with their friends. To go home.

The pony seemed to feel the urgency of their mission. She didn't slow until they were at the edge of Langesford's vast Georgia pine forest. That's when Elena first heard the other set of hooves close behind her.

It was too late to run for the cover of the low-lying pine boughs that would slow a larger pursuer; but wearing her own clothes and mounted on an Indian pony, she felt brave and strong. Apache. She turned Sprit Dancer to face their pursuer and reached for the knife on her belt.

Clay was wrong about Sean being in the cotton field. It had rained during the night and the field was too wet to work, so he headed back early to catch up on paperwork. Then he planned to see Mary Louise before she left with her Auntie Margaret to be fitted for her trousseau in Atlanta. He frowned at the thought of spending the best part of this clear, cool day listening to Mary Louise prattle on about her wardrobe, but it was part of his penance for the embarrassing scene at the ball.

Her nervous giggling drove him to distraction, and the way she pulled away as if she'd been burned every time he touched her, reminded him of Elena's accusation that she was afraid of him. Why? He only meant to keep her safe for the rest of her life and run her business so their children would have a proper inheritance.

It didn't sound like a terrifying proposition to him, but the sting of Elena's words wouldn't go away. He remembered Mary Louise's face when she was with Clay at the ball. Her eyes were bright then, her smile sweet, not forced. She obviously wasn't afraid of Clay.

So how could she be afraid of him? Even Elena, whom he admitted to treating badly, wasn't afraid of him. In fact, she looked like she wanted to scalp him every time they crossed paths. "Confounding women," he muttered. "What do they want?"

The words were barely out of his mouth when the new pinto made a mad dash out of the magnolia-lined drive, heading north. All he caught of the rider was a glimpse of bright colors and flying black hair. When Orion reared, Sean shared his frustration at being held to a walk. Without nudging the powerful stallion's side, they followed the clouds of red dust kicked up by the mare.

He knew she was heading for the river when the trail narrowed and the clouds of dust ahead of them settled. He wasn't surprised. It was his favorite place, and he knew every hidden break in the dense forest that would fit a pony. Orion slowed, as if knowing his master would lead him safely through.

Instead of a wild Mexican ranch hand trying to steal his pony, Sean faced Elena, her mount pawing the ground as if prepared to battle, and a lethal-looking bowie knife in her hand. "I come in peace." he said, raising his hands in surrender.

She was even more beautiful than at the train station, and dressed in the loose-fitting clothes with her hair floating in the breeze, she was more alluring than she'd been in the revealing ball gown. Here in the forest she was a part of the sunlit, natural world; fresh, honest, and free. Something he could yearn for, but never be. He pulled off his wide-brimmed hat and leaned forward to bow to the Princess of the forest, while his well-trained mount did the same.

He heard her laugh for the first time. Surprisingly deep, throaty, yet with the lilt of a bird in flight. His heart skipped a beat knowing the sound would haunt him forever.

He waited until she nodded, making the truce. She returned the blade to its sheath and they both dismounted to face each other in the dappled sunlight, as if meeting for the first time.

She gestured toward the knife, mischief sparking from her dark eyes. "If I wanted your scalp, Gringo, you would be bald already." She tugged Spirit Dancer into a slow walk toward the forest. The jump from the horse had hiked her skirt up above the tops of her leggings, and Sean admired the length of leg he'd inadvertently begun to explore at the ball.

Easy boy, he told himself. This one is a virgin, not a vixen. He should turn around, but Orion smelled water and tugged at his lead to follow the little mare. Taking care of his mount had been bred into him and, despite the warning from the part of him that always got him into trouble, he followed her.

The horses found a trail run by deer and moved at their own pace over the thick carpet of pine needles covering the ground, their steps barely making a sound. They stepped into a clearing near a feeder stream leading to the winding Ogemaw River that gave life to three counties.

Sensing they were in Elena's place of worship, Sean kept his voice low. "I apologize for the scene with Roscoe. I didn't mean for you to become involved in our... differences."

Her answering gaze told him an apology wasn't enough, and he again cursed himself for being the fool she said he was. Worrying about Roscoe had apparently addled his brain. But how could he explain the depth of Roscoe's greed, cruelty, and corruption without digging his own hole deeper?

"Pre-wedding jitters, I suppose," he lied. "The closer it gets, the worse it gets."

At least that was true. Roscoe would be getting desperate soon.

The horses stood side-by-side at the river's edge and Elena faced him. "You should see a Shaman. Perhaps this marriage is a mistake." Then she frowned at the stream. "The water is brown."

Saved from responding to her suggestion to see a medicine man about his upcoming marriage, Sean breathed easier. "The silt gets kicked up after a rain. When it settles, the water's as clear as any Rocky Mountain stream." He frowned. "I'm told. I've never seen a Rocky Mounbtain stream."

She nodded and looked up at him with eyes as dark and unfathomable as the riverbed. "I have also stayed close to my home. Before this journey, I have only seen New Mexico, the reservation in Arizona, and some of Mexico, when we ran from the soldiers."

He knew they weren't talking about geography. Fate had put them both in places and situations without their say. A gust of wind swirled through the tall pines, blowing strands of ebony hair into her eyes. He couldn't resist the temptation to again touch the black silk wave cascading below her shoulders. His palm cupped her cheek.

"Then we're not so very different after all, are we? We're both bound to the land of our birth."

She blinked but didn't pull away. "The land is a hard master to serve. It can keep you alive, but it cannot return your love."

As if drawn into her magic spell, he leaned toward her to whisper, "What do you know of love, little Hummingbird?" Then his lips touched hers.

Once again, she neither fought nor encouraged his embrace. Her mouth opened with a surprised, "Oh" and she slipped into the circle of his embrace, molding perfectly to the hard planes of his body. Her scent

of the forest intoxicated his senses until he felt as if he was finally...
home.

This time, the hand she placed against his chest posed no threat. She
spread her fingers against the soft black mat beneath the open shirt, tracing
the lines of his chest until his heart beat fast against her palm.

She raised her arms to his shoulders, pressing against him, the firm tips
of her breasts coming alive between the thin fabric of her shirt and his skin.
As it had on the dance floor, her body seemed to anticipate his every move,
and he knew if he lifted her just a little, she'd fit perfectly over his throbbing
need. Then...what?

Then he'd be no better than Roscoe. Defiling an innocent Indian girl.
Her hesitant kisses and curious hands told him she was just waking up to
the knowledge that she was a woman. If he took her, it would be her
first time.

He'd read enough dime novels to know that an Indian girl who had
been with a white man was unfit to wed one of her own people. He was
promised to someone else and knew she was too proud to be his mistress.
Neither one of them could take the risk.

Almost, Roscoe old boy, he thought, but he had only himself to blame
for this close call. Decency overruled his desires and he pulled away
painfully, a little at a time.

When he removed her arms from his neck and stepped away, Elena's
questioning eyes seemed to penetrate his very soul. He wondered, is this
what love feels like, or is it only lust? Nothing as beautiful as the moment
they'd just shared could be wrong. However, it could never be love. They
were from different worlds still at war with each other. He could never live
in her world, and she couldn't survive in his.

Sean smoothed her hair against her cheek and whispered so close to her
ear it could have been a kiss, "Why couldn't you be Mary Louise?" Why
couldn't he be the Apache brave who eventually would claim her? His hands
fell to his sides and he turned to the stream that patiently followed the
course nature had carved out for it.

She stood next to him, their reflections shimmering in the water. "We
can only be who we are and follow the path the spirits have laid before us."

He kissed her cheek, saying good-bye to something he'd sorely miss.
"You're right about that. It appears you have a ride to finish and I'm
expected at Rosewood." He took Orion's reins.

"Yes," she called after him. "I would like to see more of your *Rancheria*
—before I return to my home."

He tipped a finger to his brow in mock salute. "Whatever the Princess of the forest wishes." He pointed across the stream. "Up that rise, there's a thicket. You'll have to look for it, but there's a path wide enough for the pony to go through, just below a big gnarled pine. At the end of the path, down the hill, there's a hot spring. You may find it interesting."

She shaded her eyes against the sun peeking through the leafy canopy above them. "I know hot springs. We have them near the headwaters of the Gila River where I was born."

"Well, no surprises then." He winked, "Another time and place perhaps, and we could have enjoyed it together."

"That is something you can only dream about, Gringo."

Knowing he would do just that for the rest of his life, he turned in the saddle to watch her mount Spirit Dancer and turn the pony toward the rise to the hot spring.

CHAPTER TEN

*E*lena had rekindled his old dreams of freedom and adventure. Her eyes, her words, and her innocent embrace showed him the beauty of a people he'd been told were wild savages. A world he'd never seen and likely never would. Still, there was some wisdom in her words. He couldn't see a shaman as she'd suggested, but he could visit what he considered to be the heart of Langesford. Before he saw Mary Louise, who had never soiled a dainty slipper in a cotton field or walked along a muddy stream, he needed to remind himself that this was his home, and she was his fate.

He returned home to change clothes and took the long way to Rosewood Plantation, through the fallow fields. He stopped now and then to watch wildflowers sway in the gentle breeze and smell the rich aroma of earth at rest. Despite his reputation as a rogue who wallowed in smoke-filled saloons and shadowy brothels, he felt most content alone, in Langesford's remote, uncultivated fields.

There, he could lean against an old, scarred stump with a dime novel and a flask of brandy, to dream of higher hills, wider meadows, towering mountains, and raging rivers. There, his dreams could live in peace with his reality. He could pick up a handful of sweet, black topsoil mixed with rich, Georgia clay and feel the pulse of his family's blood coursing through it. It gave him the strength to endure his destiny.

He was two hours late arriving at Rosewood. Mary Louise met him with tears brimming her eyes. "Sean you're late. Auntie Margaret is nearly ready for us to leave. Any longer and we'll miss the train to Atlanta."

His apologies went unheeded as she wasted another quarter-hour whining about his tardiness, the decorations, and other details of the wedding that didn't interest him in the least.

"Well, just go then. Your auntie makes all your decisions anyway." It caused a torrent of sobs.

He stood helplessly silent until Mary Louise gulped back her tears. "How cruel you are. Our wedding is the most important event in my life, and Auntie Margaret is the only family I have. Sometimes I think you don't care about it at all. Why, you paid more attention to that Spanish woman at our engagement ball than me. Must I twist an ankle to gain your interest?"

His patience finally snapped. Instead of the usual mumbled apology for one of his numerous lapses into what she called boorish behavior, he countered her attack. "I'm surprised you noticed, Mary Louise. While you could barely speak to me all night, you had quite a little tête-à-tête on the dance floor with my brother. Perhaps you're the one whose interest has wandered."

The accusation was only a reflex. He never believed anything was going on between her and his brother. Clay only cared about horses, and Mary Louise was a baby when it came to the sins of the flesh. The first time he kissed her, she'd pressed her lips together until it felt like he was kissing a dead fish. Since then, if he tried anything more than a quick peck on the cheek, she pushed him aside with blushes and, "Wait until after the wedding for that."

The encounter with Elena told him just how long he'd waited. Impulsively, he pulled Mary Louise close and kissed her the way he had Elena. Instead of melting into his arms and responding to the embrace with her entire body, Mary Louise stiffened like a stick. When his hand wandered down her back to push her hips against him, she squealed with outrage, shoving him away from her.

Flushing bright pink, she wiped the kiss from her lips with one hand and slapped him with the other. "Animal," she shrieked. "A gentleman would never do that. It's disgusting. I may have to submit to your pawing after the wedding, but for now, you should treat me as your fiancée, not a Spanish harlot. Or should I say, Indian squaw?" She clapped her hands to her mouth the moment the words were out, the anger in her eyes turning to fear when Sean touched his reddening cheek.

"I see you know absolutely nothing about men, gentle or otherwise,

Mary Louise," he said quietly. "Unfortunately for both of us, I'm the one who is going to have to teach you."

Fear glazed her eyes as she backed away, upsetting a table topped by an antique Chinese vase that shattered on the slate floor.

When he bent to help her pick up the broken pottery, she pushed him away again. "No. Stay away. Clay would never have said that."

Sean straightened, looking down at her. Suddenly, his deep laugh echoed in the enormous room. "So it's true. I was gone a few days and your heart has been stolen by my brother." He sighed, knowing it never really belonged to him.

She ignored the mess on the floor to face him. "Well, yes..." she stammered. "I mean no. Well, sort of." Blonde curls bobbed as she shook her head in confusion. Finally, she stared at her tiny, white satin slippers. "When Clay came over in your place, we remembered what it was like when we were children with our ponies, and..."

"Ah, yes. Those ponies you were both so fond of. I can still see you two, always clucking over some new foal, talking incessantly about bloodlines and races. I should have seen it before. We all should." It would have changed so much. Now it was too late.

Once again, his fiancée misunderstood. "Clay didn't do anything wrong. He's never touched me except to dance. He, at least, is a perfect gentleman."

Her defiant stance, with her hands on her narrow, bony hips, brought a chuckle from deep inside Sean. He sat on the brocade settee and sighed. "Well, my dear, it's true that no one would ever accuse me of being perfect at anything. It seems we're in a hell of a pickle here, wouldn't you say?"

Mary Louise forgot to rebuke him for the profanity to sit next to him. Curls drooping around her cherubic face, she avoided his eyes. "You don't have to worry Sean," she said softly. "I am honored that you want to marry me." Her nervous giggle showed no humor. "After all, you are considered the catch of the county, and my father always wanted you as his son-in-law."

She sniffed and swiped at a tear. "I will be a good wife. I-I just don't know what you expect of me. You're such a puzzle. Sometimes, I'm just a little afraid of you."

So, Elena was right. He gently touched a blonde ringlet, trying not to compare its coarseness to Elena's sun-scented, ebony silk. "Don't be afraid. We go back a long way, you and I. In fact, I remember you as a baby."

He smiled at the memory. "I thought you were a china doll brought to life by old Grammy Flora's magic, but I wondered why she wasted it on one that cried so much."

Rewarded by Mary Louise's weak smile, he risked touching her chin, raising it so she could see that he meant his word. "So, there's no need to fear. I'll do my gentlemanly best to demand as little as possible of you."

Elena's words from the forest haunted him. "The land cannot return your love."

Apparently unable to tolerate his touch for more than a moment, Mary Louise pulled away and brightened. "Then everything will be fine." She rose to join her Auntie Margaret, who smiled at them from the doorway like the cat that swallowed the canary.

Auntie Margaret's ludicrous grin annoyed Sean more than Mary Louise's incessant chatter on her way to the carriage. He saw them safely on their way to the train, making sure that guards from Langesford followed at a safe distance behind their carriage. When they were out of sight, he rode Orion hard back home. All he wanted was dinner, a stiff drink, and to put the whole dismal day behind him.

He knew it wouldn't happen when Clay confronted him at the stable door. "Elena isn't back with Spirit Dancer yet. That horse hasn't run in a while. I figured she'd know enough to take it easy and come back long before this."

Sean shrugged. He felt no hard feelings toward Clay for stealing his fiancée's affections, because they were never his to claim. They'd made a bargain, he and Mary Louise, and now all three of them had to abide by it, for better or worse.

Now, his brother barred the stable door like a worried father fretting about a four-legged animal with next to no brains at all, Orion being the one exception. Saint Clay, he thought. Always clean. Always sober. Always the gentleman. Perfect in every way.

After a lifetime of being the rogue to Clay's angel, he glared down at his brother. "So, what do you think? Elena stole the horse and rode off to New Mexico?"

Clay responded to the flippant remark by stepping closer to Orion. His normally laughing, blue eyes were dark with anger as he looked up at his mounted bother. "No, but Indians aren't known for caring for their mounts. She took out of here like a bat out of Hell. Since you had to have passed her on the road this morning, I thought you might have some idea where she went."

With his brother holding his fists clenched at his side, ready to fight over something that had nothing to do with horses, Sean realized he had a raging headache. He'd spent most of the day on horseback, discovered that the woman he'd like to spend his life with could never be his, and the one he would spend it with, wanted his brother. A good scuffle could ease his tension, but he refused the bait.

He sighed, dismounted, and patted Orion's neck to let him know he'd have to be patient. "She took the path to the hot spring. Maybe she decided to spend the night under the stars." He couldn't resist one more barb. "Unless you figure she took the horse into Jeffers to sell it for train fare."

"With only the clothes on her back?" came from a feminine voice on the path between the stable and the house. Camilla O'Grady's angry green eyes and taut lips accused them both of a crime they didn't know had been committed.

"Mother," they said in unison, once again two little boys caught sparring in the stable by a mother whose footsteps never made a sound.

"Elena is missing," she said, as if she'd heard them talking from the house.

Sean tried to lighten the mood. "According to Clay, it's Spirit Dancer who's missing."

Camilla closed her eyes and rubbed her temples. When she opened them to look at Sean, they shone with concern bordering on panic. "Where is she?"

"Why ask me? Am I responsible for everything that happens around here?" He instantly regretted the juvenile outburst. It wasn't like his mother to show agitation; she prided herself on her composure.

He ignored the tickle of tiny hairs standing up on the back of his neck and answered more civilly, "I gave her directions to the hot spring and she headed that way."

When his mother looked at him skeptically, he raised his arms in surrender. "She went alone while I visited Mary Louise. That's it. I don't know any more."

"When?"

He sighed. "Mid-morning." He looked from his mother to Clay. "What is the matter with you two? Elena knows horses and she can take care of herself." He didn't mention the wicked looking knife she carried in her belt. "She's an Indian."

For the second time that day, Sean felt the sting of a woman's palm on his cheek. "She is a woman," his mother shouted.

Clay stepped back to avoid any residual blows for his role in Elena's disappearance, but Camilla never took her attention away from her oldest son. "Only a girl, really. Thousands of miles from home in a place full of frightening strangers. Since she won't borrow from us, she's virtually a prisoner here until Judith's money arrives."

She stepped closer and Sean backed away, only to meet with Orion's solid flank. Her eyes were filled with tears as she jabbed a finger into his chest. "You, of all people, know what kind of scum roams this countryside at all hours of the day and night. For some reason, except for your rescue at the station, you've been nothing but rude to her. It's time for you to behave like a gentleman."

He couldn't believe he was once again being accused of not being a gentleman; while LaPorte, who debauched young girls, swindled farmers, and killed with fanatical glee, was fawned on by women and considered to be the epitome of a gentleman. Still, he reasoned, it was odd that Elena wasn't back by now. She always helped Chloe with supper and he knew she wouldn't run away. She probably just wanted to be alone. He looked at his mother and brother. Away from all the clucking mother hens.

The idea of finding her sleeping peacefully in the grass by the hot spring suddenly appealed to him, and he surrendered. "Very well, it'll be light for a while. I'll go fetch her."

He smiled at his mother to ease the panic etched in the taught lines of her face. "I'll find your little lost dove, Mother." He turned to frown at Clay, "And your horse. We'll be back before supper is cold."

CHAPTER ELEVEN

The light stayed with him until Sean crossed the stream where he'd left Elena in the morning. Orion's sure feet negotiated the steep terrain easily as the blue and orange sunset slipped below the hill. They were midway up when a scream pierced the growing darkness.

Orion shied, pawing the air with his powerful hooves, and Sean's stomach tightened in alarm. Night owl, he told himself without believing it. Every ache in his body disappeared and every tired muscle tensed as he spurred Orion toward a thicket he should have gone through on foot. The only thought driving both him and his horse as they charged through thorny bushes that scratched Orion's gleaming sides and tore at his arms and legs, was to reach the all-too-human cry for help.

After the scream, all of nature went silent. His own ragged breathing loud in his ears, he reined the stallion to a halt just before they crested the hill. He dismounted to crawl the rest of the way up, listening for signs of the danger he knew lay on the other side.

Finally, he heard the grunting and panting sounds of a struggle, accompanied by the dull thud of bone meeting flesh. He could barely make out two figures rolling on the ground along the edge of the spring-fed pool in the tiny valley below him. His breath caught in his throat when he recognized the bright colors of Elena's skirt on the ground under a tree, and the animal-like grunts that could only belong to Billy Berens.

Please God, no. His mind fought against what he knew was happening.

He didn't feel the brambles flay his arms as he struggled through the undergrowth, slipping on leaves and grass already wet with evening dew. He rolled, more than ran, down the embankment as another scream tore through the air. This time he prayed out loud to a god he'd ignored too long, "Let me get there in time."

Another crack of the attacker's fist ended Elena's screams.

"No!" Sean yelled as Billy pushed his pants down to his ankles, the last rays of sunlight highlighting his erection. Elena lay motionless on the ground. When Billy lowered himself to feast on the treasure between her legs, Sean crashed into him, sending Billy into the bubbling hot spring instead.

He thrashed helplessly in the shallow pond, his legs entangled in his trousers, until Sean pulled him out by his shirt and threw him onto the ground.

"Jesus," Billy swore, struggling under the boot firmly planted on his groin.

"You again," Sean said over his gun pointed at Billy's nose. "I warned you that you might not be so lucky the next time I caught you insulting a lady. Now move, and give me a reason to rid the earth of you forever."

With his gap-toothed smile, Billy looked like a hideous, human jack-o-lantern. "Wait. Wait just a minute, Seany. I was just havin' some fun." He squealed when the boot ground into his abdomen. "She's just a Injun, Seany. Let me have her. You can have her next. I won't tell Roscoe."

His colt revolver aimed between Billy's watery eyes, Sean eased the pressure on his groin. "What does Roscoe have to do with this?"

Billy shivered as the damp night air blew over his wet body, and urine trickled onto the ground beneath him. "It was Roscoe's idea. He had me watch the house fer her. I was ready to give up, but when she left this morning, I followed her. Then you come up and had yer little bit of fun." His voice grew sly. "I can't believe you left her alone. I wanted to watch. Roscoe said I could when he did it."

Bile rose in Sean's throat at the thought of Billy watching the innocent, tender moments he and Elena had shared. And his stomach lurched thinking of Roscoe's cruel fingers touching Elena's satin skin. He fought the wave of black rage that washed over him to ease his boot back a little. This was his chance to finally find out Roscoe's purpose in Jeffers.

"Tell me more." He flexed his finger over the trigger.

Billy's eyes bulged in terror and pain. He emptied the rest of his bladder, then struggled to move out of the puddle of his own making. "Okay, okay.

When you left, I followed her here. Roscoe told me to wait 'til sunset to take her, on account o' he didn't want nobody to see. I watched her all the damn day, swimmin' without no clothes on an' nappin' in the sun. But when she come out of the water the last time, I couldn't wait no more. I figured Roscoe wouldn't care if I used her a little—broke her in for 'im. She'll be doin' it reg'lar after he's done with her anyway. She's a Injun, after all."

"Hey," he screeched when the barrel of Sean's gun cracked against his jaw, opening the cut his ring had carved at the train station. "It's the truth man. If'n you don't like it, then kill me." Billy spat through the blood covering his face. "Kill me now you son of a bitch and get it over with. I'll see you in Hell soon enough."

"Not until I know why Roscoe wants Elena."

Billy moaned, tears spilling from the corners of his eyes. "Roscoe don't tell nobody why he does the shit he does, an' you know it. He tol' me to git the girl an' that's what I come out here to do." His sallow face looked ghoulish in the moonlight with blood dripping from his chin. "You know he'll git you fer this."

Sean raised his boot. "I'm counting on him to try. Get up." Pointing the pistol at Billy's head, he continued. "Tell Roscoe I've bested him twice, and not to try for three. We both know I'd as soon put a bullet in your head as look at you, but spilling your blood here would spoil the pleasant memories I have of this place."

When Billy bent to pull up his pants, Sean kicked his bare backside. "Leave them here. Your shirt too."

"What?" His bloody mouth gaped open. "I'm nekid here."

Sean nodded toward Elena. "So is she. You heard me. Leave your clothes here." With a scornful frown at Billy's bruised private parts, Sean lowered the pistol to aim squarely at his now shriveled penis. "Nobody would probably even notice, but if you want to lose what little you have of your manhood, you'll keep standing there, looking stupid. Now, strip."

"Throw them on the rocks. I don't want your vermin tainting our pool," he ordered when Billy finished. "Now go back to your master, you mangy dog." He fired above Billy's already retreating head.

When Billy disappeared into the thicket, Sean holstered his gun. Orion stepped carefully through a break in the brush toward Elena and nudged her with his soft nose until she moaned.

She's alive, Sean rejoiced, and ran to her side. He blamed himself. He'd concentrated all his efforts on protecting Mary Louise, without considering that Roscoe might take his revenge on Elena. He'd sent her right into the bastard's den. Underestimating Roscoe had almost cost Elena her life.

As a full moon took its place to rule the night sky, pale beams bathed the glade with just enough light for him to see that blood covered most of Elena's beautiful body. He hesitated, not knowing what to address first, her nudity, or her injuries. Then she began to tremble.

He put his jacket over her, then retrieved the blanket behind Orion's saddle. Placing her gently onto it, he knelt to assess Billy's damage.

"Damn," he swore again. There was enough light to see she was injured, but not enough to know how badly. He couldn't see her eyes or the color of her lips to tell if she was bleeding inside. Hell, he didn't even know if he'd stopped Billy from raping her.

Until he knew how badly she was hurt, he couldn't risk putting her on a horse, and a look at the deep scratches on Orion's flanks told him it would be hell getting back through the thicket in the dark. The pony would do better, but she could never hold the two of them, especially bareback.

Instead of risking it, he wrapped Elena in the blanket and built a fire. When a healthy flame caused the little glade to glow, he peeled the blanket back, a little at a time.

The rush of night air on her skin brought her back to life with a start. Her eyes were glazed with fear and pain, her words an unintelligible combination of Apache, Spanish, and English as she fought him off with limbs she could barely move.

Sean held her close, repeating her name over and over, until she sank into his embrace, exhausted. Now that he could see her injuries, he was grateful she'd passed out again. But even unconscious, she flinched when a gentle finger touched the deep purple bruise forming on one side of her face.

"I'm so sorry, Hummingbird," he whispered. "I should never have let you ride alone." Should never have left her at all.

She stirred and whispered, "Loco Gringo." He didn't know if she meant him or Billy.

"Hush, Elena," he whispered back. "I need to see if there's anything broken before I move you again."

His fingers traced the lines of her body, feeling for broken bones in the semi-darkness. She's so small, he thought. Even smaller than Mary Louise. It occurred to him that while they had all been so worried about his delicate fiancée, they had virtually left this tiny Indian girl to fend for herself in a world filled with her enemies.

Not they, he corrected himself. Me. It wasn't her enemy that attacked her. It was his. Her wounds would heal, but would her beautiful, brave, and untamed spirit? All he could do was hope the Apache were as indomitable as Ned Butler wrote in his novels.

His hand came away from her left thigh wet and sticky. Billy had been busy with his knife. He cursed himself for shooting that bullet into the air. Keeping her covered as much as possible, he used an old blueberry bucket filled with the warm, healing waters of the hot spring, to cleanse her wounds.

The deep cut might need some sewing if the bandage made from his sleeve didn't stop the bleeding; but most of the other lacerations were from the struggle and not from the deadly blade Billy enjoyed so much.

Finally satisfied he'd done all he could in the dark, Sean pulled his jacket tighter around her, wrapped her back up in the extra blanket, and covered them both with the one from under Orion's saddle.

Lying next to the fire, he held her close, whispering, "Hush," whenever she thrashed in her tortured sleep. "He won't bother you again," he repeated over and over. "I promise."

CHAPTER TWELVE

*T*hin fingers of light reached through the leafy canopy surrounding the glen, chasing the darkness into the forest. The sound of a horse nickering nearby woke Elena.

She struggled against her blanket cocoon, groaning at the agony every movement caused. She couldn't open her left eye at all, or move her right arm without sending shafts of pain up through her shoulder. It felt as if a hot poker lay across her thigh. Finally, unable to escape the imprisoning shroud, she stopped fighting and closed her one good eye.

As she lay there half awake, confused, and wracked with pain, the dream she'd had during the night came back. An evil turkey buzzard attacked her, tearing at her flesh with its talons and sharp beak. Just as it was about to carry her away, a black panther with silver eyes came out of the darkness. The panther threw the bird into the water, then plucked it out to play with it like a kitten with a mouse.

When it tired of the game, the panther roared and let the crippled scavenger run into the woods to be prey for another, hungrier, hunter. Then the big cat came to her and licked her wounds with its warm, healing tongue. Finally, it curled up beside her to shield her from the cold night air with its thick, soft coat and soothing purr.

Now, hearing a familiar low voice, she realized it hadn't been a dream. Somehow, Sean O'Grady had come for her when she needed help and became the panther of her dream. Then who was the turkey buzzard? All she could recall was the glow of evil gold eyes and the stench of death in his fetid breath. Then she remembered a horrible, jagged-toothed knife. She'd seen it before, at the train station, during Sean's fight in the alley.

Her good eye opened again, focusing on Sean tending Orion's wounds. "Billy?" she choked out in a hoarse whisper.

Sean turned to see that she was awake. He left Orion to kneel at her side. His fingers smelled of the healing aloe plant of her homeland as he tilted her face to the light, waving a finger from side to side. "How many fingers do you see?"

Her head felt like a rock wobbling on top of her neck. Only his steadying hand allowed her to raise it. "One," she whispered and closed her eye.

"Good," he answered. "Now stay with me. Do you know your name?"

Yes, her mind screamed but her mouth could only breathe, "Elena Sant...," before she tasted blood from a split in her lip.

"Shhh," Sean soothed. "Don't try to talk. Your vision is clear and you know who you are. Those are good signs." He rolled up the blanket used to cover them both and put it under her head.

"Bill...?" she choked again. She had to know.

"Yes, but he's gone now. He won't be back."

The hard edge in his voice chased away visions of turkey buzzards and panthers so she could concentrate on what really happened. She remembered getting out of the water to return to Langesford when a man rushed from the low bushes surrounding the glade.

He blocked the way to her clothes and danced around her, taunting her with filthy language and waving his long, jagged blade like a sword. His gap-toothed grin looked like a jack-o-lantern, his feral gold eyes glowing with lust and violence. She'd desperately fought to avoid the knife until his other fist slammed against her face. She fell, the breath knocked out of her, unable to move under the heavy weight of his body. Then the weight was released and she heard splashing sounds from the spring. The last thing she heard was the roar of the panther.

Now, her one-eyed gaze focused on the holstered gun Sean wore on his hip like a Western outlaw, and she knew what the roar really was. He had saved her life and now she was indebted to him forever. She groaned, thinking she'd rather have died than owe her life to the Gringo who turned her heart upside down and was going to marry another woman. Suddenly, she didn't want to think any more. She just wanted to leave this place.

"My clothes."

"Right here." Sean put the neatly folded bundle next to her and touched her forehead with the palm of his hand. "I don't think you're busted up any inside or you'd have a raging fever by now and you're cool as a cucumber."

"Cucumber?"

"Yes. A long, pickle-like thing that's… It's just a saying. You'll mend. Now lay still and I'll get some water for your lips and cuts.

The thought of him seeing her naked and helpless humiliated her, but struggling to move had taken all her strength. Please let me die right now, she prayed, but her mother's god ignored her, forcing her to continue to take in painful breaths of air until she closed her eyes again.

"He…Billy…came out of the bushes. Before I could get to my knife, he…"

"Don't say any more," Sean whispered from behind her and slowly raised her shoulders to lean back against him. Then he offered her a canteen filled with fresh water. "Here. Drink. Try to forget."

She did as he asked, but her swollen lips were clumsy and her battered throat refused to swallow. Sean rubbed her back to ease her choking. When she quieted and leaned against him, he explained. "When I got back to the house, my mother said you were missing. I figured you'd come here. I heard you scream, and when I reached the top of the hill, you were fighting Billy with everything you had." He stopped there.

She didn't have to ask what happened next. She'd seen it in her dream and didn't care if Billy was dead or alive so long as he was gone. With Sean's strong body as warm and solid as an old adobe wall behind her, she rested against him until the sun heated the glade and her strength began to return.

She told herself she'd been through worse. The effort to keep the memory of the San Carlos massacre in the shadows of her mind made her head pound. She survived that and she would survive this. "This man, Billy, he works for your enemy?"

"Yes." He cleared his throat and nodded into her hair, "Yes. He was going to kidnap you."

"Why? I have no money."

"Neither do I, but I have land."

She again remembered the hate in Billy's voice when he vowed to make Sean pay for his missing teeth and the cut on his face. She had a right to curse Sean for not protecting her, but she cursed herself even more for fool-ishly leaving her knife so far from her side. She had behaved like a stupid young maiden and gave Sean's enemy the opportunity to use her for his revenge. Sean may have been the reason for the attack, but he was also the only reason she was still alive.

"Twice I have been saved from a white man by another white," she said. "But this time is very different from when Marcus took me from the soldier." She shivered despite the warm spring sun and the blanket around her. "This Billy, he did not care if I was alive or dead when he took me. He is a devil."

"Billy's a demon, all right, but the devil is his boss." Sean shifted behind her to prop her up against his saddle and kneel at her side. "It was dark when I got to you. Will you let me look at your wounds?"

She would have said the same thing to him, had she found him naked and bleeding on the trail. He had saved her life. He was right. She needed his help. "Si," she whispered and leaned back.

She settled against the curve of the saddle while he peeled back the blanket to check the one place where Billy's knife had found its mark. The stain on the bandage that had once been his sleeve was dark and crusty. A good sign. It had stopped bleeding.

"Try not to put too much weight on that leg," he warned when she tried to stand and still keep the blanket around her. "We need to get you to a doctor before it gets infected." He put his arm around her to help her up.

As soon as she put her weight on her good leg, the earth lurched. She threw her uninjured arm up to his shoulder to catch her balance and lost her grip on the blanket.

Sean caught her by the waist, his callused hands against her bare back held her close until the world stopped its crazy shifting. Her hand slid slowly down his bare shoulder and she saw that he would also carry scars from her battle. Red welts on his arms and chest were raw and jagged, and some of the deeper ones still bled when he moved. He risked going through the thorns to reach her. Why? She was nothing but a nuisance to him. Besides, he belonged to another.

She heard his sharp breath when her breasts brushed against his skin. When she looked up, the clear, silver-gray eyes of the panther in her dream looked back at her without sarcasm, anger, lust, or even sadness. They told her that while Sean O'Grady held her helpless and naked in his arms, he felt only her pain.

He gently touched her bruised cheek. "No man will ever do this to you again and live, Hummingbird." He kissed her forehead and repeated her words from the station. "You don't know how badly you are hurt. Let me help you."

His hands well acquainted with women's garments, he dressed her in her simple clothing, again wrapped her with the blanket, and carried her into the full sunlight. She lay back down and closed her eyes for what only seemed a heartbeat, but when he whispered, "Wake up Sleeping Beauty, it's time to go home," he had changed into a fresh shirt and saddled Orion, with Spirit Dancer attached to the big horse's lead.

The water, tender care and rest had done her good. Her bruised eye could even open enough to let her know she wasn't blind. And he'd sacrificed another sleeve to redress her knife wound. "Who is this Sleeping Beauty, and how long did I..."

"A while," he smiled. He reached into his seemingly bottomless saddlebag and pulled out a red bandanna, tying it around her neck as a sling for her injured arm. "Like you, Sleeping Beauty is the Princess of the forest, and I am your humble servant."

He lifted her easily into Orion's saddle before mounting behind her. "No, I can ride."

He leaned around her to take Orion's reins. "With no saddle, a leg wound and one hand? Maybe you are a little addled after all. Orion and I have this under control. Just lean back and enjoy the ride."

She couldn't argue with that logic. Spirit Dancer was unfamiliar with carrying an injured rider. Without a strong hand, anything could spook her. "Si," she conceded again. When she was settled comfortably against him, her hips between his body and the horn of his Western saddle, she looked at the top of the hill surrounded by a thicket. "The thorns," she said, worried about Orion.

"Relax Hummingbird. There's another way out. It's longer, but a lot less painful."

Despite the pain of her beating and the fact that a white man had just dressed her like a child, Elena did relax. Her head rested against Sean's chest as his strong arm supported her, and the gentle motion of Orion's slow, even strides rocked her like a cradle.

They were out of the grove and on the trail back to Langesford when she spoke. "What will we tell your parents? If your Mary Louise learns you were with me last night, we will both be ruined. You will lose this Rosewood you desire so much and I will be a *puta*."

Sean's silence told her he didn't have to know Spanish to understand what she meant. Whore was whore in any language, and a woman who spent the night alone with a man was guilty without a trial. His voice sounded worried when he answered. "We can tell the truth. That you were attacked by Billy Berens and I fought him off."

She turned to catch his eye and he chuckled. "That's right. We already used that one."

They rode in silence as Elena set aside her revulsion to lying to think of one that would work as well as the truth. "We can tell them I fell from Spirit Dancer and landed on my knife. That would explain the bruises on my face and the cut on my leg. You had trouble finding me in the dark and sat with me until I could ride."

"Ah yes, a half-truth is always a good option. I'm impressed, but will they believe an Apache fell from her horse?"

She thought of the man who had saved her from certain death. She'd seen him brutal, sarcastic, and arrogant, and had felt the heat of passion in his embrace. Now, cradled against him, she felt truly safe for the first time in her life. But it would be only for a little while, she remembered. Until he married the white woman with yellow hair.

Tears filled her eyes, blurring the path in front of them. Sean O'Grady's touch had changed her more than Billy's attack ever could. Suddenly exhausted, she sighed. "An Apache doesn't scream, but that is how you found me. The half of me that is white has won the battle for my spirit. I have lost the right to say I am Apache.

CHAPTER THIRTEEN

*A*fter Dr. Montrose left Elena, Chloe barred Sean from her room by standing in front of the door, her hands on her hips, lips pressed into a thin angry line. "You ain't steppin' one foot inside 'til you tell me what is goin' on here. Dem bruises ain't from no fall. An' I knows the marks of a guttin' knife when I sees 'em. You tell me right now what happen to dat girl."

He knew he'd never see Elena again if he didn't answer so he confessed. "I came on the scene just as Billy Berens was attacking her."

"Billy Berens," she whispered softly, as if like the devil, saying his name out loud would make him appear. She shook her head in wonderment and crossed herself for protection. "Den she be lucky fo' sho' you come along when you did." Her eyes narrowed. "But did you git to her in time? Before that demon....?" She swallowed hard. "What if you saved only her life?"

That very question was eating him alive, but he couldn't ask Dr. Montrose without revealing their lie or causing Elena more pain. "Isn't that enough?"

"What if that devil left her with child?"

He ran his fingers over the dark stubble on his face. "I don't know." Only time would tell, and there wasn't much of it left before he married Mary Louise, leaving Elena to deal with her fate alone. What would happen to her if she went back to New Mexico pregnant? The Spanish word *puta* echoed in his mind.

"If I married her, no one would ever know," escaped his lips before he even thought about it, but it didn't sound like a bad idea. Mary Louise obviously wasn't excited about marrying him. And if Clay's behavior at the ball was any indication of his feelings for her, it was a safe bet that he'd be more than happy to replace him at the altar.

A wide smile replaced the cunning Caribbean woman's frown when she cuffed him on the shoulder. "Now you be the hothead for sure. I sho' hopes you know what you be doin'."

Sean's head ached with a whole new set of problems. His wedding to Mary Louise was barely two weeks away. Even Elena wouldn't know by then if she was pregnant. And if she was, he doubted she'd tell him. "You know me better than that."

It was three days before Elena's fever broke from an infection in her leg wound and Dr. Montrose gave her permission to get out of bed. "I can walk," she protested when Sean scooped her into his arms to take her out to the verandah. She touched her robe, one of Lily's theatrical dressing gowns of violet silk with white, feather trim. "Please let me get dressed. I am fine."

"Is that so?" Sean carried her to the mirror. The bruise on the side of her face was a colorful rainbow of blue, green, purple and yellow. Her golden skin was sallow from the fever, and dark circles rimmed her expressive brown eyes. "I think you need some sunshine and fresh air, he continued. "And you look beautiful in feathers, Hummingbird."

Elena grimaced at both her reflection and the nickname. She pressed her face into his shoulder, inhaling deeply of his now familiar scent of cinnamon cologne and maleness. "The feathers tickle, but the sun is a healer."

He settled her into the padded wicker chair he'd enjoyed not long ago and sat next to her in an old, wooden rocker. While he looked out on the still blooming magnolia trees lining the drive, and the vibrant, green lawn spread out like a carpet in front of them, Elena again reflected that in another place and time, he would be a handsome Apache brave.

When he returned her gaze, silver eyes shattered her fantasy of a kinsman. He was no Apache warrior. He was white. Her enemy. Yet he had also saved her life. Unable to endure his gaze any longer, she finally spoke. "I was foolish to stay so long at the spring. If you had not come for me, I would be dead, or wish I was."

He covered her hand with his and searched her face for the answer to his question. "Did I save you? Really?"

Realizing that Billy had come close enough to raping her for Sean to wonder about it made her feel dirty. She looked away. "It is not proper to talk of such things to a man who is about to be married."

The reminder sent Sean's hand back to the arm of his chair. "I'm so sorry, Elena. To say you've been treated very badly here is an understatement."

"I am not used to being treated well by whites. The only years I have known without fear are the ones with Judith and Marcus. I will put this behind me when I return home. Then I will be well again. Until then, I will remember the quail and wild turkey, the giant cactus and paloverde trees of New Mexico."

His eyes, so sad whenever he looked at her, hurt almost as much as Billy's attack. She missed the mischief, even the suspicious curiosity that made him so challenging, so interesting, so attractive to her. She admitted that his eyes and strong body drew her to him in ways she never thought possible with any man. Now she saw only pity and sympathy in his gaze. It made her sad and angry at the same time. No matter what she'd said on the trail, she was still Apache. She did not want, or need a white man's sympathy.

She would have told him so, but at the mention of her homeland, his eyebrows rose, and a spark of interest brightened his eyes. The crooked smile returned. "Well if that's all it takes to make you feel better, perhaps I can be of use to you after all."

He reached into his pocket and pulled out the ragged book he'd been reading the day of the engagement ball. "It's one of Lily's Western novels. My mother takes offense to them, and they're strictly forbidden around the house, but Lily hides them here and there, just like I used to. I found it behind the palm the night we…talked."

With just one blink, the mischief in his eyes turned to shame. "Elena, I'm so sorry for the things I said to you that night… and at the ball. I… just…well, there are things going on in my life. I'm not sure who to trust."

Touching his hand, she nodded toward the book. "I don't want to talk about bad things anymore. Tell me about this Western novel or yours."

"Well, this one is really quite interesting. It's about New Mexico. I thought you might like to hear about a mystery involving gold hidden in the caves of the Taos Pueblos."

Elena ignored the healing cracks in her lips to smile for the first time in days. She straightened in her chair. "I know Taos. It is north of Santa Fe. My people went there in the Fall for the trading fairs."

She blinked away other memories that threatened her delight at hearing about her homeland. "There are places in the Sangre de Cristo Mountains that are holy to the Apache as well as to the Pueblas. The spirits from the White Mountain are our protectors. There is a sacred blue lake at its peak and a ceremony is…was…held there every year."

"You tell me then," he said. "I'd like to hear everything about your sacred mountain with the blue lake. I've dreamed of going there, but…it seems unlikely now."

"What about your book?"

"I don't need a book," he winked. "I have a very beautiful expert right here."

She blushed at the compliment, but welcomed the chance to put aside her masquerade for a little while and talk about her life as it had been when her mother was alive and they roamed freely from Mexico to the northern plains. Her heart swelled with pride when she told him about Little Wolf and what promise he had as a hunter. For this day only, she allowed him to be alive in her mind and in her heart.

She talked for nearly an hour. Sean's delight and interest made her forget her pain and the sadness that seemed to follow her like a shadow. His eyes widened as she explained the contrasts between his world of gently rolling hills and misty valleys, and the western desert of flat ground giving rise to mountains thousands of feet high. They laughed together at the plants as foreign to him as the cucumber was to her.

His deep, throaty laugh touched her soul and she knew she would never forget this moment. "Now tell me your story," she said, suddenly tired.

She leaned toward him to see the cover. The robe loosened with her movement, exposing her delicate white linen gown with embroidered flowers around the fluted bodice. She closed it quickly, painfully aware that he'd seen every part her body.

"Rebel Treasure." She sniffed and pointed to the pile of gold bullion under the title. "We have known about the yellow rock for centuries, but we leave it where the gods put it. Now the Gringos come with their dynamite and think they can pull it from the mountain's heart."

"Simmer down," he smiled. "This story is about gold bars that were stolen by the Confederacy from the Denver Mint, that is Southern soldiers, from the Yankees…the North, during the War of Northern Agression."

She pretended to be offended by his assumption of her ignorance. "I know about the war between the whites. It was before I was born, but I heard about battles they fought over our gold even then."

Sean ignored her derisive tone to clear his throat. "Well then you know the background." He settled back in his chair and began to read in a deep, soothing voice, "*Rebel Treasure*: a story of hidden gold from the late War of the Rebellion", as told to Ned Butler by Corporal Eldon Mills, Fort Union, New Mexico."

He sniffed. "That's what the Yankees called it. For us it was an invasion."

She nodded. "It was the same for my people, even while the Whites fought each other."

"Yes, I suppose it was." he acknowledged, then turned the page to begin, "Somewhere in the ancient caves of the Sangre de Cristo Mountains a fortune in gold bullion stolen by a small cadre of daring Confederates..."

"Someone is coming," Elena interrupted. One hand pulled the dressing gown tight against her throat, the other squeezed Sean's arm.

He looked up to see a lone rider coming up the drive fast, and put the book back inside his breast pocket. "It has to be important to push an animal that hard in the heat of the day," he said with a worried frown. "I'll get the old man."

"There's no need," Patrick said from the doorway. "I saw him from my study." He squinted at the bay he'd sold the sheriff a few years back. "Coulter," he said flatly, before the rider's face even came into view.

The man halted abruptly and dismounted clumsily. He brushed red dust from his trousers and swaggered forward, his fat belly bouncing over his belt, sweat pouring from his florid face. Patrick's frown answered the dislike in the man's watery, blue eyes.

Camilla O'Grady spoke politely from the top step of Langesford's verandah. "Why, Sheriff Coulter, I heard someone was riding in, but never imagined it was you." She glided past her husband, her warning glance telling them all to be wary of the snake in their yard, at least until they found a club big enough to crush it.

Apparently oblivious to her cold glare and forced smile, the sheriff smiled broadly with tobacco-stained teeth. He bowed as much as his bulging belly would allow to kiss her outstretched hand and didn't seem to notice that she wiped the hand on her apron after he released it.

"To what do we owe this honor?" she said in a voice as smooth as fresh cream. "Can we offer you an ice?"

The sheriff's arrogance disappeared in the face of her gentility. "No, ma'am. I'm here on bizness. Law bizness." He looked at Sean, then puffed out his chest. "Rupert Berens found the body of his brother Billy last night in a gully just over from your property, not far from the hot spring."

Camilla broke the silence that followed his announcement. "How horrible. What happened to him?"

Coulter seemed more than happy to explain, "Shot he was, right through the head, and left lyin' naked as the day he was born for the wild animals. Been dead three days, more-or-less. Doc Montrose says he was beat up pretty bad first. Found his clothes folded up on a rock by the spring."

With a quick look at Sean, Patrick stepped closer to his wife. "Berens was scum. If he was swimming in the spring, he was trespassing. Are you looking for a burial donation?"

Coulter's eyes narrowed until they were little more than tiny, blue marbles surrounded by greasy, pink fat. "I'm here investigatin' his murder, O'Grady." His voice crowed with triumph. "An' yer son here is my main suspect."

Camilla put her hand on her husband's arm for support. "Sean has had his differences with Billy Sheriff, but so have most of the other decent people in Jeffers County. You are mistaken."

The sheriff refused to be dismissed, even by Mrs. O'Grady. "I have evidence, ma'am," he huffed and held up a gold button. "This was in his hand when Rupert found his body."

He strutted up the steps to face Patrick. "It's from a white jacket, just like the ones favored by you and your cub here, Mister O'Grady. "

Only Camilla's hand on her husband's arm, and Elena's on Sean's, kept them from leaping on the corpulent officer of the law. As if he knew it, Coulter added, "Everyone knows yer son threatened Billy after a fight at the train station." He held the incriminating button out to Sean. "This look familiar, boy?"

Sean looked at it incredulously. "A button. You're accusing me of murder because of a button? You're crazy."

"Then you don't mind if I take a look-see around, do ye?" Coulter swaggered toward the open doors.

"You'll not set foot in my house!" Patrick roared, taking a threatening step toward him.

Coulter halted, a sly smile on his bloodless lips. "Mind if I check the barn?"

Patrick looked as if he was about to tell him to check Hell, when Sean stood. "Go ahead. If I wanted to kill Berens, it would be in a fair fight."

"You got a gun, Seany?"

"Doesn't everyone?"

"What kind?"

"Forty-four. Colt revolver."

They all knew the Colt .44 was one of the most common guns in the country, but Coulter smiled as if Sean was already convicted. "Berens was shot with a .44. Fired yours lately?"

Sean's expertise at lying showed in his shrug. "Only at a skunk that's been hanging around the house."

"Mind if I see it?" Coulter held up his hands in the face of any argument.

Sean smiled, toying with the scorpion in their midst. "The skunk? It took off."

Coulter's face reddened to the color of an over-ripe watermelon and his hand slid to the gun in his holster. "The gun, boy." He raised the other at Patrick's approach with clenched fists. "Just doin' my job."

Sean nodded to his father and faced Coulter. "Your job according to Roscoe LaPorte. It's in the barn with my saddle and gear. I'll go with you."

CHAPTER FOURTEEN

Sean handed the gun to the sheriff who sniffed it and flipped the carriage open, revealing the missing bullet. "I told you I shot at a skunk the other day," Sean repeated and leaned against a stall door while Sheriff Coulter searched the carriage he'd taken to the station to meet Elena.

"Well, well, looka here," the sheriff gloated, pulling out Sean's jacket. It was ripped and stained with blood, and when Coulter held the button to the space on the front, where one was missing, it matched the others.

Sean tried not to show his alarm. "That was from the fight at the station. I put it in there on the way back."

"Or on the way back from beatin' the life outa poor Billy an' killin' 'im dead. Looks like old Roscoe was right. You ain't only a brawler and a deadbeat, yer a murderer to boot." He put his fat face close to Sean's. "I'm gonna enjoy takin' this to the judge, boy. I knew ye'd mess yerself up sometime. Now I got ye."

Sean didn't hear anything beyond the name Roscoe. It kept popping up everywhere. Rupert must have picked up the button with Billy's knife after the fight and gave it to Roscoe. Then Roscoe killed Billy for letting Elena escape and put the button in his cold, dead hand for the sheriff to find. He had to hand it to the man. It was nice and tidy. He could never prove LaPorte's part in Billy's murder, and all the evidence they needed to charge him was in Sheriff Coulter's hands.

After he left, Sean stayed alone in the barn to ponder his fate. The idea that he could be hung for murdering a worthless piece of scum like Billy Berens was inconceivable, even with Roscoe behind it. There had to be something more at stake than Rosewood for him to risk exposing his illicit business ventures by kidnapping Elena. What?

He concentrated on his enemy. Roscoe had a devious mind and the patience to wait out a plan. His rise in politics, based on a largely fabricated reputation of killing Indians during his Army career, was evidence of that. He was mostly just cunning and sly. And damned lucky. But every gambler's luck ran out eventually. Given time, the truth would come out.

The problem was that it wouldn't take Judge Harding long to declare that the button matched his coat, because it did. They already knew the murder weapon was the same caliber as his gun. While men had been hung on less evidence, he knew his social position would protect him for a little while.

He recalled Roscoe's warning that they were far from even. The bastard had no intention of letting him live with the dangerous knowledge he possessed. He'd waited too long to call Roscoe's bluff. He left the barn knowing that if Coulter arrested him, he wouldn't live to see a trial.

Everyone was gone from the verandah. A look down the drive showed the dust from a departing horse. Chloe stood alone in the doorway, her light coffee complexion tinted with rose.

He hugged her. "Don't worry, I didn't kill the son of a bitch." When she didn't respond, he smiled. "You know I always land on my feet."

"I know," she sputtered. "But you missed Ben Simms from de telegraph." "Another death." "Dey be in de office."

He found his mother sobbing in his father's arms. Elena sat in a chair by the fireplace, staring at something only she could see. He knelt in front of her, seeing pain in her eyes that went beyond the comfort of tears.

Stunned by the change that had come over them all in such a short time, he stood and faced his father. Patrick's expression confirmed that something devastating had happened. While he was in the barn worrying about his own neck, their world had shattered.

Patrick nodded toward the telegram on his desk and Sean picked it up. It was from the Williams' partner, Jesse Woods, in New Mexico. "Oh God, how much more can she take?" He ignored his mother's sobs to stare at the stricken figure of Elena Santiago, orphaned for the second time by the death of her adopted mother, Judith Williams.

The telegram said the missionary was murdered in an attempted robbery at the school the day after Elena left Santa Fe. It had taken some time to get word to Jesse Woods, and then on to them.

Camilla wiped her tears with Patrick's handkerchief. "We must end this before that gold destroys more innocent people."

Patrick cleared his throat and sat behind the partners' desk. "Yes, my dear, but it's much more complicated than that. Even if we wired Washington, after so many years, how would they find it? All those cliff dwellings look alike. If there's been a rock slide or a cave-in since then, it could be impossible to find, even if we went there ourselves."

Camilla slumped into her chair. "So, there's no way to atone for the sins of my father, brother, or my own selfish wish to leave the gold and what happened in the Pueblos behind me." She didn't bother to stop the tears dripping onto her day dress. "But I can't ever go back there."

Patrick reached across the desk to hold her hand. "I know, darling."

Sean watched them in confused silence. Then he realized the dime novel in his pocket wasn't one of Lily's. It must have fallen out of Elena's envelope, along with Marcus Williams' letter. His world suddenly turned inside out as the passages he'd read from *Rebel Treasure* with such amusement raced through his mind, mocking him with a truth he didn't know.

The realization that he had been reading about his own family sickened him. If it was true, his parents had been living a lie all these years by perpetuating the myth of his Uncle Brent's heroic death at the battle of Chickamauga. And if the author told the truth, the worst secret of all was that his very delicate and refined mother had given birth to him in a Comanche winter camp.

The panic in Camilla's eyes told him she read his thoughts. Her voice trembled when she spoke. "We must explain this to Sean."

He hid his pain in sarcasm. "There's no need," he answered, reached into his pocket and dropped the old book onto the desk. "It's all in here, as told by a Corporal Eldon Mills, the only survivor of the recovery mission to collect gold stolen from the Denver Mint in 1862. It was rumored that the raid was led by the son of a prominent Georgia family."

Camilla gasped and more tears stained her dress until Patrick offered a fresh handkerchief. Elena just stared as Sean continued. "Five years later, the year I was born, a white woman captive with a child on her back, and the husband who had rescued her, turned it over to the Army."

His voice sharp with anger and pain, he looked at his mother. "Corporal Mills was especially complimentary to the beautiful captive with wild, chestnut-colored hair and green eyes." He turned to his father, "He was less amiable toward her dark, Irish husband who had a bad temper and a deep shoulder wound in the same one you favor during cold or damp weather.

"It ended with the revelation that the Yankee husband was a former government agent assigned to the robbery. He got an added reward for solving his case. A baby boy named Storm Cloud. Mills left it up to his readers to decide whether he was white or a half-breed."

Fury contorted his features as he stared at Patrick. "Is that why I have never felt like one of you? Is it why my brother and sister are fair-skinned and I'm dark? And why you, sir, treat me like a thorn in your side?"

"Silence." Patrick rose slowly from his chair. His face mirrored Sean's own rage. The muscle in his jaw tensed as he took a deep breath, meeting the angry gray gaze with his own. "Talk to me in that tone again... son, and you'll find out what damage I can do to a thorn in my side, even with a bad shoulder. There is a great deal you don't know, you insolent young whelp."

He paused to let his words sink in and sighed. "There is also a great deal to do very soon if we're to stop the bloodshed brought about by that book." He sat down again. "For what it's worth, from the first moment I saw you, I've never thought of you as anything other than my son. It's only to my own great shame that I've been unable to stop you from making the same mistakes I did as a youth."

He took his wife's hand again, looking into her eyes while speaking to Sean. "You'll never know the indignities your mother suffered at the hands of Three Feathers, any more than you will know the reasons why your Uncle Brent hid the gold in the Pueblos. But know this. We turned those gold bars over to the Army and left New Mexico behind us forever. Until now, there has been no need to speek of it again."

Finally, he turned to Sean. "Marcus' letter will explain that we have a much more serious problem on our hands than the identity of your sire."

Sean bit back the questions that taunted him. Storm Cloud. His legal name was Sean C. O'Grady, but no one ever told him what the "C" stood for. Aside from the color of their eyes, how could Patrick be so sure he was his son? And if he really belonged in Georgia, why did the West call him so strongly?

He held his breath as Patrick opened the center drawer of the desk and removed the packet Elena had delivered what seemed a lifetime ago. He read out loud.

"My dear old friend, if you are reading this, then I'm dead as a prairie dog in a

rattler's jaw. That don't bother me, but I fear you and your family will be in danger after I'm gone.

First off, I need to confess I never got the reward money on that pile o' gold you wanted me to keep for young Storm Cloud. I figured my papers got lost,

But a couple years ago, I got to feelin' guilty about not livin' up to my promise, so I wrote to Fort Dodge. They wrote back that the soldiers we met were kilt by the Indians, or each other. A Corporal Mills was the only survivor, but he deserted before they could go back.

A few months ago, a book called, "Rebel Treasure" started makin' the rounds of the saloons. Mills told his story to a writer named Ned Butler, who peddled it around Tucson and Santa Fe with a fake map inside. It ended up with a gambler named Anscombe, who moved into the territory a few months ago.

He was a clerk in Fort Dodge before he quit the army and knew about my letter. He's in with a passel of lawyers usin' phony land grants to cheat the Mexicans and Indians out of their own land. He killed Ed Torres to get title to his place up near Rancho de Taos, but nobody can prove it. Then he applied for a mining permit in the southeast end of the Taos Pueblos. I figure he's looking for the gold.

The varmint found me a few days ago, an' offered me a deal to lead him there. When I tol' him I'd sooner lead him to Hell, he tracked down Jesse. Ambushed, and almost kilt him. I 'spect I'm next. With the book and my letter, it won't take him long to find out about you.

Anscombe is deadly, but he ain't smart enough to know about mining permits. His boss goes by the name of Colonel. He's slippery. Nobody knows his name or what he looks like.

I poked around some and found out Anscombe's been sending regular telegrams to Jeffers. The Colonel or whoever's bank-rollin' the fake mining operation is in your own backyard.

I told Judith if anything happens to me, she should send this with someone that won't likely be followed. It may be one of the students, and I trust you and the Missus will treat him well.

Watch your back, amigo.

Adios, Marcus."

Patrick put the pages down and looked at his audience. Camilla wrung his handkerchief in her hand. Elena now stood next to Sean, her hand on his arm, whispering the names, "Anscombe and Colonel," over and over.

"I led them to you," she sobbed. "Junior Anscombe has been paying attention to me. The day I left Santa Fe, I saw him at the depot. He looked at my ticket. And the man who murdered my village was called Colonel. He vowed to kill Marcus and Judith for saving me. If he is here, he knows why I came and who you are."

Her voice lowered with hatred. "And Junior Anscombe murdered Judith."

"Roscoe," Sean announced, putting the final piece of the puzzle into place. "It has to be him. He has businesses in Santa Fe and spent time at Fort Dodge during his Indian fighting days. He's even bragged about gold mining as a possible venture.

"That's why he's courting Mary Louise. He needs her money to bankroll his scheme, and her connections to win the Senate seat and get approval to open the Pueblos to his mining company."

Patrick nodded. "I suspected he was up to no good. Six years with Allen Pinkerton taught me to recognize an actor when I see one. I wrote letters and wired old colleagues in Washington and Santa Fe as soon as we got this, but it's too soon to hear back. All I know is that the New Mexico Rangers and Federal Marshalls have been chasing their tails trying to find out who's behind a group of swindlers who call themselves The Santa Fe Ring. If Roscoe is behind it, then he's holding the aces right now. And I'm sure he's not above using a murder charge against you as a distraction to squeeze the whereabouts of the gold from us."

Patrick folded his hands on the desk, once again an investigator with the uncanny ability to enter the mind of a criminal. "Blackmail," he concluded. "Marcus and Judith wouldn't tell Anscombe anything and he got stupid and killed them. Now we're the only ones left with the information Roscoe needs. He'll propose a bargain when he figures he's got us by the short hairs."

Sean was suddenly proud to be this man's son. If his father was like him as a young man, perhaps there was hope for him after all. "It's Roscoe all right, he's been bragging about his ring of partners who are above the law. So, don't underestimate him. He's resourceful, as well as dangerous and evil. He adapts. He had Billy watching the house to kidnap Elena, but when I foiled that plan, Billy became the victim instead. I played right into his hand. A murder charge beats a ransom demand any day."

Patrick looked at Elena. "I didn't think you fell off your mount."

He looked older when he crossed the room and took her hand. "Please accept my humblest apologies. Until now, I never believed in the curse my wife and Morning Bird insisted lingered over those caves and the gold. They warned me to leave all of it behind as a sacrifice to the Anasazi gods, but I had to close the case. By trying to keep the reward money for my son, I brought this trouble on my family and my closest friends."

He turned to Sean. "Your mother is right. It's time to put an end to it once and for all. I can't have you hang because I offended some Indian ghosts."

He returned to his chair and for the first time in Sean's life, invited him to sit on the other side. When he did, Patrick spoke to the ladies. "Elena, you need your rest; and Camilla, it's important we behave as normally as possible. I know you have things to arrange for the upcoming wedding, so if you'll excuse us, we have some plans of our own to make."

CHAPTER FIFTEEN

t took Sheriff Coulter several days to locate Dr. Montrose who was in Darbyville delivering twins. It took a couple more days after that to get him to confirm that the bullet found in Billy's body was the same caliber as Sean's gun.

Then Judge Harding was reluctant to issue an arrest warrant for his friend's son based on a button and a bullet from a gun as common as cockroaches in the South. He only relented when Coulter threatened to find a Yankee judge who'd happily try a pillar of Southern aristocracy for murder.

Finally, armed with a warrant to arrest Sean O'Grady for murder, Coulter arrived at Langesford. Several carriages lined the drive and a formally dressed ex-slave guarded the front door.

"Let me in, Cato," he demanded.

The massive black man with a head of silver hair, shook his head. "Sorry suh. They's a weddin' goin' on in there. I cain't let nobody in who weren't invited."

It caught Coulter off guard. "You mean Mary Louise is still goin' ahead with the weddin'?"

Cato nodded this time. "She come back early from her shoppin' trip and say they got to get wed afore the law comes for her man. Says she be waitin' right here 'til the jury lets him off."

That didn't sound at all like the Mary Louise Fairchild Coulter knew.

"This is a trick. I don't believe it. It's just to keep me from arrestin' O'Grady. I want to see for myself."

Cato stepped closer to him, his height and broad build dwarfing the corpulent sheriff as well as blocking the entrance to the mansion. "Waaall, you'll jes' have to wait until after the 'I do's' is done afore havin' your looksee."

Coulter backed away as if it finally dawned on him that if the carriages in the yard could be believed, most of Jeffers County society was inside the house. Even with Roscoe behind him, he didn't want to make a scene by arresting one of them in the act of marrying into the county's second most prominent family, especially for shooting trash like Billy. His eyes narrowed shrewdly. If he couldn't barge in and stop the ceremony, he'd just bide his time until Sean tried to leave for the honeymoon.

Twenty minutes later, Judge Harding joined him on the verandah steps. "Let him be for a while, son," he cautioned. "The boy has promised to put himself under house arrest until his trial."

The Judge smiled through a bushy white mustache. "No sense puttin' a newly married man in the pokey, now is there?" He laughed and patted the sputtering sheriff on the back. "Come on now. Let's leave the family to their celebratin'."

A stunned Coulter moved along with the Judge's prodding. It wasn't going at all like Roscoe told him it would. He stopped, "Mary Louise really married an accused murderer?"

The judge's old top hat bobbed. "I kissed the bride myself. It brought tears to my eyes to see that handsome young couple, knowin' this little altercation lies in the path of their happiness."

Then with a warning that couldn't be misunderstood, the judge told him, "You don't really think Sean O'Grady would soil his hands to murder Berens, do you? You'll have to come up with more than a button, and a better witness than Rupert Berens if you want to convict that boy in front of a jury of his peers."

He slapped the Sheriff's back. "Don't fret. You'll have your day in court." He saw Coulter to his horse and watched him ride down the drive before climbing into his brougham and following at a safe enough distance to avoid the bay's dust.

∼

Elena took a deep breath in the privacy of her room, suffocating in Mary

Louise Fairchild's silk wedding gown. After yet another masquerade, this time in a sham wedding ceremony, she desperately wanted out of it. But her strength was slow to return. She'd only unbuttoned half the tiny buttons lining the back of the dress before feeling exhausted. She knew if she wanted to be strong when she reached New Mexico, she'd have to take things slow and looked forward to a long nap on the train.

The O'Gradys had answered her prayers for a way to return home when they asked her to pretend to be Mary Louise in their plan to fool the sheriff. It would buy them more time for Senor O'Grady to trap Roscoe. In return, she considered her debt to Sean for saving her life paid in full.

Now she could concentrate on paying her one remaining debt. She had caused Judith's death because she let Junior Anscombe know where she was going. As soon as she got to Santa Fe, she would pay that debt in full—with his blood.

A knock on her door ended her clumsy struggle with the buttons. She opened it to Sean's smiling face. Grateful she hadn't finished undressing, she backed up toward the mirror. "What do you want of me now?"

He smiled at the reflection of her naked back tapering down to the silk cord of her pantalets. "I came to thank you for becoming by bride."

She moved away from the mirror. "The wedding was a lie. I am not your bride. I will never marry." Who would want her? She was no longer Apache and she would never be white.

"Whatever the lady wishes." He stepped behind her to finish her buttons. The featherlike touch of his fingertips against her skin awakened something deep inside her, heating her feminine core until she felt damp, but his deep voice kept her still.

"You are a remarkable woman, Elena," he whispered against her neck. "You may consider yourself a coward because you screamed at the hot spring, but I saw you fight like a demon for your life. I'm forever in your debt for what you did today."

When he finally loosed the last tiny pearl button, he put his hands on her bare shoulders and turned her to face him. His warm lips brushed lightly against hers. "You could stay and we could honor our marriage. I don't think Mary Louise will be upset." He winked. "I'm sure we could come up with a convincing story."

The lingering feel of his lips on hers, even from the light kiss, his smile, and the heat in his eyes tempted her, but what he asked was impossible. If she didn't leave now, the comfort of his arms would make her forget the crimes committed against her family. Then she would lose her honor as well as her heritage.

She fought the temptation with anger, stepping away from his mesmerizing touch and gaze. "More lies. Ever since I came to this place, I have been surrounded by lies. You lie to each other and to your friends. Your parents lied to you about your birth and your uncle's death. I have lied for you and you for me, and now we have lied before your god. Even those who will judge you are part of the lie."

She waved her arm. "*Madre de Dios*. You are all *loco* here. If I stay, I will become *loco* too."

Her careless gesture made the top of the dress fall away, revealing the filmy camisole beneath her corset that barely shielded the dark tips of her breasts. The more she fumbled to pull the bodice back up, the farther the satin cloud slid down her body, until she stood wearing only her pantalets, the corset and camisole.

The amusement in Sean's eyes told her he hadn't heard a word. Then his gaze grew hungry and he stepped toward her again. The last time a man had come after her with lust in his eyes, she had fought and suffered the consequences. With no knife strapped to her wounded leg, she stiffened when Sean raised her chin to meet his eyes.

He repeated what he'd said at the river. "Another time perhaps. In Another place." He helped her into Lily's dressing gown, making sure she was modestly covered when he tied the belt around her waist. "Don't judge all whites by us, Elena. Or all men by me."

He opened the door, and turned back to face her. "Your train leaves in two hours. My mother is packing a trunk of clothing and supplies for the school. Your ticket is under the name of Mrs. O'Grady and the ring will show you're a married woman, even though you're traveling alone. Once you get to Santa Fe, it'll be up to you if you want to keep either one."

He tapped a finger to his forehead in mock salute and his eyes sparkled with mischief once again. "Take care of yourself, Hummingbird."

Lily burst through the door that Sean had barely closed and jumped up onto to the feather bed. "Can you believe it?" she said between ecstatic giggles.

"We did it. Sheriff Coulter is gone and now we can work on finding out what old Roscoe is doing." She stood on the mattress to assume a dramatic pose, narrowed her eyes, and lowered her voice. "He disappeared, you know. Right after Sheriff Coulter claimed Billy's body. It won't be long before we find him though. Papa used to be a Pinkerton man."

When Elena shook her head in confusion, Lily slowed down to explain. "Pinkerton is a big detective agency now. Papa worked with them and Uncle Marcus during the war. Oh, I'm sorry," she said when the name brought a stabbing look of pain to Elena's face.

"It is all right," Elena comforted her. "My people believe you must never speak a person's name after they die, or their ghost will hurt you. But Marcus would never hurt me. So, I think of him often and Judith too." Especially Judith.

Lily chattered while Elena packed her little carpetbag and put on the green traveling dress Judith had given her with such high hopes. "Do you want to know how I got the gown away from Rosewood?" Lily asked.

Elena looked at the expensive wedding gown, now a heap on the floor. It was obscene. The cost of it would have fed Judith's school children for a year. She couldn't bring herself to touch it again, and Lily didn't seem interested. "Yes, how did you do it?"

The rest of her packing was accompanied by Lily's enthusiastic and detailed narration of how that very morning, she'd been smuggled over to Rosewood to impersonate the bride in case Roscoe or the sheriff was watching. "I told Mary Louise's maid I needed the gown to match it to some decorations. From a distance, I look a lot like her, so I just made sure my back was to the window on the way back. It went without a hitch."

"Without a hitch?" Elena repeated. No one at Langesford talked like that. "Where did you learn that?"

Lily laughed. "In the novels Mama doesn't know I read. I know all about the West. About Billy the Kid and the Lincoln County Wars and Geronimo and Indians and—"

She stopped when Elena raised her eyebrows and crossed her arms over her chest. "Well maybe not real Indians. But when I'm on tour with the theater someday, I can visit you and—" A knock on the door made her jump off the bed. "…meet some."

The next knock was louder and Cato spoke from the other side. "The buggy is ready ma'am, if you is."

Elena hugged Lily. "I'm afraid all the real Indians are dead." She took her bag to follow Cato.

On the steps of the wide front porch, Camilla's swollen and red eyes were filled with concern. "It's too soon, Elena," she said. "You should stay until you heal properly and get your strength back. You'll be safer…" She stopped at the absurdity of the statement. "I'm so sorry. None of this should have happened."

Loneliness made Elena's heart skip a beat when Camilla leaned into her husband for support. She touched the older woman's hand. "My wounds are healing. I will only be strong when I am back home."

Patrick left his wife to embrace Elena and whisper in her ear. "Don't do anything foolish. Remember, Judith always said that everything happens for a purpose. We'll find the ones responsible for this. We just need some time."

She clung to him a moment, but couldn't meet his eyes when she answered. "Judith also said that God helps those who help themselves." Then she climbed into the carriage to begin her journey back to where her spirit lived. To where she'd avenge the deaths of her white family the Apache way.

CHAPTER SIXTEEN

The conductor adjusted his spectacles on the tip of his nose and looked at Elena's ticket. He leaned in as if trying to see her face under the black mourning veil and hooded shawl. "Mrs. O'Grady?" he drawled.

Silently cursing Sean for not putting the ticket in her real name, she tried not to show her fear of being thrown off the train as an impostor. "Yes."

He nodded. "Heard there was a weddin' up Langesford way. Congratulations." He looked around, "Not that it's any of my business, but where's the happy groom?"

Imitating Mary Louise's little girl voice, she held a handkerchief to her lips. "My...Auntie has died. He will join me later."

"Yeah, I heard old Sean's got hisself in a peck o' trouble." Then he apologized, "Oh, sorry ma'am. My condolences on the passing of your loved one." He tipped his hat and moved along the seats, glancing at the remaining passengers' tickets as he punched them through to Savannah.

She let out a long breath when the conductor left the car. As the train finally started to move, she again felt the fatigue from her fever and slow-healing leg wound, but she wouldn't give in to it, or to the grief that made her heart feel like a stone in her chest. She wouldn't grieve for Judith until her murderer had been sent to Hell.

Instead, she'd sleep as much as possible on the way home, knowing that her strength would return when she reached her mountains. With that thought in mind, she released the hood of her cape and raised the suffocating veil. Then she stretched her still-bandaged leg under the seat in front of her and closed her eyes, barely noticing when a man came from the rear of the car to sit beside her on the aisle.

She woke at the Savannah stop to find her hand pressed against the white silk shirt of the man sitting next to her, her cheek against the sleeve of his gray tweed jacket. She snapped back to her seat so fast her head banged against the window.

"I am so sorry," she said, afraid to look at him. "I fell asleep."

When he didn't answer, she realized he was sleeping too, a bowler hat over his face. His slow, even breathing gave her hope that he hadn't noticed she'd used him as a pillow.

She moved as far away as she could and stared through the dirty window as smoke settled around the slowing train. She hoped he'd claim his carpetbag and leave the car before she had to face him wearing guilt all over her face for the wrinkles on his shirt.

But he continued to doze while the other passengers rose and stood in line to leave the car. Elena wanted to leave too, before the single rooms for overnight stay were gone and she had to stay in a dormitory with several women in one bed. Finally, the man stirred, but made no effort to remove his hat from his face or to get up. She gently nudged him.

"Please sir, I must get out or the rooms will be gone."

He straightened slowly before lifting the hat. "No need to worry about a room, Elena, we're booked at the Savannah House." Sean O'Grady smiled at her shock. "The honeymoon suite."

She recovered faster than he anticipated, delivering one gloved punch to his shoulder before he caught her hand in an iron grip. Satisfied she wouldn't cause a scene, he set it down in her lap, covering both her hands with his one.

"You don't want to call attention to us," he whispered.

She looked at him as if he was a snake and hissed. "You. You lied again. You are wanted for murder and if you follow me, you will drag me deeper into your trouble." Her voice rose with her level of agitation. "I have pretended in front of God to be your wife. What more do I have to do?"

She stood in the small space, pulled her hood back over her head and tried to step over him. "Please, go away."

He rose too, standing so close to her she could smell the scent of his shaving cream and feel the heat of his breath on her cheek. "You pretended nothing in front of God, Hummingbird. The license we signed was real. We're married."

"No," she moaned, and dropped back into the seat, shaking her head in disbelief. "Now I have been lied to about lying." She rested her aching head in her hands. She was a Gringo devil's wife.

Sean's low chuckle was the only sound in the now empty car. He tucked his bag under his arm and picked up her little one. "I'll explain it all to you at the hotel."

When he put his free hand under her arm to help her up, the look she gave him erased his smile. His grip on her arm tightened and his voice lowered. "I didn't lie about your ticket. You're Mrs. O'Grady as far as Santa Fe. After that, if my company is so distasteful, you may do whatever you wish with the name, the ring, and the marriage license."

"Santa Fe?" Her voice sounded high to her own ears. She cautiously looked around to make sure they were alone. "Why are you going to Santa Fe? You are running from the law. You'll get us both ki—"

Sean's sudden kiss met her partially open mouth. Shock at the sensation of both pleasure and pain made her forget to struggle as his tongue gently teased her lips into responding.

The conductor, who had entered the car from behind Elena, cleared his throat to announce his presence. He winked at Sean over Elena's shoulder. "Got that little mess back in Jeffers cleaned up O'Grady?"

"Clean as a whistle, Jack," Sean answered, adjusting her hood over her hair. "We're just starting on our honeymoon." Jack whistled as he turned to leave, and Sean and Elena walked slowly to the other exit.

She was furious that her own body had betrayed her by responding to Sean's kiss and the power of his embrace. She reminded her traitorous heart that the mountain lion hunted alone. If she wanted to catch Anscombe, she had to be free of Sean. Once off the train, she tried to step away from him, but his grip on her arm was firm.

"I could scream and they would arrest you," she threatened.

"An Apache doesn't scream," he reminded her. "I saved your life. I'll see you safely to Santa Fe and hold to my offer. The rest is up to you. Right now, all I want to do is catch Roscoe."

She stopped short and turned to him within the confines of his arm. "I saved you from the sheriff. The debt is paid. You cannot expect me to honor this marriage. I came here alone and I will return alone."

He tightened his hold. "All I expect from you is to keep your beautiful mouth shut and pretend to be my loving bride until we get to Santa Fe. Let me take care of Anscombe and LaPorte. Or maybe you don't really want them brought to justice?"

The barb hit its mark. More than his strong hands, his cruel accusation kept her from running to the stationmaster. "You are evil," she whispered, wondering what on earth she had found attractive about this conniving, self-serving, white man.

"You know I am going back to Santa Fe to punish Anscombe for his crimes. But you lie all the time. Maybe you did kill Billy Berens and are only using me to escape. I remember a gunshot that night." She stopped suddenly, knowing that if he killed Billy, it was to save her life.

She was as responsible for Berens' death as Sean, and it was her fault he was now a fugitive. How could anyone ever truly repay someone for saving their life? Among the People, it was only when the act was repeated in kind. Did she save Sean's life by pretending to marry him? She doubted it. His family would never let him hang for killing Billy Berens. So her debt was not paid.

She couldn't let Sean know she still owed him. Yet she couldn't stay with him all the way to Santa Fe. She'd never be able to resist his smile, his eyes, and his touch until then. She tried a different approach. "What do you think you can do in Santa Fe? You are a tenderfoot, a greenhorn. The desperadoes will spit you out like bad tiswin to dry up on the desert and be blown away with the wind."

"I may not know what tiswin is, but wouldn't it be worth the trip to see that happen?" he teased.

She weighed the thought of spending four more days in the company of this loco Gringo against seeing him humiliated by desperados. Neither was a pleasant thought. For a time, she reasoned she could pretend she was still Apache and sleep with her knife at her side. "I will live for the day you go running back to your home, Senor," she lied and stepped away from his loosened grip.

"Well, it's settled then," he said with an air of satisfaction. "Just remember, we're in my territory until Santa Fe." His finger traced a warm path along her jaw. "I'm not as bloodthirsty as you and will see that no harm comes to you."

She touched her mother's talisman and hoped that this time it would protect her from both his charms and his lies. As they walked to the depot office, she again thought of the great Manitou, who could appear and disappear at will.

"How did you get on the train without being seen?"

He winked and confessed to being human. "You had a rather large trunk of donated clothing. It seems some of those clothes just happened to be on my back. It was easy to get from the baggage car to the passenger car."

"I see." She had her first doubts about the wisdom of her bargain, but comforted herself with the thought that while he knew his way around iron horses and city places, in the West, without his fine stallion, he would be like a prairie dog looking for a hole to hide from the circling hawk.

Sean purchased new tickets on the Santa Fe Railway to St. Louis. He turned to her, smiling like a little boy who had just stolen candy. "Everything's taken care of Hummingbird. From here on, you won't have to sleep in your seat while you bounce around the rails. We've got a private car all to ourselves."

At her questioning look, he explained. "It seems that a Colonel Roscoe LaPorte reserved the Ambassador car, but changed his plans and left early for St. Louis. Not only are we right on the bastard's heels, but his car is ours for the taking." He took her by the arm, lightly this time. "I hear it has full-sized sleeping accommodations. We should be quite comfortable."

Her contempt turned to grudging respect for his knowledge of his territory when he hailed a hansom cab to take them to the Savannah House Hotel. The giant pillars, huge potted palms, and gleaming marble floors held her spellbound while he checked them in. As they turned from the desk to face the massive, curving stairway up to their second-floor room, she moaned. She'd foolishly refused the hickory walking stick Chloe had offered and the climb would be grueling on her already throbbing leg.

Suddenly, in keeping with his newlywed charade, Sean picked her up and followed the bellboy up the stairs. He put her down inside a suite of rooms nearly as big as the Charles Carter School for Indians.

The carpet almost covered the tops of their shoes with its soft, gray nap. A canopied bed so high there were steps leading up to it dominated the main room. When Sean pushed a button on the wall, two sconces above the bed glowed with light.

"*Madre de Dios*," she exclaimed, witnessing the miracle of light that shined without fire for the first time in her life. "This place is like a palace." The palace of the devil, she reminded herself, following cautiously when he led her into another room.

A huge white bathtub big enough for two people, filled the room. Two shining golden handles on either side of a large spigot told her hot and cold water could be summoned at the same time with the turn of a wrist. A commode with a chain hanging from a large tank was suspended on the wall in the corner. And above the big white sink, a mirror framed by gilt leaves reflected her amazement and Sean's amusement.

Spellbound by the opulence, she watched Sean turn one of the handles in the tub until steaming water poured from the spigot. When he took his jacket off and began unbuttoning his shirt, she ran out to the sitting room.

"Don't you want to freshen up and get something to eat?" he said when he found her sitting on the window seat. His new shirt hung open and his chest muscles flexed as he dried his face on a thick, Savannah House towel. Rather than let him see what she truly hungered for, she turned away to look down at the busy street below.

He ignored her efforts to ignore him. "Suit yourself. I'm starving and need to meet...someone. I'll send food up to you." He sounded almost sincere when he lightly kissed her cheek. "I won't be late. Get some rest, my darling."

CHAPTER SEVENTEEN

The sun rose from the sea like a huge, orange ball of fire, replacing the cool night breezes with the heat and humidity of the Georgia summer day. Sean couldn't resist the call of the bustling, adventurous city two stories below him. He left the soft feather bed and glanced at the pocket doors separating the sitting room from the bridal suite's bedchamber.

Elena had closed those doors tight against him before he'd left her the evening before. Just in case she tried to bolt, he hired a porter to stay close to the door and find him if she came down.

When he returned well-past midnight, the porter confirmed she hadn't come down. He frowned at the meal he'd ordered for her sitting untouched in front of the door to their room. Annoyed that she wouldn't eat, he peeked into the sitting room to see her curled up on the divan, sound asleep. Rather than disturb her rest, he slept alone on top of the step-bed's silk coverlet.

Now, he shook his head clear of the grogginess left over from a night of playing cards and drinking watered down whiskey. The headache was worth it. By patronizing some of Roscoe's haunts, he'd gained a great deal of information about his cadre of crooked businessmen and a gambler from Santa Fe who fit Elena's description of Junior Anscombe.

It seemed that Roscoe had come across a land grant from the King of Spain in the 1600s. It belonged to a long-dead Mexican named Miguelito Peralto, with no known heirs. He forged a bill of sale and by enforcing

Peralto's grant he and his partners evicted a dozen or more families from their homes in Rancho de Taos, near the entrance to the ancient Ansazi cliff dwellings. It confirmed Sean's suspicions.

Corporal Mills wrote that the gold from the Denver Mint was hidden inside an ancient pueblo somewhere within the thousands of acres covered by Peralto's Grant. The person who owned that grant could legally "mine" the Federal gold, melt it down, and sell it anywhere in the world. However, even with a map, the right cave would be harder to find than a mustard seed in a grain bin.

Without the exact location, Roscoe and his ring of thieves and greedy businessmen were faced with spending vast sums of money and time searching the caves, one by one. Sean realized again that it was money he'd planned to get from Mary Louise—until the connection between his family and the missionaries dropped into the bastard's lap. Then he changed his plan in favor of extortion.

The cat and mouse game they were playing was far from over. Sean was as certain of that as he was of his own name. His own name. He finally knew his name was Storm Cloud when his mother passed him off as the son of a sub-chief named Three Feathers. The "C" as his middle initial meant Cloud, in recognition of where he'd been born. His parents were was right. There were more important things at stake than his sire.

While he believed Patrick was his father, he wondered if the West was somehow still a part of him. If so, he hoped he could he be as cunning and fierce as Three Feathers when the time came to battle his enemy. He'd have to be if he planned to take down Roscoe and avoid the law at the same time.

With no time to waste, he knocked on the sitting room door to wake Elena, then entered the bath to begin preparations for the next phase of his fugitive flight into the outlaw West. He had to admit he enjoyed the idea of spending the journey in a private railroad car with a beautiful woman who was legally his wife. When doubts intruded, he reassured himself by thinking Roscoe would trip himself up eventually and when he did, Sean would be there.

As he washed, shaved, and splashed toilet water on his cheeks, he admitted he'd never felt so alive. For the first time in his life, despite being a hunted man, he felt free. Whatever the outcome and however long it took, he was finally going to live the life he'd always dreamed about. He smiled as he knocked again on the sitting room door.

"Elena. You have to come out of there sometime."

Her silence dampened his good humor. She had to go along with the charade, at least until he knew for sure she wasn't carrying Billy's child. His jaw set as he slid the huge double doors apart. When they opened wide enough for him to enter, he was hit by a wall of heat.

Elena was still curled up in a tight ball on the divan, fully dressed. "Jesus, now what?" He crossed the room in a few strides and doused the smoldering coals in the grate with water from a vase of wilted flowers.

Unable to budge the swollen window frame, he closed the thick curtains against the heat of the morning sun. Sweat poured down his face and his clean shirt clung to him by the time he scooped her into his arms and carried her to the bed.

The jostling never roused her. Her black hair was damp with perspiration; yet her face looked gray against the white sheets. He filled the china basin next to the bed with cool water and soaked a towel in it. When he unbuttoned her dress, the heat from her fever warmed the towel. Finally, when the water and towel were nearly as warm as her skin, he watched helplessly as her breathing grew more and more shallow.

Again, he blamed himself. She was just an innocent pawn in Roscoe's lust for gold. He realized Billy wasn't at the station looking for him the day she arrived. The bastard was after Elena, even then.

There was only one more thing he could do. Chloe had done it with all the O'Grady children when they came down with fevers and he smiled a little, picturing the sting of Elena's sharp tongue when she woke up.

He removed her heavy dress, scooped her up in his arms and laid her, petticoats and all, into the bathtub. Then he climbed in with her and whispered, "Forgive me, Hummingbird, but I can't have my wife expiring after our wedding night."

He bathed her face and neck with the cool water that filled the tub, watching for a reaction and praying she wouldn't go into shock. Suddenly, she opened her eyes, and her mouth moved without a sound as she gasped for air. Her cheeks flushed and she began to shiver.

Fighting the urge to shout, "Alleluia," he turned off the water. Now all he had to do was get her temperature back to normal, fill her with water and food, and she'd be right as rain. They were both drenched by the time he had her leaning against him on the thick Turkish mat, a big Savannah House towel wrapped around her.

~

"No," she cried as the cold water and friction from the towel he rubbed over her arms and legs brought her back to the painful world of life. Accepting defeat, she rested her head against him, feeling the familiar beat of his heart beneath her cheek, remembering the night before.

She didn't believe he'd leave her alone and had shut the door between them. Then she checked her bandage on her leg. Chloe had cleaned the wound with hot water and vinegar and wrapped a poultice of honey tightly around her thigh. When the doctor arrived, he was furious and pulled off the poultice, insisting on closing the wound with a hot poker.

Chloe saved her from his savagery by shrieking in a mix of three languages and bodily forcing him out the door. While the O'Grady's tried to convince him to try another method, she barred the door until he was gone. The infection had responded slowly to Chloe's honey and herb poultices, but chills and fever from blood loss still plagued her. When she returned home, she would heal her wound with Apache medicine and the curative power of the aloe plant.

She curled up on the divan to rest her head and remembered Chloe's warning, "Eet is too soon to go. De chills and de fever, dey will come and go until your body makes up more blood." She woke up shivering around midnight, and lit the coals in the little grate to ease the chill that had replaced her soul.

Then there were no more thoughts, just a silence deeper than any she'd known before. As she sank into it, the peacefulness beckoned her to stay. Is it death, she wondered, feeling awake and asleep at the same time. Yet as she wandered the darkness, she saw no welcoming faces from her ancestors, no endless hunting ground teeming with game and flowing with water.

It could only be the place where lost souls went to wander endlessly in the dark silence of the underworld. Still, it was a world without pain and she wanted to stay. Then the howl of the panther again shattered her peace. His giant paws dragged her from her slumber back into the painful light of life and gnawing grief.

First, he threw her into icy water, his rough tongue scratching her tender skin, forcing her to open her eyes, but it wasn't the panther who brought her back into the human world of pain and suffering. It was the man who claimed to be her husband. Trapped in his strong arms, she began to cry. She couldn't stop, though the effort made her muscles ache, her wound throb, and her lungs burn.

"Don't cry, Elena," he whispered through his own tears, shuddering with her as if he felt her pain. Holding her soaked body to him, he kissed the salty trail of her tears. "You're all right now. I won't leave you again. Ever."

It was a promise they both knew he couldn't keep, especially if Roscoe found them. She pressed a finger against his lips. "Just hold me, for a little while," she whispered. "We don't know what the future will be."

He smiled, smoothing her hair from her face. "I do. I know we were meant to be together. So don't pull any more stunts like last night." He tucked a fresh towel securely around her shoulders and squeezed the moisture out of her hair with another towel before wrapping it in a turban. Sounding like Chloe, he said, "You need to get your strength back." Then he carried her to the bed.

He obeyed her order to close his eyes when she shed the soggy underclothes and snuggled between the cool, linen sheets on the feather mattress. She was still incredibly weak, but no longer felt as though she'd slipped into a bottomless black hole devoid of both the pearly gates reserved for whites and the beautiful hunting grounds of her people. She once more owed a debt to this man who fought his passions every time he looked at her. She closed her eyes so he wouldn't recognize that she fought the same battle every time he touched her.

"What is a stunt?" she demanded when her teeth finally stopped chattering.

He made sure she was comfortably propped up against two goose-down pillows with the sheet up to her neck and brought her a glass of cool water. "Drink this," he ordered, steadying her shaking hands as she emptied it.

She choked half way through it, but he waited patiently, urging her to fill her body with the life-giving moisture she'd lost to the coals and the closed-up room. After one more glass, he set it aside and ransacked her suitcase for a change of clothes.

"A stunt is doing something stupid that could get you killed," he said over his shoulder, pointing toward the ruined dinner plate. "Like not eating perfectly good food. The Savannah House has one of the finest restaurants on the Eastern Seaboard."

He picked up her ruined dress and threw it into a corner. "And sleeping in those heavy clothes with a coal heater. This is Georgia, for God's sake. The humidity here is so thick you can chew it. You have to wear clothes that let your sweat evaporate, or you'll end up poaching inside them."

Small clothes and stockings flew everywhere until he found something to his liking. He held up a white, organdy dress trimmed with navy silk stripes on the puffed sleeves. "This should do," he said and laid it on the bed.

"My guess is you haven't had anything to eat or drink since our skimpy little wedding fare. No wonder you've got the vapors. We have a long road ahead of us and you can't be passing out all the time. If you can get up, let's get you dressed and get some breakfast."

She was wide awake now, though if the truth were told, weak as a kitten. She wanted nothing more than to stay in that magnificent bed and sleep the sleep of the living. Yet she couldn't show him her weakness. She looked at the clothes he'd laid on her bed, wondering why he was still there.

"Do you want me to help you dress—again?" he offered with a sly grin.

It brought a flush to her cheeks that had nothing to do with her injury. For a little while, she'd imagined their lives weren't doomed and they really were on a honeymoon. At the mention of their mission, the dream dissolved. He'd saved her life twice. It was impossible to repay him now. She could only pray he wouldn't demand more than she could give.

She forced her lungs to fill with air, wincing at the effort the simple act of breathing took. "No. I am fine now." Afraid to meet his eyes, she lowered hers and saw that his trousers were soaked through, revealing his strong thighs as well as other attributes she didn't care to think about. She moaned and turned away, "You are all wet and need to change too. I can manage."

Smiling, Sean leaned over to feel her forehead for signs of a fever. "You're cool as a cucumber again, Mrs. O'Grady, but I'll leave you to it, only if you promise to eat a healthy breakfast with me afterward."

Holding the sheet to her chin, she reached for the dress. "I don't think doing anything with you is healthy."

CHAPTER EIGHTEEN

Sean's hand rested protectively at her waist as they descended the staircase. She looked down at a lobby filling up with other hotel guests bent on breakfast. A few of them nodded in polite greeting when her gaze met theirs. "Honeymooners," floated up to them from the front desk.

Midway down the stairs, Elena swayed against him. "I cannot do this. I am not hungry and I cannot eat with these people. They are staring at us." She blinked away the tears that had betrayed her too many times. "Please, can't we just board our private car and wait until the train leaves before we eat?"

"They're just fellow travelers," he assured her. "We'll probably see some of them on the train." Leaning down, Sean nearly completed the trip to her trembling lips. "The clerk has told people we're on our honeymoon," he whispered. "They're happy for us. We mustn't disappoint them by arguing or running away. Besides, we both missed dinner last night. It would be too much to stay in our room through breakfast too."

He kissed her lightly on the cheek. "Even for a couple as much in love as we are."

Her cheek warmed at his touch and the more she tried to stop it, the hotter it burned. She couldn't risk meeting his hypnotic eyes again. "Very well," she muttered. "I will go with you, but I will not eat."

He chuckled. "Oh, yes you will. If you don't, you'll probably faint and have those mother hens down there clucking all over you. They may even think you're with child. Then we'll miss our train entirely and have to spend another night in the bridal suite."

Measured against another night upstairs, where she knew she wouldn't be so lucky to have doors separate them again, the lobby didn't look so frightening. She searched his face for signs of his intentions.

"You can't make me do that. I must get home."

~

Once safe on level ground, Sean slipped her hand through the crook of his arm. He wanted to tell her that he only wanted to hold her until the terrible hurt in her eyes disappeared and they sparkled with mischief and laughter again. Even her anger was better than the emptiness that had haunted her eyes since the news of Judith's death.

No matter how much he wanted an excuse to spend another night in Savannah, they didn't have the time. He needed to get her to safety and find Roscoe before the law that was surely on his trail by now, found them.

He patted her stone-cold hand. "No, Elena. I wouldn't make you do that. I want to get away from here every bit as much as you do. If we're going to help to each other, you've got to get your strength back."

She nodded to his logic and breathed deeply of the aromas coming from the nearby dining room. Her stomach responded with growls they could both hear. "Until Santa Fe," she answered his smile as he ushered her into a huge, light-filled room with enough tables to seat a hundred.

She nearly missed a step while staring at palms and other full-grown trees rooted in huge pots, lending privacy between the tables. Ferns hanging from hooks in the ceiling beams shielded the diners from the sun shining through tinted skylights in the ceiling. Here and there, fans hung from those same beams, their blades lazily stirring the air, dispersing the delicious aromas of the food.

He led her to a table in a secluded corner behind a potted palm and a giant Boston fern. He ordered each of them a Planter's breakfast that began with a basket of honey-covered sticky buns and a bowl of fresh butter.

Elena eyed the pastries as if she wanted to attack the entire basket. Instead, she watched him take one and open it, letting the steam escape before spreading soft butter on each half. Then she did the same, nibbling on it in a completely civilized manner. By the time a bowl of fruit was set before them with a pitcher of fresh squeezed juice, she smiled as if her only thought was to see and taste the next delicacy.

She was savoring a strawberry dipped in thick, rich cream when she noticed him watching her. She froze with the strawberry partly imprisoned between her lips, then bit it and swallowed hard. "Don't."

"Don't worry," he answered, feeling hurt by her lack of trust. "You're a very lovely woman. You should be used to men looking at you. I'm just glad you're mine...for the time being. I'll keep the others at bay."

He wiped a bit of cream from her lips with the tip of his finger and pressed it to his own. "At least until you eat the restaurant out of food and they have to roll you out of here in a freight wagon."

She blushed and lifted her napkin to her lips as if to avoid any more of his help. "A moment ago, you said if I did not eat, you would send me to your squaws for torture. Now you say I am eating too much."

He leaned back and smiled as the feisty old Elena returned. "Not at all, but save room. These are only appetizers." He nodded toward a waiter who was holding a huge tray laden with plates of steaming white grits, eggs, cheeses and meats.

"This would feed a village," Elena exclaimed, leaning back as the busboy cleared the other dishes away and the waiter put new platters in front of them.

Sean was nearly finished with his bacon and ham before he noticed she hadn't touched hers. "You need to eat meat. It's the best slab bacon and honey-cured ham you'll find anywhere."

She grimaced. "No. The fruit was enough. I feel much better now."

He saw the lie in her eyes. She'd only eaten one sweet roll, some fruit, and her grits and eggs. And she looked at the meat as if it was about to bite her. "What's really the problem?"

"Hog eaters," she announced as if it more than explained why she wouldn't eat the ham.

"What?"

Her eyes narrowed at his stupidity. "Hog Eaters. White-eyes. Gringos. The same thing. Apache don't eat pigs."

Sean's laugh drew a few curious glances and he quieted to lean in. "Why?"

She folded her napkin neatly and placed it on the table. "We just don't. Fish either."

"Again, why? Please tell me. I was born in the West and I want to know about the customs...my mother lived with."

"Why? You are not going to the reservation, and we will be parting soon."

His hand caught hers when she started to rise. "Please."

She pulled away but remained seated. "Our people became ill once, with spots on their skin. The medicine men said they were the same as the spots on the fish they had eaten from the sacred lake, high in the White Mountains. Eating the fish had made the mountain gods angry and they punished us by making us sick. We learn fast. We don't eat fish."

Sean lifted the offending slab of ham off her plate and dropped it onto his. She grimaced as he sliced a piece off and placed it on his fork. "And pork?"

"Hogs are cousins to the wild boar, a bad manitou. It is bad magic to eat one." She leaned forward, a challenge in her dark eyes. "There. Now you know why the Apache do not eat hogs, or fish."

"I see." He put the fork down and touched her hand, encouraged when she didn't pull away. "Well, then what foods would you suggest they serve here?"

She shrugged. "This food is fine for white-eyes."

"All right, then what delicious foods can I look forward to once we get into your territory?"

She seemed to welcome the question and straightened her shoulders. With a sly smile, she leaned toward him in what anyone watching would consider an intimate moment. "If you go into the desert or the mountains that are home to my people, you may eat rattlesnake, prairie dog, wild turkey, or even a rat. Or maybe a horse or dog if you need it to live." Her eyes sparked with mischief, and a hint of rose crept back into her golden complexion.

This time Sean's face puckered in revulsion. He would never be hungry enough to eat Orion. Or a cute little prairie dog. "Rat?"

She paused to sip her spring water. "Of course, but good fat rats are hard to find in the desert. They prefer the company of whites. With another frown at the uneaten ham and bacon, she added. "Where waste is more plentiful. After a week in the mountains, you will run like a rabbit for the nearest town. Then my debt to you for saving my life—again, will be paid and we will both be...where we belong."

His ability to survive in the desert didn't matter to him. He wouldn't find Roscoe there. The man preferred the comforts of civilization. "Rat," he repeated. "Imagine that."

He used the information to fill in his mother's life during the months she was with the Comanche. It was very hard to imagine her killing, eating, or even cooking, a rat—or a prairie dog, and especially a snake. Marveling at the adaptive powers of the human spirit, he felt a new respect for the mother he'd always considered pampered by his father.

While Sean pictured his mother as a captive, Elena left the subject of Apache cuisine. "We must hurry. Senor Anscombe will try to hide in the mountains."

He doubted it. At least for now, Anscombe had no reason to run. He hadn't been charged with any crimes, and couldn't know they'd connected him to Roscoe. "Maybe. Do you know someone who can track him?"

"*Si*," she answered. "Me. I know the mountains and I can track. Marcus taught me. Junior cannot hide from me."

She seemed stronger, as if merely talking about the West helped her heal. While it pleased him, the savagery in her voice made Sean set aside the rest of his food. He watched her eyes turn from the color of rich, brown earth to cold, hard obsidian. "How would the little Apache woman known as Hummingbird punish him?"

She frowned at the delicate nickname. "I would do what my fathers did to the Mexicans and freighters who first invaded our land."

"Enlighten me." He pushed his plate aside, leaning his forearms on the table, his hands knitted in front of her.

She leaned toward him. "First, I would start a fire in a large pit so deep only the tops of the flames would rise above it. Then I would strip my enemy naked, lash him upside down to the wheel of a wagon, and flail the flesh from his body with rawhide thongs."

Her eyes seemed to reflect the glow of the fire in her imagination. "Then I would roll the wagon wheel over the fire pit and watch his hair burn to the roots, hissing in the fire when it left his scalp. And I would watch his blood boil inside his skull until it was cooked and he was silent."

She sat back with a final wave of her napkin. "Then I would feed him to the dogs."

She sipped the cool milk placed in front of her by a thoroughly shaken waiter. "That is how the Apache woman foolishly called Hummingbird, would punish her enemy. Do you still feel it is wise to travel with me?"

Sean was so captivated with her animation, however misdirected, that he'd paid little attention to the savage details, thinking that like Lily, she would have made a wonderful actress. He smiled and patted her hand when he answered "More than ever. I'd rather have you with me than against me."

He laid enough money on the table to cover their breakfast and a tip for the horrified waiter. Then he stood and bowed slightly, taking her delicate hand in his. "I'll steer clear of wagon wheels and keep shovels out of your reach, my dear, but I think we've eaten enough. Shall we go to the depot?"

Smiling back at him, she rose and accepted his arm. "You were right about the food here. I am feeling much better now. I look forward to the comfort of our private car. We must remember to properly thank Senor LaPorte when we meet him."

CHAPTER NINETEEN

hey boarded Roscoe LaPorte's private railroad car before the heat of the day set in. Elena remarked about the coolness. "These windows open wider than the passenger cars," Sean explained. "We'll have to close them to keep out the smoke and sparks at first, but once we're on our way we can enjoy the breeze."

She stood with her hands on her hips, admiring the rich brocade furnishings and velvet draperies in what looked like the parlor of a rich man's mansion. "I know that," she answered testily. "I have traveled many miles by train, you know."

"Pardon me. I forgot what a seasoned traveler you are." Sean's smile made her heart beat faster. "So, you won't mind if I do a little exploring before we embark on our grand adventure."

"Your grand adventure," she reminded him as he tested the softness of the large bed opposite a brocade divan. Next to the bed, she parted a velvet drapery on a circular, gilded curtain rod and discovered a small sink and commode for their personal use. One look at the gilt-framed mirror above the sink showed her that she was so pale from her stay in the white man's world she looked like one of them.

"I am fading away," she whispered, touching a trembling finger to her paper-dry cheeks. Like a flower wilting in winter. She turned to him. "Only the sun can make me whole."

He kissed her lightly on her cheek. "Not to worry, darling. In only a few days, you'll be back in New Mexico. I hear the sun shines there most every day."

Her face lit up at his knowledge. "*Si,* it does. And the stars are brighter than anywhere. I can't wait to show...I mean, you will soon see for yourself."

"With you by my side, I hope."

"That is not for us to decide." she said. "Now go. You have our bags to collect and a train to explore. I am suddenly very tired. I will lay down a while by the window."

He kissed her on the cheek this time. "Whatever the Princess of the forest desires. I won't be long."

She was sound asleep when he returned a short while later with their bags. The top buttons of the lightweight dress were open to the swell of her breasts. He set the bags down in the middle of the room, and looked at her closely, smiling at the slow rise and fall of her breasts beneath the lacy chemise. Then he closed the window against the smoke and noise of the train as it began to move.

Figuring she'd sleep most of the day, leaving him free to explore the wonders of transcontinental rail travel on his own, he gently kissed her forehead. "Sleep well, Beauty," he whispered. "The beast has a busy day planned."

He entered the curtained washroom, splashed his face with fresh water, straightened his cravat, and smiled at the deceptive image of youthful innocence in the mirror. His youth had often caused more experienced gamblers to underestimate him, and, more often than not, came out a winner at the tables. "But it'll take more than, 'Aw shucks Mister' to win this time O'Grady," he told the face in the mirror. He'd need every ace he ever held to even come out alive.

As he explored the train from end to end, Sean learned there were several passenger cars, a couple old Pullman cars for the immigrants flooding the West, two baggage cars, the private car, and a palace car that served as a socializing place for travelers tired of their cramped seats.

It was filled with comfortable chairs arranged in cozy circles for conversation, and plants to provide the illusion of coolness. A large round table at one end allowed the passengers their choice of games, and a fully stocked bar with all manner of liquid refreshments stood nearby.

A chatty porter told him that mid-afternoon, a buffet would be set up with cold meats, cheeses, and fresh breads, along with cold coffee or tea. There was even a piano for entertainment before Nashville, where the train would stop only long enough to refuel before going on to St. Louis.

He was also pleased that the palace car was reserved for those passengers who paid extra in their tickets, or traveled in the comfort of private cars. The unwashed immigrants traveling in the Pullman cars wouldn't enjoy champagne or play a high stakes poker game dealt by gamblers wearing diamond and pearl cufflinks.

One such gentleman was already preparing for the games. A few years older than Sean, he had dark, heavily oiled hair, and diamond-laden fingers that moved with amazing speed over the table's green felt surface. He wore a jewel-toned striped silk vest with a gold chain and a diamond horseshoe clip over a hand-tailored silk shirt. Smoke from a thick, Cuban cigar circled his head. Like an athlete warming up before a competition, he shuffled and dealt the cards out to the empty table while he watched the door for "comers."

The gambler's lips curled upward while his cunning blue eyes took in every inch of Sean's deceptively naive appearance. "Smile?" He asked, offering his newest mark a drink.

Sean returned his greeting with a nod, but hesitated before stepping forward. The gaudy vest, slicked back hair, and fast, callous-free hands looked familiar. He realized with an eerie sensation, that except for the color of the gambler's eyes, he could be looking at himself in ten years. In fact, given the chance, this was probably the very life he'd have chosen. Until Elena. Now the thought sickened him.

Still, a man had to do what he had to do. He smiled his well-practiced, boyish grin and approached the table. "Don't mind if I do," he said, pulling up a chair to watch the gambler pour two fingers of bourbon into a clean glass.

"Gladstone." The gambler offered his name without extending his hand.

Sean didn't take offense. Gladstone's hands were his livelihood, the tools of his trade. He couldn't risk one of them being crushed in an over-zealous handshake. "Grande," Sean responded. "Seth Grande."

He accepted a cigar from Gladstone and sipped the amber liquid slowly as they warmed up for the afternoon games by playing low stakes, five-card draw.

"Traveling through?" Gladstone said without looking up, most likely assuming Sean was going to Denver, San Francisco, El Paso, or Santa Fe.

"Maybe. I'm on my honeymoon. We're touring the West until my father says I have to go back East and work in the family business. You?"

He noticed the spark of interest in Gladstone's eyes before he shrugged. "St. Louis, maybe. I'll see what's what there."

Again, Sean understood. If the pickings were good in St. Louis, the gambler would stay. If not, he'd move along. No roots. No ties. No boundaries. It was the kind of free life he always thought he wanted.

After several hours, Sean felt stiff in his seat. Afternoon shadows cooled the car and passengers began coming in to sample the buffet. Someone suggested they get a glee going with some music, and one gentleman produced a banjo, strumming the ever-popular, "Oh, Susannah."

Gladstone went for another bottle behind the bar and Sean rose to see if Elena was awake yet. She had to eat again or she'd be forever passing out or sleeping on him. He needed her for more than that, he admitted with a twinge of guilt.

She was coiling her thick hair into a twist at the back of her head when he entered their car. The cooler, more sophisticated hairstyle suited her and he paused to admire her delicate features, dominated by those expressive, dark eyes.

She smiled when he closed the door. "I am hungry again. Is there food on the train?"

He was surprised at how much she'd improved since her second brush with death and wondered if perhaps she was right about her home. It seemed she recovered a little more with every mile they traveled toward it.

"That's what I came to tell you. They're getting a glee together in the palace car and the buffet is ready." He winked. "They have cold ham on the platter but it wouldn't be a good idea to make any of your 'Hog Eater' comments to the other passengers. You might frighten them and spoil our disguise."

"Your disguise," she said pointedly. "What if the conductor recognizes you when he comes for our tickets?"

He parried the challenge in her eyes. "Our tickets were punched through at the station. We're on our honeymoon. We won't be disturbed."

Her slight flinch at the thought of being alone with him made him frown. Would she never learn to trust him? Then he admitted he hadn't really given her much reason to.

"But the people in the palace car, what if someone knows about you?"

"Gamblers, politicians, and socialites. I don't think they'd be very interested in the skeletons in my closet." He gently caressed the length of her satiny cheek and felt her pulse quicken. "Why not forget for a little while that we're fugitives from the law and try to enjoy the time we have together?"

"We?"

The alarm in her voice made him regret the comment, but there was no turning back. She had to understand her position. "When you married me, you became an accomplice in my alleged crime. Now that we've both disappeared, they'll think you helped me escape."

Her hand flew to her throat as if she could already feel the noose around it. "But I didn't know I was really marrying you, and I didn't know you were on the train. Why can't you just let me go home alone?"

He lay on the bed, his hands behind his head. "Roscoe knows he can't prove I killed Billy. I figure he was banking on my mother's obsession with the family honor to blackmail her for the gold."

Elena's hands rested on her hips like a frustrated school teacher. "If you knew you would not be found guilty, you could have stayed to prove his other crimes. Now you are an outlaw...and so am I."

He sat up, smiling at her naiveté. "I was never meant to come out of this alive, darlin'. It never mattered whether he could prove I murdered Billy. Once I was in jail, even if my family paid the ransom, I'd never make it out. For Roscoe, it's the game that counts, and he's still holding the best cards."

He stood, taking her hands in his. "Anyone with half a brain could see how much you wanted to leave Jeffers. With me in jail, all he had to do was intercept you on your way home and he'd have two ways to convince my mother to give up the gold. You're an intelligent girl, Elena. Tell me if you don't see it that way."

Understanding flickered in her eyes. She nodded and sat down beside him. "This Roscoe. He has many people to do his bidding?"

"Yes. How many, I can't be sure."

"Even now, they could be following us?"

"I'm sure of it. Roscoe knows where you're going and that I'll come after you—him. It's just a race to see if I find him before his henchmen find me."

She looked up at him. "The Apache have been hunters and we have been prey. My father, Wah-Kee, told my brother and me that to be a good hunter, you must become your prey. See with its eyes. Hear with its ears. Then even without tracks, you will find it. I know now that I cannot hunt Junior Anscombe until I know him and his kind better. Please help me."

Sean tried to imagine her childhood spent running from an enemy who hated her simply because of who she was. He squeezed her hand. "Well, I know Roscoe. He cancelled this car for a purpose. He's leaving a trail for us to follow as wide as a Kentucky rainbow. He'll try to stop us along the way and separate us. If he can, he'll use one of us against the other, and both of us against my family."

"How?"

"By now Sheriff Coulter knows I'm gone. I'm sure he's gotten word to Roscoe, who has already told him to wire all the main stops on the way to St. Louis. They in turn, will telegraph the trains heading west using the box relays they carry in case of a breakdown." He patted her hand. "In fact, they've already wired this one."

He couldn't resist a smile at his own audacity. "I told the box boy I was an officer looking for a wire about a fugitive. It had just come." He pulled a piece of paper from his breast pocket.

Elena looked at it and gasped. It described a man being sought for murder in Georgia. "It is you and your name. Why haven't you run? They will kill you."

He appreciated her concern after all he'd put her through, especially after her human fire pit story. Putting his arm around her shoulder, he said, "I couldn't run. Read on."

He felt her shudder when she read the description of the murderer's accomplice: a small, half-breed Apache squaw named Elena Santiago.

"There is no escape now," she gasped and rose. "But I am not ready to die. This game you play is a white man's game. If you know the rules as well as you say, tell me what we will do now."

He hadn't expected her to give her life over to him so easily and paced the tiny corridor in the center of the car. "I convinced the box boy there was no need to see the conductor and cause a panic. That I'd take care of it myself. The descriptions are a little vague and I'm using the name Seth Grande. Your name is Helen by the way, and you don't look very Apache right now. So, for the time being, we're still safe. I think."

"You think? What about the next stop?" The paper shook in her hand. "This will be at every stop along the way."

The time for lies and half-truths had long since passed. Sean told her what they both knew. "In Nashville, the depot will be full of lawmen ready to invade our little car."

"Then we are trapped." She turned to the open window. "My father saw his own death in the clouds the morning he sent me away with the women, before the soldiers came. Little Wolf was supposed to be with me, but he forgot his knife and went back to get it. I believe Judith saw hers in the dirt falling on her husband's grave. We can no more stop our fate than we can slow a cyclone."

The sorrow in her eyes nearly crippled Sean. He pulled her close. "We're only trapped for a little while, Hummingbird. I have a plan."

When a faint ray of hope lit her dark eyes, he smiled. "Now, let's go eat."

CHAPTER TWENTY

A plan. Elena wanted to believe him, but her heart told her this would be her last night alive. She had a plan too. Her Spanish knife was tucked safely against her calf again, under her skirts. When the white police boarded the train in the morning, she would slit her own throat.

It wasn't the Apache way, but she wasn't afraid of death any more. She was just sad that she'd never had the chance to live. Another place and time, Sean had once said. Now, they'd never know. She kissed him. "What will be, will be."

Gladstone's long-awaited poker game was well underway when Sean and Elena entered the palace car. The gambler dealt the cards with lightning speed and smiled when he saw Sean. Then he turned back to the table and raised the bet, challenging his opponents to call his bluff.

Sean acknowledged Gladstone's smile with a nod and turned to Elena. "Trust me," he told her as he led her to the piano. "Why don't you play something that will liven things up a bit?"

"I only know hymns."

He rolled his eyes. "Missionaries. Well try one. A little guilt might clear out the room."

She followed his glance toward the gambler. "Poker? You can't be thinking about that now. We need to..."

"Shh. Just do as I ask, for once."

People had looked up at their voices and she bit back a caustic reply before sitting at the piano. After only one verse of, "Nearer My God to Thee," several people clustered around her to sing along.

"Bets everyone," Mr. Gladstone announced. "Ante is a fiver."

When a stylish young woman offered to play some of the more popular songs from the musicales that never made it to Santa Fe, Elena happily surrendered the piano and strolled to the buffet. She picked up a china plate decorated with hand-painted, purple flowers. Carefully avoiding the ham, she took generously of the sliced chicken, turkey, and thick slices of fresh bread.

"You play real good, ma'am."

The deep voice startled her just as she took a bite of chicken and she turned to face an enormous man whose broad body was stuffed into a suit that didn't look the least bit comfortable. Her eyes only reached the top button of his wool vest and she looked up to see the brightest red hair she'd ever seen. Then she lowered her gaze to meet the brightest blue eyes she'd ever seen.

His smile was friendly beneath a thick red mustache matching his vibrant hair. "It reminded me of services when I was a young pup," he added in a Southwestern drawl.

Hearing her homeland in his voice made her breath catch in her throat, and she choked. Unfazed, he gently thumped her on the back to dislodge the tiny piece of chicken, offering her a glass of water to wash it down.

Sean appeared at her side almost instantly and helped her to a chair away from the buffet. The red-haired man followed them like a giant shadow with the glass of water and her plate.

Elena took it from him and the man reached his hand out toward Sean. "Pruitt," he said. "Sam Pruitt."

Sean took the measure of Sam Pruitt. He judged him to be somewhere in his thirties, despite lines that the sun and wind had carved into his face. His answering smile never revealed that he recognized the big man who had tipped a finger to his Stetson as they were coming down the Savannah House stairs. Coincidence? He doubted it.

He squeezed Elena's hand hard while he extended his other one to the Westerner. "Grande," he said with a wide, fake smile. "Seth Grande. This is my wife...Helen. We're on our honeymoon. I'm afraid after all the excitement of the wedding, she's a bit unwell. If you'll excuse us, I think I'll take her back to our car." He pretended to support Elena with his arm around her waist while propelling her through the door to the vestibule between cars.

Speechless at his rudeness to the stranger, Elena had the presence of mind to grasp her plate of food before being pulled away. Once back in their car, she turned to him, furious with his display of childish jealousy. "Why did you do that? That man was just being nice to me. You made a scene. People noticed. I could feel their white eyes on our backs." She sat on the bed to finish her food.

He paced in front of her, running his fingers through his hair. "He was nice all right. Nice enough to get us both hanged."

She shook her head as she savored the last bite of her delicious bread. "You are loco. His clothes and voice are from the West. He can't be a policeman from Georgia."

"Exactly. His suit looks old and he was wearing a Stetson hat not long ago. His boots have worn spots where there used to be spurs. It's too early in the year for the kind of suntan he has. It looks permanent."

"*Si*. That proves you are wrong." She licked the last of the sweet butter from her fingers. "We need to worry about tomorrow, not tonight. You said so yourself."

He sat beside her. "I recognized him from when we came down the stairs at the hotel this morning. He looked out of place and when I went back for our bags, the clerk told me he wasn't a guest. If Pruitt isn't a lawman, then he's Roscoe's man. I just don't know how he got to Savannah so soon."

"You're...."

He covered her mouth with his hand. "Don't say I'm crazy again or I might just believe you."

She pulled away, frightened by the worry in his eyes. It was too soon for him to break and run. She needed him to get her out of the white territory safely. Most of all, she didn't want Senor Pruitt to be one of Roscoe's men. He walked straight and tall, like a warrior or a chief, not like a cowardly dog in the shadows. His eyes held none of the cunning or lust that shone from Roscoe and Junior's eyes.

"How could that be? Senor Pruitt is from the West. Your lawmen and Senor LaPorte's men are looking from the East," she insisted.

"If he was in El Paso or New Orleans, he could have made it to Savannah in time to meet with Roscoe, and then waited, figuring we'd come through eventually."

Elena again felt chilled to her bones. These whites were so cunning. They could lie with their words, their eyes, and even their voice. None of them could be trusted. Yet she had to trust Sean, even though he had tricked her into becoming his wife.

As if she'd voiced her thoughts, Sean squeezed her hand. "Whether Pruitt is the law or Roscoe's man, he'll follow us until we either lead him to the gold or he arrests us." He touched her cheek. "If I'm gone, you can say you were kidnapped. My parents will stand by you." He rose to sort through their bags, deciding which one to take with him.

Panic gripped Elena as she watched him prepare to leave. He had never harmed her as others would have done, and he'd saved her life twice. It was true he'd used her to escape the law, but only to find the real murderer. She gripped his arm and stood between him and the window. "You can't jump. We are going too fast."

He looked out at the swiftly moving shadows, then back at her. "The longer I stay with you the more involved you'll be."

"If you leave, they will arrest me anyway. I am Apache. They won't believe I was kidnapped. We must stay together."

The train rocked gently on the rails and the oil lamps on the walls flickered while her gaze held him prisoner. He leaned over to kiss her on the forehead. "Are you sure?"

"Yes," she whispered, circling his waist with her arms. "Together is our only hope." She raised her head to meet his eyes. "Judith wished for us to be together and your priest has declared it so. We agreed it will be that way until we reach the land of the White Mountain Apache. Then I will listen to voices of the four winds and the gods of my people. They will lead me."

With both hands cupping her face, Sean kissed her eyes, cheeks, and lips. Her mouth opened to taste his tongue and her arms wrapped tightly around his neck until she pressed against his arousal. Overcome with an emotion as old as time, and more powerful than magic, Sean's fingers found the soft tips of her breasts and teased them until they puckered, waiting for the touch of his lips.

Elena arched her back as his palms slid down her hips to cup her buttocks and raise her until only the thin fabric of their clothing prevented her from receiving the gift of his seed. In the flickering light of the lamps, his face buried between her breasts and her legs wrapped around his hips, she moaned into his neck and rocked back and forth against him. With each quickening breath, she prayed to be closer to him, part of him, to feel him inside of her. Instead he set her down and pulled away.

"You know how much I want you." His voice was hoarse. "The longer we're together, the harder it will be to deny it."

A blush crept up her cheeks as she sat on the bed's satin comforter. The aching need between her legs throbbed and her swollen breasts begged for his lips. She couldn't meet his eyes because he'd see how much she needed him to fill the emptiness within her and finish what his embrace had begun.

"What will we do now?" She didn't know if she meant about Pruitt or the passion that grew between them with every passing moment.

"I had a plan," he said, his voice still husky with passion. "But I thought we'd have all night to accomplish it. Now, I don't know. Still, Pruitt can't do much until daybreak."

"What is your plan?" What better way to die than in the arms of the man the gods had made for her?

"It's better if you don't know too much right now. Just follow my lead and pretend we're honeymooners with a weakness for gambling." He winked like a little boy plotting a prank. "I'm going back to the palace car to bring home a friend for a little private game. Do me a favor and clear off that table over there under the lamp. And maybe rumple up the bed, for a little realism," he teased before opening the door to the vestibule. "Oh, and set out some whiskey. It's in that cabinet by the washroom."

Elena stared at him. How could he think of gambling when they had so little time before the lawmen came for them? Doubts raced through her mind, but before she could express them, he kissed her lightly on the cheek.

"Don't worry. I won't let anything happen to you, Hummingbird."

Hours later, Sean returned with his clothes disheveled, his cravat askew, and his shirt stained with whiskey-colored splotches. He wobbled unsteadily on his feet and grinned drunkenly at her. "Hello there, sweetie," he slurred, exhaling the odors of cigar smoke and bourbon into her face.

She recoiled and stepped away to let him lurch inside with a grinning Mr. Gladstone in tow. When Sean bumped into the bed, Gladstone looked at the rumpled covers and smiled. The fact that they had come so close to doing what he was thinking made her blush and she glared at Sean. This plan better work. Whatever it was.

Gladstone looked again from the bed to her. The touch of his ice blue gaze made her flesh crawl until she realized why he was so important to their plan. Without the mustache, he could easily be mistaken for Sean.

She turned from his leering grin and threw her arms around her husband, sobbing. "Seth, darling. I was so worried about you dearest. Where have you been?"

Sean accepted her embrace and smiled when she whispered, "I have Chloe's sleeping powders in my reticule."

"Enough of that Helen," he said thickly and slapped her backside. "Fiz us sum drinks. We gonna play some real poker now." He pulled a cigar from his vest pocket and offered it to Gladstone.

The gambler waved it under his nose. "Cuban," he pronounced. "Very good." Then he sat at the table while Elena went behind the curtain.

Sean sipped his whiskey slowly while Gladstone won a staggering amount of the money he carried in a hidden compartment in his belt. Yet despite the straight up whiskey and Chloe's sleeping powders, the gambler never faltered as he dealt the cards time after time, bluffing with only a pair and winning on the draw. The pile of money in front of him grew worrisome.

"Your glass is nearly empty" Elena said. "Let me pour you another." She shrugged to show Sean she had no idea why the sleeping powder hadn't taken effect, except that this man had an amazing tolerance for liquor.

She checked the ship's clock atop the stove in the corner. One-thirty. Hours until dawn, but they had no time to waste. Sean had let Gladstone win nearly everything he had and the bastard was still conscious. She considered using the poker from the stove to knock him out, but it was important they find his substitute alone and drunk.

Finally, Gladstone rose unsteadily from his chair. "Got to take a break partner. My old pot's 'bout to burst." He looked at Elena. "In more way's 'n one," then lurched for the curtained room.

"What the..." was followed by a thud as Gladstone spilled through the curtain, out cold.

They dragged him out to the center of the room. Sean re-buttoned the man's pants and removed the silk vest so their clothes were almost identical. He pulled off Gladstone's diamond rings and tie chain, putting his own signet ring on the well-manicured tools of the gambler's trade. Then he ordered, "Get my razor."

Elena froze. "Your razor? Why? You can't kill him."

He looked up from the unconscious gambler. "No. I was going to leave that up to you. You seem to have some novel ideas in that area."

"That isn't funny. He hasn't hurt us."

"The mustache, Elena," he said as he worked to get Mr. Gladstone into bed with his clothes thrown haphazardly around the room. "We've got to get rid of it now."

She felt stupid. How could she have forgotten the mustache? She hurried to get the razor from Sean's carpetbag, but when she reached out to give it to him he pulled away. "You do it. I'm clumsy."

"Me?" she whispered as if the sleeping man could hear. "What if I cut him?"

Sean was busy combining the contents of several carpetbags into one bag and answered sharply, "Just do it. Then put the razor in here. We need to be gone. Now."

Fear steadied her hands as she shaved the man's mustache. Then she looked at her work and found it lacking. His upper lip was smooth and white, while his chin showed the stubble of a new day's growth. She took a few precious moments to shave the rest of his face.

"I admire your restraint, my dear," Sean smiled, and threw the bag with the razor and some clothing in it out of the window.

"What are you doing?" Elena cried. "We can't jump. If we aren't killed, they will find us in a few hours."

"We're not jumping," he assured her while he gathered a satin drapery cord, tied the two other satchels to the ends and hung them around his neck. "We just want them to think that. Get your hat and come with me."

She did as he asked and they stepped into the vestibule between their car and the last Pullman car. They entered it quietly and she felt the judging white eyes on her, telling herself they were only curious.

"Hiding in here won't help," she whispered. "Pruitt knows what we look like."

He paused. "This is for later. If people are asked, they'll remember us. Just do what I say." He put his arm around her. "Sit down here," he whispered. "In a minute, pretend to feel faint. I'll offer to take you outside for a breath of fresh air."

While a few people looked up and nodded at their arrival, no one even noticed when they rose again to leave the car.

CHAPTER TWENTY-ONE

A hot wind sent gravel and cinders swirling around them when they stepped onto the open platform at the rear of the Pullman passenger car. Elena's little bowler hat blew off, and her hair flew into her eyes as she held Sean's hand to jump the gap to the baggage car. He motioned toward the top of the door and shouted above the noise of the train and the howling wind, "Take down that lamp."

A sudden lurch of the train jerked the rusted lamp in Elena's hand and jarred Sean's lock pick out of the keyhole. It cut his hand before falling into the darkness at their feet.

"Damn," he swore as he pressed his handkerchief to the wound and shouted, "Hairpin."

Elena stared at him in horror, thinking they were coming up to one of the dangerous turns in the tracks that had been named after the U-shaped female accessory. More than one train had derailed trying to negotiate a hairpin curve too fast, and there was nothing between them and the rocky rail bed but the rusty platform.

When she didn't answer, Sean repeated. "Hairpin. Hatpin. Do you have one?"

Finally understanding, she wrapped the arm holding the lantern around the swaying railing and fished an ineffective pin from her hair with the other.

"Ouch," Sean said when it poked him in the dark. "I'm not a pincushion."

"I only have two hands," she snapped back, and heard a low chuckle as the lock clicked and the door opened wide enough for him to push her inside.

After several failed attempts, he got the lantern to light. The pale glow through the sooty glass showed stacks of freight, mail, and baggage piled haphazardly inside the rolling cavern. Sweat beaded on Elena's forehead as she remembered the caves where her Apache family was killed. She fought the pressure that threatened to crush her chest by taking a deep breath.

"This is like a tomb," she whispered, reaching out to find Sean's arm. "Let's go back and jump off the train. At least we would die in the night air with Mother Earth at our feet and Father Moon over our heads."

He pulled her into his arms, stroking her hair. "It's just a train car, Elena. I have no intention of dying, with or without Mother Earth and Father Moon, and neither should you. Follow me."

Holding the lantern up to eye level, he negotiated the narrow pathway through a labyrinth of immigrant and merchant goods, along with piles of blankets on their way west to be traded to the Indians.

Her eyes adjusting to the semi-darkness, she put aside her fear to sniff derisively at the threadbare rags passing as blankets. "The soldiers take away our way of life and the merchants make us trade for what we could have made for ourselves. Then they laugh and call us Blanket Indians." Her voice grew husky. "I think they would rather have us be Naked Indians, and then we would all freeze to death and become Good Indians."

"Whoa there," Sean said. "Stop the speechifying. We're fugitives remember, not politicians. Maybe someday it'll change, but right now, there's nothing we can do about that. We have more pressing concerns."

He swung the lamp toward the trunks piled around them. "Beginning with our clothes. At least we shouldn't have any trouble finding a new disguise from of all of this."

"No." If not for her wound, Elena would have stamped her foot. "You are not going to rob these people like you did the gambler."

Sean was already moving around the car, picking out the luggage that would hold the best disguises. "I only took the money I let him win. And his rings. And I gave him mine in exchange."

She admitted it was true, but what they did to him was wrong. She sat on a trunk and looked at the floor. "When the police find out Gladstone isn't you, we'll be wanted for stealing his jewelry and the money he thought he won. Maybe we do not have to do this. Billy was nothing. You said they wouldn't hang you for killing him. Maybe the lawmen are not really after us."

He balanced the lamp on a flour barrel and went to her, tilting her chin to face him. "You don't know small towns and the South. If I'd stayed, I wouldn't have lived long enough to prove my innocence, and now that I'm gone, the wagging tongues will paint Billy as a model citizen whose throat you and I slit just for the fun of it.

"Believe me, with Coulter fueling the flames and Roscoe backing him, the law will chase us to the ends of the Earth. Even my father's influence won't make a difference. I can't go back unless I bring in Roscoe."

The truth settled like a lump in the pit of Elena's stomach. What they'd just done to Gladstone would likely put them both on wanted posters from Savannah to Santa Fe. Somehow, they had to prove that Roscoe ordered the missionaries' deaths, as well as his role in the Santa Fe Ring—soon.

He waited until she nodded before explaining, "We'll be known in these clothes. They don't exactly blend into the crowd, if you know what I mean."

Elena still resisted the idea of stealing from innocent travelers. "I have my own clothes. I will be fine."

He remembered how beautiful she was in the blue shirt and striped skirt. How natural. How Apache. "You'd be arrested the moment you got off the train. We need to blend in with the crowd. Be invisible."

He pointed toward a pair of battered old trunks. "What better disguise than as one of the nameless pilgrims in homespun?"

The first trunk he opened revealed several neatly folded cotton work shirts and homespun trousers. There was even a pair of long underwear and a set of suspenders. He held them up, pleased that they would fit him very well; but before he could close the lid, Elena held his arm.

"No."

He ran his fingers through his hair. "I thought I explained. We have no choice."

"Then leave something in return."

"These clothes? We may as well paint a sign."

"They won't open their trunks until they reach the West," she answered, matching his frustrated tone with her own. "And our clothes won't help them there. Leave money."

"But we may need..."

She folded her arms across her chest. "Pay for them."

With another sigh, he reached into his pocket and unfolded bills until she nodded for him to stop. "Could have bought a whole wardrobe with that," he muttered.

"It will come back to you someday." She took a similar sum from him to another trunk full of women's utilitarian clothing. Without examining them, she chose a blue gingham dress with white lace trim and a wide-brimmed bonnet, tucking the money into the pocket of a starched apron.

"What will we do with these?" She indicated the clothes they wore.

"We can pack them back in our bags and use them when we're safe."

Elena turned her back to the man who had already seen her naked and prepared to change into the emigrant's dress, until Sean's hand rested on her shoulder. "Leave that for later. You're exhausted. What do you say to breaking in that pile of blankets over there and catching a little sleep before Nashville?"

Now that they were safe, at least for a few hours, fatigue again washed over her. She accepted his suggestion without considering the danger of sharing a blanket with the man who awakened desires in her she'd never felt before. "What then?"

"In Nashville, we can board a train to Texas. So far, we've obediently followed every crumb Roscoe's dropped along the trail. He thinks we'll chase him to St. Louis, so if we go directly to Texas, it may throw Pruitt and whoever else is looking for us, off our trail. From there, we can try a stage or go on horseback into New Mexico."

She shook her head, knowing only too well that Texas and New Mexico were full of desperados. Mexican bandits, and outlaws who preyed on innocent travelers. Even as an Apache, she was loath to making the trek across the desert alone. With a tinhorn gringo, they'd both be doomed the moment they crossed the Pecos River.

"What about outlaws?"

He kissed the nape of her neck. "We're the outlaws, darling."

She knew she should resist his hands when they circled her waist, but she was too tired, too frightened, to bother. He was her only comfort in this dark and dangerous place. Lawmen or bandits, their fate would be the same. This could be her last chance to become a woman. She sighed as his fingers slid through her hair to the bottom of her spine, tracing soothing circles on her back with his fingertips.

Fear and fatigue slipped away with each tender touch, to be replaced by a physical hunger she couldn't deny. She stepped into his embrace and her body came alive, arching to meet the hand that cupped her breast. His thumb found the supple, sensitive tip and it swelled in response. His other palm rested below her buttocks, pushing her against him. Instinctively, she slid up the length of his erection.

His tongue left her responsive mouth to caress the length of her neck and nibble on her earlobes. "We really are married," he whispered. "This was meant to be."

With the taste of him filling her, and her breasts aching for more of his touch, she agreed. If he had stayed with the People and remained Storm Cloud, they could be together like this forever. Accepting that fate had led her to this strange and exciting man, she relaxed against him.

He lifted her up to the bundle of blankets and slowly unbuttoned her shoes. Then, as he'd done at the ball, his hands ran up the length of her calves until they reached the top of her stockings.

One by one, he pulled them off, his hands returning to glide up her legs until her knees parted. He traced the line of her thighs with his hands, following them with his lips.

She trembled as his curious fingers found her center, and moaned when his tongue tasted her. Her fingers biting into his shoulders, she lay back, opening herself to him.

He raised his head. "Not yet, darling. You're not ready." He stood above her then, his thumb lightly rubbing the nub just inside her cleft.

Her eyes rolled with pleasure and her hands reached out for him. "Please," she sighed.

"Soon, my love," he whispered as he kissed her with her own taste on his lips. Then he lay down beside her and slowly opened the buttons of her dress until it spread beneath her like a filmy, white sheet on the musty-smelling blankets. He loosened the ribbon of the camisole to free her breasts to his hungry lips and tongue. Then, naked in the light of the cloudy lantern, with only a thin shaft of moonlight breaching the boarded windows, she reached out for him to cover her.

Instead, he hypnotized her with soft caresses, and seductive whispers while he removed his own garments. When he was naked as well, he guided her hands over his body.

She was clumsy at first as she threaded her fingers through the matt of soft hair on his chest, tracing circles around his nipples and tasting them with her tongue. She smiled when they reacted to her touch as hers had to his, and he sighed with pleasure.

Gaining confidence, her palm pressed against the strong muscles of his abdomen, following the dark curling hair to the base of his manhood. It responded to her touch to grow hard.

His body trembling in both agony and ecstasy, Sean sat up.

"Did I do something wrong?"

He shook his head and rolled her onto her back. Straddling her, his knees placed so he wouldn't touch her still-tender wound, his fingers traced a fiery trail from her lips, down the smooth line of her throat to her breasts. He rested there, filling his hands with them, suckling them even as he tested the opening to her womb.

Her body responded to his gentle probes to slowly open for him. When she was ready and he could wait no longer, his hands cupped her buttocks. Instinctively, she rose with him, wrapping her legs around his hips, her virgin womb inviting him inside as her mouth had invited his tongue the first time they kissed.

"Now?" she whispered.

"Soon," he pulled away and lowered his head to kiss the lips between her legs that waited, wet and ready to receive him. In a moment, there would be no turning back. He looked up at her. "Are you sure?"

Her hips bucked to swallow him. There was no stopping now. He swelled within her and her legs held tight to receive him. Before the blinding pleasure of release consumed them, he broke the thin barrier guarding her innocence. They rocked as one body to the rhythm of the train, their pleasure skyrocketing at the same time, calling out each other's name before collapsing, out of breath.

Elena's breath came in gasps, her heart pounding in time with his. He moved to separate, but she held tightly to him. "Stay." She whispered. "In me. For a while."

They dozed like that until Elena moved and he rolled away. "Did I hurt you?" he asked.

She rose to her elbows and with a smile as old as Eve and rolled on top of him. He moaned in surprise and pleasure when she did the same things to him as he'd done to her. When she felt him move beneath her, she raised to her knees, placing herself over him. "Here is my answer, *Querido.*"

She smiled watching him watch her through half-closed eyes. First, she rocked back and forth gently, her head swaying to some primal music only she could hear. As he grew inside her, she pressed down until he felt her climax a moment before his release.

They rode together above white-capped mountains in a clear blue sky. As the wind shrieked, the earth trembled and lightning flashed from the clouds, Elena heard Judith's words, "The choice is yours, Elena."

She answered, "Yes," at his release and collapsed onto his chest. For a short time at least, they were truly one. When they reached Santa Fe, she would keep Sean's name. And somehow, she'd find a way to keep him safe. Jesse would help her.

~

Too spent to dress, they lay beside each other, breathing to the rhythm of each other's heart. Sean watched her sleep on his chest. He couldn't let her go now. While he knew she wasn't carrying Billy's child, she could well be carrying his. He thought he heard Chloe's laughter in the thunder that grumbled in the distance. He couldn't live knowing she was in danger. He had to keep her safe. Jesse, his father's old partner, would help him.

CHAPTER TWENTY-TWO

*T*he train pulled into to the Nashville station more than an hour late. Loose track twenty miles outside of town forced the locomotive to a crawl sometime after midnight. When the smoke cleared, Chief of Police Clarence Hobbs positioned a man at each exit door until the conductor verified all the passengers were off except for the private car.

Hobbs crowed to his men, "Well, it looks like the son of a bitch and his squaw are still hidin' in their little den, boys." He waved his men in from the now-empty train to surround the Ambassador car.

Just as he was about to send the first officer in, a man dressed like a cowboy, with bushy red hair sticking out from under a stained Stetson hat, stepped between him and his duty. "Looking for someone, Old Timer?" the cowboy asked with a smile.

Hobbs turned red from the base of his neck up to the roots of his thinning, mud and salt-colored hair. The rolls of fat hanging over his belt testified that he lived well on what the citizens of Nashville paid him; but his scowl showed that for every ounce of fat, he had a pound of mean. It also showed that he didn't much like folks getting in his way when he was about to make an arrest.

Hobbs' bulging eyes squinted at the man who had called him an old timer. He'd taken down bigger, smarter and tougher looking men for less than that in his younger years, but what he had in bad temper and girth, the cowboy had in height, breadth, and youth. He was more interested in catching a murderer than scrapping with this young, red-haired grizzly.

"An' who might be askin', boy?" he growled with his gun drawn.

The cowboy's granite face split beneath the red mustache, and white teeth flashed in another smile. "Sam Pruitt." He held a hand up in deference to the other man's weapon while he opened his coat to show a shiny, five-pointed star. "New Mexico Rangers."

"Damned cowboy lawmen," the Chief grunted and holstered his gun. The one thing he didn't need right now was a busybody New Mexico Ranger sticking his nose into how he did his job.

"I'm busy, boy," he dismissed Pruitt. "My office is down the road. If y'all need to talk with me, you kin wait for me there. Right now, I got me a murderer and his Injun bitch to arrest." He moved to step around the Ranger, only to find himself closer to the wall of the big man's chest.

"Out of my way, sonny," thundered through the depot.

Pruitt continued to smile in the face of Hobbs' rage as he shook open an official looking document in front of the flustered lawman. "Sorry, Chief, but so do I. I have a warrant from the territory of New Mexico for the arrest of Sean O'Grady and his woman, Elena Santiago. It could be we're after the same folks."

"Damn it all to hell," Hobbs' cursed. He had two murderers holed up in a train and he couldn't wait all day to see who had jurisdiction. He squinted to read the cursed fine print everyone used these days and all he could make out was the date. A week ago. "Goddamn sons o' bitches." He swore again and handed it back.

Still, something smelled bad. He squinted up again at Pruitt. "This O'Grady fella's a popinjay from down Georgia way. What's New Mexico want with him?"

"He's wanted on suspicion of land fraud. He and the woman may be in cahoots on a couple of murders in Santa Fe." He leaned forward. "Missionaries."

Hobbs spat a wad of chew onto the ground. "You don't say?" It looked like Coulter would have to get in line. Two murdered missionaries beat a dead bum any day of the week.

"Caught is caught," he finally admitted. "It'll save me a load o' cursed paperwork." Just for show, he waved a fist in the big man's face. "But this is my town and they go to my jail before we figure out if you or Coulter gets 'em."

Pruitt nodded and stepped aside for Chief Hobbs to finish the performance of his duty. He watched intently as Hobbs and two deputies burst into the car with their guns drawn. They emerged moments later with a terrified, half-naked man writhing on the end of their tether, his hands tied behind his back, suspenders flopping around his thighs.

"There's been a mistake," the prisoner cried. "I'm no murderer." He stumbled off the last step of the platform to land face down in the gravel alongside the track. He struggled to his bare feet, dirt and blood streaking his face, he saw Sam and grinned.

"My name is Gladstone. I'm a gambler. Ask him." He pointed his elbow at Pruitt. "Tell them. I been set up. I'm innocent."

Pruitt shrugged. "If I had a nickel for every time I heard that one."

Hobbs grunted in agreement. As his men marched Gladstone to the Nashville jail, he watched the Ranger head back to the private car. "Where you goin'?" he said, starting to take a liking to the big galoot from New Mexico. "The fun's just startin'."

Pruitt nodded at the empty railroad car. "The girl?"

Hobbs scowled and shook his head. He'd looked forward to taking her into his own personal custody. "It was jest him in there. Window's open. Maybe she jumped."

Sam nodded at the possibility and waited for Hobbs to turn his attention back to the prisoner. Then he scanned the faces of the departing passengers as they made their way through the station. Southern dirt farmers seeking greener pastures in Texas or California, mingled with miners still looking for that pot of gold in the Western mountains. There were also gamblers like poor Gladstone, tourists out to see the wonders of the American Wilderness, and salesmen plying their wares to a new market west of the Mississippi.

They were all ages, sizes, and shapes, all dressed in the uniform of their class. It was impossible to distinguish the German farmer from the redneck sharecropper in their homespun or cambric suits; while their equally nondescript women wore gingham or calico dresses, and wide-brimmed hats to protect them from the sun. The socialites from New York looked just like the Southern Belles from Atlanta in their impossibly frilly dresses, feathered hats, and flimsy parasols. If they wanted, Sean and Elena could blend in with any of them like snakes on a rock.

He rubbed his eyes. He'd waited all night for O'Grady to make his move. It surprised him when Sean let himself get drunk and left the Palace car with Gladstone. He didn't seem the kind to drink and play cards with two lives in the balance. Now it looked like he'd underestimated the boy. The girl too.

He watched one of the last couples join the thinning crowd. More homesteaders. Between them, they had only two little carpetbags. The young man's clothes were worn, but clean, still showing the creases of an iron. His little straw hat sat at a cocky angle on his neatly barbered dark hair.

The woman with him looked like a little girl playing dress-up in her mother's clothes. Her blue and white gingham dress hung on her tiny frame and she held the skirt up to keep from tripping on it while her free hand tried desperately to keep her oversized sunbonnet from falling backward.

Sam shook his head and muttered, "Greenhorns. They get younger and greener all the time." Then he reached into his pocket for a cheroot.

Smoke from the cigar circled his head as he climbed into the empty Ambassador car. LaPorte's car. How Sean O'Grady came to be in possession of it was something he'd planned to ask him this very morning, but the boy was wiser than he thought. He'd smelled the law on him the moment they laid eyes on each other. Must have been the suit. Damn thing never did fit right.

He stood in the middle of the car next to the rumpled bed where Gladstone was found. There was no sign of a female inhabitant. The window was open, but it wouldn't be easy to get out of, even for someone as small as Miss Santiago. His forehead furrowed in displeasure when he left the private car.

He walked through the empty Pullman and stood on the tiny platform between it and the baggage car, puffing on the cigar. The noise of the station faded to a dull hum as he concentrated on Sean O'Grady and Elena Santiago.

The girl was an Indian out of her element. She'd depend on Sean. He was a scrapper, a gambler, and a smooth-talking ladies' man. He was also a landowner with the moral code of a gentleman drummed into him as a child. Sean O'Grady might take chances with his own life, but not with an innocent woman's, Apache or White. Somehow, he found a way for them to get off the train together.

He reviewed the events of the night before. It was late when O'Grady and Gladstone left the Palace car, only a few hours left for them to escape certain capture in the morning. The weather was clear. The moon and stars would have illuminated the rails they were racing over at a breakneck speed approaching thirty-five miles per hour. From the platform, it would seem much faster. Even after the train slowed for the loose rails, the gravel on the side of the tracks would cut like knives if someone jumped shy and missed the grassy slope on the other side.

A man might make it with little or no damage, but a woman no bigger than a girl, hampered with a skirt, would be another story. He remembered Sean's attention to Elena on the stairs of the Savannah House and again when she choked on her little piece of chicken. His concern was more than an act. No. O'Grady would never risk her life to save his own.

He squatted in front of the baggage car door and smiled when the sun glinted off a thin shaft of silver sticking out of the coupling below the deck. A lock pick. The lock was scraped and scratched, as if someone was in a hurry to get it open. Further inspection of the floor revealed tiny rust colored stains. Haste and darkness had resulted in a wound. Sam tipped his Stetson back on his head. Not a bad one though.

He stepped inside. It was a converted passenger car. A board hung askew from a window that allowed fresh air and a thin shaft of sunlight to stab the darkness. As more light poured in from the open door behind him, Sam's sharp eyes scanned the car from top to bottom.

He bent to examine fresh marks on the dirty floor, following the barely discernible trail through the dust to a couple of trunks set slightly apart from the others. He opened one of them and whistled low when he found five dollars stuffed into the pocket of an apron. He wasn't surprised to find five more hidden in a pocket of men's clothing in the trunk next to it.

Feeling close to them now, he moved faster through the baggage car and slapped his hat against his thigh when he found the pile of mussed, musky smelling blankets. His deep laughter echoed in the gloom as he recalled the girl in the ill-fitting blue dress, and the young man leaning close to her, exactly the way Sean O'Grady had leaned over Elena Santiago in Savannah.

"Damn, if they didn't pull it off," he announced to the empty car and stepped out into the light of a beautiful, Tennessee morning.

He whistled as he made his way to the jailhouse. There was no rush to find them. He knew what they looked like and where they were going. It wouldn't be long before the three of them had their little talk.

He found Mr. Gladstone/O'Grady simpering in a corner of his cell. One eye was purple and swollen shut. His slick, handsome features were barely recognizable from his fall and the Chief's fists.

"Hobbs?" Sam said to a young deputy when he entered the office.

"Uncle—I mean Chief Hobbs, is down at the cafe havin' a cup of coffee. This is pretty early in the day for him to be up and around."

Sam nodded and folded his long body into Hobbs' chair. He lit another cheroot and cocked his head toward the prisoner. "He confess yet?"

The boy ran his fingers through sand-colored hair and gave up when the wayward mop immediately flopped back down over his eyes. "Nope. Funniest thing, though. Swears he's some gambler what rides the rails. Said he won a bundle from a rube named Grande and went with him for a game in his private car. Then Grande and a girl drugged and robbed him. Even says they took the time to swap jewelry and give him a shave." He howled with laughter.

Sam laughed too, at the idea of cold-blooded killers grooming their victim after they robbed him. Poor Gladstone, a wild story like that would get him nowhere, even if it was true. He noted that without the mustache, Gladstone's resemblance to Sean was close enough to fool anyone who hadn't seen Sean's stockier body and gray eyes.

As if the prisoner might hear them above the sound of his own wails, Hobbs' nephew leaned close to Sam. "Says you know he's not O'Grady."

Sam's eyes narrowed and he suppressed a smile. The boy was smarter than he looked and knew better than to accept things at face value. He took a long look at the prisoner. Then he settled back again, crossing his ankles on the desk, balancing on the two back legs of the Chief Hobbs' chair.

"Nope, can't say as I've made the acquaintance. He fits the description of the man I'm after; but it's a long trip to Santa Fe and he looks a bit sickly. I'd hate to have to explain his body when I got back. I still got the woman to track down."

As if deep in thought, Sam rubbed the red stubble on his unshaven cheeks. "You got someone comin' for him?"

"Yeah, Sheriff Coulter's sendin' a man up from Jeffers. Should be here in a day or so. You want me to stop him?"

"Nah. It's like your uncle said, 'caught is caught.' He'll hang either way, so you can have him."

He stood. "I'll sign over my warrant to Chief Hobbs and be on my way. Cities don't agree with me. Too much smoke," he said from behind a cloud of his own making. "When's the next train South to Texas? I'd as soon be gone as settin' around here listening to that whining jackass."

The boy stood too, his gaze traveling upward to meet Sam's. "Train's gone by now. Next one is first thing in the morning. I can get you a ticket if you want to stay and, uh...question the suspect before you turn him over to Coulter's man."

"No, thanks. I have all the answers I need. I'll take care of the ticket myself." He nodded toward Gladstone. "Take care o' him, mind you. I'd hate to have to come back if he got away between here and Georgia."

"Don't worry, Mr. Ranger, sir. He won't see the light o' day 'til he climbs up the gallows."

CHAPTER TWENTY-THREE

*W*hen the sun filtered through the slats on the windows, Sean woke Elena with a kiss. She opened her eyes and saw he was already dressed in his farmer's clothes. Concern filled his eyes when he saw the stain from her virgin blood on the ruined dress beneath her. Then he kissed her again. "Good morning, Mrs. O'Grady."

He misunderstood her hesitation. "Elena, you didn't do anything wrong. We're married."

Shame at his reminder of their sham marriage dulled her happiness and she flashed him an angry look. "The marriage vow is not for easing a guilty conscience. It is a vow of love and faithfulness between two people who become one in God's eyes for all their lives. We have mocked it and we will pay dearly for it."

He lifted her down from the blankets. "I don't take it lightly, Elena. I never did."

She was glad the shadows hid the blush that crept up her cheeks as she remembered the explosive moment when their souls had touched. Though her heart would always belong to him, it didn't change their circumstances. She didn't deserve a life with him or anyone, until she made Junior Anscombe pay for his murders.

"It was only our bodies," she lied and reached for the farmer's dress. "A marriage is much more than that. If you do not know that, then—"

He finished her sentence for her. "I can learn."

She turned to pull on her stolen clothing. "There isn't time."

"We have until Santa Fe."

There was no time to explain the real meaning of a marriage. The train had stopped and a look outside showed people already spilling from the passenger cars onto the depot landing. The police were spread out along the track. Then her heart fell. The red-haired man was talking to the Sheriff. Again, Sean was right about the white man's ability to deceive.

His hand touched her elbow. "We have to hurry. The train will be empty soon and we need to blend in with the others."

She nodded and skipped in her overlong dress to keep up with him through the Pullman car behind the other farmers and settlers. It was a short walk to the ticket agent. Her heart racing, she fought the urge to turn around and see if the police had found Gladstone.

The ticket agent peered over the top of his spectacles and smiled at the young couple. "What can I do ye for?"

"Two tickets on the next train to Texas," Sean said.

"Ah." The agent shook his head. "Now that won't be 'til tomorrow at seven o'clock in the mornin'. Ye just missed it. The Southern Pacific keeps an early schedule. On the Santa Fe, you can count on an hour or two wait, but if yer in a hurry, you want the S.P. an' you better be on time."

Sean pulled together what he could of the Irish brogue his father slipped into when he had too much brandy. "Well, I do admire punctuality. So, two tickets it is for the mornin' train, my man. On the S.P."

He looked at his pocket watch. They had twenty-one hours to rest up for the final part of their journey. "We'll need a room. Me wife here, is mighty tired." He winked and added, "We're expecting a babe."

"She does look a mite peaked," he agreed. "The Harrow House is three blocks east and one north of here. Clean and quiet."

"I thank ye for that bit o' information sir," Sean answered with a bright smile and took the tickets.

The agent smiled at the young farmer and his pregnant bride. "Go with God, son. Next," he called to the man behind them.

While she was stunned at Sean's story, Elena couldn't stay angry with him. On those rough woolen blankets, he'd shown her a tenderness she'd never thought possible between a man and a woman. Apache villages are very small, and she learned early that it was a woman's place to give pleasure to her brave, no matter how it hurt. Instead, Sean had put her needs before his, holding his own passion in check until she was ready to receive it.

When they left the station, and Sean turned west instead of east to find a room, she tugged at his arm. "You're going the wrong way."

"Just being careful. That old man was a little too curious for my taste. Besides, the Harrow House probably pays him to send people over there. It's best to find a place on our own."

She nodded. The old man's cunning blue eyes behind his tiny spectacles had darted like a snake. Her confidence in Sean's ability to negotiate the white world returned. She nearly tripped on her own skirt trying to match his long strides. "I must alter this," she said finally. "Stop so I can buy some thread."

He stopped in front of a little general store and winked, "We can do better than that."

"No. We will spend too much. There won't be any money left for supplies, or to buy information about Junior Anscombe. We must be careful."

He laughed and reached into his pocket, pulling out Gladstone's rings. "Well, we have these."

Elena gasped and snatched them from him, dropping them in her little reticule before anyone could see them. "Are you loco? You can't sell these. You stole them."

"I told you I had to take them. The ring I gave him is worth more than these added together."

"Well you can't sell them."

His frown was soon replaced by a boyish grin. "Well, we still have enough to buy something that fits you better than that sack. And now is a fine time to be worrying about money after what you made me put in those trunks."

"It was only fair," she said to his back as she followed him into the shop.

"My wife has been ill and she needs something that fits her better," Sean explained her ill-fitting dress to the clerk. "For chores," he added with a wink at Elena. They selected two simple shifts in dark calico prints. He added a soft cotton nightgown with satin laces to their purchase.

Then they checked into the Blue Dawn rooming house. It couldn't compare to the opulence of the Savannah House, but did have plastered walls, a clean looking bed, and a basin of fresh water for washing. They used the communal privy at the back of the building and ventured out for something to eat.

Elena had no moral code against eating fried chicken and ate ravenously.

"Maybe you are eating for two." Sean smiled as if the idea pleased him a great deal.

"You give yourself too much credit," she fired back, ignoring the leap her heart took at his smile. "This food is delicious."

"It certainly is," he said, letting her know that his appetite was for anything but the food. "Let's take some back to our room."

She stopped eating. The taste of freedom and the knowledge that she would soon be in Texas had made her forget they were on the run from both lawmen and criminals.

"The red-haired man," she said. "He was with the sheriff. I saw him watching the crowd. Have you seen him? Is he following us?" Panic made her start to rise from the table, but Sean's steady hand stopped her.

"No and no." He checked his pocket watch. "I'm sure Gladstone has spilled his story a hundred times by now, but they'll still be looking for a woman." He leaned forward and whispered, "You are very beautiful. Even in that feed sack, people notice. It's safer to stay out of sight until the train leaves in the morning."

Safer? Another night alone with him would only make it harder to leave him in Santa Fe. Yet she had no choice. To be alone here would be to die and to stay with him there would get him killed. "You may be right," she said and rose with him when the cook brought them a basket filled with more food.

Sean grinned. "Hurry. I have a surprise for you."

When they returned to the hotel, he rushed Elena up the stairs to their room. Once inside, she gasped at a bathtub full of steaming water.

A bar of lavender soap and a towel lay on the bed next to it. She dipped a hesitant hand into the bath, longing to strip off her borrowed clothes and soak in it forever.

A look at Sean told her he would have liked to join her, and she fought her own urge to invite him by saying, "We can't."

He chuckled and gathered her into a hug. "Don't worry. This is my gift to you." Then he grabbed his carpetbag and went to the door. "I'm going to the public bathhouse down the street. Lock the door when I leave and don't let anyone in."

He laughed again at her smile. "Well, don't look so happy. I will be back, you know."

Her smile remained. "I know."

The bath was heavenly. She inhaled deeply of the delicate scent of lavender soap on her skin, washed her hair, and sank deeper into the tub, closing her eyes and letting her spirit soar in the blue skies of her home. For the first time in weeks, she slept peacefully.

~

Sean's heart hammered in his chest when he returned from the bathhouse and the door to their room opened without the key. He stepped inside to see only the top of Elena's head above the bathtub rim, her eyes closed. He swallowed hard and said a silent, unfamiliar, prayer as he closed and locked the door behind him. Then he approached her.

Her chin rested in water that floated like an opaque veil across the rosy tips of her breasts, shrouding the deeper, sweeter, regions of her body. He watched the silky cloud ebb and flow across her satin-smooth skin with the rhythm of her breath, and knew she was safe.

When she opened her eyes to meet his, he added a prayer of thanks to his store of rare conversations with God. He even forgot to scold her for leaving the door unlocked. "I thought you'd be done by now."

"I fell asleep." She waited for him as he waited for her.

"You should get out. You'll catch cold."

"Will you help me out?" she smiled and took his hand to rise slowly, letting the sheer, lavender-scented, liquid silk slide from her skin in a shimmering wave.

Once again, Sean wrapped her in a big, soft towel and carried her to the bed. She helped him out of his sodden shirt and trousers, exploring his body by candlelight.

Just the touch of her smooth skin against his aroused him. When her fingers circled him, he grew hard in her small hand. She settled over it with a sigh like a silk glove over a familiar hand. Her eyes grew large with pleasure and her body set the pace of their lovemaking.

His fingertips coaxed her breasts to attention, and their eyes locked to enjoy the other's pleasure. This time, he rocked her until she stiffened from the spasm deep within her. Their eyes closed and hands locked, they rode together to a place that belonged to only them.

With their appetite for the basket of cold chicken and biscuits renewed and a single candle their only light, Elena sat on the floor in her new nightgown. The open laces revealed the swell of her breasts, the narrowing V pointing the way to the only place where Sean had ever known real peace.

He stared at her as if he'd never touched a woman before. Indeed, she felt like his first. The first he'd ever truly cared about, the first and the last he ever wanted to be with for the rest of his life.

"I've never known a woman like you," he said between bites of a crispy drumstick. It was true. The whores and unhappy wives he'd bedded in the past were puppets compared to this beautiful, innocent, and passionate child-woman. "I thought all virgins...I mean ladies, were like Mary Louise," he said. "She hardly let me touch her and I doubt it would have changed if we'd married."

"Then the ladies you have known are fools." Elena waved her own drumstick to emphasize her words. Her eyes suddenly misted in the candle-light. "Perhaps one day you will find a white lady who is not a fool."

He took the chicken leg from her and cupped her face in his hands. "Can't you understand, Elena? I'm not looking for a white lady." His kiss showed her he'd found what he was looking for.

CHAPTER TWENTY-FOUR

Sean watched in awe as the Southern Pacific train bound for El Paso rolled through Texas under a high yellow moon playing hide and seek with the ghostly shadows of storm clouds. A steady rush of rain against the windows muted the midnight symphony of clacking metal wheels, flashing lightning bolts, and roaring thunder claps. It was Nature's fury as he'd never seen it before.

A farmer traveling west to retire in sunny Southern California remarked, "After the last couple years of drought, the ranchers hereabouts should be mighty happy to see this." His voice woke Elena from her doze on Sean's shoulder.

"Happy?" a cowboy responded. "I suppose so, but they don't call this country, God Forsaken fer nothin'. I hope the engineer's lookin' out fer flash floods. Too much rain out here after a drought can turn a little gully into a deathtrap."

Suddenly, heads turned and eyes widened in fear. "I was in Las Cruces once, and a storm like this come up out of nowhere. It was like the end of the world." Pleased with his audience's rapt attention, he explained, "Las Cruces back then was built around a little natural gully they used for the main street. Well, after that storm, there wasn't no main street an' there wasn't no Las Cruces. Flood washed the whole damn shootin' match a mile downstream. Been there ever since."

He paused for effect. "Seen a man and horse jest swallered up and washed away. Prob'ly ended up fish food somewheres in the Rio Grande."

Worried whispers turned to panic and someone insisted they stop the train.

As the panic began to spread, he assured them, "Then again, these storms kin dry up faster'n spit. Jest have to wait 'em out." He leaned back in his seat, crossed his arms over his chest, and closed his eyes.

The car grew silent again as people wrestled with the information. Whole towns moving downstream? How was that possible? The story was generally dismissed as poppycock and passengers slowly returned to their rest, if not slumber.

Sean winced from a cramp in his leg as Elena snuggled back into his shoulder. He'd heard enough about the weather from sodbusters and cowboys, as they complained first about the dust and now about the rain.

He moved enough to disturb Elena and she released him so he could stretch. "Looks like a long night, love," he said. "My legs are about to break off. How about if I stroll back to the smoking car and see if I can find a little exercise there?" He cracked his fingers to limber them up for the type of exercise he had in mind.

He was eager to test out his new guise as a raw country-boy with baggy clothes and two-day's growth of beard. Likely, the so-called card-sharps on their way to San Francisco would underestimate him and he'd empty their pockets. He'd have to be careful though. While they could use the money, calling attention to himself as a big winner would only increase their danger.

She glanced warily around them. "Be careful," she answered, as if reading his thoughts.

Her moist, sleepy eyes awoke Sean's passion enough to keep him from rising for a moment. It was nearly unbearable to sit so close to her and not be able to kiss her. To have her breasts pressed against him and not be able to caress them. To feel the warmth of her body without the smooth, satin touch of her skin, was torture.

In the last two days, she'd given herself so completely to him that he would gladly have died in her embrace. While she insisted they had to separate in Santa Fe, he knew better. Only death could part them, and he had no intention of letting that happen.

Her whispered warning told him she was still afraid of being captured. He risked a quick kiss on a warm cheek that bore creases from his sleeve. "You worry too much. We're almost there." He rose and stretched again before carefully working his way around legs, skirts and bags to the back of the car.

He almost tripped over a big, rumpled cowboy with a sombrero pulled over his face, his long legs sticking out into the aisle. "Pardon me," Sean said, but the cowboy only grunted before pulling his booted feet back out of the way.

Sean frowned. Drunk, no doubt. Everyone said cowboys were a rough lot. It was a reputation he had yet to see proved beyond fierce expressions, dirty clothes, and big guns. Quick draws aside, he doubted these clumsy, clanking buffoons could outrun a flying knife. Then he opened the door, lowered his head against the driving rain and quickstepped across the vestibule into the smoking car.

~

When the door closed behind him, the cowboy unfolded his lanky frame from the narrow seat and moved toward the empty one next to Elena. She saw his wavy reflection on the window. "I'm sorry, this is my husband's seat."

A deep voice with a southwestern drawl answered. "Yes ma'am, and I think maybe we better go find him." He removed his hat to reveal a freshly cropped head of red hair and a line of pale skin above his lip where a bushy red mustache used to be.

Elena gasped. She was trapped between the window and Sam Pruitt's mammoth, buckskin-clad body. All she could do was stare into the striking blue eyes that held her in place even more than the big hand on her arm.

"Whoa, there," he said quietly. "For your own good and that wily young squirrel you call a husband, just get up slowly and walk in front of me to the end of the car." A slight shift of his position revealed a Colt .45 peacemaker in his gun belt.

She didn't believe he'd shoot her in a moving railroad car full of cowboys, ex-soldiers, women, and small children, but she couldn't risk it. Despair deadened her will to escape. They almost made it.

She stood, taking a deep breath to control the terror gripping her soul. Smelling of buckskin and saddle soap, Sam stepped close behind her, and like a huge rolling boulder, prodded her to the exit. Once there, he threw his woolen poncho over her head and opened the door to the chilly downpour outside.

She took advantage of his kindness to turn to him and plead. "*Por*

Favor, Senor..." just as the train lurched under their feet. A grinding sound rose above the raging storm, followed by the groan of metal grinding against metal that sounded like screams from the demons of Hell. Then the car teetered crazily back and forth.

"The bridge is goin' down," Sam shouted and scooped Elena under his arm. He took one big step out onto the wildly swaying platform, gripped the slippery rail with his free hand and stepped onto the edge. "Hold on to me," he shouted above the din as the car behind them derailed. Then he propelled them both through the wall of rain, into the oblivion that lay beyond the tracks.

Elena landed on top of Sam, his weight alternately crushing and cushioning her as they rolled down the side of the steep embankment. When they stopped, Sam grabbed her by his poncho and dragged her up a rocky incline. Lifting her head slowly, she raised a shaky hand to wipe away wet clumps of mud and hair from her face. Please let him be dead, she prayed and turned to look at the man who had just thrown her from the train.

Sam Pruitt sat next to her, panting from the bone-crushing roll. A dark streak ran from his forehead down the side of his sharply etched jaw. "You all right, Ma'am?" he said as if he'd just lifted her over a mud puddle instead of throwing her headlong off a moving train above a river that shouldn't have been there.

Trembling from the shock of the fall and the fear of being alone with this dangerous man, she nodded slowly. Then they both looked back at the train. Sam's curse was drowned out by screams as the passenger car toppled off the broken trestle and dangled like a toy on a string above the raging water.

Flames shot from the windows as the lamps caught the interior on fire. The shrieks of trapped passengers rose above the sounds of the rain, thunder, and swirling water. Each flash of lightning bathed the scene in a white light that branded it forever in Elena's memory.

Clawing the air and pounding the hands that held her, she shouted. "Sean, Sean," and finally, "Storm Cloud," until her voice died in her throat. When the smoking car tipped over and exploded into flames before following the passenger car into the draw, she would have followed it. Then what felt like a brick crashed into her head and she no longer felt the rain or heard the screams of the dying train passengers.

CHAPTER TWENTY-FIVE

*H*er head felt like it was clamped in a vise. The wet cloth pressed over her eyes did little to ease the throbbing pain, and when she moaned, invisible hands took it away. One of her eyes refused to open and the other was slow to focus on the shiny, five-pointed star pinned to a leather vest stretching across a wide chest.

She didn't have to ask. She'd seen enough of the little tin stars to know the words "New Mexico," and "Ranger," were engraved on it. She also remembered enough of the previous night to know if she looked up, she'd see clear blue eyes in a weathered face topped by red hair.

Sean was wrong. Pruitt wasn't one of Roscoe's men. He was the law. Either way, he was their enemy. Yet he had thrown her from the train only moments before it crashed into the raging river.

She closed her eyes to the memory of the burning smoking car and refused to believe she was a widow before she'd had a chance to be a wife. There was some comfort in knowing it would only be for a short time.

"Kill me now, Gringo, while you still have the chance."

Sam balled his wet bandanna in his hand and rocked back on his heels. A smile split his features like a gorge cutting through the Texas plains. He bet that, at barely a hundred pounds, battered and bruised, and one eye swollen shut, she'd make good on the threat if she had the chance. Like her husband, she had more guts than good sense.

His smile disappeared at the thought of Sean O'Grady. Dead probably, in the fire, or drowned in the Salt Draw. He gave the boy credit for trying to outwit Roscoe LaPorte alone. It was a right noble act, if also a foolish one. A dirty shame they'd never know if he could have pulled it off.

It seemed unlikely. For more years than Sam cared to count, New Mexico and Texas Rangers had been chasing the bunch of scalawags and thieves who were murdering and cheating poor Mexicans and small ranchers out of their lands. All they had for their efforts were saddle sores and dead witnesses. Now, thanks to Patrick O'Grady and his Washington connections, they finally had a name. Roscoe LaPorte. However, it had cost Sam's old friend Camilla O'Grady, her son.

"I went through a lot just to save your little hide, ma'am. What makes you think I want to kill you?"

She struggled to sit up in the narrow cot in a corner of the one-room shack. "Then what do you want with me, Ranger Pruitt, if that is who you really are."

Despite the bruise from his powerful backhand, the love for Sean O'Grady that he'd seen written all over her face at the Savannah House was still there. It melted his resolve to keep his real mission from her. She deserved to know.

He'd spent much of his adult life on the trail, or with company he didn't care to engage in conversation, and words came hard for him. He rose from his squat next to the cot, handed the rag to her and pulled up a wobbly three-legged stool to sit next to her. "I never lie about who I am, ma'am."

She winced at the accusation in his voice. "Then you are really a Ranger?"

"Yep."

"Are you going to arrest me?"

The rumble of his laughter filled the old line-shack. "No, ma'am."

Instead of relief, Elena's eyes widened in terror. "Then you work for Senor Roscoe."

He was more than a little hurt by the accusation. Had the years he'd spent on the trail made him look like the men he hunted? He covered her hand with his own giant paw.

"No, ma'am. I'm lookin' to arrest the son of a bitch, pardon my language."

"Then why were you following us?" Her voice caught at the word "us".

Her good eye filled with tears at the realization that Sean was likely dead. Her moan said it all when she lay back down.

"Well, ma'am..." Failure didn't come often or easy to him. For ten years, he'd never lost a witness or a prisoner in his custody. It may have been an act of God, but the boy was dead and he felt responsible for it. "I was helping some old friends named O'Grady, to see that no harm came to their son and his bride..."

Her disdainful glare silenced him. If he'd collared them before Nashville, none of this would have happened. But there was no going back. "Well, you see, back when I was a youngster, my folks came West with Marcus Williams, Judith, and her husband Charles Carter."

Her cold stare turned into one of curiosity, and he continued. "Camilla O'Grady was with them. On the riverboat from St. Louis to Independence, she and Marcus saved my life. I'll never forget that day." He paused at the memory.

"I was running wild on the deck and tripped on a rope. Woulda flown right into the paddle wheels if her scream hadn'ta woke up old Marcus who was dozin' on the deck. For a second, I felt like a bird flying through the air. Then I saw those paddle wheels comin' at me, and for as much as a seven-year-old kid can understand death, I knew I was a gonner.

"That was when what seemed like the hand of God reached out and brought me back." He smiled. "Only it wasn't God. It was Marcus. One of the most ornery codgers I ever met and one of the best men I'll ever meet."

"Si," Elena answered. She sat up, leaning on her elbows. "Marcus was strong. When I first saw him with his white beard, I thought he was the Manitou of the white eyes."

Her soft, feminine smile reminded Sam of the sacrifices he'd made in choosing the life of a lawman, but he had a job to do. One he'd managed to completely botch up. He cleared his throat. "Well, that was a long time ago. I owe a debt to both Camilla and Marcus, and Jesse Woods is my friend."

She kept silent while he continued. "Anscombe jumped Jesse on his way to visit his mother. When he didn't tell him where the gold was, Junior left him for dead. Somehow, he made it to her lodge and when Marcus came lookin' for him they worked out a plan. Marcus headed back to warn Judith and the O'Gradys, and Jesse high-tailed it up to my folks' ranch to find me."

"So that is what kept him from being with Judith," Elena whispered.

Sam nodded. "Anscombe is just a hired gun. It was Marcus who found his connection to Georgia. While Jesse was tracking me down, Judith took things into her own hands and sent you to the O'Grady's. I left right away, but by the time I got to Jeffers and met with Patrick. Marcus and Judith were both dead, young O'Grady was in a peck o' trouble, and they knew that Roscoe LaPorte was our man."

"Then why didn't you arrest him?" She remembered Roscoe boldly socializing at the engagement ball. "He wasn't hard to find."

He took the blow in stride. "We didn't have any real proof. After young Sean killed that piece of scum Berens, he convinced his old man to let him go on his own. His Pa and I figured it'd be best if I stayed outta sight, but close by, so nothin' happened to you two whilst he and his Washington pals investigated LaPorte."

The grief etched on Elena's beautiful face made him scowl. He should never have let them out of his sight. Now, this pretty, little gal was a widow and he had to wire Camilla O'Grady that he let her son get killed.

"I brought this trouble upon the O'Gradys." Elena's voice was suddenly deep with self-loathing. "I should have convinced Judith to wait for Jesse… and you." She looked at him, her good eye clear, her chin set with purpose. "Senor and Senora O'Grady, are they safe?"

He nodded. "Patrick's got more tricks up his sleeve than I'll ever know. He didn't want to use his son as bait, but Sean figured if it was personal for Roscoe, he'd get sloppy. 'Sides, somebody had to look after you."

"I can take care of myself," she snapped without acknowledging she was losing count of the times a white man had saved her life.

"What is this 'Ring' that can commit many murders and not be punished? Is it like the army?"

Sam understood how she could compare it to the army that had continued to exterminate her race long after it was defeated in war—for the benefit of rich, greedy men who would do anything to get richer.

"No, it's worse. The Ring is a secret circle of influential businessmen and politicians who use false land grants and deeds to claim land in the West. Then they sell it at huge profits to European investors who think there's gold in every mountain. We figure Roscoe's using the Ring to cover his search for that missing gold from the Mint."

She seemed to shrink in front of him as her only hope of finding justice for the murders of both her Apache and white families, dissolved. "They are so powerful. How can they be stopped?"

"They're greedy, so when it comes to a showdown, they won't back each other up. If we get LaPorte, we can get the Ring too."

Unfortunately, the possibility of that was fading by the minute. Without Sean as bait, it was anybody's guess what Roscoe would do. Damn.

"You think you have failed."

Her hand felt cold on his. "It looks that way now. Roscoe will likely lay low until things cool off. If he does, our chances of busting up the Ring are gone too, and I just let an innocent man die for nothing."

Elena swung her legs over the edge of the cot, clinging to his hand to fight the dizziness that followed. "What about me?"

He looked away from the hope shining in her battered face. "What about you?"

"Senor LaPorte likes me. I can pretend to join him. We can catch him that way if Sean is really—."

Sam took her by the shoulders and pulled her to her feet. "Don't you even think about it. I ain't about to let one more person I'm supposed to be protectin' die. I'm goin' to deliver you safe and sound to Jesse Woods, and then I'm going to find Roscoe and make him pay for what he did any way I need to."

"But you are the law of the white eyes. You cannot murder."

He let go of her to pull the star off his vest and toss it onto the scarred table in the center of the room. "Now I'm the law of the West, the law of the fittest and the fastest. It's Roscoe or me."

"No," Elena shouted. "A wise woman once told me that a woman has weapons against such a man. Weapons more powerful than guns." She touched Sam's arm. "First, we do not know what happened to Sean. You were sent to protect him, and I am his wife. We cannot leave until we know."

Knowing it would be a while before Roscoe figured out if Sean was a victim of the train crash, Sam let her cling to her one last hope. "Won't know 'til the rain stops."

She slowly crossed the room toward the filthy glass of the only window in the shack and rubbed a spot clean with Sam's bandana. "Then we wait until the rain stops."

CHAPTER TWENTY-SIX

By noon the next day, the rain stopped as it began, suddenly and without warning. The sky cleared to a brilliant blue and the ground steamed under the heat of the summer sun. Soon the water in the Salt Draw would flow away, leaving the charred skeletons of burned-out train cars half-buried in the mud. Some bodies would be trapped in the limbs of dead trees that were stripped from their sandy soil along the draw; but most of the victims would simply wash downstream to be buried in the mud of the Rio Grande or devoured by scavengers.

"I need new clothes," Elena told Sam.

He looked up from the map of Texas and New Mexico he was studying. "We're a far piece from a dressmaker's shop, ma'am."

She frowned at his ignorance. "All I have is this dress, and it is torn. No good for the desert. I need buckskins. Leggings. A poncho. *Comprende?*"

He finally understood and smiled at this brave and practical little woman. She hadn't complained once about the bruises on her face, or the many more he was sure she wouldn't show him. She'd even cleaned up the shack, sweeping years of dirt and debris into the old hearth.

Concentrating on their immediate needs over the sorrow that the future held, she rifled through the saddlebag Sam had retrieved from his dead horse, finding only a little jerky and some brown boot polish. "We need food. Is it far to a town?"

He stood and reached for his hat. "Pecos is only a few miles away. The horse I rescued from the livestock car wasn't hurt, so it won't take me long to get there and back." He stopped at the door. "You sure you don't want any frills? You'll look like a boy."

She paused from washing their few cooking utensils in an old bucket filled with rainwater. Her frown told him she wondered if all Gringos were stupid. "I don't think it would be good for Elena Santiago to be walking around while she is still wanted for murder."

She arched an eyebrow. "A Mexican boy would get little attention, no?"

He didn't think anyone would take her delicate features for a Mexican boy, but couldn't fault her logic about the disguise. The law would be looking for an Indian girl posing as a white woman. Still, there was something about the set of her jaw and the tone of her voice that made his gut ache. She was up to something.

First things first. He determined she wouldn't be going anywhere with just the clothes on her back. He'd check out Pecos and get supplies. After that, he sure as hell wouldn't let her out of his sight.

The road to Pecos that was a muddy quagmire the night before was already dry and turning hard. The town, if it could be called that, consisted of little more than a couple saloons, a general store, telegraph, and few scattered houses.

He went first to the tiny general grocery in the center of town where he purchased some flour, salt, sugar and coffee. Salted bacon was the only meat in stock, and he settled for that, along with more jerky. He could hunt something else up on the trail. "I'll take a half-dozen of them canned beans," he told the storekeeper.

The grocer was busy tallying up Sam's sale when a little Mexican boy came in shouting they'd found more survivors washed up on a sandbar. "Miguel, git yer Greaser ass outta here," the storekeeper ordered with an impatient wave of his arm. "Doc McAllister is over at the Nugget. Go tell him." The boy hung around to stare at the tall Gringo with red hair.

Sam paid for his purchases and tossed a nickel to Miguel who caught it, but was too slow to escape Sam Pruitt's long reach.

"Hey, Gringo," he shrieked when Sam pulled him back. "I no steal. You give."

"You like American dollars, boy?" Sam laughed.

The boy's eyes widened. "*Si*," he answered, smiling.

Sam looked at the boy's white peasant pants with their drawstring waist, and the buckskin leggings on his feet. The homespun shirt was worn, but looked clean. His floppy hat nearly covered his eager brown face. This was no street urchin. "You got a home, boy?"

"*Si.*" He pointed down the street. "Rosa's. The Cantina."

Sam fingered Miguel's shirt. "You got more clothes like this? Clean?"

His shrewd eyes narrowed. "*Si.* For church."

Sam laughed at the lie. There was no church in Pecos and he doubted God cared very much about the bedraggled little Mexican brat. "I'll buy them if you promise to keep your mouth shut." He flashed a dollar gold piece in front of Miguel's bright brown eyes, only to pull it away when he reached for it.

"Take me to Rosa's. I get the clothes, and you get paid."

"*Si.*" Miguel tugged on Sam's sleeve.

The boy led him to a brothel, currently crowded with cots occupied by wounded survivors of the train wreck. On their way to Miguel's tiny closet, Sam's gaze scanned the beds without finding Sean O'Grady.

He took his attention away from what looked like an Army field hospital, to watch the boy reach into a box under his cot and hold out a set of clothes identical to the ones he wore, including leggings, a poncho, and a wide-brimmed sombrero.

Sam smiled. Miguel had told the truth. The clothes were louse free and smelled of lye soap. He flipped the promised gold piece, into the air and chuckled when Miguel caught it before it hit the floor. Then he blocked the boy's effort to rush out and spend his money.

"Now tell me about the new survivors."

A trip to the livery provided Sam with a mount more to his liking than the chestnut mare from the livestock car. It was a big roan that could carry his weight easily and wouldn't tire on the desert. Elena could have the mare. With the new horse, food, clothes for Elena, and news that two men had been found a mile downstream, Sam's spirits lifted. Maybe he wouldn't have to send that telegram after all.

He didn't waste any more time checking beds. Elena wouldn't believe him unless she saw for herself, and there was never any good in doing something twice. If Sean was still alive, he'd be at Rosa's, the Nugget Saloon, or Doc McAllister's office, where they'd taken the two new men. If not, he'd either be in the makeshift morgue in the icehouse behind the general store or they'd never find him.

He entered the cabin and noticed Elena had managed to prepare an eating space on the propped up, three-legged table. She'd also washed her dress and her hair, which now lay in two neat braids along her back. A sudden pang from more than hunger hit him in the midsection. A lawman's chances of having a lovely young woman to greet him at the door was only a dream.

Elena's worried frown at Sam's scowl gave way to a smile when he tossed the bundle of clothing onto the cot. "Found a Mexican boy about your size," he said. "He had a spare set."

She squinted doubtfully at him. The words, "Mexican" and "spare" rarely went together when it came to clothing or anything else—and one other thing. "Clean?"

～

During Sam's absence, she had spoken to the four winds about her husband. Sitting naked on the cot with her legs crossed beneath her, her clothes drying on a hook over the fireplace, she tried to feel his presence. In her trance, she saw him circle over her like an eagle, and "Storm Cloud," whispered in the breeze from the open door. She knew then he was alive.

Now, she smiled up at Sam. Disguised as a boy, she could see Sean one last time before she left. Then things would be as they should be. He would go back to his home and a life with the white child-woman, and she could find Junior Anscombe while Sam searched for Roscoe LaPorte. There was no time to delay.

"I will put these on and we can find my husband," she announced.

"Not so fast," Sam said. "I sure ain't gonna eat my only meal in two days opposite a woman dressed like a Mexican boy." He produced the bundle of food. "How about a little grub before we leave?"

Elena finally realized how hungry she was. If it meant finding Sean, she could happily ignore the familiar rumble in her stomach, but a man as big as Sam Pruitt needed food. He'd saved her life. She could cook him a meal. Besides, Sean would wait for her.

"*Sí*, I cook for you," she said, sounding enough like Miguel to make Sam frown.

After a meal of bacon, beans and biscuits, Sam went out to get the horses ready for another trip into town. He took his time so he wouldn't interrupt Elena while she changed her clothes. When he was finished, he knocked on the cabin door. It was opened a moment later by a young Apache buck. Only Elena's smile and her shining brown eyes kept him from reaching for his gun.

"Well, I'll be..." he whistled. She was the spitting image of a young

Apache brave, right down to the short, chin-length hair she kept out of her eyes with his red bandanna tied around her forehead. The remains of her silky black braids were feeding the hungry flames that had cooked their food. Though her face was too delicate to really be a boy's, boiled boot polish had darkened her skin, blending into the telltale bruise around her eye.

"Is good, no? No one will know who I am?"

She was right. Now, she'd never be suspected as Sean's accomplice. He nodded at his new friend. "You got that right. No one will know. Uh...what do we call you?"

"Call me Mah-go-Chee," She smiled triumphantly. "It means Little Wolf. I am no longer the hunted. Now I am the hunter."

CHAPTER TWENTY-SEVEN

*A*t dusk, shadows stretched out from the alleys across the wide dirt road running through the center of Pecos. Despite the cots filling the dance floor, the piano played, singers sang, and gamblers dealt cards to anyone who could walk to their tables. Pecos residents and survivors waiting for a new train to take them back to Fort Worth, strolled the plank sidewalks in the cool night air. No one noticed the big man who rode into town with a young Indian boy in tow.

Sam and Elena stopped in front of the Nugget Saloon. Neither women nor Indians were welcome there, and since Elena had no wish to be discovered as both, she waited outside. She searched the faces of every passerby for the smile that would always warm her heart. None of the frontiersmen, farmers, and cowboys looked at her with smoldering gray eyes or carried themselves with the grace and power of a panther.

Sam reappeared after a few minutes and mounted his roan. He shook his head. Sean wasn't at Rosa's place or the Nugget. The Doc's house was their last hope. They both knew that if he was lucky enough to be one of the last two survivors, he could be badly maimed.

In his hurry to check the doctor's house and be done with it, Sam pulled hard on the reins, and his horse reared, spooking Elena's mount back into the traffic on the street. Suddenly, a barrage of curses filled the early evening air and she stared down at a stinking, gap-toothed, range hand.

The rage in her answering glare silenced him and he turned to Sam.

"You better keep that Injun tied up, Ranger. Or he'll be slittin' yer throat fer sure, the bloody savage." Then he ambled drunkenly into the Nugget.

Sam flushed but let it go. The drunk didn't know he was talking to a lady. Her disguise was just too damn good. It could get them into trouble if a cowpoke decided to pick a fight with what he thought was an Apache buck with a chip on his shoulder.

"Sorry," was all he could say to Elena, since his action had caused the confrontation.

She answered him with a smile no one would have mistaken for an Apache brave's. "I have heard worse. This is a good disguise."

"Well don't get cocky," he warned. "The man was so drunk he couldn't see straight." He urged the roan forward and called over his shoulder. "Let's get this over with once and for all. Follow me."

They stopped in front of a white, clapboard-sided house with a wide front porch. A simple wood sign painted with the words, "Medical Doctor," hung from the arch over the front steps.

"Wait here," Sam told her, hoping to shield her from what might be inside. She shook her head. "No. If my husband is in there, I will see him."

He relented to her Apache resolve. "All right, but you don't say a word, understand? From this moment on, you don't speak, even if your life depends on it. The clothes and hair may fool some people, but your voice is a dead giveaway."

When she opened her mouth to protest, he stood firm. "That's the deal. You're dumb or you don't go in."

Her lips tight, she nodded and slid off the mare to follow him up the steps.

A short, thin man wearing a blood-spattered butcher's apron wiped his hands on a stained towel after answering Sam's knock. He was only a few inches taller than Elena, with lines of fatigue etched in his face beneath a thin layer of graying brown hair. He stared at them from above eyeglasses sitting at the end of his nose, his thin lips puckered into a frown.

"Doc McAllister?" Sam's deep voice sounded official and the star Elena had convinced him to put back on his vest met the doctor at eye level.

"Aye, Ranger," he answered.

"I heard more survivors were found today."

Doctor McAllister's attention was diverted by a thumping noise, followed by a curse, from deep within the house. He looked back at Sam. "Aye. Two, but one's gone."

When he heard Elena's gasp from behind Sam, his lips pursed even more to peer around Sam's broad back. "I'm full up with patients right now, Ranger," he said curtly. "If the boy's sick, take him to Rosa's. I'll see him in the morning." He stepped back to close the door.

Sam's strong arm reached above the Doctor's head and held it open. "It's not the boy, Doc. It's the other survivor. Could we see him?"

"This official?"

Sam nodded. "One of my men was on that train. This is our last hope."

The Doc's gaze strayed again to Elena. "The boy yours?"

"No. He's my man's adopted brother," Sam lied with ease. "He ran away from his Indian School in St. Louis. We were takin' him back home to Santa Fe." He winked. "He's a handful, even if he can't talk."

The little man adjusted his spectacles to look more closely at Elena. "Dumb you say?"

"Yep."

"Deaf too?"

"Nope. Hears like a cat. Sleeps like one too."

The doctor seemed to forget all about his critical patient as he stared at Elena. "I've never seen an Indian that couldn't whoop or screech to raise the dead. Born that way?"

Sam's huge body kept the Doctor from getting too close. "Nope. He was the only survivor of Colonel Compton's raid at Sand Ridge. Saw his whole village massacred. He was just a tyke then, but he howled so much the folks who took him in called him Little Wolf. Then one day, he stopped howlin'. Ain't uttered a sound since, hardly."

"What happened to his eye?"

The doctor was a little too observant for Sam's taste, so he ended the game. "He's scrappy. Don't like bein' called dumb just 'cause he don't talk."

He let Little Wolf's tragic story sink in a moment, and then finished. "My man is all the boy's got left. It was his folks that took him in. If he's inside, we'd appreciate a look-see. He's young. Twenty-five or so. Dark hair. Gray eyes. Strong build."

The doctor listened to the tale, gave Elena one last look, then nodded and backed away from the door. "One was older, and bald. Died right after they brought him in."

"The other one?"

"Fits your description. He's real busted up. Didn't know which to treat first, burns or breaks. He swallowed a lot of water too, and after a night in the flood, I don't know how good his lungs are. If he makes it through the night and the fever doesn't get worse, he may make it."

Sam towered over the little doctor who looked like he was tired enough to keel over. "If it's my man, Doc, we'll watch him and you can rest, so you can help him in the morning."

Dr. McAllister nearly choked. "You mean you plan to stay here? Both of you?"

Sam nodded. "If it's him, he's a Ranger. We stick together. And Little Wolf here is his...brother."

The doctor mulled over the proposition. Finally, he nodded. "He's in here. If he's your man, I'll take you at your word. I'm up to my neck in patients and could use some sleep."

They followed him to a room behind the stairs crowded with a narrow bed and a straight-backed chair, along with a basin and pitcher on a table. There was a pile of burned and bloody clothes in a corner waiting to be carried out, and a body covered with a thin sheet up to his waist, lying on the bed. Elena pushed ahead of Sam. The tears in her eyes when she looked back at him confirmed Sean O'Grady as the last survivor of the Salt Draw train wreck.

Sam stepped into the room and stood over the bed. He'd seen a lot of injuries in his day, from gut-shot to scalping and cat mauling. This bandaged creature with splints on an arm and leg, his hands wrapped in two huge white mittens, and stitches on his head, looked as near dead as anyone he'd ever seen. Yet the patient's chest, red and blistered from burns, stubbornly rose and fell with each shallow, raspy breath.

Elena gently touched the unmarred flesh above Sean's heart and felt its struggle to beat. She turned to the doctor, forbidden to ask the questions in her heart.

McAllister apparently forgot his dislike of Indians to speak to the pain in Elena's eyes. "I don't know."

He blinked and turned to Sam. "It's a fair bet his lungs are burned from smoke. He's got a broken right leg and left arm, burns on his hands and a good part of his body, along with multiple cuts and bruises, and now a fever."

He edged Sam toward the door. "It'll only be by God's good grace that your man survives the night."

Sam looked back at Sean. He'd sworn an oath to Camilla to protect her son. "You're wrong, Doc," he said. "He'll live." He prodded the doctor out of the room so he wouldn't see the wild Indian on his knees, hands folded neatly in prayer.

"If he does survive, with those burns, will he be all right? Afterward, I mean."

The doctor sighed. "I admire your optimism, young man." He nodded toward Elena. "And the…boy's devotion is touching, but I been patching bullet wounds and mending broken bones for twenty-five years, and have seen precious few miracles. The only blessing from being in the cold water so long was that it kept those blisters from festering. 'Course, all the wreckage floating around is what busted him up. If he comes through the fever, and that is a very big 'if' mind you, and we can keep those wounds clean, he could be fine in a couple months."

"Months?"

The doctor stepped back at Sam's shout. "Bones don't heal overnight, Ranger. If he wants to walk straight and use that arm, he'll give 'em the time they need." He pointed a bony finger at the larger man's chest and nodded to Elena. "Understand?"

All Sam understood was that he'd just been sentenced to months as a nursemaid to this tenderfoot while LaPorte and the Ring went on murdering innocent people. He tried to think of a way out, including shipping the invalid back to Georgia. "When will he be able to travel?"

"He'd never make it in and out of a train. I wouldn't recommend travel until he's fully healed."

Sam's shoulders sagged under the weight of his new responsibility. He looked back at Elena. His only hope was to convince her to put aside her silly masquerade and do the nursing so he could head out to Santa Fe.

CHAPTER TWENTY-EIGHT

*S*itting in the little straight-backed chair was torture for Sam, and listening to every ragged breath coming from Sean O'Grady's still form drove him to distraction. Satisfied that Elena would keep her vow of silence during what looked like a death watch, he excused himself to pay a visit to Rosa's Cantina. "Send for me if anything happens," he said without explaining how an illiterate, mute Indian boy would manage that.

Throughout the night, Elena was left alone to pray for her husband's life. Her mother had taught her the rosary, but Judith encouraged a more personal relationship with God. She wrapped her fingers around the silver crucifix under her shirt and offered her own happiness with her husband, in exchange for his life.

Sam returned just after dawn, rested from a night in Rosa Contrero's soft arms and carrying a sack breakfast for Elena. She was asleep, half on the floor and half on the edge of the narrow bed. He scooped her up and gently settled her in the chair.

"You'll get all cramped up sleeping like that," he muttered when she woke.

She rubbed her eyes like a disoriented child, then pushed Sam away to stumble back to the bedside on cramped limbs. She sighed with relief when she found no change in Sean's shallow, but steady, breathing.

She took the sack from Sam's outstretched arm and sat cross-legged on the floor next to the bed to spread the contents in front of her. There was a covered dish of eggs, along with a steak and rolls still warm from the oven. Without cutlery, she picked the steak up in her hands, making appreciative sounds as she gnawed it to the bone. When she finished, she graced Sam with a greasy grin.

"Ahem," Doc McAllister stood in the doorway staring at her in revulsion. She swallowed hard, rubbed her hands on her pants and used her shirttail to wipe her mouth.

The doctor strode directly over to Sean without noticing the telltale stain left on the shirt or the slight change in the color of the Apache boy's skin. He put an ear to the patient's chest and a hand to his forehead.

"Lungs sound a little better. Fever's down a bit too," he addressed Sam. "Nothing we can do but wait. It could be days before we know for sure." He nodded toward Elena. "You two planning to stay here that long?"

"I'll never get him outa here until we know."

The doctor's thin, perpetually frowning lips puckered again. "The boy's a filthy savage. He can't stay here."

"Shhh," Sam cautioned. "I told you, he can hear everything you say. Understands it too."

"Well, I can't have a wild Injun livin' just below me."

Sam saw anger darken Elena's eyes and spoke before she could ruin his plan. "Oh," he laughed. "You mean his table manners. That was my fault. I brought him breakfast from Rosa's, but forgot the table service. He spent a year in a St. Louis school. He's tame and he's clean. Once we get a spare set o' clothes, he can wash these."

McAllister still didn't seem convinced.

"What if we set him to doing a few odd jobs around here to pay for his keep?" Sam bargained. "We already know he'll take care of the patient here all by himself. And he's quiet. You won't even know he's around. He can sleep right here on the floor."

The doctor's eyes narrowed. "What about you? I don't run a boarding house."

Sam crossed his arms over his barrel chest. "Don't worry. I'll be staying at Rosa's. I'll bring his food from there."

Doc McAllister's skeptical gaze wandered toward Elena, to be met by sparkling brown eyes and a smile that could charm the Devil. He scratched the few hairs on his pointed chin and adjusted the spectacles on the end of his nose.

"Well, I suppose I could scare up some clothes that would fit the boy. If he takes care of this one while I'm at the Nugget and Rosa's, and maybe does a little cleaning around here...well, I'll give it a try."

Then, like an old woman scolding a child, he wagged a finger in front of the big man's nose. "But no more eatin' on my floor."

Sam and Elena both nodded.

With the negotiations out of the way, McAllister finally spoke to his new Apache nurse directly, "He'll need a bath every morning and evening, and the linens must be changed every time there's a need. They're in the chest in the hall and the washtub's in the kitchen in the back." Then, seemingly as an afterthought, he continued, "There's a cot in the shed for you. Sleeping on the floor just isn't civilized."

He turned to Sam again. "The boy'll have to keep a kettle on day and night for boiling bandages and bed clothes. I'll take care of the dressings and medicine, but the rest is up to you two. As soon as your Ranger can get out of bed, I want you all out of here." He jabbed a finger at Sam's chest. Understand?"

Sam was of no mind to stay in this dusty little town any longer than necessary. He clenched his jaw at being ordered around by a scrawny small-town saw-bones and didn't bother to hide his sarcasm. "Yes, sir. We're mighty obliged for the chance to give you a hand here, Doc."

After McAllister left the room, Elena's gaze accused Sam of abandoning her.

"I had to do it," he insisted, raking his fingers through his hair. "I'll help as much as I can."

Her frustrated, "Hmmph," when she brushed past him to get a basin of fresh water and new linens for the bed told him she wasn't convinced.

"I ain't no nurse," he sputtered when the sheets hit him full in the face, and she motioned for him to gently roll Sean onto his side so she could change the bed.

~

While Sean's fever broke on the second day, eight days after the wreck, he still hadn't opened his eyes, tried to speak, or moved. Every morning, Elena bathed him and shaved the stubble that served as a dusky reminder of life within the silent, still form.

She realized that with his eyes closed, his world was dark, and with her vow not to speak in the white man's house, silent as well. When she'd gone to that silent world between life and death in Savannah, it was Sean's voice, as well as his touch, that brought her back to life. Perhaps he didn't know he was alive. Her eyes welled with angry tears at her own stupidity.

Sam was gone and the doctor was at the cantina, so she pulled up the chair close to him, took one bandaged hand in hers and placed her lips close to his ear. Then she began to sing softly. "Amazing Grace, how sweet the sound..."

Tears flowed down her cheeks and her voice faltered when she reached the end of the hymn with still no reaction from him. "*Yo te ammo mi Corazon*," she whispered, kissing his unresponsive lips.

"I knew it!" a woman's voice shrieked from the doorway.

Elena's head snapped up as Rosa Contrero bustled into the room with her customary sack breakfast. Her breasts struggling to escape the low-cut bodice of her red and black striped gown, she threw the sack onto the table and enveloped Elena in a suffocating hug.

A long moment later, Rosa sat at the foot of the bed. "I knew something wasn't right about you from the beginning," she crowed. "That Sam. After all the nights he and I, well as close as we been the last week, you'd think he'd trust me."

She gently pressed a shiny red fingernail against a cheek that had lost nearly all its boot polish stain. "You're white too," she continued. "Or part white. *Si?*"

She didn't wait for confirmation. "What is it, *Querida?* Are you in trouble? Is that why you are dressed like this? Who is this man to you? A lover? Amigo? Certainly, no *hermano.*"

"It was the only way I could be here," Elena confessed to a woman who reminded her of Chloe. Sam would be furious that she broke her word, and she had failed again. Sean lay silent and still as the dead. "He is my husband, but no one must know I am here, and when I know that he is all right, I must leave."

Rosa covered Elena's small hands with her own plump ones. "Sounds like you two are in trouble. Is it with Sam? Tell me. Maybe I can help you."

"No. Senor Pruitt saved my life. He is a friend of Sean's family."

The older woman looked closely at Sean and cocked her head. "Sean. Not Sean O'Grady?"

Fear of Roscoe LaPorte's army of police and desperados made Elena whisper. "How do you know his name?"

"The wanted posters got here yesterday. He and his woman are wanted for murder in Georgia, armed robbery in Nashville, and other crimes between there and here. There are rewards for each of them—I mean you. Dead or alive."

Elena's moan was echoed from the bed and both women turned to peer closely at Sean. Elena felt his forehead. It was still cool and dry to her touch. Her joy that he was coming back from the darkness was offset by the knowledge that she would soon be leaving him. The tears in her eyes were from both joy and sorrow.

Rosa squealed joyfully. "Don't worry *Querida*," she announced. "Your secret is safe with me. Look. Now your man is going to be all right. I'll get Sam."

Sean's head moved a little from side to side. His arms and legs struggled against the weight of splints and bandages and his eyelids fluttered wildly, as if the dim light in the heavily curtained room burned his eyes. "Elena?" he whispered hoarsely from a throat badly burned by smoke and heat.

"*Si Querido*, I am here," she whispered and kissed him. His lips curved the tiniest bit before the pain of consciousness became too much and he slipped away again, this time to sleep.

She smiled as he relaxed under her touch. The gods had answered her prayers. It would take time, but he would be whole again. A bargain was a bargain.

"*Adios mi amor,*" she whispered against his ear and left before Sam and Rosa returned with Doc McAllister.

CHAPTER TWENTY-NINE

*C*ursing greenhorns and Indians, Sam rode hard to get to the line shack before Elena faded into the desert like a water hole in July. Her mare was tethered to the old hitching post outside the shack, and he nearly pulled the door from its hinges when he opened it to stomp inside.

"What the hell is wrong with you?" he bellowed. "O'Grady's finally conscious. He wants to see you."

Elena ignored him to pack the few food items left in the cabin into a saddlebag. When she finished, she spoke in a voice so empty that the hairs on Sam's neck rose. "I must go home now. All I have from before is my knife and this little purse." That and her wedding ring that had joined the crucifix on the chain around her neck. "I think I earned the saddlebag by working for the doctor and you don't need this food since you are staying with Rosa."

She reached into the little velvet reticule that looked ridiculous dangling from the wrist of an Indian boy, and pulled out Mr. Gladstone's gaudy rings. Folding Sam's big hand around them, she explained, "This is for the mare. I do not want to be accused of horse stealing."

Sam's face turned nearly as red as his hair. "What the hell do I need with a gambler's shiny rings?" he shouted. What he needed was to get out of Pecos and get on with his job. He was about to say so when Elena hit him with a weapon far deadlier than any Winchester rifle. The truth.

"Sean is your responsibility. You swore an oath to his family. You must finish it."

"Dammit." He threw the rings onto the floor and crushed the phony gems beneath his boot. "I told you, I ain't no nurse."

"Rosa will help you."

He refused to give up so easily. "You're his wife. You swore to God to stick with him in sickness and health, until death. He's still alive, dammit."

"Yes, but Elena O'Grady is dead."

"Not by a long shot," he sputtered and played his last card. "I can still arrest you."

"You cannot arrest me without arresting the son of your friends, who is innocent. As you Whites say, I have called your bluff. You are between a rock and a hard place and have to let me go." She put Miguel's big sombrero on her head and stepped around him to go outside.

He followed, knowing if she really wanted to leave, there was nothing he could do to stop her. She was an innocent victim in all of this and he had no hold over her, either as a lawman or a friend. "Where you headed?"

The warrior, Mah-go-Chee, answered. "First, I will ask the spirits of the four winds to help me find the murderers of my family. Then I will make spirits of the murderers."

Sam caught her arm and turned her to face him. "Don't be a fool. You may think you're a tough hombre in your Indian get-up, but you ain't been an Indian for eight years, and you sure as hell ain't no hombre. So you listen to me little lady, and you listen good."

His voice rose like thunder rolling down from the peaks of the mountains and his hands bit into her shoulders. "You should stay right here and nurse that pig-headed husband of yours back to health whilst I take care of the business with Roscoe. But if your mind is set, promise me you'll find Jesse and Morning Bird in the Pueblo and tell them what happened. Then wait for me. As soon as O'Grady can board a train for home, I'll come to you. We'll get LaPorte, and the Ring too."

He choked and pulled her to his chest. "Wait for me, Elena. We'll work out a plan with Jesse, and we'll get 'em. I promise."

He brushed her cheek in a chaste kiss, and she circled her arms around his neck. Then he carefully adjusted her floppy hat over her butchered hair. "What will I tell O'Grady about you? He says he heard you singing to him. You kissed him too." His smile told her that he held no grudge against her for breaking her vow of silence.

"Spirits."

"What?"

"Tell him it was my spirit bidding him farewell. It will be the truth." She took off her hat, reached up under the neck of her shirt, pulled her mother's necklace over her head and taught the white man how to lie. "Give him this. Say you took it off my body. Then he will believe you."

One red eyebrow arched as the silver crucifix and wedding ring winked at him in the sunlight. His shoulders sagged under the weight of his surrender to her logic. "Little Wolf," he said before she mounted the mare. "Wait."

He pulled out a spare gun belt from his saddlebag with an old six-shooter in the holster and fastened it around her hips. "I can't have you out there with only a knife and a foul temper for defense. Can you shoot?"

She picked up an empty bean can, handing it to him. When he threw it up in the air, she drew the gun and shot the can before it hit the ground. He walked the few feet to retrieve it and brought it back with his finger in the bullet hole. "Well, I'll be gawd-damned. Where did you learn to shoot like that?"

She beamed at earning the Ranger's respect. "Marcus. He said in the West, a woman must know the same things as a man. He taught me how to shoot, and hunt, and track. Now I will use those lessons to find his murderer."

"After we meet in the mountains," he reminded her and kissed her on the cheek again. "*Vaya con Dios*, Mah-go-Chee. Remember to wait for me."

She tipped a finger to her sombrero before turning toward the trail leading west across the Pecos River, into New Mexico. It told him she'd do no such thing and there wasn't a damned thing he could do about it.

As Rosa fluffed Sean's pillows for what seemed like the hundredth time, he pushed her away. "Stop that and tell me what you've done with my wife," he demanded for what seemed like the thousandth time. "She was here."

Rosa stopped fussing and stood with her hands on the hips of her hour-glass figure. "It must have been me you heard, honey. I been coming and going since they brought you in."

He shook his head, grimacing when pain shot through his brain like a bullet. "No. Hummingbird was here. I heard her voice. She sang Amazing Grace."

Hands still on her hips, Rosa's smile faded. "Well, my singin's been compared to a lot of things, but a hummingbird ain't one of them." She patted a hand that was now healed enough to allow his fingertips to peek out of the gauze mitt. "And ain't it nightingales that sing?"

He sighed as Elena's words from what seemed so long ago haunted him. She was here. It was her scent, her familiar touch, and her cool, gentle fingers on his burning skin. It was Elena, not the screeching banshee that pushed and prodded him until he wanted to scream.

When he asked the doctor about his wife, he'd looked at him with pity in his eyes. "Sometimes grief takes a long time to work its way out, son. I hear she's been dead two years now. Your little brother did a good job taking care of you," he added grudgingly.

"Clay? Clay was here?"

"Didn't get his white name."

Convinced he'd been thrown into a lunatic asylum, Sean turned his frustration toward the big red-haired man when he entered the room. His angry glare focused on the star pinned to his vest. "You've been following us. I want Elena set free," he demanded. "I don't care what Roscoe does to me. If anyone hurts her, I swear I'll—"

"Whoa there." Sam pushed Rosa out of the room with a pat on her fanny and closed the door securely behind her before saying, "You got more than a few things mixed up my friend. I don't work for LaPorte."

"Well then, who the hell are you and what do you want?"

The man pulled up a chair and sat by the bed. Eyes as cool and blue as Rocky Mountain ice met Sean's molten fury. "Well, sonny boy, you could call me your guardian angel. As for what I want, thanks might be in order given you're still breathin.' And you might want to take stock of yourself before runnin' at the mouth with threats."

Sean took a long look at the craggy face and bushy red hair. "I must be in Hell."

"Could be. This is Pecos."

"Where is my wife?" Sean demanded again before the doctor's latest dose of laudanum took effect. "Please... tell me."

Staring down at the floorboards rather than Sean's face, Sam began his lie. "Elena couldn't have been here. She died in the train wreck."

"I don't believe you," was the last thing Sean said before returning to the place where Hummingbird sang to him.

CHAPTER THIRTY

*R*osa's plump fingers played with the red/gold curls on Sam's chest and kissed the creases on his tanned forehead as she slid her voluptuous body on top of his. "You worry too much," she whispered against his ear and felt him grow hard beneath her. "The boy is strong and my girl Kitty takes good care of him. His fever will break again soon. Until then, I take care of you."

Sam chuckled as he rolled over and slid into her, both his heads focused on her. A knock on the heavy oak door followed their noisy climax.

Kitty shouted through the wood, "Miss Rosa. He's awake. Looks like this time it's for good an'...uh...Ranger, Sir, if you're in there, he uh...wants to see you. He's...uh...mighty pissed off...an' I-I-I think you should come. If'n you can...uh, right away."

Kitty ended her tortured speech when Rosa opened the door. Despite living in the whorehouse for more than a year, the young girl blushed when Sam appeared, naked to the waist, his trousers only half buttoned.

"He's awake?"

She stared at the floor. "Y-yes sir. Fever's gone an' he's mad as hell, so you better...c-come quick." She smiled when her boss and a New Mexico Ranger obediently followed her and relaxed enough to explain without stuttering, "Lordy, that man has one powahful bad tempah."

Sean's fitful dreams had been haunted by Sam Pruitt's words, "She died in the train wreck." He would gladly have wandered forever in the silent blackness where he was certain Elena waited for him, if not for the voice that refused to give him a moment's peace. It was a woman, but not Elena or that harpy who called herself Rosa.

This woman talked with a flat, nasal monotone that put Rs where they didn't belong and left them out from where they did belong. Yankee, he concluded. New England. Boston maybe. And she never stopped talking, even as she poked and prodded him, rubbed him raw, forced him to swallow food, and moved his arms and legs like some evil puppeteer.

Over and over, she told him that he had to be strong if he was going to beat the devils in his dreams. A quote she read from the Bible when she wasn't torturing him finally convinced him to choose life over death.

"An eye for an eye," she had read. It gave him a reason to live. If he wanted to make Roscoe pay, he'd have to be strong.

It was a difficult climb back from the abyss where flames seemed to lick at him from a burning pit much like the one Elena had described in Savannah. The first things he saw when his eyes focused clearly were naked cherubs staring down at him. But the physical expression of the angels' joy told him he was assuredly not in heaven.

A whorehouse? How in God's name did he get from a lunatic asylum in Hell to a whorehouse? "Pruitt," he bellowed, ignoring the pain shooting through the raw wound his throat had become. "Pruitt, where the hell are you, you bastard?"

When no one responded, he reached out one bandaged hand to grasp an obscene statue of another Cupid, sending it shattering against the far wall. Another nude angel barely escaped the same fate when Kitty hesitantly poked her head around the door.

"Oh, good. You're awake," she said calmly.

He recognized the nagging voice from his dreams and relinquished his weapon to a skinny young girl with a parchment-pale complexion, and the biggest, sweetest smile he'd ever seen. "Where is Pruitt? Get him in here," he croaked.

She nodded and disappeared as quietly as she'd come. He felt the weight of the splints on his arm and leg and awkwardly lifted the sheet with his good arm. What wasn't bandaged in white linen was greased with an obnoxious smelling ointment that assailed his senses as much as the odor of his own urine staining the oiled cloth beneath him.

He moaned and dropped the sheet. Then anger gave way to horror, and horror turned into a fear he'd never experienced before. He was helpless. His hands, encased in white gauze mittens, felt like they were on fire, and memories of the train wreck flooded his mind.

He had been about to enter a friendly game at the back of the of the old palace car when an unearthly screech drowned out the laughter and loud conversations. The car jolted, throwing the gamblers out of their seats. Then it wobbled uncontrollably and dark streaks of kerosene ran down the papered walls.

One lamp broke when a hanging plant smashed against it and in seconds, flames devoured the plush furnishings, draperies and carpet. Men fell in their rush toward the exits, pushing and shoving each other on their way. Others climbed over them, jamming the doorways until no one could get out. Finally, the car stopped swaying and tipped at a crazy angle. It teetered there a moment and then slowly crashed over on its side, breaking windows and shooting flames so intense even the rain couldn't extinguish them.

Sean smashed a window before the car stopped moving and was half way out when it toppled over on its other side. Through the driving rain, he saw the passenger car dangling over a precipice above a raging river.

"Elena," he shouted and began to climb out. His hands and chest burned from contact with the hot metal as he crawled to the edge of the coupling just as the passenger car dropped into the gorge, spraying him with a tidal wave of cold water when it hit.

In moments, the flames from the passenger car were snuffed out and it bobbed like driftwood on the floodwaters. Those who could, tried to swim in the raging water while others, dead already, floated out of sight. Only a few passengers clung to the broken windows like rats on a raft. "Elena," he called again and dove into the water.

He fought to keep his head above the white, foaming waves that threw pieces of wood from the fuel car against him, sending shafts of new white-hot pain through his body. Exhausted, he gripped one of the logs and floated by a woman caught on a piece of wreckage. A shaft of lightning lit the night sky, and he screamed at the sight of her dark hair and wide, staring eyes. Then, before he could pull her to him, she was ripped from his grasp by a dislodged passenger seat.

Struggling to keep his hold on the log and his head above the swirling deluge, his mind raged against what he'd seen. It could have been any of the many women with dark hair and practical dresses, but he couldn't reach out again as a gruesome parade of charred, lifeless forms floated by him.

Exhausted, he heaved a leg over the log and gave into the blackness he'd fought for so long. His last thought before the cold water swept over him, was of a clear blue sky and the bright-colored stripes of Elena's skirt. "Storm Cloud," answered him before everything went silent.

The memory of the dead woman he'd seen floating in the water brought tears to his eyes that even the pain of his wounds couldn't accomplish. He fell back against the sweat-stained pillow and let them flow as his mind cried out, Elena. God, please. Don't let it be true.

Kitty opened his door again and Rosa pushed past her to charge into the room. She stopped short at the remains of his tears glistening in the beard left unattended since Elena's departure. Her own tears flowed freely when she reached for the cloth in the basin.

Sean's hand clamped over hers. "Where is Elena," he demanded again.

For a moment, something in her face gave him hope. Then she looked away as Sam bellowed from the doorway. "Well, well. Finally decided to join the living, did you?"

"What makes you think that?"

Once again, the pain tried to control him, pull him back into the comfortable void. But this time, he wouldn't run away into the darkness and silence where he searched for his love. She wasn't there.

That one brief glimpse into Rosa Contrero's guilt-ridden eyes told him Pruitt was hiding something. They all were, except maybe the little Yankee girl.

Now, he welcomed the pain. It meant he was alive. He no longer cared about clearing his name. He'd find Roscoe and see that he died slowly and painfully.

"Look at you," Rosa answered for Sam. "Now you are awake, and you will heal quickly. Soon you will be as good as new."

Fighting the feeling that he wasn't even attached to this weak and unfamiliar body, Sean whispered hoarsely, "As good as new? I can't even use the privy, for Chrissake."

Rosa whispered, "Do not worry. Me and my girls...we will take care of you until you are well. She dipped her handkerchief in the basin next to his bed and washed away the signs of his tears before Sam could see them.

"You have only a moment," she told the lawman. "We must change...things and apply his medicine."

Sam nodded and stepped closer to the bed, flinching at the unmistakable odor of illness. However, it was just piss and sweat, not the stench of flesh rotting on a living body. Nothing he hadn't seen before. "You're the one who called for me," he growled at Sean. "If you ain't ready to make a go at livin', what do you want from me?"

"If you're my guardian angel, why don't you know what I want?"

A deep chuckle "You got me. I'm no angel."

"So, Elena is...dead?" He swallowed the lump that suddenly collected in his throat.

Sam looked at his bare feet and nodded.

Then the sound of what Patrick O'Grady's Celtic legends called a Banshee, roared through the house, sending Kitty back into a corner with her hands over her ears. Rosa threw herself into Sam's arms and he buried his face in her hair.

"Leave me," Sean whispered when his body and soul were spent.

When the door closed behind Sam and Rosa, Kitty handed him the last naked angel. Another pain-filled cry of anguish, followed by the sound of porcelain crashing against a solid oak door, steeled Sean's soul. He would kill Roscoe LaPorte and then he would go to the mountains Elena loved and join her in the dark void of eternal death.

CHAPTER THIRTY-ONE

*S*ean convinced Kitty to send a telegram to his family saying he'd return when he could travel, with no intention of doing so. Instead, in the weeks that followed, he considered each day as one more step toward finding Roscoe. First, he mastered those tasks that had once seemed as natural to him as breathing, like feeding himself and eliminating the embarrassment of periodic linen changes. Next, he had Kitty slice open one leg of his trousers to fit over the splint.

She still had to help him into them, but at least he was dressed like a man. Buttons remained a challenge to the stiff and clumsy fingers that slowly emerged from the bandages, and he wore a cut-off nightshirt until his arm was free of its splint.

Every day, he sat on the edge of the bed with his bad leg propped up on a stool. Kitty, who had changed from devoted nurse to faithful servant, obediently tied rocks to his good ankle. She watched in fascination as he spent several sessions a day raising and lowering the weights.

"I won't lose the use of one leg while the other one heals," he answered her raised eyebrows when he sent her on the rock-hunting expedition.

As soon as the bandages came off his right hand and he could flex his fingers, he fastened a holster to the side of the bed and practiced drawing and aiming his unloaded Colt .44. As Kitty became used to facing the harmless gun when she opened the door, they invented a contest to see how far into the room she could get between her knock and his awkward quick draw.

Doc McAllister took the splint off his leg six weeks after the train wreck, saying, "You're one lucky son of a bitch. It was a clean break and looks like it mended straight." As if reading Sean's thoughts, he cautioned, "Don't push it. A bad twist or fall could snap it again like a twig. Breaks like that don't heal right the second time. You could end up a cripple."

"I'll be fine," Sean insisted, grimacing when a knee that hadn't bent in nearly two months protested the movement. "When can I ride?"

McAllister laughed. "Sonny, you got to learn how to walk before you can ride." He turned to Kitty, "See that he takes it easy."

"Th-that's like tryin' to p-p-put out a fiah with a s-s-sprinklin' can...Doc." Kitty stammered,

The next morning, she found Sean standing by the bed, washed, dressed, combed, and shaved, with the gun belt buckled around his waist. His new jeans fit his good leg snugly, proving he'd lost no muscle tone there.

"Well, well. Look at you," she observed with a wide grin. Then she crossed her arms over her tiny chest. "Jest wheah ye think ye goin'?"

He smiled at the homely little kitchen maid. She'd served him like a slave for weeks and met all his complaints with that wide, trusting grin, never once raising her own voice in protest or anger. She'd made him laugh when he wanted to cry, diffused his temper, and made him live when he wanted to die. Without her, he knew he wouldn't be standing where he was, finally ready to leave this room.

"I'm going for a walk, Kitty." He took her hand in his. "And I'd like my best girl with me."

Kitty performed a clumsy curtsy in her narrow skirt. "My pleasure, suh," she carefully enunciated and moved next to him to slip his injured arm out of its sling and over her bony shoulder. When his handmade crutch was steady under his right arm, they stepped out for the trip down the stairs to Rosa's cantina.

Sam looked up from his losing poker hand and shifted his cigar to the side of his mouth. "Well, I'll be gawd-dammed." He dropped the cards to watch Sean struggle his way down the stairs, Kitty attached to him at the hip.

Rosa made the sign of the cross over her bosom. "*Madre de Dios.*" She pushed her chair back.

Sam caught her arm. "Let him be. He's gotta do it on his own or he won't be no good at all."

Sean ignored his audience to concentrate on what looked like a hundred steps, each one moving in a different direction below him. Sweat beaded on his forehead, but he could feel Kitty's pride as she braced herself next to him. He couldn't let her down.

"Good leg. Crutch. Bad leg," he chanted through clenched teeth, pausing only for the dizziness to pass before descending to the next step.

Most of Rosa's patrons lost interest before he'd reached the bottom and crossed the room to the brass rail at the bar. When Rosa joined him, her bright smile disappeared at the sight of his shaking hands and sweat-covered face. Instead of reaching out to him, she waved at her bartender. "A bottle for the young gringo, Pepito. On the house."

Sam came to stand on Sean's other side. He nodded to Rosa and then toward the poker table. "Watch my hand, darlin'. The boy and I got things to talk about."

She nodded and returned to the table, picking up Sam's discarded cigar as well as his poker hand. She smiled, drew one card, and scooped up Sam's winnings.

She was shuffling another hand when Sam's powerful fist pounded the bar. "You callin' me a liar, boy?" he shouted.

Sean carefully balanced his weight on his good leg and turned to face him squarely. "I just said that maybe you made a mistake."

Sam poured a shot of whiskey from Sean's bottle into his own glass. "What makes you so dang blamed sure she's alive?"

To Sean, the liquor tasted more like turpentine than bourbon, but it eased some of the pain from the punishing trip down the stairs and steadied his nerves. He poured another two fingers into his glass and stared at it. "Because I'm alive."

"Bullshit," Sam roared. His empty glass slammed the bar, rattling a pyramid of newly washed ones at the other end. "That, 'can't live without you' nonsense is plain old horse shit." He leaned close to Sean, "Grow up, kid. You're behavin' like a spoiled, lovesick pup by refusing to believe the truth."

When Sean didn't move, he sighed and reached into his shirt pocket. When he opened his fist, Elena's crucifix hung from a finger between them, the diamond on her wedding ring winking under a stray sunbeam from the open doors. "What about this?"

Sean's eyes fixed on the glittering silver cross and ring. No. He blinked away the unmanly tears that clouded his vision. Elena always wore that cross. Even when she was gloriously naked beneath him, it had nestled between her breasts. The last time he'd seen the delicate, Princess cut diamond was on her hand. Yet despite the truth dangling in front of him, he refused to believe she was dead.

"Where did you get that?"

Sam looked straight ahead at the painting above the bar of a naked lady lying on a couch. "I recognized this from the parlor car the night you shang-haied Gladstone." He swallowed hard. "I took it off her body…before the burial."

Reason wouldn't let Sean doubt Sam's testimony, but his heart couldn't accept that his love lay in an unmarked grave in a dried-up snake pit called Pecos, Texas. He snatched the necklace and ring from Sam's grasp. "Then show me her grave."

With a nod toward the crutch, Sam snorted. "A set o'stairs near done you in, boy. You'd never make it to the graveyard."

Sean bristled. They both knew he was weeks ahead of Doc McAllister's predictions. He stepped away from the support of the bar. "You can stop calling me boy, Pruitt. I figure you're not much older than me."

"Out here, you're a boy 'til you earned the right to be called a man."

Fury made Sean throw his crutch to the floor. With virtually no strength in the withered muscles of his injured leg, sheer willpower held him upright, his hand poised over the holstered revolver.

"I can do that with only one arm and one leg, you besotted, loud-mouthed, cattle tramp with a tin star." The challenge gained him Sam's full attention as well as the entire cantina.

Sam's sky-blue eyes took in Sean's glare, noting the flexed fingers hovering above the gun. He turned back to the bar and poured another drink. "Hold your water, son. There's no use getting' all riled up. We're on the same side."

Sean stared at him, furious that his parents had asked this buffoon to follow him like he was some sort of schoolboy off on his first trip. So far, the lout had only managed to steal his wife's necklace; but for the time being, he was in no position to argue. He controlled his raging temper for the moment to repeat, "I want to see her grave."

Again, Sam pointed to the crutch. "Judging how long it took you to get down the stairs, it'll take all day to get there on foot. Have to rent a damned rig."

"If you really know my family, you know I'm good for any expenses."

"Only thing you're good for right now is causin' a pain in my ass," Sam muttered. "Be ready when I get back." He strode out of the cantina to rent a buckboard for Sean's tour of the new graveyard at the edge of town.

When he got back with a grain wagon, the step was too high for Sean to pull his bad leg up into the box and Sam offered no help. So rather than give up like the son of a bitch Ranger wanted him to do, he rode in the back, like a stray dog. At least there, he could stretch out the still mending leg.

At the graveyard, the pain involved in climbing into the wagon didn't compare with the agony of getting out. When his injured leg connected with the brick-hard Texas soil, the world around him turned purple and red, and he leaned against the wagon wheel to wait it out.

Sam ignored his distress as he strode across the uneven ground to stop in front of a marker standing alone on a little knoll. He squinted at it, waiting for Sean to make it up the incline. "Satisfied?" he asked when the sound of Sean's labored breathing announced his arrival.

Wiping the sweat from his forehead, Sean leaned on his crutch to examine Elena's headstone. The crude wood marker was already dry and cracking from the fierce Texas sun. Soon, the shallow carved words, "Woman - 1892," would be obliterated. No one would know that the girl who lay beneath it had a bright smile, beautiful brown eyes, and glossy black hair. Or that her lips were soft, her body yielding. They wouldn't know that she was loved beyond death.

He stared at the marker for several long moments, pondering the cruel twist of fate that had kept him from dying with her. Finally, he looked at Sam, who sat on the flat wood top of another marker, lighting a cheroot.

"Why isn't her name on the marker?" he demanded.

"Carver got tired. Half the graves here are marked like that, if there's anything at all."

"I still don't believe it."

Sam's head shot up. He forgot the burning match in his fingers and swore when it burned him. "Goddammit." He dropped it, grinding out the flame with the square tip of his boot. "You saw her necklace and now her grave. Do I have to dig her up?"

Sean shook his head. Even the sight of a half-rotted corpse wouldn't convince him. He clung to the memory of her voice and the touch of her lips as he lay in Doc McAllister's hospital bed. It was too real to be a dream and he didn't believe in guardian angels or ghosts. Still, Pruitt seemed to have all the answers, so he called the Ranger's bluff.

"The Doc said you had an Indian boy with you who claimed to be my brother. Where is he?"

Sam hid his surprise behind a well-practiced poker face and reached for another match. "Just a kid who attached himself to me at the general store. I hired him to look after you. Had to lie to the Doc so he'd let him in. He took off right after you came to." His eyes bored into Sean's, accusingly. "Your bellyachin' scared him off."

His heart broke again. If Sam was a liar, he was one of the best he'd ever seen. He bid a silent farewell to the decaying grave marker, knowing that even though the earth held Elena's body, her soul would live on in his heart.

He bent stiffly to touch the crude marker, vowing to replace it with granite after he'd killed Roscoe. "Another time and place, Hummingbird," he whispered. "LaPorte will pay for this." He turned to Sam. "When do we leave?"

Sam removed the still unlit cheroot from the corner of his mouth, shaking his head. "You'll just be in the way. He's killed better men than you without breakin' a sweat. Good men, friends of mine. He belongs to me."

"Well then you better find him before I do."

Sam's gaze slowly traveled up from Sean's crutch to the sling on his arm. "You don't look up to much of a race."

Sean smiled and slipped his left arm out of the sling. He drew his gun with his right hand and fanned the hammer with his left thumb, sending six shots into a nearby tree. "It's only the leg," he explained, holstering his weapon. "I'm going to Santa Fe, with or without you."

"Tinhorn stuff," Sam snorted. "More likely you'll shoot your own fingers off than hit the side of barn." Still, his nod showed he understood that no man with any grain in his grits could look at the grave of the woman he loved without wanting to avenge her death. He crossed his arms over his chest. "So you fancy yourself a gunfighter, eh?"

"I'm not stupid enough to think that, but I think I could beat Roscoe."

Sam nodded, acknowledging that spending years back East could make a man soft, though it wasn't likely in the Colonel's case. "In a fair fight, maybe. You know LaPorte. He fight fair?"

"Never since I've known him."

The cheroot returned to Sam's pocket and he left his perch on Elder Smith's headstone. "Then it looks like you got a few lessons to learn, O'Grady, and a short time to learn 'em in."

CHAPTER THIRTY-TWO

The batwing doors of Bowen's saloon on Santa Fe's Front Street stood open, dust from the street floating inside to settle on top of everything, including drinks. A warm August breeze dispersed the smell of whiskey, tobacco and sweat, as flies swarmed on the spittle-covered floor.

"Make yer little bets, gentlemen." The faro dealer's voice rose above the catcalls of cowboys and miners who had just witnessed Annabelle Tyler, a self-proclaimed, "Chan-To-See," sing "Oh Susannah" in two keys at the same time.

"All's set for the bets." Men turned from watching the saloon girls frolicking on the raised stage at the rear of the hall to put their dollars and gold dust over pictures of cards painted on a waxed cloth in front of the dealer.

Elena perched on a high stool at the dealer's left. Her job was to look for players who tried to shift their bets while the cards were being drawn. Mostly, she just saw the money that men had slaved for months to draw from some lonely mine whisked away from them in an instant. It made her sick that the white man's obsession with gold made young men old before their time and killed good men in their prime. Satan lived in places like Bowen's, so she watched the endless parade of winners and losers, knowing eventually, the devil named Roscoe LaPorte would come home.

It had to be soon. She'd spent her time alone in the desert praying and cleansing herself of her terrible anger so she could battle her enemy with a cool head. Surviving on rattlesnake, prairie dogs, and the juice of the cactus, strengthened her Apache blood; while the fierce western sun returned the copper glow to her skin and she had no need for Sam's boot polish.

For a month, she'd roamed the town as a young Indian boy who couldn't speak, willing to do any dirty, unpleasant job for the fancy eating establishments frequented by Santa Fe's leading businessmen and politicians. She assumed correctly that when men were served by a child who couldn't speak, they thought he was deaf as well. As she cleaned tables, emptied spittoons, and swept up ashes from expensive cigars in the gilded rooms, she heard talk of, "LaPorte's big find". Without identifying it, they grumbled about lack of proof. Some even suggested they abandon the whole enterprise and get out while the getting was good.

She followed their advice when one of the men who rented rooms above the Red Horse Gaming Club took a fancy to the light-skinned Indian boy named Little Wolf. Catching her alone in the hall, he wrapped his big hand around her slender wrist. "Where you been hidin' son?" He offered her a week's pay to meet him in his room. She demanded half up front and disappeared.

With a quarter in her purse, Elena returned to the abandoned shell of the Charles Carter School. The children were dispersed to whatever hellish reservation the Bureau of Indian Affairs chose, where they would no doubt be abused and enslaved. Standing outside the boarded door and barred windows, a wave of grief washed through her. All the people she had ever loved were dead. She was truly alone. Only her vow to avenge all their deaths, kept her heart beating.

Crawling in through the unlatched root cellar door buried beneath nearly a year of weeds, sand, and tumbleweeds, she didn't fear the ghosts of Marcus and Judith as she took up residence in the old dormitory. In fact, she welcomed them, praying for them to give her the strength to stay true to her mission and die like a warrior.

At night, covered by an old horse blanket on the red tile floor, the dreams from her past returned to haunt her. She took to sleeping during the day and prowling El Royale Street at night, watching who came and went from the saloons and brothels lining the narrow street.

When Alex Dooley, the faro dealer at Bowen's Saloon, lost his spotter to a badly aimed Colt peacemaker, she dressed in a Mexican skirt and blouse and applied for the job. After only three months away from Santa Fe, Dooley never recognized the little Indian girl from the school down the street. Instead, he stared at the curve of her breasts beneath the flimsy peasant blouse and saw the potential in having a woman for a spotter. He hired her immediately.

He wasn't disappointed. The pretty little Mexican girl named Maria kept his customers' tempers in check with just a smile. When word got out there was a girl on the stool above his table, the producers who usually played blackjack or roulette lined up as much to catch a glimpse of her slender leg as to play the game.

"Hoc's comin' up boys." Dooley used his tongue to bounce the cigar in his mouth from one corner to the other. "Last card, no pay. He winked at Elena. "Get ready gentlemen."

"Six ounces on the Ace," answered the banker's call and everyone turned toward a tall, slim man in a well-tailored black suit. He placed a buckskin pouch on the ace of hearts. "If the Queen of Hearts will descend from her throne and favor me with a dance."

Elena turned slowly toward the familiar voice. During her time as Dooley's spotter, she'd hoped her seat above the crowd would allow her to see either Anscombe's blond hair, or Roscoe's dark, slender form before they saw her. Instead, Roscoe found her.

Bowen's private entrance, she realized, angry over forgetting to guard her own back. Now he had the advantage. Unless he didn't recognize her. She didn't have to look in a mirror to know she no longer resembled the Elena Santiago who had masqueraded as a white woman at Langesford. Perhaps she could convince him she was simply Maria, a peasant girl from Sonora.

Hiding her emotions behind a flirtatious smile, she looked down to see Junior Anscombe at Roscoe's side, staring at her with naked desire. Junior winked before drifting back to the poker table. She watched his retreat wishing she could kill him with her gaze. Then Alex motioned for her to join him on the floor.

She shook her head. "I no dance, Senor," she said, clinging to her Mexican charade.

Roscoe's thin lips pushed his mustache upward, baring his teeth to more of a sneer than a smile. "Oh, but I think you dance very well, Senorita."

He handed Dooley a $5.00 gold piece. "I'm hiring your lookout for the evening."

Dooley bit the coin to see if it was real as Elena jumped to the floor in indignation. "Dooley, no," she shouted above the laughter of the crowd.

"Go with him Maria," he ordered. "Or get out."

She looked from him to Roscoe. If she left, she'd lose her chance to kill Anscombe and bring Roscoe to justice. This was what she had been waiting for. What she dreamed about, but while it was fine to pretend to be a Mexican saloon girl to find her enemy, she would be no man's whore.

She tore the gold piece from Dooley's grasp. "I am no *puta* for you to sell to anyone who comes along." She dropped the coin down the front of her blouse and looked up to meet Roscoe's amused eyes. "For the dance, Senor. Only a dance."

"Como desee, senorita," Roscoe replied in fluent Spanish. "As you wish." He led her onto a floor slippery with spittle and spilled whiskey.

Elena barely breathed in the tight circle of Roscoe's arms as the lively jig seemed to last an eternity. He held her so close she could smell his bay rum hair cream, and worried he could feel her heart beating wildly through her thin blouse.

"You dance even better unfettered by white women's clothes, Elena," Roscoe whispered.

She stiffened as his fingers bit into her waist, cringing from the breath sending little bursts of warm air onto her bare shoulder. Yet she couldn't stop dancing for fear of giving herself away. She barely controlled the tremor in her voice. "*No comprende, Senor,*" then gasped when his hand left her waist to pinch one of her breasts.

"Don't play the stupid Mexican bitch with me, Elena," he said as his hand wandered down her back to push her hips against his arousal. She squeezed her eyes shut and raised a knee to his swollen crotch, causing just enough pain for him to release his indecent hold.

"Bastard."

Roscoe didn't find her show of spirit as amusing as the other, mostly male, couples on the floor. He raised his eyebrows. "Stop the Greaser act now Elena. I recognized you the moment you asked Dooley for a job. I've just been waiting for that foolhardy husband of yours to show. Where is he? He's late."

Elena followed him off the dance floor, wondering if she should tell him that Sean was gone back to Georgia or let him think he was dead. Roscoe would know a lie. The only way to catch him was to win his trust. "They arrested him in Nashville," she tested.

The flat of his hand striking her cheek told her she was playing games with a very dangerous man. Her skin burned, but she refused to touch it as Roscoe's eyes bored into hers.

"Don't lie to me," he said. "Hobbs is a fool. He arrested the wrong man. Where is he?"

She realized then that Sean had been right about Roscoe's spies and continued to test the range of his knowledge. "It would be better if he was caught. There was a train wreck in Texas."

Roscoe's face remained expressionless, waiting to hear more. She proceeded carefully, telling as much truth as possible, using his own arrogance to fool him. "The bridge at the Salt Draw broke away in a storm. He was in the gambling car when it burst into flames and tipped over. The glaze of tears in her eyes lent credence to the lie. "Everyone inside of it died." Her voice betrayed her to choke, "The Gringo is no more."

This time Roscoe touched her face gently, caressing the red print from his palm. "Then how, pray tell, did you survive the Great Salt Draw Disaster? There were only a handful of survivors and I don't recall seeing your name among them."

So, he knew about the train wreck, but not that Sean survived. Letting the spirits guide her tongue, she told the truth. "I jumped from the train before it went off the bridge and escaped." Then she looked into death's own eyes and lied. "The Gringo is gone, and I am glad."

"You don't say?" Roscoe smiled, pulling her to a small empty table in the back of the saloon where Junior Anscombe's glare couldn't reach them. He pushed her into a seat, settled into a chair next to her, and lit a cigar. "Why are you glad Elena? The O'Grady family is a pillar of society. Though I can't imagine why, Sean is considered quite a catch."

Grateful she wasn't wearing her mother's crucifix, she spit on the floor and lied again. "They are thieves and liars."

Though Roscoe nodded in agreement, he still refused to incriminate himself, so she baited her hook. "They stole gold from the Army and used it to pay for their grand hacienda. Sean forced me to pretend to be his wife and help him escape the law."

His eyes sparked with evil amusement as he puffed more smoke into the saloon's foul air. "Did he tell you where it is before he...died?"

Confident that he didn't know Sean was alive, Elena leaned forward. "If I tell you *si*, you will kill me for the secret. If I say no, you will probably still kill me." She leaned back with a shrug, "I am just a poor half-breed girl. What do I know of gold? If I did, do you think I would be sitting lookout for Dooley?"

Roscoe closed his eyes, savoring the cigar in silence while he drummed his fingers on the table. They both knew it was time for him to call her bluff or fold his hand. Instead, he raised the bet. "Well then, perhaps we can discuss exactly what you don't know over a late supper tomorrow evening at the Tuscarora. Their food is stellar."

He reached out to touch her shortened black mane. Ignoring her shudder, he caressed it from the crown of her head down to where it ended, just above her shoulder. Then a finger continued along the line of her throat down to the gentle swell of her breasts, where a silky black tendril had once laid.

"Why did you cut your hair?"

He changed subjects so quickly she was at a loss for an answer. Then she remembered his satisfied smile when she told him Sean was dead. Forcing one to her own lips, she answered, "The O'Grady family is very rich. I am in mourning for the loss of my husband, their son."

CHAPTER THIRTY-THREE

*R*oscoe's six ounces of gold dust turned into more than ten at the Faro table. The next day, as a reward for bringing him luck, he surprised Elena with an expensive red satin gown. The French design had a plunging neckline trimmed with black lace that also dripped from the short sleeves and the hem of the wide, above-ankle-length skirt.

At her obvious aversion, he squeezed her forearm. "If you're going to help me celebrate, Elena, you have to dress the part." He pulled her close and ran his fingers across the frayed neckline of her blouse. "As much as I like the disposable quality of these rags, I prefer to see you dressed the way you should be, in luxurious satin and lace." He kissed her hard on the lips to prove his point. Though her flesh crawled and her stomach turned, she showed no reaction.

Roscoe laughed at her frigid response, cupping her face in his hand. "I can be patient, my dear. I will do my best to melt the ice in your veins, beginning with supper tonight. Meet me at the Tuscarora at nine o'clock and wear the dress."

She dreaded meeting him at the opulent Tuscarora Hotel. It was one of the newest of the fancy establishments that had sprung up as Santa Fe grew from a sleepy little Mexican village into a city of some renown. Only the richest and most stylish people went there. She'd rather run a gauntlet of braves with hatchets than face the piercing eyes and knife-edged tongues of Santa Fe society at the Tuscarora.

Her fears were confirmed when she entered the hotel alone wearing the gaudy evening gown. A room filled with well-heeled Eastern travelers and Santa Fe's elite fixed their disapproving stares on her. Her ears burned from their rude comments as she walked past them to join Roscoe at his table in the back of the establishment.

Seated far away from any doors or windows that would have provided a breeze, Elena longed for one of the Savannah House fans when she felt a droplet of sweat trickle between her breasts. She warmed even more as Roscoe, who didn't seem to be bothered by the heat, smiled and watched its descent.

"I am not the dinner, Senor," she said, straightening her shoulders. "You can stop looking at me like I am a rabbit about to be stewed."

Roscoe's laugh had a hollow ring to it. "I would hardly stew you, Elena. You are too fine a piece for that. You would be best prepared with a light basting of fresh butter, served on a bed of rice surrounded by succulent sweetmeats."

The game took Elena's mind off the uncomfortable gown. She leaned forward, ignoring his appreciative gaze at her nearly exposed bosom. "Some wild game is never fit to be eaten, no matter how well dressed."

Roscoe frowned when the waiter who brought their dinners of American steaks and fried potatoes, chuckled. "Enough sparring, Elena," he told her when the waiter was gone. "You know what I want from you, and you know I always get what I want. You may as well submit now, while you can still enjoy it."

The huge, greasy platter of food and his obscene grin sickened her. Reasoning he could only kill her once, she pushed her plate away in disgust. Then, with all the anger she'd held in check since seeing him again at Bowen's, she said, "You are a stupid, grinning jackass who thinks more with his cock than with his head."

Shocked at hearing her own voice say such vile things, she took advantage of his momentary stillness to continue. "I thought you were an adventurer who could help me find the lost treasure, but I was wrong. Your brain is in your crotch."

Roscoe paused with his fork in mid-air, and she finally saw tiny beads of sweat form on his brow. He was human after all, and humans could be killed. "If you want a whore, go back to Bowen's. If you want a partner who can help you become rich, talk to me as if I am a human and not a piece of meat. Then perhaps we can do business."

Wishing she could run from him to the safety of the mountains as Sam had begged her to do, she controlled her shaking legs to rise slowly and step around the table.

His hand shot out, gripping her wrist so tight she thought he'd pinch it off. His face turned almost purple with rage. "Sit down, cunt."

She didn't move. To obey him would be to admit her fear, and he would kill her for sure. His fingers bit deeper into her flesh and she blinked back the pain to whisper through clenched teeth. "Elena. I am Elena Concetta Santiago O'Grady. I can find your gold for you, but I will be your partner, not your whore."

She expected to feel the sharp point of his steak knife slide into her empty belly. *Que sera*. What will be, will be. If Roscoe killed her, then Sean would not be wrong in mourning her death. She would be happy to join the spirits in the mountains, to become part of the four winds, and if death was only a dark, silent place, at least there was peace.

Instead of the pain of a mortal wound, she felt the heat of Roscoe's body as he stood in front of her. He released her wrist, but she knew he would never forget or forgive, her defiance. As surely as she still drew breath, she would pay for it one day. She pulled her arm away, forcing herself to look into his evil, obsidian eyes.

Suddenly, Roscoe lowered his head and took possession of her mouth with his lips, his tongue, and his teeth, until she tasted her own blood, along with the rich sauce of the steak he'd just eaten. When he was finished, he wiped his mouth with his napkin and dabbed at the blood staining her cheek. "You can't deny me, Elena. You know that."

A strength she didn't know she possessed kept her voice steady. "That will never happen. Billy Berens taught me what it means to submit to a white man. I will take my own life first." She narrowed her eyes and glared at him. "Is taking my body worth losing your golden treasure?"

Smiling as if he'd caught her in an enormous bluff, Roscoe parried, "Why can't I have both? I have Mills' map and suicide isn't the Indian way."

"Mills was a Gringo. Every rock looked the same to him. You could spend years wandering in the mountains with his worthless map. You will be an old man before you find the gold...if you ever do. And remember, I am only half Indian."

"Point taken," Roscoe chuckled and sat again. "Please be seated, Elena. It appears we have business to discuss after all."

Feeling as if she'd just walked over a pit of heated cactus thorns, she sat in front of her congealing meal. She folded her hands together on top of the table to show that she was not trembling in fear—at least on the outside. "What do you wish to discuss?"

He spoke slowly, as a teacher might to a slightly dull student. "Gold. We were talking about gold. About how you can find it faster than I can with Corporal Mills' map. I'd like to know how, because now that O'Grady is dead, his parents are not likely to be of any help. Their friends, the missionaries, are also sadly departed from this life. Do you plan a ceremony to speak to the dead?"

He'd moved too fast. Beyond hinting that she could help him, Elena had no real plan. She only hoped she could appear more valuable to him alive than dead, at least until Sam arrived. Now it was too late. He wanted proof. Sweat dampened her satin-covered back as Roscoe waited for the answer that would seal her fate.

God forgive me, she prayed. "There was one more who saw the gold. Jesse Woods."

The swipe of Roscoe's arm sent their wineglasses flying, causing the other guests to turn their way. He ignored their stares and waved the waiter away when he appeared to clear the mess away. He reached across the table to squeeze her jaw, forcing her to see the threat in his eyes. "What kind of fool do you think I am, Elena?" he said. "Woods is dead. The idiot died before he'd tell Junior where it is. Stupidity seems to be an epidemic when it comes to friends of the O'Gradys."

He dropped his hand to lean back against the chair. "But then again, they probably would have died anyway. Sometimes my boys get a little carried away." He reached out again, covering her hand with his, painfully crushing her knuckles together inside his fist. "Think of something else Elena, or your virtue and your life are both mine—tonight."

She faced him down with the truth. "Jesse only pretended to be dead while your men kicked him and left him to the coyotes with his head in a noose and his hands and legs tied behind him."

Roscoe let go of her. He sniffed like a predator testing the air for the scent of fear. "Lived, you say? Tell me more and I may let you do the same."

Again, she used the truth to draw him into a trap she hadn't yet laid. "After dark, he cut his ropes on a rock and went to his mother's lodge to heal."

"How do you know all this?"

Realizing she'd talked herself, instead of Roscoe, into a trap, she swallowed hard. She couldn't tell him about Sam. He was her only hope if he arrived in time. Deciding she'd told enough of the truth for one night, she remembered Roscoe's suggestion about speaking to the dead.

"Judith told me. When I begged for Jesse to go to Georgia instead of me, she told me he was attacked by outlaws in the mountains."

She waited as he closed his eyes and drummed the fingers of one hand on the table while stroking the edges of his waxed mustache with the other. From beneath his hooded eyelids, he watched her breasts rise and fall with her breath. He wanted her, but she prayed that he wanted the gold more. With Jesse Woods alive, Sean's death would be just a minor inconvenience to him.

"How can you prove this?"

He believed it. She wanted to shout for joy as she took her first step into the world she planned to bring crashing down around him. Well-schooled in hiding her thoughts from white men, she folded her hands in her lap. "I can find Jesse. He will tell me where the gold is."

He laughed. "Just like that. You'll find Jesse, who is hiding somewhere in an endless wilderness, and he'll tell you the secret he nearly gave up his life keeping. You'll have to do better than that, Elena."

His skepticism crushed her newborn confidence, but she hid her fear to make things up as she went along. "Jesse is of the People and so am I. I will find him and he will tell me what I need to know."

"And have the Army waiting for me when I show up."

She leaned toward him this time. "I want this gold too, *Senor*. The white man has stolen much from me. Jesse will help me and I will help you."

Roscoe seemed momentarily satisfied by her zealousness, but demanded more. "How do you plan to do this? Exactly."

"I will go to Jesse, find the gold, and bring some of it back to you."

"If you don't return?"

She smiled. "You have Corporal Mills' map,"

"And you have Jesse."

"But no way to get the gold out. I need you to take out the gold and turn it into money for me. You need me to find it for you fast, before your mining lease runs out."

"How do you know about that?" This time he looked genuinely surprised.

Surprising him for the second time made her bold. If she could win Roscoe's trust and destroy Junior Anscombe at the same time, all her prayers would be answered. "Junior was easy to follow. Marcus knew about the permits and that time was running out on them. He figured out what Junior really wanted."

She leaned back in her chair and waved a hand in disdain. "He is a very stupid man, your Junior, and he has caused many of your troubles. He was foolish to kill the only ones who could tell him what he needed to know. You would do better with a partner who thinks more and kills less."

She listened to herself speak calmly to the man responsible for the murders of her adopted family, wondering if Judith and Marcus were guiding her tongue. "Everyone in Santa Fe knows how long a mining lease lasts and that you have to know the location of your main shaft to within a mile. Mills' map cannot do this for you, and you do not have the time to stake one claim after another until you find the right place. You will never find the gold without me. You have to trust me and I have to trust you."

"Trust," he mimicked. "Is an overused word." His eyes narrowed and he took her hand, gently this time. "You have a week, dearest. Junior will accompany you to Jesse's lodge and wait for you to convince him to tell you what we need to know."

"No," she snapped. When Roscoe's eyebrows raised, she turned his own statement back to him. "What kind of fool do you think I am? Jesse will never tell me if I go to him with Junior. I must go alone."

"Again, Elena, what if you don't return?"

"I must return," she answered, wondering what she had to do to convince this man she was as corrupt as him.

"Why?"

Using all of her will to keep from shuddering, her fingers massaged the sensitive skin of his palm. "Because after we have the treasure, I think we can become friends."

One of his hands slid up her arm, his black eyes holding hers captive. "If you're not back in a week, I'll find you myself. I guarantee you won't like the consequences if you try to double-cross me."

She pulled away from his wandering hand. "There is one thing that would ensure my quick return."

"What?"

"The Torres ranch. When I show you the gold, I want the deed to that ranch."

"There is nothing more dangerous than a woman with property." He laughed, then turned serious, "In exchange for your third of the treasure."

She shook her head. "I will be your partner, not Junior Anscombe's. For the Torres ranch, you may keep half of my half of the treasure. What you give Junior is up to you."

Roscoe smiled as they both agreed to a bargain neither intended to keep.

CHAPTER THIRTY-FOUR

hen Elena found Jesse and his mother, Morning Bird, the old woman frowned from a dark, weathered face as cracked and lined as the walls of her mountain home. For twenty-five years, she'd kept her hair short, mourning her brother. Her black, almond shaped eyes peered sadly at the world from behind folds of skin as tough as leather. The only thing keeping her from fading entirely into the sand and stone-colored landscape was the exquisitely beaded belt of bright green, fuchsia, and gold that held her woolen skirt in place.

"The spirits have claimed the white man's gold," she argued, reminding Jesse that even the Comanche weren't free of the wrath of the Pueblo gods. "Red or white," she said in a voice as soft as an evening breeze, yet clear as the lonely call of a coyote. "All who have sought the yellow rock in the Pueblo have died. It is a tomb. Leave the spirits resting there in peace."

Morning Bird's body was no larger than a young girl, her parchment-thin skin stretched tightly over bones as brittle as a raven's wing, but Elena didn't make the mistake of thinking she was weak. Rather, she was so strong she would never die. When the old woman stopped breathing, she would live on in the rocks and the earth. They could never force her to help them. Only the power of truth would sway her.

The old woman told Elena how she had watched the mutiny from her aerie across the gorge. She heard the first shot that killed Lt. Douglas, and watched as the men fought each other until the cliffs and the canyon floor were stained with their greed-tainted blood. In a matter of minutes, the only survivor was one wounded, horseless creature who crawled his way out of the Pueblos.

When Corporal Mills left, Morning Bird crept around the cliffs to the open cave, pushing the blue-clad bodies over the ledge to feed the scavengers on the canyon floor. She covered the low opening with rocks so it looked like a landslide on the side of the trail. In the nearly three decades since then, her skilled masonry had kept the cave hidden from everyone who passed through.

Elena watched the exchange between the man who had grown up without his mother, and yet was so much like her. Like Elena, Jesse was a half-blood. His mother had been captured by whites as a young girl and wasn't as fortunate as Elena to be saved from a life a slavery. She raised Jesse in the back room of his father's tavern and when he was old enough to survive without her, she returned to the People.

Jesse told Elena it was Patrick O'Grady and not Marcus who had taken him West. Patrick was searching for Camilla, who was on the missionaries' wagon train. When they found her in the Comanche camp, Jesse was reunited with his mother. Though he could take Elena to the gold, he'd never to it without his mother's permission.

He took Morning Bird's wizened brown hand in his strong, copper-colored one, speaking to her wise old eyes. "You have hidden the gold well Mother, but the killing has not stopped. Farmers, white, Mexican, and Indian, who would not leave their land when the thieves from the Santa Fe Ring stole it from them, have been killed.

"Their families have been murdered or left with nothing. They were good and honest men like Edward Torres and now our own dear friends Marcus and Judith. None of them sought the gold, but they are dead because of it. The killing will not end until either the gold or the greed for it is destroyed forever."

Morning Bird's piercing black eyes bored first into Elena's eyes, then into Jesse's. "All who enter there will die. You will die."

"You did not," Jesse countered. "You were with the gold and you did not die. Or Camilla and Patrick O'Grady."

"We did not want it."

"Neither do I." He looked from her to smile at Elena. "Neither does she."

The old woman pulled her hands from his, rose slowly on weary legs, and turned to the East as she did at the beginning of every day. "The girl has a thirst for revenge. All who enter the sacred Pueblos with hatred or greed in their hearts will die. I have seen it. When my brother followed the white woman to kill her husband and take her son, the gods allowed the white man to kill him. They lived because their love for each other and for their son was stronger than Camilla's hatred for my brother."

Suddenly, with the grace of a fawn, she turned from the ledge of her wind-hewn home and bent low over Elena, pointing a crooked finger at her face. "If you go into the cave seeking revenge for the dead missionaries, you will die and my son will die with you."

"Only the spirits know when we will die, Mother," Jesse insisted. "The time cannot be changed. If I am to die in the Pueblo, then it will be so. If it stops the gold-crazed white men from killing anyone else, it will be a good death."

The old woman snorted, turning from them again to silently watch a turkey buzzard swoop down to the desert floor, scooping up a remnant of what had once been a living creature. A single tear followed the scavenger's descent. To Jesse, she said, "Go only once to the cave and set your trap." And to Elena, "When the evil one comes, do not go in with him. If you are there when the gods speak, you will die with him, no matter how good your motives."

Jesse and Elena both nodded. Neither one had any intention of entering the cave with Roscoe. Elena's job was to lead him to it. Sam would arrest him as he brought the gold out. Sam. The unspoken name echoed in Elena's mind. They needed him. Two half-breed Indians couldn't arrest a white man, and there wasn't much time left to wait. Everything would be lost if Sam didn't arrive before Roscoe "mined" his gold.

They went to the cave the following morning. Jesse rolled away one of the larger boulders. The stench of death and ancient dust inside the opening sickened them, but it was the smell of evil, more than death, that caused Elena to tremble. For a moment, she clung to her teacher for support.

"It's all right, Elena," Jesse's deep voice whispered into her ear. "We're here out of love. We won't be harmed if we keep the love of Judith and Marcus and your Sean in our hearts. We'll simply lead the desperado to what he wants. What happens after that is up to God."

As if seeing the question in her eyes, he smiled and kissed her gently on the forehead. "Our God. The Great Creator who loves us, Elena. Not angry spirits conjured up in an ancient imagination and kept alive by fear and superstition."

Elena nodded bravely, hoping he was right. She crawled inside the cave, stopping only when it seemed that her heart had ceased to beat. She fought dizziness and nausea as memories of another cave and other deaths sapped her strength and threatened her courage.

As usual, the scene was shrouded in smoke, the sound of keening, the smell of gunpowder, and the colors red and blue flashing through her paralyzed mind. When she looked down at the scuffed dirt floor, shiny black boots entered her vision and she again heard a deep, commanding voice order, "Round up the women. Leave the rest."

"Elena," chased the unbidden memory from her mind.

Her legs trembling, she followed Jesse's dim light farther inside, toward a shadow cowering against the back wall. He held the light and raised the canvas from a pile of golden bricks. "Take only one," he told her."

For one brief, terrifying moment, the pile of gold groaned at the separation, threatening to add her bones to the others who'd tried to wrest it from the mountain spirits. Then with a sigh, it settled around the gap, and the cave became still.

The heavy bar was almost too much for her to lift, but somehow, her small body gave her the strength. It felt cold despite the stifling heat and the thought that such a heavy, lifeless thing had caused the deaths of so many people sickened her again. Unwilling to turn her back on the evil that existed there, she backed out of the cave while Jesse set his trap.

Elena returned from the mountains on time and met Roscoe in his room at the Tuscarora. When she presented him with one solid gold bar bearing the seal of the Denver Mint, his black eyes glowed with its reflection. He took it from her, weighing the heavy bar in his hands.

"Well done," he purred while he stroked it, smelled it, walked with it, and finally tucked it into a niche carved inside a book titled, *Treasure Island.*

She looked away in disgust. His greed would never be satisfied. Once he saw the immense treasure stored inside the ancient Anasazi pueblo, he would never share it. While gold fever corrupted innocent souls, it fueled the flames of greed in those who were already corrupt until it became an inferno, devouring everything in its path.

Even Lt. Douglas and the soldiers who came to take it back to the Denver Mint so many years ago, were victims of the white man's lust for gold, killing each other for it.

Roscoe put his treasured book on his bookshelf and turned to her. Like the drawings of the Devil in Judith's Bible, his long, narrow face and black eyes glowed with lust. His teeth flashed like fangs when he smiled. She cringed at the touch of his hand on the back of her head, and nearly wretched when he pressed lips that seemed too cold to be alive, against hers.

She backed away demanding, "My payment, *Senor*."

His eyes flashed with anger before he pulled a document from his inside breast pocket and presented her with a signed deed to Edward Torres' ranch, titled to her. "We're partners now, Elena."

His sly smile reminded her of their dinner conversation. "I look forward to becoming friends with you."

"Patience, *Senor*," she whispered. "We have much to do." She ignored the fact that she hated everything about Roscoe and lightly brushed his lips with hers.

"I know," he agreed as his fingers forced her lips apart. He kissed her again, nearly gagging her with his thick, probing tongue that tasted of malt liquor and tobacco. "Stop struggling," he hissed when she twisted away.

"Later," she insisted, resisting the urge to spit until her mouth felt clean again. Instead, she forced a seductive smile. "There is much work to be done first. It will not be easy to remove and smelt all that gold without being noticed. The trail is dangerous. It will take time if you do not want many people to know what you are doing."

Roscoe rallied quickly and fondled her breast. "Work. Work. Work. It can wait. First we celebrate."

"Are you crazy?" she hissed. "You cannot tell people about this."

"No, but I can celebrate my engagement to the most beautiful half-breed in New Mexico."

"What are you saying?" The laughter in his eyes baffled her, but the set of his cruel mouth told her he was serious.

"What would you have me say? That I've fallen in love with you and want you to be the queen of my kingdom after we get the gold?" He chuckled dryly, pouring two drinks. His eyes held her captive as he forced a glass into her hand and lightly clicked it against his own. "I'm sealing our partnership. A wife cannot testify against her husband in court."

Elena's fingers involuntarily reached up to touch the crucifix that no longer circled her neck, no longer protected her from evil. "I cannot marry you."

Roscoe ran his fingers through her hair, curling it into a ball at the nape of her neck. He kissed her there, sending shivers down her spine. "Why not? Your most recent husband is dead, I believe."

At her stony silence, he yanked on his fist full of hair and faced her. "It's just a formality, my dear. Since we will be lovers anyway very shortly, I thought you would be pleased to have our relationship legitimized. We can even use a priest if you like."

"You don't think I have enough names already?" she said, playing out the farce.

"The best for last, of course." He finished both their drinks. "So when shall we tie the knot my love? Tonight? Tomorrow?"

She tried to hide her panic. Where was Sam?

She prayed he'd return soon and that he and Jesse would have time to put their plan into motion, but she couldn't stall forever. She had to take Roscoe to the gold soon. It wouldn't take long after that to loot the cave and move the gold to where he had a legal lease and a smelter to make it look like it was legally mined—if one didn't look too closely.

"Not so fast," she countered. "Our bargain is to be friends after the gold is out.

He shrugged. "Very well, but I don't favor long engagements. You have a week. You prepare for the wedding, and I'll prepare for the mining expedition. No one will suspect a thing when the happy bride and groom return from their honeymoon with the richest find in New Mexico history."

He laughed at the enormous joke he was playing on the world and tucked her arm beneath his. "Tonight, we celebrate our betrothal."

CHAPTER THIRTY-FIVE

Sean and Sam arrived in Santa Fe well after dark. They took rooms at the Tuscarora Hotel, intending to clean up, spend a long overdue night in a real bed, and leave in the morning to meet Jesse Woods in Taos.

"I need a drink," Sean said when they met again after getting baths and changing clothes.

Sam shook his head. "Not a good idea. Better lay low until Taos. If you mouth it around you're looking for LaPorte, he'll run for cover and we'll never find him."

After weeks being cooped up with Sam in Pecos and the seemingly endless trek across the desert to Santa Fe, Sean could barely stand the sight of the Ranger. He was grateful for the lessons in Western-style pistoleering, and his advice on how to blend in with the rough characters roaming the West. But Sam never hid his opinion that Sean was holding them back and would end up getting them both killed.

Now, in what passed for civilization in New Mexico, Sam's order to stay away from the one place where Sean was the expert, was the last straw. "I'm not stupid, Pruitt," he snapped. "You have the law written all over your face, but I'm just a drifter looking for a game. I might be able to pick up some information."

"That's what I'm afraid of," Sam growled. "You're still obsessed with revenge and if you go off half-cocked, we could lose him for good."

He knew Sam was right. His hatred and thirst for revenge was all that kept him going through the heat and cold of the desert. The pain of every time he mounted his horse, and the agony of every step he took along the way carved new lines on his face, but he wouldn't quit. Couldn't quit. And Sam knew it, goddam it.

"That won't happen," he growled back.

"Just take it easy," Sam conceded. "Folks in these parts can smell a greenhorn a mile away. A fresh growth of beard ain't gonna hide it. I'm gone for Taos at dawn, with or without you."

"Don't wait up." Sean jammed his new Stetson onto his head, knowing the Ranger would like nothing better than to leave him behind. He'd sure as hell be back and saddled up by the time Sam Pruitt had his big ugly belly filled with breakfast.

He felt at home the moment he walked into Bowen's. Savannah, Pecos, or Santa Fe, a saloon was a saloon, and gambling was gambling. He could predict the turn of a card better than most men and could read a table like a book.

He approached the bartender. "Rye. Double shot." He'd gotten used to the rotgut whiskey at Rosa's and didn't want to call attention to himself by ordering quality, Old Crow Bourbon.

When he laid his Morgan Silver dollar on the bar, the burly barkeep in a stained vest and banker's cuffs on his sleeves, pushed it back at him. "No need. All you can handle is on the happy groom-to-be over yonder, so order the good stuff my friend." His smile showed a row of whiskey-rotted teeth under a bushy handlebar mustache as he poured a double shot of Old Crow.

"Then leave the bottle," Sean said before he took it away. The barkeep nodded and stepped away to sop up a spilled tankard of beer at the other end of the bar.

Sean smiled into his glass. Most of the men were drunk already. Tongues would be loose and so would purses. He had no doubt that by the end of the night he'd have the information he needed to find Roscoe.

His drink stopped part way to his lips when the crowd at the end of the bar parted and he saw the man he hated most in the world propose a toast to a woman in a red dress. His vision blurred when she turned toward the crowd and he watched his wife smile the dazzling smile of his dreams at his enemy. It was like seeing her in Hell.

The loud chorus of cheers and bawdy wedding night comments were drowned out by the sound of blood pounding through a heart that shattered a little more with every painful beat. His only thought for months was avenging Elena's death. So much so, he ignored Doc McAllister's warnings and left with Sam as soon as he could walk without crutches. Each day on the desert was agony as the dry, suffocating heat left him weak, and the cold night air chilled him to the bone. And while he was exhausted beyond endurance, the pain in his leg kept him from sleeping.

Through each endless night, the cry of the coyote echoed the emptiness of living without her. In his fitful dreams, she was with her people on the reservation, or working in one of the cantinas. In those dreams, he saw her smile, tasted her lips, and felt her body against his as they began their new life together. Never, even in his fever-filled nightmares, did he imagine finding her in Roscoe's arms.

Trapped in a waking nightmare, he watched the celebration and knocked back several more drinks without even feeling the strong, smooth bourbon sear his parched throat. Though his heart protested, his eyes answered his question on the first day they met. She may have been a virgin then, but she was a vixen now.

She was also one of the best actresses he'd ever seen. She'd fooled his entire family, including Chloe, who claimed to be able to read minds. How could they all have been so wrong about her? No longer thirsty, he took his place at the end of the line of men waiting to congratulate the happy couple.

Two places ahead of him in line, a tall, blond man with garters on the full sleeves of his white silk shirt kissed Elena full on the mouth. Her smile wavered at his approach and she took a drink after, as if to cleanse her lips. When he tried to sneak another, she pushed him away.

It took a sharp word from Roscoe to make him step aside, and Sean swore under his breath. Junior Anscombe. From Elena's vivid descriptions, he'd know the man anywhere. She may have fooled Roscoe, but the hatred that burned in her heart for Anscombe was second only to his own lust for LaPorte's blood.

Love may fade, he thought, but hate never died. What the hell kind of game was she playing? If she was working her own plan of revenge alone, it could get her killed.

He was last in line and Elena, tired of being manhandled by every shaggy, smelly, ranch-hand in the place, put her hand to his chest to stop his approach. At the contact, she raised her head. In the space of an instant, hope, disbelief, doubt, and fear followed each other in her eyes as she searched his bearded face.

The momentary flicker of joy when she first recognized him answered Sean's questions. She wasn't that good an actress after all. He watched her joy turn into terror and longed to kiss her trembling lips just one more time. If he did, he'd never be able to let her go and would get them both killed.

For once, he listened to his better sense. With a wink and a chaste kiss on her soft cheek, he whispered, "I see you made your choice." Then he turned slowly, favoring his right leg as he strode toward the batwing doors.

He needed time to think. So many questions raced through his mind that his head pounded from the chatter. How did she survive the train wreck? He'd seen the passenger car fall into the gorge. Heard her scream. Yet it was Elena's voice, her touch, her kiss, that brought him back to life. Was she the Indian boy who tended him? How did Pruitt get her necklace? Why did he say he buried her himself? Why did she leave?

Damn Pruitt's soul to hell, he wanted to scream when he turned to leave. The Ranger had something to do with Elena's disappearance and he'd damn well find out why. Had she gone willingly? No matter, he decided. Even if she didn't love him enough to stay with him, she was still the reason he lived. She loved him then and she loved him now. He just had to figure a way to get her away from LaPorte.

One step short of the batwing doors, "O'Grady," rose above the music and voices in the saloon. The silence that followed crackled with the tension of an electrical storm.

Sean turned slowly, and Bowen's patrons scurried to the corners of the saloon, leaving a space between him and Roscoe, with Elena in the middle.

He stared past her ashen face into the pitiless black eyes of his enemy and suddenly felt more alive than any day since the train wreck. This was why he was saved.

Even if Elena really chose Roscoe over him, he could never let her become a part of that murdering bastard's stable of used women. "What do you want, LaPorte?" he replied, knowing the answer.

The older man smiled and put an arm around Elena's waist, pulling her against him. "How good of you to rise from the grave and come all this way to celebrate my wedding, O'Grady."

Elena winced under Roscoe's touch. He was right. Whatever was holding her to him wasn't love. It was his only ray of hope while he played his hand one card at a time.

"You know better than that LaPorte. It'll take more than a thunderstorm to keep me from settling things with you. It's time you paid for your dirty work."

Roscoe sneered, his amused gaze scanning the room for support. "I suppose you have a way to make me?"

Anyone who knew Roscoe knew he wore a derringer mounted on a spring attached to his sleeve, ready to be released with a twist of his wrist; and every gun hand in the place seemed to be poised over its holster. Sean had learned from the desert that it wasn't wise to attack a snake in its nest. Without bothering to answer, he turned to step outside.

Roscoe betrayed his anger when he shouted, "Don't turn your back on me, you cowardly son of a bitch."

"Thought I'd help you out," Sean tossed over his shoulder. "Backs seem to be your favorite target, after old men and helpless women, of course." The doors flapped behind him.

Pausing just outside the saloon, he heard Roscoe say, "Give me your iron."

With a slow smile, Sean walked to the center of the street and turned to face the saloon as Roscoe stepped through the still swinging doors to face him.

"What took you so long?" Sean said. Though his life hung in the balance, he'd never felt more calm.

Roscoe was vermin and had to be stopped before he ruined more lives. Sean no longer felt the constant ache in his leg and his hand itched to try the fast draw he'd practiced so diligently at Rosa's and along the trail. He was fast, but if he rushed, his injured trigger finger sometimes jerked and made him miss his target. He could only hope to clear his holster fast enough to aim one true shot. There wouldn't be a second one.

Roscoe adjusted his borrowed gun belt on his hips and shook his arms to limber them up. "I'm here now."

"Give up, LaPorte. You're after a lost cause." Sean tried to reason with his enemy. "Elena has nothing to do with what's between us."

"If she belonged to you, she has everything to do with what's between us."

"Is that what this is all about?" Sean laughed cruelly. "Revenge for Mary Louise? You can't compare a lady like Mary Louise Fairchild to a little greaser like Elena. She got me out of Georgia, that's all. She doesn't matter." He prayed that someday Elena would understand why he said that, and forgive him.

"I disagree." Roscoe's face was an angry mask, his voice cold as death itself. "She matters a great deal, or you wouldn't be here. Face it, you can't beat me."

"I can try."

Elena had run out of the saloon in time to hear Sean call her a greaser. He saw the insult burn through to her heart and her face darken in the moonlight. They were in Santa Fe now, he realized, and because of his words, their love, as well as their marriage, was over. Worst of all, she believed he hadn't come for her, but for his revenge against Roscoe, and the treasure his parents had found so long ago.

Still, she protected him, running to Roscoe, wrapping her arms around his waist. "The Gringo isn't worth the lead from your bullet," she told him. "We don't need him." Then she turned to Sean. "It is over. If you want to stay alive, go home."

"Over?" Sean's voice carried through the now empty street. "This man has murdered countless people, including Marcus and Judith Williams. He won't rest until he has what he wants, and he doesn't care how many people die in the meantime."

Elena tipped her head toward the alley to Sean's right. "You are wrong," she shouted before Roscoe could reach for his gun. "Marcus died in an accident and Judith was killed by a robber. I know that now."

"You can't believe that." She couldn't have changed that much in only a few months. Even in the dim yellow glow from the saloon, her face called her words false. "You are still my wife."

"Until Santa Fe," mocked him. Another time and place echoed in his mind.

She spat toward his boot and her voice turned hoarse. "You used me to escape the law. I used you to come home. Go back now to your white lady and raise your soft, white-eyed brats. We do not want you here." She whispered something into Roscoe's ear and stepped aside, between Sean and the opening to the alley.

Roscoe's hand left his gun and he smiled. "The little lady just saved your life, O'Grady. I suggest you take her advice and skedaddle back to your mama and pa." Without waiting for an answer, he circled Elena's shoulders with his arm and led her back into the saloon.

Sean was immobilized with rage and confusion. Roscoe would never give up looking for that gold. Elena couldn't have fallen for his lies so quickly. Feeling totally exasperated and more than a little foolish, he headed toward the Tuscarora.

A movement in the alley caught his attention and he turned just as Anscombe stepped out carrying a Remington rifle and following Elena and Roscoe back inside Bowen's. "I'll be gawd-damned," he mimicked Sam. Elena had saved his life—again. Now his step was light as he returned to his room. He had some planning to do.

CHAPTER THIRTY-SIX

*R*oscoe walked Elena back to the abandoned Indian school. She was so exhausted she could barely walk, yet he, after drinking most of Bowen's customers into a stupor, strolled without so much as a waver in his step. He kept a steady hand on her elbow. "It's dangerous staying here alone," he said in a voice as sober as a preacher on Sunday morning. "Why not take up residence in my rooms at the Tuscarora? In a week, I'll have your marriage to O'Grady annulled, and we'll be legally married anyway. No one will even care."

She used the last of her strength to summon an angry response. "I will care. We made a bargain. I will not live with you until my share of the gold is safe. If we find the gold while the Gringo is still my husband, he can take it away from me. I won't risk that."

Roscoe's head rose, like a wolf sensing his prey and his smile caught the moonlight. "I know a way to eliminate that risk much easier, faster, and cheaper than an annulment. In fact, Junior was most distressed over your intervention this evening." *He had a clear shot and you blocked it.* He grasped her shoulders, making her face him. "Could it be you weren't such a merry widow after all?"

Hands biting into her bare shoulders, he shrugged. "No matter. I leave your husband's fate in your hands, for now. I'm also holding you to your bargain. If O'Grady isn't out of Santa Fe in a week, he won't be anywhere."

Despite his threat, Elena's heart filled with joy. She was right about

227

Anscombe waiting in the shadows to kill Sean. Her Apache instincts were coming back. When you think like your enemy, you know what he will do before he does it. She no longer feared the soulless darkness in Roscoe's eyes. She was beginning to understand the thoughts behind them.

Still, her blood chilled as she felt his hatred for Sean, and smelled blood-lust on his whiskey-tainted breath. He was lying about giving Sean a week to leave Santa Fe. He'd be dead before another night fell, unless she convinced him to leave.

"If you kill him, lawmen will come looking for his killer." Her voice held more confidence than she felt. "His father is very powerful and would never stop until he avenged his son's death. After the annulment is signed and I see him board the Eastern train, we can go after the gold."

Her frantic mind again screamed, where is Sam? He was supposed to be watching over Sean. They needed him soon or Sean would be dead and she would be Roscoe's wife.

Roscoe's eyebrows raised at her temerity to question him. "The arrogant cur needs his ass whipped and I will be only too happy to oblige."

She was tired of lying, of fighting off Roscoe's advances, of worrying about Sean O'Grady, and wondering about Sam Pruitt. She only wanted to slip out of the hated dress, wash off the stink of Bowen's Saloon, and fall into as deep a sleep as her troubled mind would allow.

She turned to open her door. "You are both acting like jealous little boys. I don't have time for children."

Roscoe's hand caught her elbow. "You flatter yourself, Elena. You belong to me. We wed in a week, with or without an annulment, and then we go after the gold. See that O'Grady is gone before the nuptials, or I will."

She pulled her arm away. Her bluff had given Sean a week to live and Sam seven more days to come to their rescue. "You forget why we became partners. It was to get the gold, and not to argue about Sean O'Grady. If the Gringo is fool enough to interfere, then his fate is with the gods. I do not care."

She stepped inside the school, grateful the lie in her eyes was hidden in the darkness. With her back against the door, she inhaled deeply of the dry, still air inside the empty building. As she did, Judith's love and Marcus' strength filled her body with the resolve she needed to avenge their deaths. She would sacrifice even her own life for that purpose if need be, but first she had to save the love of her life.

Roscoe chuckled on the other side of the door, and she watched from her tiny window as he ambled back toward Bowen's. His low, satisfied whistle told her she had just gained her enemy's trust by betraying her love.

When the darkness swallowed him, she released the invisible strings holding her up since she first saw Sean. A cry tore from deep within her as she slid down the wall to sit cross-legged on the floor.

Tears she'd promised not to shed until Judith's murderer hung from the gallows filled her eyes. She made no effort to dry them as they ran down her cheeks, staining the expensive crimson gown with streaks as dark as blood. As her people had done for centuries, she swayed back and forth, her arms outstretched as she beseeched the spirits of her people to receive her when her mission was complete.

When she could cry and sing no more, she curled into a ball on the floor and slept. And as she slept, the window in her mind opened to the day her life as an Apache ended. This time, no fog protected her from the horror. This time, she surrendered to the power of the mind to be in the past and the present at the same time.

In her dream, she floated above the smoke shrouding her younger self and the bodies littering the cave's floor. Then the smoke cleared and she saw herself rise from Little Wolf's dead body. The sun flashed on her blade as she moved with the speed of a snake to plunge it into the gut of the soldier who had scalped him. Her cry of vengeance and his of pain, rose to the mountain peaks.

For a moment, the ever-flashing signal lights that told of the white man's victory over an unarmed village of old men, women, and children, stopped. The women ceased their keening and even the wounded lay silent as the soldier tried to pull his organs back into his body. Suddenly, a dark shadow blocked the light. Strong hands pulled her hair and dragged her from the cave.

"No," the adult Elena screamed while the younger one could only whimper as she was dragged away from her dead family into the painful light of day.

She thrashed in her sleep, gasping for breath as the soldier carried the child Elena like a sack of grain under his arm. "You belong to me," he said. Then, for the first time, she saw her captor's face. It was long and thin. Bloodless lips curled upward in an arrogant sneer masquerading as a smile. Though years of greed, corruption, and depravity had made their marks, the face belonged to Roscoe LaPorte. He finally had his revenge. He had killed Marcus and Judith and now he had her too.

He was truly the Devil. Voices in the dream told her she could never beat him at his own game. Her only way to escape was to follow the bright light that suddenly surrounded her. To grasp the shadowy, ghost fingers reaching out to lead her into the world beyond death.

Opening her eyes to begin her passage, her mind cleared. She realized the hand touching her was human and the light which had been so bright in her dream, was simply a lantern held close to her face. Before she could scream, a sweet-smelling cloth pressed against her mouth. Then everything became dark and quiet.

CHAPTER THIRTY-SEVEN

*S*he woke choking from the effects of chloroform and pulled herself up onto her elbows, gulping in the fresh morning air, hoping it would stop the churning in her stomach. When she could breathe without retching, she lay back down and watched a turkey vulture hover motionless in the bright blue sky while she floated below it in lazy circles drawing her ever closer to its razor-sharp beak.

This is all wrong, her bewildered mind told her as she gripped the blanket to keep from falling into the sky. She closed her eyes until the earth eventually ceased its crazy spinning and the buzzard left her to search for a more cooperative meal. Her mind cleared slowly, recalling that a faceless intruder had robbed her of her senses.

It was night then, she remembered. She was at the school. Now it was near noon, if the position of the sun could be trusted. She didn't have to move her aching head to know she was in the foothills of the Sangre de Christo Mountains, about as far north of Santa Fe a man riding double could travel in a half day.

"Kill me now," she repeated to another unknown captor she sensed no more than a few feet from her. "While you still can." Then she closed her eyes and surrendered to a new, dreamless sleep.

She woke again to cool water being poured by droplets into her mouth. With the sickness gone and her mind clear, anger gave her the strength to fight for her life. She pushed the hand away to scramble unsteadily to her feet. Her head ached, her eyes burned, and the sudden movement made her stomach lurch, but she forced herself to speak.

"Stay away from me," she told several identical male images drifting in and out of her line of vision. Finally, the images blended into one form that looked like Sean O'Grady, but was a stranger to her. His face was darker, his shoulders broader, his thighs more muscular. Tiny lines along the corners of his eyes, made him look older, like a desperado, but the steel glint in his clear gray eyes could only belong to him. She moaned, grieving for the man with a crooked, little-boy smile who laughed at rules, and looked at life as an adventure to be enjoyed, not endured.

Then it came. It was slow to show itself, hidden behind an unkempt beard, but it was her husband's smile. His head tilted, making the smile even more mischievous. "Good morning Sleeping Beauty," he said in a slow, Southern drawl.

Yes, he was still the man she married, and the clarity in his gaze told her she was safe…for the moment. Suddenly, anger replaced her fear. "You." She pulled her fist back to strike his grinning jaw.

Unstable on her feet and aiming at a target that seemed to be every-where at once, she only succeeded in creating a breeze. Sean's body kept her from falling face down in the desert brush. She fought, cursing him in Apache, Spanish, and English, but the struggle only made her more aware of the new, harder planes of his body. As she twisted to get away, his shirt split open.

Just as her fear disappeared at the sight of his smile, her anger dissolved at the sight of the rough, sun-reddened scars crisscrossing his chest like a hastily scrawled treasure map. She reached out to trace the new landscape of his body. He flinched at her touch and her breath caught in her throat when she saw more than the pain of his injuries in his eyes.

Then the pain turned into passion and she couldn't deny her own body's reaction to it. It was as if nothing else existed in the world. Not the heat that caused the stained and wrinkled satin dress to stick to her skin like a sausage casing; not the danger they were both in if Roscoe found them together. Not even the knowledge that their union was an affront to the God who instituted marriage.

Only the cry of a distant eagle and the moan of the wind funneling down from the mountains disturbed the quiet of the desert floor as they stared at each other. Their hearts spoke what their lips could not. Even the nickers of the two Indian ponies tethered nearby couldn't break the spell that lasted until Sean's lips touched hers.

She melted into him, her hands struggling to touch every part of his face at once, her lips and tongue hungering for the taste of him. She opened her eyes to again see the circling vulture and pushed away before she lost complete control of her actions.

Her lips tingling and her heart racing from just being near him, her mind reeled with questions about this new Sean O'Grady. He was her husband, but he had also called her a greaser and confessed that he had only used her to escape the law. She didn't matter, he said. Yet now, he'd kidnapped her. She couldn't give herself to him again until she knew what he wanted. Was she his wife, or his hostage? A pawn to beat Roscoe to the rebel treasure.

The slap of her palm branding his cheek sent a prairie dog scurrying to its burrow and she faced him with her fists clenched at the sides of the ruined dress. Staring into eyes now as cold as an ancient dagger, she saw the violence she always knew lay just beneath the surface of his arrogance.

It was justified, she reasoned. She had abandoned him when he needed her, forced others to tell him she was dead, and he'd found her in his enemy's arms. She couldn't blame him if he'd brought her out to the desert to kill her.

When he raised his hand to touch his cheek, she braced for a blow that never came. Instead, he smiled, his white teeth contrasting with the dark fringe above and below his lips. "Why did you do that?"

The teasing lilt in his voice told her he hadn't changed so much after all. Neither had she. With just a smile, he could still ignite both her anger and her passion beyond the bounds of her common sense.

While his touch had taught her how to be a woman, except for those moments of exquisite pleasure, he'd brought nothing but pain and trouble into her life. Now he was about to get them both killed before she could accomplish her revenge. She answered his question with another tirade in Spanish and Apache that she couldn't express in the English words taught by missionaries.

Still he smiled. As if he didn't care that she was insulting him in two languages and damning him to every hell known to exist. She had every right. He'd gotten her mixed up in his own mess to the point that they would both likely be killed.

Apparently enjoying the sound of her voice, the flush in her cheeks and the fire in her eyes, he cut down one of the balls of fruit growing near the top of an old saguaro cactus and sat on the blanket to carefully peel back the thick skin of the fruit.

When he reached the soft, juicy flesh underneath, he fixed his eyes on hers, slowly sucking on the ripe tip of the rose-colored fruit. When he'd drawn the nectar that the cactus stored for its own survival to the surface, he offered it to her, a slow smile curving his moist lips.

She acknowledged that he'd learned quickly how to live in the desert. Except for the beard, he could have been an Apache brave sitting cross-legged on the bright-colored blanket. His lips, moist now from the fruit of the desert, tempted her. She knew how they would taste, how they would feel on the parts of her body that thirsted for more than a cool drink.

As his eyes roamed slowly over Roscoe's dress, she lost her train of thought, forgetting the words of her own native tongue until she could only stand in front of him, the heat from her body matching the scorching heat of the day.

Refusing to acknowledge that she felt the same hunger, she batted the succulent fruit out of his hand, letting the precious syrup spill into the white sand at the base of the mother plant. Hands on her hips, she repeated his question. "Why did I slap you? You are a clever *Gringo* who can squeeze the milk from a cactus. I think you know why. No," she ordered when he started to rise. "Don't move."

She reached to where her Spanish knife would be riding at her waist—if she had been wearing her own clothes. Instead, it was hidden in a strap around her thigh, beneath layers of silk. She could never reach it before he was upon her, and they both knew it.

He rose slowly to stand in front of her, the slightest wince of pain as he put his weight on his right leg. His expression grave, he reached into his own sheath to pull out the familiar knife with a handmade silver hilt. The blade found its way to the hem of her skirt, lifting it to reveal her slender ankle. Then it rose to calf height and continued to just above her knee.

"Looking for this?" He raised the skirt higher to reveal a stretch of firm, golden thigh encircled by an empty leather strap beneath the fading scar of Billy's wound.

"Bastard," she spit, stepping away. She waved a fist at the smug smile that said he'd like nothing better than to unsheathe another, far more dangerous, weapon. Memories of the times she had welcomed it shamed her.

"You are a fool," she attacked, honing her tongue on the sharp edges of her own broken heart. "How long do you think it will be before Roscoe knows I am gone? He won't trust me anymore, and we will lose him forever."

She glared at the cruelest, most selfish man she'd ever known—ever loved. "Then you will be sent to Georgia to hang for murder."

Sean acknowledged the truth of her words with a nod and put her knife back on his belt. He left her to go to the extra pony and reach into the saddlebag, tossing a bundle onto the blanket. "You better get out of that dress before you pass out. I have chloroform but no smelling salts."

She couldn't argue with his logic. The dress felt like it was shrinking around her body and she finally understood the snake's desire to shed its skin from time to time. She looked inside the package and found her own blue shirt and striped skirt, along with her doeskin leggings and her knife belt. Her joy at seeing her own clothes made her forget her anger.

"Where did you get these?"

"The baggage car didn't go into the gully. I made Sam retrieve your bag." His voice cracked when he added, "As a memento."

Her heart broke at the pain she'd caused him. She wanted to answer the question in his gaze. To tell him why she had to leave him; that he was better off without her, and she had a duty as ancient as life itself to perform. Yet she couldn't speak without shedding the tears pooling in her tired eyes. There was no time to weep.

He would never understand that revenge was more than her duty to Marcus and Judith. It was her right and her destiny. She'd been spared from the massacre of her village to kill the Colonel, who she now knew as Roscoe LaPorte. Because she was a weak child who shut out the memory of his face, the spirits allowed him to kill her adopted family as a reminder of her duty. Her purpose on the earth.

If she failed in her purpose now, he would kill the man she loved more than her own life. It had to stop. Roscoe had to die. She was ready to die doing it. Before her resolve weakened, she unfolded her clothes. "Turn around."

She felt his breath on her shoulder when he whispered, "But Elena, I've seen you without clothes."

She shook her head, tossing hair that now dipped below her shoulders. "When I was your wife."

"You are still my wife," he answered, emotion thickening his tongue.

"Until Santa Fe."

He sighed and stepped away. She peeled off the gown, leaving it in a heap on the ground to pull on her Indian clothes saying, "If we were ever married at all, it is over now." It surprised her she could lie so easily. Perhaps if she said it often enough, it would become the truth. A part of her would always belong to Storm Cloud. Finally, she said, "You can turn around now."

~

Sean's heart skipped a beat when he saw her in the familiar clothes. Only her hair was different from the day he fell in love with her by the forest stream. The shorter length emphasized her long neck and made her look older. No, stronger, he admitted, finally believing what she'd said about the source of her strength. It came from the faded earth, the bleached rocks, and the bright New Mexico sun. She was strong because she was finally where she belonged. She was home.

Only one thing was missing. He smiled. "Now it's your turn to turn around."

"Why?"

"Just trust me for one little minute."

With a sigh, she obeyed, shivering at the touch of his fingers along her neck, lifting her hair. When the familiar weight of her mother's silver chain returned to its home above her heart she turned to him, tears shining in her eyes.

The hope and gratitude in her eyes needed no words, and for the first time since convincing Sam Pruitt to let him fight Roscoe his own way, Sean's confidence faltered. Maybe the Ranger was right after all. Roscoe had fought the Indians in Arizona and in some of the most desolate regions of New Mexico. He lived like them, ate like them, and thought like them. He had tracked them until they were too tired to run and too hungry to fight. It would be next to impossible to beat a man who had beaten the Apache on their own ground.

Another look at Elena's innocent, brown eyes strengthened his resolve. Roscoe knew the territory, but he knew Roscoe and he was learning the lay of the land.

He was surprised at how quickly he'd adapted to everyday life in the west. He'd had no problem killing and eating rattlesnakes, prairie dogs, and even an ugly lizard called a Gila monster. The cactus, aloe, and pita bushes seemed familiar. Perhaps because they had nurtured him in the womb. His first breath was of the dry desert air, his first sight the cloudless, sapphire sky. By the time he and Sam reached Santa Fe, he'd felt as if he was finally coming home.

"You must go," interrupted his thoughts. "I may be able to explain if I get back to Santa Fe quickly." When he didn't answer, she shouted "Did you hear me?"

He nodded, looking at the flat, featureless landscape slowly rising to meet purple hills at the foot of the red mountains the Spanish priests had named, "Sangre de Christo." Blood of Christ.

"Yes, I heard you, along with anyone within a hundred acres. We're not going anywhere until we straighten a few things out."

"What things?" Her hands went to her head in frustration. "There is nothing but the danger we are in. *Madre de Dios*, what did I do to deserve this? Why did you come here?"

He smiled and took her hand to lead her to the shade of nearby boulders. Still holding it, he leaned against the relics of a world that existed long before man. "I came here to save your life."

She pulled her hand away. "You lie. You thought I was dead already."

"All right. I came here to avenge your death."

"Another lie." She folded her arms across her chest. "You came for the gold. Just like all the rest. You are no different from Roscoe." Her voice cracked at the lie.

He touched her knee. "I may be like Roscoe in many more ways than I care to be, but I don't care about that gold. It's nearly destroyed my family. I'd be happy to let it lie where it is forever if I could." The back of his hand caressed her cheek. "You made me see that there are things more valuable than gold, Hummingbird."

She relaxed like a cat against his gentle caress, the soft look in her eyes telling him she was listening. Maybe one day she'd believe him.

"It's because I am...was...so much like Roscoe that I'm here. I met him after I left college four years ago. He was exciting, dangerous, and he'd been places and seen things I could never hope to if I stayed at Langesford. I was as seduced as any innocent by his tales of adventure and fortune in the Wild West. It wasn't until I visited his New Orleans brothel that I saw him for what he was, a low-life panderer and pimp; a whoremonger and slave merchant dealing in the flesh of innocent young Indian girls."

He couldn't elaborate on the things he'd seen at, "La Fleur de L'Ouest," Roscoe's private club for men. The "flowers of the West" were ten and twelve-year-old Apache, Sioux, and Cherokee orphans. The same age as Elena when Marcus and Judith rescued her.

He risked touching her shoulder. "You can't fight him, my darling. He's a master of the game. The only reason he's let you live this long is that he thinks you can help him find the gold. Most of all, he's let you alone because he wants me to see him ravage and kill you, before he kills me."

CHAPTER THIRTY-EIGHT

*E*lena knew he was right. If Roscoe really wanted her, she could never have stopped him. Perhaps he knew Sean was alive and was just waiting for him to step into his trap—using her as bait.

"*Sí*. He hates you as he hated Marcus and Judith. He has wanted me for eight years. Only now, his hatred for you burns hotter than his lust for me."

As sudden as a winter storm in the mountains, Sean's eyes darkened. "What do you mean he's wanted you for eight years?" His cold, deadly tone frightened her more than the look of murder in his eyes, and it hurt to think he still didn't trust her.

That couldn't matter anymore. Roscoe was accustomed to getting what he wanted, and he never forgot a wrong done to him. It was only a matter of time before he tracked them down and killed them both. Sean had a right to know why.

She told him about the massacre of her village and that Marcus and Judith were not murdered solely because of the gold. She shuddered at the end of her tale and looked up at him.

"Holy Jesus," he swore. "The bastard's worse than I thought." He faced her with blood lust in his eyes. "Hanging's too good for him. He should be castrated and hung by his thumbs over a beehive and then...what?" He stopped ranting when Elena smiled

"Who is bloodthirsty now?" she said, reminding him of his reaction to her story at the Savannah House Hotel.

Silent now, he stared at her as she sat on a wind-worn rock in her blue shirt and bright skirt that barely covered the tops of her Apache leggings. He was so close. She knew he would lower his head to kiss her and she wouldn't resist him. But before she surrendered to him, she had to know more about this man who held her emotions prisoner with just his gaze. So far, he'd admitted to a dissolute life of drinking, gambling, and womanizing, without apologizing for it. She had to know how deep into Roscoe's pit he'd sunk.

She turned to watch a lizard sun himself on a small rock nearby. "Why does Senor LaPorte hate you so? You were his *compadre*, no?"

Sean's finger gently raised her chin and she was forced to see the honesty in his gaze. "Yes, Roscoe taught me everything I know about cards, dice, knives, small guns, and fighting dirty."

His answer crushed her heart, but she had to know the truth. "And the...women?"

"No. I was fascinated by where they came from, but I don't believe in paying a woman to pretend pleasure with me."

The lizard sidled away for a quieter resting place "I never knew how Roscoe's exotic Western beauties came to be with him.

"You never asked?" pronounced him guilty.

He shook his head at his own stupidity. "I thought they were there because they liked the gifts, the clothes, and the money. I never guessed they were forced, and no, I never asked. I could have helped them and never did."

He blinked back tears. "I'm so sorry, Elena. I know I've probably killed whatever spark of love you may have ever had for me. My motto was always, 'Live and let live.' I guess it only counted if I was the one living well."

She watched the play of emotions on his face. Shock, guilt, and anger at the evil he'd condoned, all registered in his eyes and the set of his jaw. She believed him, but before she could forgive him, she had one more question. "If you did not try to stop Senor LaPorte's business, why does he hate you?"

"It's a long story."

The sun moved away from them, tinting the landscape a soft, golden tan before moving west to paint the walls of the distant cliffs gold before the sun set. Elena no longer knew which god to trust, the one whom the priests had called the Son of God or the one who had painted the desert and the mountains. The one her people called, the Sun God.

She slid onto the warm ground and leaned back against the rock. "I am sure it is no longer than mine. It is too late for me to go back to Santa Fe now."

He joined her, covering her small hand with his. "I wish I could say I got an attack of morals, but I just plain got scared. I was pretty deep in the life when I figured out Roscoe was using prostitution and his crooked gambling money to buy respectability. He bragged about becoming a Senator and began buying political support, first with money and other services, and finally with blackmail. He got elected to the Georgia State Legislature by a mostly dead constituency, but no one demanded a recount. Then, he used his fame as an Indian fighter. I'm sorry," he said when Elena moaned.

"Go on," she answered through clenched teeth.

"You sure?"

"Yes," was barely audible.

He wasn't any more anxious to continue his confession than she seemed to be to hear it, but they had to pool their knowledge of their enemy before they could begin to fight him. "I had a long time in Pecos to review my life. You were right, the desert is the closest thing I've seen to both Heaven and Hell. It teaches you a whole lot about yourself, good and bad.

She nodded and he went back to the subject of the only thing they had in common now, Roscoe LaPorte. "Once Roscoe thought he was a respected public figure, he decided to expand his interests to the developing western territories through mining. Of course, I had no idea about the gold then or that I was…born here…."

"How did he plan to do that?"

Her voice brought him back from thoughts about what his parents had gone through to survive in this harsh and beautiful land. He blinked and took her hand. "Mining takes money. It's common knowledge that old money is the cleanest kind. After the Fairchilds' so-called accident, Roscoe started courting Mary Louise."

"Oh, no," she whispered, and squeezed his hand. "She would have died with him."

He nodded. "That was the plan. Then Roscoe would own Redfern Plantation and the Fairchild fortune. He'd also be a stone's throw from Langesford."

He laughed again at his own expense. "However, it seemed that while I could lay down with pigs in Atlanta, living with one right next door was another matter entirely. I've known Mary Louise since she was born. I couldn't let Roscoe get hold of her, so I took a page out of his own book and blackmailed him."

"How?"

"I threatened to expose his whorehouses, ballot fixing, and gambling operations. I had no idea what he was up to out here. He covered his tracks so well I had very little proof of what I knew; but I knew enough to raise some important eyebrows. A few well-placed rumors, and I could have stopped his political career in its tracks long enough to ruin his courtship."

She touched the coarse black beard covering his cheek. "To challenge a desperado as bad as Roscoe out of love for a childhood friend took a great deal of courage, and you are not alone in your guilt.

"When I came to Langesford, I gave Roscoe a way around your plan. By sending Billy Berens to steal me, he knew you would seek revenge. If he had succeeded, Miss Fairchild would be at Roscoe's mercy. You stopped him. Mary Louise is safe, and he can never be a senator."

He turned his head, kissing the soft skin of her palm. "Does it really look like I stopped him?" He answered for her. "No, my threats just succeeded in killing my neighbors, my parents' best friends and nearly a beautiful and innocent Apache girl. I can't say I've done anybody a whole lot of good."

"You couldn't let him marry Miss Fairchild. You had no choice."

He shook his head. "Instead, two other people have died. Three, if you call Billy a person. That's not counting those ranchers out here. There won't be an end to it, Elena, unless we find a way to trap him."

"We can kill him first. He will follow me. We can ambush him."

Her eyes glowed like they had at the Savannah House when she described the fire pit torture. Only this time it looked like she'd like to skin Roscoe before putting him on the wagon wheel. If he could, he'd start the fire himself.

He snapped his fingers in front of her glazed eyes. "It's too late for that. I'm in too deep. Catching Roscoe in the act of stealing the gold is the only way to clear my name. My father once told me that the only thing separating a fugitive from the law is the ability to think clearly."

"Be the wolf," she whispered.

He squeezed her hand. "I can think like Roscoe, but I'm not him."

"I know," she drew closer to him until their lips met.

He lifted her from the sand and carried her to the blanket. Before putting her down, she answered the question in his eyes with a nod. In moments, they lay naked together under the stars.

Sean's lovemaking was as gentle and unhurried as their night at the Blue Dawn Hotel. He took his time exploring her skin with his fingers and her mouth with his lips and tongue, until she wrapped her legs around his thighs, inviting him inside her. He kissed her lips, her throat, her breasts, with every thrust until they arched together.

They rested until the sun slowly made its way behind the mountains, and the moon took its place in the sky. Sean's fingers traced a gentle circle around the still-aroused tips of her breasts, and Elena sighed at the tickle of his breath along her throat. Then she rolled on top of him to return the pleasure his body had given hers.

He watched her. Her hair shimmering in the moonlight, her body a golden silhouette against the sand and sky as she slowly rocked back and forth to the rhythm of an eagle's wings, until passion gripped them both once again. Then they lay quietly, watching the azure sky turn purple, giving way to inky blackness.

CHAPTER THIRTY-NINE

The moon was high when a chilly breeze brushed Elena's shoulder. She woke from her comfortable slumber on Sean's chest and smiled. Her body was rested and relaxed. She felt strong again, and it was all because of the extraordinary gentleness of the man who lay sleeping beneath her.

She had thought their night together in Nashville was like a dream, but the ecstasy she experienced then was only an introduction to what a deeper knowledge of each other could bring. This was their wedding night. Their bodies had spoken their vows under the clear night sky. They were acknowledged by the four winds and sent to God on the wings of an eagle. That it might be their last taste of happiness brought another chill, and she moved to wake Sean.

Eyes the color of a wolf's pelt met hers. Though contentment had replaced passion in his silver gaze, she felt him harden beneath her, ready to once again claim her as his and his alone. He winked at what they both knew was happening. She kissed his neck and felt her own private place prepare to receive him.

Plant your seed, she prayed. Then if their lives were spared, she would have something of him after he returned to his world. Once again, they ignored the danger stalking them to claim a lifetime of love in the short time they had together.

"What's this?" Sean said as a tear trailed down her cheek. "Did I hurt you?"

"No, *Querido*," she whispered. "You would never hurt me." Remembering how much Roscoe would enjoy hurting them both cooled her passion, and she wriggled away to reach for her clothes. "We have wasted a whole day. We must hurry."

Sean rolled over onto his side, like a panther lounging after a satisfying meal. He leaned on one elbow, his long, muscled legs extending beyond the blanket and the ruined satin dress. Moonlight accented the ridges of his chest down to the shadow of his sex. It was shameless, she thought, that just looking at him made her want to feel him inside her again, breathing life into her body.

"Stop that," she said weakly. "Roscoe will kill us both just for sport. The Torres ranch belongs to me now. It is not far. We can go there to make our plan." She turned away to break the spell of his gaze and gasped when his warm length pressed against her back, sending waves of pleasure through her once again.

He made no move to touch her with his hands, though his chest, hips, and thighs molded to her curves. "Not until you admit you are my wife," he said, his voice heavy with the passion he'd just spent, and the desire they both still felt. "In Georgia, Santa Fe, and anywhere else in the world, for as long as we both shall live."

At her nod, he kissed her neck and withdrew to dress. "How long do you think we have before Roscoe comes after you?"

"He gave me a week to prepare for the wedding…"

"That won't happen."

"*Si*, but he may not wait that long," she cautioned. "Since you are also gone from Santa Fe, he will know we're together. He is as sly as he is evil. Sometimes I think he can see into the mind."

"A gambler's trick," Sean laughed. "It's a good thing you have me around. I can read Roscoe's mind like a book."

The unexpected burst of his old arrogance annoyed her and she faced him, hands on her hips. "How well can he read yours?"

He put a hand to his heart. "After all we've been through, you still doubt me?" Then the mocking lilt in his voice disappeared. "I came back from Hell for you, Elena. I felt your presence even when I couldn't feel my own body. No matter what they told me, I couldn't believe you were dead. It was the only thing keeping me alive. I refuse to let Roscoe win. It's past time for his elaborate house of cards to cave in on him, and I will bring it down, even if I die trying."

She wanted to believe him, but couldn't put aside her fears. Roscoe always seemed one step ahead of them, no matter what they did, foiling their attempts to trap him at every turn. He never gave anything without getting more back. When he gave her the Torres ranch, she knew she'd pay for it—with interest.

Sean attributed her shudder to the cool, night air. "Wear this." He tossed her a woolen poncho while he slid another one over his head. "I brought food. Can I trust you to keep the fire small enough for a pot of beans instead of a loco Gringo?"

Welcoming the warm poncho, Elena shook her head. "There is no time for a fire. We're still too close to Santa Fe. If you can read Roscoe's mind so well, then you know he will be on his way to follow us soon, if not already. We can eat cold beans and travel by the moon."

She gestured at the full moon and a sky studded with more stars than could ever be counted. "It is bright enough to keep the horses out of prairie dog holes and away from snakes. We are close to the old Taos Road. It heads true north and is wide and smooth."

All the way from Pecos, Sean hadn't seen anything resembling a real road, let alone a straight one. "Out here? How's that possible?"

"Legends say the ancient Anasazi built it. Yet they were already long dead when the conquistadors brought horses here. So no one knows how they did it or why, but it is still there for those who are willing to look for it."

"Maybe they built it for us." He put his arm around her, smiling at the thought of fate working so long ago to provide them with safe passage out of the desert.

"Perhaps." She sighed above the sound of her stomach rumbling. "Where are those beans? I'm hungry."

He opened a can and handed her a fork. "There's pork in there."

"I'm too hungry to care."

"You could be eating for two, you know." The teasing, half-smile was back.

"You give yourself too much credit, *Gringo*," she answered, praying he was right.

They packed their horses quickly for the trail. "What are you doing?" she asked when he balled up her ruined gown and pushed it behind a rock instead of stuffing it into his saddlebag. "He'll find that and know we're together. He will know where we are going."

Sean nodded while arranging the dress so it would appear hidden, but still attract the attention of someone looking for signs. "We don't want to make it too hard for him to find us," he answered. "No point stretching this out any longer than it needs to be."

She watched him, wondering if on the way from Texas, the sun had made him crazy. That happened to white men sometimes. "If you want us both to be killed so soon, why leave at all?"

"Just trust me…this once." He flexed his right leg before springing up onto the big Chestnut's back, waiting for Elena to mount the smaller pony. He handed her the knife that belonged in her Spanish belt. "We can't run from him forever. Roscoe thinks you want the gold and he knows I want you. It's time to let our prey catch us on our own terms."

She took the knife and placed it in the sheath that now rested at her waist, instead of her calf, knowing she'd have no trouble using it on either Roscoe or herself, whichever way the battle turned. With the blade resting comfortably at her side, she listened as Sean laid out his plan.

"Roscoe has no sense of right or wrong. He lives by the principle that if it benefits him, it's right. He only understands greed and cannot comprehend honesty or decency. Everything, and everyone, is a tool put on this earth to help him get what he wants, which is everything. That's why he let you live. He plans to use you to find me, and me to find the gold; and afterward, he'll kill us both and live like the king he feels he should be."

"How did you know about my plan to work with Roscoe? Did Sam tell you?"

"You mean Pruitt knew your plan and he still let you go?"

"He didn't have a choice. His duty was to protect you. I can take care of myself. I'm an—"

"Apache, yes, so you've said." He shook his head. "You're not as good an actress as you think. One look at you at Bowen's and I knew you were up to something. If I could do it, you can sure bet that Roscoe knows you're out to double-cross him. It just doesn't matter to him. He'd win either way."

"How so?"

"It was a safe bet. Roscoe knew that if I was alive, I'd show up and give him the gold to save you. If I was dead, he'd let you lead him to it. A gambler's dream come true. A hand that can't lose."

She felt stupid and naive. She thought she was so clever, and all the time, Roscoe knew she was waiting for Sean. But he was wrong. She was looking for him. The thought gave her hope. He didn't know about Sam Pruitt.

"Perhaps," she said. "But we still have one card to play. Where is Sam?"

He smiled. "I shouldn't underestimate you. You're right about Sam being our wildcard. I convinced him to let me do this my way. He's probably half way to Taos by now, to meet up with Jesse Woods."

She breathed easier, knowing Sam and Jesse were out there somewhere, waiting to save them. Still, Taos was a long way away and worry knotted her gut. "You said we shouldn't ambush Roscoe. That murder isn't the answer. We can't arrest him without Sam."

Sean's laugh joined the sounds of the night. "As much as I'd like to wait by the side of the road and feed an ounce of lead into his perverted brain, I still have a murder charge on my head. And I'm wanted for evading a law officer. Someday, I'd like to visit my family without fear of the noose."

Visit? Despite their danger, her heart filled with hope. Did that mean he planned to stay in the West? She waited for him to tell her more of his plan.

"The way I see it, Elena, the only way to stop Roscoe is to give him what he wants."

"The gold?" she whispered to avoid upsetting the spirits who guarded the Pueblos and whatever lay within them.

"The same."

CHAPTER FORTY

The Torres *rancheria* lay just south of Rancho de Taos, near the entrance to the old Taos Pueblo that protected the ancient mountain dwellings deep inside the canyons and cliffs of the Sangre de Christo Mountains. Riding was easy on the ancient, Old Taos Road, but the terrain grew increasingly rugged as it rose toward higher elevations. Traveling through the night, it was their second sunrise together before they finally saw the sturdy adobe walls built to protect the hacienda and its inhabitants from raiders and outlaws.

"It has been empty for more than a year," she told Sean. "The newspapers blamed the Apache, but Eduardo Torres and his family were no threat to them. They were good Mexican people, friends with all travelers. They shared whatever they had with those who needed help. That is also the Apache way."

They moved forward cautiously, both hoping Roscoe hadn't out-thought them to come directly to their haven. While much of the wall surrounding the Spanish style ranch house was intact, the wooden gate to the courtyard was torn from its stone moorings, lying like a fallen soldier in the wake of an enemy invasion.

Still in the shelter of the mountain aspens, Elena dismounted to check for tracks of shod horses, white men's boots, or any other sign that someone else had been there recently. Her smile signaled it was safe to move forward. Stepping over the gate, she shuddered as if she'd stepped on a grave. Grief settled around her heart the moment they entered a courtyard lush with flowers grown wild. This was once a happy home and would be still, if not for Roscoe LaPorte's lust for gold.

Her hatred for him strengthened her resolve as they walked past another door torn from its hinges lying beneath a tile roof supported by strong, adobe pillars. Then she circled the house to the back wall of carefully fitted desert stones. It rose solid and uninterrupted above her head to the edge of a steep ravine separating the nearly flat plateau from the cliffs to the East.

Protected by the ravine and the wall, that side of the house seemed untouched by the violence so evident inside the courtyard. The unbroken line of red clay roof tiles gleamed at her in the sunlight and the soft, sand-colored walls spoke to her of strength and courage.

Sean followed her silently back to the front of the house, assessing the place where they'd confront Roscoe. Their backs were adequately protected by the rear courtyard wall and ravine. Only a few small windows faced the front.

He looked out at the steep, colorful cliffs surrounding them. "Why don't any windows face that spectacular view?"

"Defense."

"I see." His smile was slow. "It's a fortress."

She was lost in thoughts of finding wood to replace the rotted poles supporting the roof between pillars, and how to repair the old adobe walls if they survived Roscoe. "*Si*. It is difficult to breach a house when there are few ways in." Not wanting Sean to feel too secure in the little hacienda, she pointed to the gate. "Still, it can be done. Anyone who knows the Apache could do it." The set of her jaw told him she knew that Roscoe could do anything an Apache could do.

Sean dismounted to kiss the worried furrow in her brow. "It doesn't matter. We're not hiding. We're waiting." He scooped her into his arms. "It may be your house, Mrs. O'Grady," he said lightly. "But I'm still carrying you over the threshold."

"Why? I can walk."

He twirled her around to face the sagging door and pushed it open with his boot. "It's white man's magic for good luck, a long marriage, and many children."

"I hope it is strong magic." She buried her head in his shoulder.

"Oh, it is." He settled her on her soft moccasins inside a room that had nearly returned to the wilderness from which it was carved. Dust, tumble-weeds, and animal signs marred the once polished tile floor. Plastered walls, once fresh with whitewash, were stained dark by blood from the Torres family's struggle and rain pouring through bullet holes in the roof. What few furnishings remained were broken and ruined, horsehair stuffing skittering around the floor like tumbleweeds.

Elena stared at the shambles for which she had sold her soul. The blood on the walls belied rumors of the Torres family being murdered in their beds by renegade Apache, but she wasn't prepared for the violence that had been done here. She shivered from the family's terror as the enemy overwhelmed them. She could almost see Anscombe's evil smile as he destroyed their precious possessions, and killed their children before torturing Eduardo and his wife Celia. She closed her eyes before another scene of violence clouded her senses entirely.

Sean steadied her with a hand on her waist. He waved the other at the mess. "Never mind this. A broom and a good scrubbing will take care of it. We're not going to be here long anyway. I'm hungry, and we could use some sleep. Let's find the kitchen and bedroom."

His wink told her which room would satisfy both his needs. She nodded, leading him down a short corridor to a closed door still solid on hinges that had protected it from the larger mountain creatures.

She let out a long-held breath when Sean pushed the door open to reveal that the bedroom, though dirty, was intact. Two of the legs of a huge four-poster bed were broken, but could be easily set back into place. The trunk at the foot had been looted, linens strewn about the room. Stepping inside, she no longer felt fear. No violence had been done there. Looking from the bed to her husband, she only felt love.

Sean woke just before dawn the next morning in a bed made with freshly aired linens still carrying the scent of pine and pinion. He washed and dressed quickly, following the delicious aroma of food and fresh coffee from a room off one of the corridors that ran like a maze through the hacienda.

After a few dead ends, he found a cheerful little room with a fire in the grate and water heating on the stove. It was free of debris, smelling faintly of lye soap and the presence of a woman; but it was a phantom presence. The room was empty. He turned at a soft voice singing in the courtyard and followed it to find Elena wearing Mrs. Torres' white cotton wrapper.

She stood outside the gate, her arms raised, facing the sun just rising above mountains fringed by poplars tipped with early autumn gold. Her back to him, she sang to it in her ancient tongue. Finally, her song finished, she held her arms above her head until the shimmering golden orb leaped into their circle to rule over a sky blushing pink in its presence.

As if at her bidding, the earth brightened under the rising sun's gaze, sending shadows scurrying to the depths of the forest until the dull gray landscape was painted in hues that only God could imagine. Accustomed to the slow, somber sunrises of Georgia, where night retreated leisurely into a cotton-colored mist, and a lazy pink sun hovered over the pastel landscape, Sean stood in awe.

The sky had turned to azure by the time Elena finished her final prayer. He stepped up behind her. His body pressed against her curves, he caressed her warm cheek and soft hair. "Good morning Hummingbird," he whispered as his lips followed the path of his fingers.

She turned to him with a sigh. Then she jumped back, stifling a scream. He'd shaved, with only slightly lighter skin on his jaw as evidence that a beard had once shielded his skin from the sun. Instead of his own blue shirt and denim jeans, he wore a peasant shirt and leggings covered by an Apache loincloth. A red bandanna around his forehead held back his thick black hair long overdue for a trim.

"Storm Cloud," Elena gasped. Then her eyes narrowed. It was only a masquerade. He couldn't hope to believe that if he dressed like an Apache, he would be an Apache, any more than dressing up in a ball gown had made her a white lady.

"What are you doing?"

He nodded toward a tiny column of dust rising from the lowlands to their south. "Company is coming."

The worry in his gaze betrayed the smile on his lips, telling Elena that their play at being *hacendados*, the Patron and his Lady, was finished before it began. A rare cloud crossed the newly risen sun as fear crippled her.

"Roscoe?" She couldn't let Sean, or Roscoe know how much she feared him. Sean would make her hide and Roscoe would kill them both. Sean pulled her into his arms and she felt his heart beat steady against her cheek. "Trust me," he whispered, and led her into the house.

Later, wearing her skirt and shirt, Elena stood in the shade of the covered porch, watching Roscoe ride through the broken gate, his horse's hooves scattering purple and yellow flowers. He reined in his lathered animal so suddenly it reared, almost unseating the experienced ex-cavalryman before he leaped to the ground and strode toward her.

She couldn't resist a smirk at his new growth of beard and sweat-stained silk shirt. The smile disappeared when his hate-filled black eyes met hers. He passed her without acknowledgment, kicking the front door and sending it slamming to the floor.

"Where the hell are you, O'Grady?" he roared on his way through the house, sending more doors crashing into walls. Without finding him, he stomped back out to face Elena. "Where is the son of a bitch? I know he's here. I can smell him."

He leaned over her. "I can smell him on you. You should think twice before you lie to me, bitch. I don't give second chances."

She now saw him for what he was. He was the wolf her father had taught her to understand. It pleased her that despite his snarl, he was confused. He could smell his prey, but he couldn't find it. Their victory was small, yet they had fooled him. Perhaps they could confuse him enough to triumph against him.

She put her hands on her hips. "You have been in the sun too long, *Senor*. It is but a week until our wedding and I came here to prepare my home for afterward, when I am free. I planned to return to Santa Fe today, but now I have a door to repair or the coyotes will be sleeping in my bed."

~

Roscoe was still breathing hard from the ride that began when Elena didn't show up to spot for Dooley the night after his showdown with O'Grady. He asked around and found that the big, red-haired cowboy, who rode into Santa Fe with Sean, had ridden out alone that morning. There was a bad smell about both Sean and Elena missing; and the cowboy sounded a lot like the man who confronted Hobbs in Nashville. He quickly mobilized Junior and four Mexicans for a skunk and beaver hunt.

Instinct told him they were together and they'd hole up at the Torres place. He swore he'd get what he wanted out of Elena in front of Sean. He'd do a little fancy knife work on the boy and let him watch Anscombe and his men do what they wanted with her. Then he'd slit the uppity Sean O'Grady's throat and let her watch him die—before tying her naked to a stake in the desert for the buzzards to finish.

With Sean nowhere to be found, Roscoe slapped her hard across her mouth. He stepped back, smiling as a mark shaped like his hand reddened her face and a thin line of blood trickled from the corner of her lips. "Don't lie to me, cunt," he shouted, sniffing the air for the scent of her fear and listening for signs of her hero coming to her rescue.

Only the sound of breezes rustling through the aspens answered him, while Elena faced him woodenly, letting the blood drip onto her shirt. Disgusted, he pushed her out of his way and crossed the courtyard to where her pony stood alone. The tracks of his own horse made it impossible to see if another one had been in the courtyard. O'Grady was there. He knew it.

"Come out you coward," he shouted. "Watch me kill your whore." Silence. The wind stopped and not even the birds dared trill. He turned then and strode back to Elena, brushing the dust of the trail off his clothes along the way.

Touching her swollen lip tenderly, as if he'd forgotten the print on her face was caused by his own hand, he sighed. "Well, it seems I was mistaken." Then brighter, "No matter. Since we're here, we may as well get on with it." He pushed her roughly off the porch into the courtyard, then stepped toward her.

She spit blood onto his expensive shirt. "Get on with what?"

His fist slammed against the other side of her jaw. She stumbled, but refused to fall. "Stupid Indian whore," he hissed through pressed lips. "What do you think? The gold. Take me to it. Now."

"What about our wedding? It was what you wanted."

Roscoe cocked his head at the violence done to her beautiful face. His mouth twisted and his laugh was cruel. "You don't expect me to marry you looking like this, do you?" Disgust colored his voice. "You're a filthy Indian beggar. How could you presume I would ever marry you and take you to Washington?"

"Then what do you want?" Her feet spread apart, bracing for the next blow.

He smiled at her flinch when his long finger traced the cheek he'd battered so efficiently. "Don't play the stupid greaser with me, Elena, lead me to the gold now or—"

"Or what?" A deep, and equally threatening voice spoke from the darkness inside the house.

Roscoe swatted Elena's battered cheek one more time before he turned around to crow, "I knew you were here. Where did you hide?" His hand inched toward the pistol strapped to his thigh.

Sean stepped into the light brandishing a shotgun. "I was paying a little visit to your men down the slope," Sean answered. "Now unbuckle the gun belt."

CHAPTER FORTY-ONE

*E*lena rushed to take Roscoe's holster.

"And his boot and right sleeve," Sean told her curtly. "A knife and pistol." She followed his orders silently.

The ice in his voice puzzled her, and when she looked up, her stomach lurched. Sean's eyes now glowed with the same madness as Roscoe's. Confused, she stood in the center of her courtyard, staring from the man she hated to the man she loved and seeing little difference.

Roscoe crossed his arms over his chest staring at Sean. "A visit you say? Junior's men are trained assassins, cunning as wolves, so I find that hard to believe, old friend."

"I thought you might feel that way, old friend," Sean mimicked, and stepped back into the shadows of the house.

Though her heart trusted Sean with her life, Elena wondered if he too, had caught the gold fever. She considered running away from both crazy white men, but lost her chance to bolt when Sean dropped four gun belts onto the wood floor.

The pearl handles of Junior Anscombe's pistols winked at them in a rainbow of reflected colors from the sun directly overhead. "Proof enough?" Sean said, raising Roscoe's bet.

The older man raised his hands. "You're holding the cards, son," he growled back. A breath later, he called Sean's bluff, pushing Elena closer so Sean could see the bruises on her face. "What's next?" he taunted. "Did you tire of the squaw already and want the gold for yourself and that sweet little piece of tail back in Georgia? I won't forgive you for that, you know.

"I worked hard to make her available to me. Arranging an accident for members of one of Georgia's founding families is very expensive; but all is not lost. Everything happens for the good, it seems. Now I won't have to put up with her incessant whining while I sell off her inheritance for my... expedition.

"Your expedition is cancelled La Porte. The only place you're going is Hell at the end of a rope."

Roscoe didn't blink. "How do you plan to do that. The last I heard, you were being hunted for murder." He nodded toward Elena. "If you're not here for the chit, you're here for the gold." He stepped forward, stopping when Sean cocked the rifle.

Roscoe grabbed Elena's arm, pulling her in front him. "Your parents must have told you where it is. Tell me, how do you plan to get it out? And when you do, what will you do with it? You are a fugitive. There are even wanted posters for you in Santa Fe. Dead or alive."

His voice lowered, "You need a partner, O'Grady. I've already laid the legal groundwork for mining leases, I just need the location. You can have Elena's share, twenty-five percent of the profits. It would set you up like a king in Mexico City."

Sean cast a stranger's gaze at Elena and shrugged. "Fifty percent of the whole take. Tell me how you plan to get it out."

Roscoe kicked Elena's backside, this time sending her sprawling face first onto the ground. "The little bitch was supposed to lead me to it, but your cock got in the way. The minute I register the location on my lease, we're good to start melting down those bars and shipping it down to Mexico."

He sidestepped Elena as if she were a horse pile, taking one slow step at a time toward Sean. "You're a bright boy, Seany. Berens was scum. I can make that murder charge go away with a single telegram. With your family's connections to Washington, you can keep the inspectors off our backs. I'm willing to let bygones be bygones if you are. I'll even throw in the girl," he chuckled. "Though she seems a little the worse for wear."

Sean appraised Elena as if she were naked on the block in a Mexican slave market and shook his head. "I've had my fill. You can have her."

Her soul died the moment Sean rejected her, but her body refused to stop breathing. He had asked her to trust him no matter what, but she could see nothing in his eyes to call his statement false. No man who truly loved a woman could lie that well. Not even a white man. None of this was going according to the plan they'd laid out at dawn.

Sean had planned to use his Indian disguise to run off Anscombe's horses. While they were chasing them, he would go to Taos for Sam. In the meantime, if Roscoe appeared, she was supposed to convince him she planned to go ahead with their agreement. Then, on the way back to Santa Fe for the wedding, Sam and Sean would arrest Roscoe for kidnapping another man's wife. That was how it was supposed to be. Not like this.

"No thanks," Roscoe laughed.

Insults no longer wounded her. She was already dead. Gold sickness had replaced her husband with a demon and Sam Pruitt wasn't coming. Morning Bird was right. They would all die because of that cursed gold. Stepping back into the courtyard, she shouted, "S-stay away from me, both of you. You are on my land. Get off it now." She waved an arm toward the impotent gate.

Both men smiled and spoke with one voice, "Not without the gold."

Sean loaded the extra weapons onto a packhorse and rode behind Elena and Roscoe along a trail rising steadily upward, until it became a narrow, rocky path only Elena could see. His heart broke at the sight of her drooping shoulders and the stricken glances she stole under the guise of checking the ancient trail.

He saw that his betrayal hurt her more than the bruises on her face; but their lives depended on them both playing their roles convincingly. She may have thought she was a good actress, but she wore her love, her honor, and her decency on her face. She'd never make Roscoe believe they weren't together. This way, she had no choice.

He rode silently, praying their plan would work. For trained assassins, Anscombe and the Mexicans had been embarrassingly easy to ambush. They didn't even post a guard as they sat around their little camp joking about what they would do with Elena when Roscoe was finished with her.

When he ran off their horses, they were easy for him to pick off. The ones he didn't kill took off running. He let them go, except for Anscombe. They needed him alive to testify at Roscoe trial; but alive was all he had to be, so after making sure Anscombe's pretty face would no longer attract innocent girls, and his body ever debauch a virgin again, Sean tied him up as they had Jesse, and left him tethered to a tree. If they survived Roscoe,

Junior would rot in prison instead of hanging. If not, well, they'd all meet again in Hell—except Elena.

Still, a gunslinger's testimony against an ex-cavalry hero wouldn't carry a lot of weight with a judge who was controlled by the Santa Fe Ring, and getting a confession out of Roscoe was as likely as getting a snake to spit out a mouse. They had to give him enough rope to warrant a trial in the states. They had to catch him in the act of stealing Federal gold.

Two hours into the trail, Roscoe chuckled over his shoulder. "Looks like you broke her little heart, son. Be careful or she'll get even by taking your scalp."

"I'll take care of her when this is all over. The San Carlos Reservation should keep her urges for scalping under control."

Elena's back stiffened and Roscoe howled in amusement. "How fitting. After eight years, she'll be back where she started. If those missionaries hadn't interfered, she'd be the queen of my Flowers of the West. Now it's too late. Thanks to you, she's damaged goods."

As each lash of Roscoe's cruel tongue scoured Elena's heart, Sean fought the urge to shoot him and throw his body over one of the ever-deepening ravines, but Roscoe was the only one who could clear him of the murder charge. The cards had been dealt, and the game had to be played out.

"Shut up before I shoot you now," he ordered.

"Temper, temper," Roscoe taunted.

Elena stopped at a place on the trail that widened onto a little mesa and turned on them, speaking for the first time since taking to the trail. "Be quiet, both of you. Your voices will wake the spirits who guard the pueblos," she said with a venomous stare at Roscoe. Then to Sean, "Your gun will bring the whole mountain down on us. I do not wish to die with two loco Gringos."

Sean smiled at the anger flashing from her beautiful eyes. She wasn't out of the game yet. With Roscoe in tow, he rode up next to her and looked across the chasm. A circular series of mesas and buttes cut into the mountain range by wind and rain, formed what the Indians called the Enchanted Circle. Even from far away, they could see the dark recesses of caves carved by the ancient Anasazi into the red, sandstone cliffs.

"There are your caves," she told him flatly. "Where we will all die."

More primitive than the many-storied cliff homes below them in Rancho de Taos, they still showed the ancient foot trails leading from one to the other, as well as the crudely cut toe and hand-holds leading to the upper level homes. Yet while they could see them clearly, there seemed to be no way to reach them across the canyon.

"Bitch!" Roscoe's shriek bounced off the rocks and returned to them several times. "You tricked us. We'll never get to the gold from here."

Sean pulled Elena's knife from his own belt, turning it over in his palm. Then he held it up to his forehead, like a knight saluting her with his sword. The sun reflected off the polished silver blade, in a flashing yellow and white light. "A fine weapon," he said before giving it to her.

Surprise lit her eyes as she realized Sean had not left her after all. She remembered the flashing reflections the soldiers had used to signal each other in the canyons. Was he signaling Sam and Jesse? She could only pray it was so.

With a regal nod, she took the weapon and placed it in her moccasin boot. Then she turned her pony away from the outcropping to plunge through a narrow opening between solid rocks, disappearing into the thin mountain air. Roscoe forced his reluctant horse to follow, and Sean went in last, wondering if Elena really would lead them all to their deaths rather than the gold.

Instead of falling hundreds of feet to the rocky ground below, their horses found sure footing on a new trail. It dipped dramatically, then rose, widening out again toward another level of cliff dwellings, and descending from there to the floor of a box canyon.

He marveled that the ancient trail along the canyon walls was suddenly wide enough for a team of horses and a wagon, until they came to a rockslide that was too treacherous to ride through. "We walk the horses from here," Elena ordered, jumping off her mount.

"Easy, LaPorte," Sean reminded Roscoe as he leaped from his mount and nearly pushed past them to search the caves on his own.

Elena faced Sean with a plea in her eyes, begging him to end this madness. It also told him that despite his betrayal, she loved him. "Let him go," she begged. "He can spend his life searching, even this close, and still never find the gold."

She faced Roscoe and spit at his feet. "The Ancient ones were very clever. There are hundreds of caves in these mesas that cannot be seen. Even if you stand right in front of them. Your gold is in such a one."

Ignoring Sean, she waved him on his way. "Go, look for it until you die of thirst. Until the buzzards claim your body and the Devil claims your soul."

Sean's heart broke for her, but for the sake of finishing the charade, he looked down at her and growled, "Don't play with us, Elena. Show us the cave and I may reconsider San Carlos."

"Enough sweet talk O'Grady," Roscoe shouted. "Make the bitch do her job. Let's get going."

Elena searched Sean's face one last time, but he kept his lips drawn in a thin line, until she bowed her head. "I will show you the gold, Gringos, but you will die for it." Turning her back to them, he heard her whisper, "We all will."

As they picked their way through the debris blocking the old trail, Sean turned pale. His breath came in shallow gasps, and dizziness threatened to throw him off the cliff. Crawling hand over hand around a rock barrier, his lungs seemed to empty of air, his skin chilled beneath his clothes. He stopped to lean against the warm stone wall behind him. He'd been here before.

As impossible as it was for him to remember something from when he was little more than a baby, he realized they were close to where his parents had faced Three Feathers. The place where his father had found his missing gold, and his mother found the brother she thought was buried at Langesford.

"That gold is cursed," his mother had cried in the Langesford study. He didn't believe her then. Now her words throbbed in his head.

The wall finally stopped spinning and he met Elena's stare. "Humming-bird," was all he could say to her beautiful, sad face.

She ignored Roscoe to scramble back to help him take the final steps of their journey together.

"Very touching," Roscoe spoke from behind them. Anscombe's pistol from Sean's saddlebag was pointed at Elena's head. "Drop the scattergun, O'Grady or I'll kill her first."

Holding tight to Elena with one arm, Sean tossed the shotgun over the cliff. It clattered against the rocks in its downward spiral, to land without a sound on the canyon floor hundreds of feet below them.

"Looks like you can't take heights boy," Roscoe taunted. "Don't worry. You'll be down there before long." He turned his attention to Elena. "Now you, my little Indian whore. Lead me to the gold."

At Sean's nod, she smiled into Roscoe's hate-distorted face. "You stupid, white-eyed Gringo. You are standing right in front of it and still you do not see it." She pointed behind him to what looked like another pile of rubble from a rockslide. "In there, just beyond those rocks. Go. Your treasure is calling for you."

Roscoe's gun hand never wavered as he watched them pull away the rocks Elena and Jesse had so carefully placed after their visit. As the sun slid lower in the sky and the mountains turned from blood-red to brilliant gold, they opened a space big enough for one person to enter at a time. Roscoe gestured for them to crawl inside first.

"Let her go, LaPorte," Sean said before taking a step. "She did what you wanted. Let her go back to her ranch. She earned it."

Roscoe's black eyes reflected the dying sun. "Or, since I don't need her anymore, or you for that matter, I could just shoot you both here and let the buzzards pick at both your scrawny bones down below. Now move."

"No." The strength in Elena's voice made both men pause. "I am one of the People. If you want to live, you must follow me."

"Ladies' first," Roscoe chuckled, pushing Sean in after her and following them both into the semi-darkness. He motioned toward a torch lying near the opening. "Light it," he ordered Sean

The oil-soaked rags on the torch she and Jesse had used in setting their trap still smelled of smoke as Sean's match ignited them. Roscoe smiled as he took the light and slowly crossed to the center of the spacious cavern.

Just a few feet away, near the entrance, lay the skeletons of two men with a few metal buttons still clinging to the rotted threads of their clothing. Soldiers. Yankee or Rebel, they couldn't tell. Two other bodies farther back in the cave revealed the horror of their deaths, arrows still imbedded between their bones. Opposite the entrance, against the far back wall, stood the canvas-covered stack of gold bricks that had cost them their lives.

A flash of sulfur and the smell of more oily rags burning filled the room when Roscoe lit another torch in its niche. Then two more lighted the cave like a cozy evening fire. Finally, with the smoke curling upward through the ancient ventilation system, Roscoe approached the golden goddess of his dreams. Like a priest at an altar, he bent to one knee and bowed his head. A moment later, he removed the canvas with the flourish of a magician on a stage.

Sean's jaw tensed in the flickering light, watching Roscoe like a hunter watches its prey. When he moved, it wasn't with the sudden spring of a panther that Elena had dreamed him to be. Rather, he swaggered noisily toward Roscoe. He reached toward one of the gold bricks, praying she would trust him this one last time.

"Don't," she and Roscoe shouted at the same time. He froze and bats took to flight from the darkness beyond the torches.

Then Roscoe reached out to touch the gold bar and, "No," again sent bats screaming to the deeper recesses of their home.

Roscoe turned, his fingers just inches away from his treasure. His dark eyes were empty black holes in a face shiny with sweat. His breathing was labored in the high mountain air, his smile rapturous at being so close to what had been his obsession for so long. Then rapture turned to cunning, and cunning became evil. He waved the pistol at Sean.

"Get back. It's mine."

Sean fixed his gaze on his enemy. In a low voice, like a mesmerist putting his subject into a trance, he spoke. "How do you figure that, Roscoe?"

Safe behind Anscombe's pistol, the older man bragged, "I earned it."

"How?"

"You just get stupid, O'Grady? That gold has been like the Holy Grail for half the army officers out here since '62. For me, it's personal. I was in charge of the mint guard when it was robbed. It ruined my career. Killin' Indians gave me an excuse to track down the gray-bellied cowards who stole my future along with the gold.

"I knew those no-good Rebs wouldn't get far hauling a wagon loaded with gold bars. We followed them to the base of Sangre de Christos until their tracks disappeared into thin air. It was like they went through a hole in the mountain and never came out. The Army gave up but I kept searching, making a little money on the side sellin' squaws and scalps."

He grinned at Elena's gasp, then bragged, "When Anscombe came to me with Ned Butler's little book and Mills' map, I was closer than I'd been in twenty years."

Under the flickering torchlight, his smile looked like the fangs of a mountain lion. "Then your little pet here gave me the last piece of the puzzle."

"What puzzle?" Sean said, encouraging Roscoe to think he was indeed stupid, urging him to confess to what they already knew.

"The puzzle of who was behind the robbery," he crowed. "Butler's story gave me the breed and the missionaries early on, but no idea of the couple who turned the gold over to Douglas and his men. After Anscombe mistakenly told me the breed died without talking, I had no choice but to go after the old man and the bitch."

Elena eyes widened in horror as he gloated, "When Anscombe wired me that the little cunt was heading your way, it was like Christmas. There I was, practically sitting right on top of the goose with the golden egg."

His voice deepened. "Then that imbecile Berens got horny and you interfered with my plans again." He pointed a finger. "It's the last time you will, by the way."

Sean kept his voice low and uninterested. "So, it was you who killed Berens." He held his breath for the confession that would free him of the murder charge.

Roscoe's laugh echoed through the many chambers of the cave. "Put him out of his misery is more like it. You used him pretty hard. He came stumbling into my kitchen naked, his balls and prick bruised up, his face a bloody pulp. Made a mess on my floor. Well, I couldn't let him get away with that, could I?"

"I suppose not," Sean agreed, fueling Roscoe's descent into insanity. They needed more facts that they could prove so he could hand him over to Sam with his fate sealed. If nothing else, he'd at least go to jail for Billy's murder.

Roscoe's head bobbed in agreement. "Damn right, I couldn't, so I took him outside. One bullet in the space between his ears where his brain should have been ended his suffering, and I was back in the game. That fool Sheriff Coulter was only too happy to go after you."

Sean held his breath as he slid one foot after the other, closer and closer to Roscoe, encouraging him to brag more about his crimes. When he was close enough, instead of taking the gun, he again reached past Roscoe to one of gold bars that extended a little askew from the others.

"No." Roscoe and Elena both shouted again and he pulled back. Elena rushed to take his arm, while Roscoe waved the pistol madly, shouting, "Get away."

Sean laughed in his enemy's face. "You don't think I'd leave loaded weapons in my saddlebag, do you? You have a very bad habit of underestimating me."

To test his word, Roscoe pointed the gun at Sean's chest and pulled the impotent trigger. The light faded from his eyes when Sean snatched the weapon, flipped the empty carriage open and began methodically loading bullets into it. "Now, this is what we're going to do..."

"No," echoed again, this time from deeper inside the rock chamber. Elena stood in the back of the cave holding the last torch in one hand and a stick of dynamite in the other. The images in front of her flickered in the thin air that fed the flame, but her voice was steady.

Just behind her lay the skeleton of a packhorse. Four leather bags strewn open around the bones exposed the rest of the dynamite used to blow the wall out of the Denver Mint nearly thirty years ago. She knew old dynamite could sputter out like a dead cigar, or it could blow just from the thought of lighting it. So be it.

"Put it down, Elena," Sean said quietly. "There's no need."

"She's bluffing," Roscoe yelled.

Once again, centuries of racial hatred burned in Elena's blood as she faced the cold-blooded murderer of her family. She was no longer afraid of Morning Bird's warning. She would have her revenge, even if she died for it. Even if her love died for it.

"The spirits of my people say there is a need," she spat at them both. "The spirits of my father and my brother say there is a need." She lowered the torch closer to the fuse. "The spirits of my adopted parents say there is a need. So, this is what we are going to do."

"Elena," Sean shouted. "Don't…"

"No," a deep voice echoed from the darkness where the bats had fled, "I'll tell you what we're going to do."

Sean reached Elena before she could light the fuse. He pried the explosive, slick with the yellow residue of nitroglycerin that could have exploded without lighting the fuse. Laying it gently on the ground, he pulled her away from it while Roscoe paced back and forth in front of the gold, looking for the source of the voice.

"Who are you?" he shouted "Show yourself. I'm a Colonel of the US Army. You are under arrest for trespassing."

Sam Pruitt stepped out of what seemed to be a solid rock wall, into the light of the sputtering torches. "No, LaPorte. You are under arrest. For multiple murders, corruption, trafficking in Indian slaves, and kidnapping."

His features slowly came into view, his smile visible in the semi-darkness. "That's all that comes to mind now, but I'm sure I'll think of more between here and Santa Fe."

Stunned at Sam's appearance and shaking from what she'd almost done, Elena looked from him to Roscoe, and finally to Sean, seeing what she needed to see. His eyes were clear. The spell of the gold was gone.

"Elena," the Sean she knew said softly and she fell into his open arms.

Roscoe took the distraction to pick up another discarded stick of dynamite. "Get out," he shouted, parrying and thrusting the explosive like a sword. "The gold is mine."

Sean backed Elena toward the entrance of the cave.

"Now what're you going to do with that little stick, LaPorte?" Sam's deep voice said. "Drop it and you'll blow us all to kingdom come, along with the gold. What good will that do?"

Roscoe eyes glowed with feral glee, his teeth bared. "It doesn't matter. If I die, you all die too. You're a decent man, Pruitt. You won't let an innocent woman die, will you?" he keened.

Sam's hesitation gave him his answer. "Now back away."

"Do it Sam." Elena had stepped out of the protective circle of Sean's arm to face Roscoe from across the cave. "You are right. It is yours. You wanted it even before it was stolen from the Mint. You have searched for it for a generation. You have earned it."

Sam put a hand on Sean's arm when he would have stopped her, and they listened to her voice sooth the savage beast. Softly, in a mystical, musical rhythm, she purred. "See how she glows in the torchlight for you, *Senor*. Only you. It is cold here by the trail, but where you are, by the gold, it is warm. *Si?*"

He nodded. Entranced by the music of her voice, he stopped waving the dangerous explosive. "Yes, I feel it. It's been waiting for me all these years."

"Don't you long to touch it?" Elena coaxed. "Put down that stick and touch her. She is hot for you, waiting for you, begging for your caress. See how she has reached out for you with her golden hand?"

All three men followed the wave of her hand to the wayward bar Sean had nearly removed. In the quiet voice that tamed wild horses, Elena continued. "The stick, it frightens her. Before you can touch her, you must put it down."

She approached the stack. "Come here, and kneel before her, your golden queen. Then, and only then, you can embrace your love. She will be yours forever."

"Yes," he crooned back and pushed her back toward Sean. "She wants me." Then a moment of clarity returned to his eyes and he seemed surprised they were still there. He laughed, taunting them again with the stick. "Get out! Leave us alone."

Sean, Elena and Sam obeyed, edging closer to the cave opening while Roscoe faced his idol, dropped to his knees and reached for the beckoning hand of his siren. He pulled it out, so thrilled with its smooth skin shimmering in the flickering torchlight, he didn't feel the tremor of the pyramid wall shifting in front of him. Still kneeling, he looked up just as the bar at the top hit his collarbone, breaking it.

One-by-one, then two-by-two, they tumbled toward him like golden dominos, gaining speed as they moved forward. He leaned back, stretching out his good arm as the bricks engulfed him. "No," he screamed as they battered his head and face, advancing on him as if they were alive, until they covered him like a torn, golden blanket.

Dust from the collapse snuffed out the torches as the three bystanders covered their faces. When it settled, they stepped forward to find that only Roscoe's bloody and broken right hand had escaped the crushing gold bars. Like his life, it was empty.

During the few moments that ended Roscoe LaPorte's life, the sun gave way to a full harvest moon and the three survivors stepped from the darkness into its light. The rubble inside the cave seemed to shimmer in homage to Father Moon.

Sean wiped the sweat and dust from his face. "Looks like it was rigged to fall when that lower brick was moved." He understood then that Elena's scream when he reached for it had nothing to do with mountain spirits. He pulled her into his arms. "Your handiwork, I suppose."

"No," she confessed. "Jesse studied engineering from Judith's books. He knew how to stack them so they would fall exactly where Roscoe would be standing."

He kissed her, whispering in her ear, "We've got to start trusting each other my love or we may very well kill each other."

She pulled away first and looked at Sam, who was leaning against the sun-warmed mountain wall, lighting a cigar in the corner of his mouth. "Finish it."

He shook his head and nodded toward Sean. "Not my call."

Sean heard his mother's voice again, urging him, "If you find it, destroy it." Her fingers had bit into his arms, her eyes boring into his soul. "Melt it, bury it, throw it down to the canyon floor, but don't take it, any of it, with you." At the time, the intensity of her plea and the fact that he never really expected to find it, made him agree.

Now they'd found it. A king's fortune in pure, minted gold. More than any man could earn in a hundred lifetimes as a planter or a rancher. And the cave was safer than any bank on earth.

His eyes sparked with mischief when he turned to Elena. "That's a lot of money, Hummingbird." Then he used the same argument his father had twenty-five years ago. "The reward alone is more than we could ever make on your ranch."

Like his mother, she stood firm, Father Moon glowing like a halo behind her head. He took it as a sign. She was his gold; her love his treasure. Like his father before him, he sighed. "What do you want me to do?"

"Blow it up."

He looked at her in surprise. "You want me to go back in there?"

"No." She bent to move a stone near the cave entrance and picked up a new fuse. "It leads to the dead pack horse." At his raised eyebrow, she explained, "Jesse and I planted it in case Roscoe didn't risk pulling the loose brick."

When they were safely away from the opening, at the end of the new fuse, Sam handed him his lit cigar.

They were well along the wide trail leading down to the canyon when the mountain belched rock, earth and golden rain from the sacred Pueblos down to the canyon floor. Sean turned toward the explosion, but Elena stopped him with a touch. "Don't look back."

He squeezed her hand. "I just blew up a king's fortune. Can't I at least see the spectacle?"

She shook her head. "Look at me and see the future, not the past."

CHAPTER FORTY-TWO

*S*now dusted the courtyard of Elena's hacienda. It shimmered under a sun just rising above white-capped mountain peaks as she and Sean stepped outside to watch two riders approach. She was wrapped in a bright woolen blanket and Sean wore a sheepskin jacket against the late November chill. He shielded his eyes against the sun's glare.

"I'll be damned," he said.

He left Elena staring at his back as he ran out toward the riders.

She followed at a slower pace, matching her moccasins to his widely-spaced boot prints. One of the riders gave a whoop and removed his Stetson hat.

"Sam," she shouted and forgot the wet snow to run to him. When the second rider approached, she stopped short. "Clay," she whispered when her brother-in-law leaped off a huge black stallion and embraced Sean.

The walk back to the house was filled with a blend of masculine voices, overwhelming the one female in the group. Elena finally stopped trying to be heard and let them take care of the horses while she went inside to prepare coffee and a breakfast of eggs, chilies, and tortillas. "Do not talk of anything that you will only have to repeat to me later," she ordered. "I do not want to miss a thing."

Later, while Sam and Clay ate ravenously, she waited impatiently to hear what had happened since they left Sam on the trail after the explosion. For two months, they'd been waiting for word on whether Sam's testimony about Roscoe's confession would clear Sean of the murder charge against him.

Clay finished eating first. "Mother insisted I bring Orion out here. I met Sam in Pecos. The trestle over the Salt Draw is back up, by the way."

He winked at Sam who had a mouthful of eggs. "I met the woman who helped my brother get well. Her name is Petunia, or Daisy. I don't know. It was some kind of flower I think," he said grinning at Sam's discomfort.

"Rosa," Elena said. "You met Rosa? How is she?" She realized how fond she'd become of the Mexican saloonkeeper. A glance at Sam, who concentrated a little too intently on washing down his food with a big swig of hot coffee, told her he was too.

Clay answered for him. "Mighty fine, I'd say. She's quite the lady. If she wasn't spoken for, I might go for her myself."

Elena was growing frustrated with all three men. Clay seemed to speak in riddles and neither Sean nor Sam spoke at all. She rose. "Must I repeat everything you say? Rosa is getting married?" No wonder Sam was so silent. His heart must be broken. "Who is he?" She sat down, waiting for Clay's explanation.

Instead, Sam cleared his throat. "Why, me, I guess." His blush heightened when Elena threw her arms around his shoulders, kissing him on his red-whiskered cheek.

"When? You will bring her here. Say you will."

"Hold on." He waited for Sean to pull her off. "I spent two weeks testifying against the Ring at hearings in Washington. Then I had to take a side trip down to Georgia to get murder charges on that rascal of yours dropped. Not to mention havin' to watchdog this overgrown pup you call a brother and keep the desperados from killin' him for that fine animal out there.

"There's still some housekeeping to be done in Santa Fe, but after that's finished, I'm for Pecos. Rosa sold the cantina to Pepito, and we'll be comin' back to settle down on my folks' ranch. Now that the ring is busted up, we need honest lawyers in the territory and after nearly thirty years since his practice before the War, my Pa is opening up a practice in Santa Fe. He and Ma already bought a house near the Indian school."

Aside from the news that her husband had been vindicated for Billy's murder, Elena didn't know which announcement was more wonderful: that her two friends were finally going to find happiness together, or that the Santa Fe Ring's decade-old reign of terror in New Mexico was finally over. Both, she decided, clapping her hands. "Tell me what has happened since we left the mountain."

"Well, Jesse's got the school pretty near good as new and his students will be comin' back from the San Carlos Reservation soon," Sam said. "He even talked Morning Bird into comin' down from the mountain to help."

Elena crossed herself, thanking Judith's god for bringing Jesse's family together again. Then her smile faded. "Anscombe?"

Sam grinned at her. "He sang like a little birdie after Jesse found him and got a little...well...creative on the way to Taos. Washington's handing out indictments right and left to the Ring's leaders. Half of New Mexico's legislators are up on charges of fraud or worse. The rest are packing their carpet bags and heading for safer digs down South America way.

"Anscombe is charged with more than a dozen murders, including the Torres family, Marcus, and Judith." He nodded toward Sean. "The rope will be around his neck before the new year."

After dreaming of avenging their deaths for so long, Elena found no joy in Anscombe's execution. Only peace. She would see her loved ones again someday—Marcus, Judith, Wah-Kee, Little Wolf, and Maria Santiago.

She finally understood that the God of Judith and Marcus was the same as the God of the Apache. The God of the sky, the four winds, and of the mountains. The God that bled for the souls of all people, white, red, or brown.

Sean broke the silence that paid homage to the dead. "Clay has some news of his own, Elena. Besides bringing Orion out here, he came to announce his engagement to Mary Louise."

After the bittersweet news that justice had finally been served for the evil done by the Santa Fe Ring, knowing that Clay and Mary Louise would be together made her happy. She hugged Clay. "When did this happen?"

His bright blue eyes showed his love for Miss Fairchild. He poked Sean playfully in the shoulder and grinned. "Once she found out she didn't have to marry this old bull, well, we made our feelings known and one thing led to another...and, well, we'll say our vows when I get back."

Elena gave Clay one more hug, meeting the Ranger's honest blue eyes over his shoulder.

"Did you bring it?" she asked.

"Yep."

"Bring what?" Sean said.

"Roscoe's wedding gift."

Sean's fist hit the table. "You were never going to marry that bastard."

"Whatever he gave you, I'll give you double...someday."

His jealousy was both unfounded and unbacked, since he was mighty shy in the asset department. When he'd left Langesford, he'd signed over his ownership of the plantation to Clay. And the Torres ranch belonged to Elena, even if the law recognized him as the legal owner.

Right now, the only things he could rightfully call his own were Orion and his new job as a Deputy New Mexico Ranger. That position wasn't likely to help him give Elena the things a rich gambler or a plantation owner could.

"Simmer down, man," Sam told him, and reached for a package in his saddlebag. He handed it to Elena. "It's just a book."

"A book?" Sean stared at it, obviously baffled that a book would be so important to her she'd ask a Ranger to deliver it. "What kind of book?"

Smiling at her husband's misplaced jealousy, she sat down and opened the wrapper. Pausing a moment, she told them, "This is a very special book."

Three pairs of male eyes peered at the large, leather-bound tome on her lap. "Treasure Island?" they said in unison.

Clay voiced the question in all their minds. "Why would an Apache... I mean you... be interested in a tale of pirates and buried treasure, especially after what you've just done with one.

"It's a first edition," Elena answered, knowing Clay's reverence for fine literature. Before she could stop him, he reached over her head to open the front cover. "Look, it's even signed," he pointed out.

"Yes," she agreed, closing it quickly and holding the heavy tome close to her chest. "It is one of a kind." She smiled at Sam's warm, knowing gaze. "It is very valuable. Thank you for bringing it to me."

The big Ranger winked at her. "You earned it." He turned again to reach back into his seemingly bottomless saddlebag and give her another package. "Your mother-in-law sent you this."

"Hey," Clay shouted in frustration. "Who put you in charge of all the gifts?"

"You were in such a rush to deliver that horse and high-tail it back home to that little filly of yours, you'd have left them in Santa Fe," Sam joked.

"And you're in no hurry to get back to Rosa?" he fired back while Elena opened the gift from Camilla O'Grady. They stopped their good-natured banter when they noticed tears streaming down her face as she read the note tucked inside.

Sean went to her side and saw, despite the tears, pure joy shining from her eyes. She held up an exquisitely hand-beaded, white, buckskin dress.

"Your mother was wearing this when she presented you to your father," she said through happy tears. "She has given this to me to wear when I give you your first child."

She took a deep breath. "She says she cannot come to us because of the painful memories, but she sends this symbol of the one truly good thing that came from her time here. You."

Sean wrapped her in his arms and Sam and Clay made excuses to leave the room. "Your mother, she is like a Shaman. She has the sight," she told him.

He remembered the night his mother had known Elena was in danger, sending him back to the hot spring. There were other times when she'd warned him of things about to happen. Even though he mostly ignored them, her gift of intuition had saved his sorry skin more times than he cared to admit.

"How do you know?"

Her smile was wide when she answered. "Because, in the summer, I will wear this dress for you."

～

Join Doris Lemcke's mailing list and never miss a new release!

dorislemckebooks.com

~

THANK YOU FOR READING

~

Did you enjoy this book?

We invite you to leave a review at your favorite book site, such as
Goodreads, Amazon, Barnes & Noble, etc.

DID YOU KNOW THAT LEAVING A REVIEW...

- Helps other readers find books they may enjoy.
- Gives you a chance to let your voice be heard.
- Gives authors recognition for their hard work.
- Doesn't have to be long. A sentence or two about why you liked
  the book will do.

Eager to hear what's next for Doris Lemcke?

Join her mailing list!

www.dorislemckebooks.com

~

Don't miss out on your next favorite book!

~

Join the Satin Romance mailing list
www.satinromance.com/mail.html

Subscriber Perks Include:

- First peeks at upcoming releases.
- Exclusive giveaways.
- News of book sales and freebies right in your inbox.
- And more!

ABOUT THE AUTHOR

A native Michigander whose great-grandmother was a member of the Saginaw Ojibwa tribe, Doris is fascinated by American history and Native American culture. Sources for this book included first-hand accounts from early Western pioneers and from the Civil War and Reconstruction eras.

Now retired in Southeast Michigan, Doris loves spending time with family, friends and other writers while writing and researching fast-paced historical and contemporary novels about strong, intelligent women caught in the web of, *Love, Lies and Family Secrets.*

For more information:
www.dorislemckebooks.com
Doris@DorisLemckeBooks.com

ALSO BY DORIS LEMCKE

WITH SATIN ROMANCE

The Langesford Legacy

Rebel Treasure

White Mountain Spirit

Novels

Legacy of Lies